On
STARLIT
Seas

On STARLIT *Seas*

Sara SHERIDAN

BLACK & WHITE PUBLISHING

First published 2016
by Black & White Publishing Ltd
29 Ocean Drive, Edinburgh EH6 6JL

3 5 7 9 10 8 6 4 2   16 17 18 19

Reprinted 2016

ISBN: 978 1 78530 038 7

A CIP catalogue record for this book is available from the British Library.

ALBA | CHRUTHACHAIL

Typeset by Iolaire Typesetting, Newtonmore.
Printed and bound by CPI Group (UK) Ltd, Croydon, CR0 4YY

This book is dedicated to the many women who have fought for change. Feminists all of us.

Those who visit foreign nations, but who associate only with their own countrymen, change their climate, but not their customs... they see new meridians, but the same men, and with heads as empty as their pockets, return home, with travelled bodies, but untravelled minds.

Charles Caleb Colton, *Lacon*

PROLOGUE

Outside Valparaíso, Chile, 1823

At dawn, Maria Graham stood in the drawing room of the cottage she had lived in for the last year. Outside, the trees swayed in the unseasonable breeze as the sky lightened. The hem of her grey travelling dress trailed as she crouched on the wooden boards with her eyes on the empty grate. She had loved this room. They said it was too far from town here, for an English lady alone. But the moment she had seen the low building, its walls wreathed in flowers, she knew it was the perfect place. She had strewn her papers across the comfortable chairs and laid them in a pile beside her bed. At the dining table she had eaten as she studied a vellum map of the Chilean highlands, and from the veranda she had sat contentedly and watched the swathes of green all around, and then, of course, she had witnessed the earthquakes. With quill in hand, she inspected the damage. It had been a matter of trigonometry to notate the tremors.

She knew what they said in Valparaíso. *It isn't natural. The English widow is an odd fish.* But she didn't care. The consul had troubled her with constant offers to send her home. To keep her safe. Her aunt, the august Lady Dundas, had written repeatedly. In a tone that could only be described as testy, she demanded Maria come back to London. *You are a widow now and your place is here,* she insisted. *A woman cannot travel by herself, Maria. We are most dreadfully embarrassed by your gallivanting.* Maria set the fire. The air was thick already with the heat of the day still to come. Lighting a spill, she sat back to watch the paper burn – the twenty-two pages of her journal that were simply too private. The evidence of her mourning for Thomas. Her eyes were still as she watched the thick paper curl and flame. Then she fed the fire with her aunt's letters and watched them burn.

The sound of a door opening echoed from the other side of the cottage. Maria poked the ashes to make sure all vestiges of the unwelcome words were gone. She stood up, brushing the rise of her skirt with the palm of her hand as if it might have creased. The maid came into the room – a young girl from the nearby village. Her skin was the colour of ginger, smooth and plump. She had kept the house well. She had cried when Maria had told her that she was leaving. Now she bobbed a curtsey, ready to face this last day. 'The men will come later,' Maria said, indicating with a nod the trunks and cases packed and piled high in the hallway. She removed a coin from her purse and handed it over. The maid's dark eyes filled up as if she would weep again, but Maria didn't wait to see.

In the hallway she fixed her hat and scooped up the blousy white roses she had picked before the sun came up, the over-grown bushes the legacy of an earlier occupant of the cottage. 'He will come for the key,' she instructed.

Maria had arrived on a cart she had hired from an ostler in Valparaíso. Two of the *Doris*'s young officers had driven it. She had been a mother to them for almost a year on the voyage from England, and Thomas a father too. Now she stowed the roses in one saddlebag and her precious manuscript, the *History of Chile* – the prize she had spent her year of mourning writing – in the other. She pulled herself onto the horse, side-saddle, and set off down the track, rough hewn out of the woodland, the maid standing on the shady veranda, watching her leave. The girl raised a hand and Maria waved back.

In moments the house was obscured and, at a steady trot, Maria's cheeks were beaten pink by the warm spring squall that cut through the branches. The ride left her breathless. There was nothing like a journey to quicken the blood and feed the spirit. Maria was a natural traveller and today she would set out across the continent, or at least around it. The trees were a blur of green, thinning here and there into farmland, and as she came over the crest of the hill she caught a tantalising glimpse of the ocean. From here she could just make out the frantic, sweaty port with its tangle of sailors and rigging in a straggle along the shoreline. Beyond it, the sea sparkled. One of these ships would take her on the first leg of her journey, but first she had something to do.

As the town drew into view, a flock of small birds took off from the wall of the fort. They moved like a length of dark silk caught by the breeze as they headed out to sea. Behind them, the sky was the colour of forget-me-nots. The sun blazed. Maria kept to the fringes, approaching the vantage point of the bone-dry cemetery on the hill. Had it been a year? Several of the British community and the entire crew of the *Doris* had turned out for Thomas's funeral. Two of the younger officers, both midshipmen, lads of eleven, had blubbed. It seemed long ago and very far away.

3

A thin bougainvillea plant trailed across three chalky grave-stones by the gate. Maria, still breathless, her heart pounding, tied up her mount and took out the wild mountain roses. The gate creaked as she pushed it aside. *Captain Thomas Graham* it said on her husband's gravestone. It still seemed strange that he was gone. Many years before, when her father had passed away in Bombay, she had been thousands of miles off and the news had arrived in a letter weeks later. 'Maria, you are a strange, solitary creature,' her aunt had scolded, as if it was selfish of the girl to lock herself in her room to mourn him. 'We are all upset,' Aunt Dundas had sniffed, although Maria recalled dinner had proceeded and the main portion of her aunt's grief appeared to revolve around the organisation of appropriate, black-silk attire. For her part, Maria had never forgiven herself for not being in Bombay when it happened. This time she had held Thomas's hand as he jolted out of this life into the next. She preferred to be present and play her part. When her husband lay still at last, she had crouched beside the berth with the ship creaking around her and sat with his body for an hour in contemplation before she informed the second in command. This death was hers to grieve and now she had done so. She laid the flowers on the yellow earth and stood for a moment. It was unlikely she would revisit Valparaíso. 'Goodbye,' she said stoutly, turning to leave him behind.

In town, Maria visited her only friend, Mrs Campbell, a Spanish woman who had married one of Valparaíso's Scottish merchants. Woman to woman, Rosa Campbell had under-stood Maria's grief. She had hosted Thomas's wake. She had not asked Maria when she might be leaving Chile. Slowly, as the Englishwoman recovered, Mrs Campbell had visited.

'You are so very kind to me.' Maria had smiled.

4

'I'm an admirer,' Mrs Campbell admitted. 'I have read all of your books. Such wonderful adventures, one almost feels as if one has travelled with you.'

Today, the maid led Maria inside where it was cool. The Campbells had planted honeysuckle in the garden. The scent of an English summer wafted into the shady house. Maria hovered by a satinwood desk, glad to be out of the heat. She shifted on the tiled floor and lifted a goose-feather quill from Mrs Campbell's inkpot. The desk was used for preparing the household accounts. Maria had never run a household for Thomas or anyone else. Most naval wives stayed at home, but she had always travelled, either with her husband or independently. He had seen to British interests and she had written about everywhere they had visited. Rosa Campbell came into the room, her satin shoes clicking as she crossed the tiles.

'Mrs Graham.' Rosa put her arms around her friend. 'Today?' she asked.

Maria nodded. The women sat down.

'Tea,' Rosa said, as if it were a matter of plain fact rather than an offer. She had adopted the ways of her husband's country.

The maid had scarcely been sent to fetch a pot when the sound of knocking disturbed the women and the girl returned to the room with the card of the British consul. Maria sighed audibly. Rosa shrugged. Valparaíso was a small town.

The consul was smug as he entered. He had wanted Maria to leave for months on end and now he would have his way. The man bowed. 'Will you do me the honour, madam, of allowing me to organise your passage home at last?' Straight to business.

Rosa curtseyed, but Maria only inclined her head. She feigned shock. 'Why, sir, what made you think I was going home? To London, you mean?'

The consul blustered. 'But you have given up your property, Mrs Graham. You have packed your things.'

News travelled so fast here. The maid returned with a tray of tea. The porcelain cups tinkled as she set it down.

'Today is the anniversary of my husband's death,' Maria announced. It was a dramatic statement, but the occasion seemed to demand it. 'And I am going to leave,' she assured him. 'Though not for London.'

Rosa picked up the teapot and began to pour. She was enjoying this tremendously, but she didn't show it. The consul was out of his depth and Maria, in her opinion, magnificent.

'Pray, where will you direct yourself next, Mrs Graham? It is not safe or seemly for a woman—' the man started.

Maria raised a gloved hand. 'Brazil, sir. Mr Murray has commissioned me to write a book about Brazil.'

This was not entirely true. Maria had suggested it to John Murray. She was not ready to go home yet.

The consul appeared unsure of how to take this news. Mrs Graham had been a thorn in his side. A British woman alone was his responsibility. In Brazil she would at least be out of his jurisdiction.

'Have you visited Brazil? Do you know it?'

'Why, not at all, sir. I have plans, though. My maps. That is the pleasure of it, don't you see?'

'I shall write a letter of introduction,' he announced.

Maria inclined her head once more. John Murray had already furnished her with several such letters, but it would be churlish to refuse. 'Thank you,' she said.

The consul eyed the tea tray and got to his feet. 'Matters to attend,' he announced. 'I wanted to see you safely off, Mrs Graham.'

'So kind.'

As the door closed behind him, the women waited a moment before a wave of laughter overtook them.

'Pompous fool,' Rosa declared with unaccustomed boldness.

Maria took her teacup and sipped. 'They cannot help it, I suppose,' she said, more kindly than she felt. It was good to have dispatched him. And she hadn't lied. Murray, after all, was expecting her manuscript.

Far further east, London

The Old Street Bridge Club kept two sombre rooms on the first floor of the little house opposite the Rose Tavern. These were cleaned and provisioned by Betty Wylie, the landlady at the Rose. A fine piece of Regency mutton dressed as English lamb, Mrs Wylie left a monthly account folded carefully on the slate mantelpiece, which was paid promptly in cash.

The club emanated an air of permanence and authority. The rooms boasted panelled walls, leather chairs and a lush baize card table. The air was heavy with the stale smoke of late-night cigars over which the illustrious members lingered during the last rubbers of the evening. A bucket of oyster shells lay shucked and discarded, and the occasional carelessly abandoned leather glove or gentleman's silk scarf spoke of another area of town, to the west, where life was more generous and the quality left tips. Mrs Wylie hoped one day to live there, or at least closer.

The club was discreet in its habits and its existence was not generally known. From outside it looked like lots of other buildings in the run-down laneways off the main road. There was no nameplate on the shabby door to announce this den of gentlemen to the world. The shutters to the three filthy windows were kept resolutely shut, secured by iron bars. Some days when Mrs Wylie crossed the filthy walkway and used her key, it was evident that the place had lain deserted all night. Other times there was a riot of abandoned cards and drained port bottles. The members were not predictable in their habits. However, they never brought women to their premises – not a single tatty painted street girl from nearby Shoreditch or even one of the better-looking whores that foraged a meagre living on the fringes of the Mile End Road. Nor was there brawling, apart from once a smashed chair.

'Money for jam,' Mrs Wylie often observed to herself, for she never spoke of the Old Street Bridge Club to another soul. Her husband's mother, Old Mrs Wylie, had instructed her most particularly in that matter. The old woman had retired to a coastal resort in Kent and left the running of the Rose to her son and his family. Before she went, Old Mrs Wylie neglected to impart how long the Old Street Bridge Club had been in operation, but it seemed an almost ancient institution – one that was simply there, like Hampton Court up the river or the grand palace at Whitehall. What the present Mrs Wylie and indeed her forebears had neglected to ask was why.

It was a brisk spring afternoon, and too early for the gentlemen to be taking their places round the table, when a tall fellow no more than five and twenty cut off the busy highway. Will Simmons had travelled a long way – catching an overladen coach from Falmouth and riding thirty-six hours alongside the jostling baggage on the roof. Once he made London, he walked the last few miles. He passed a spate of newspaper boys, shouting their wares, but didn't pay any attention to the headlines of the sudden uprising thousands of miles away in Brazil. Will had never learned to read and as far as he was concerned foreign affairs were unimportant. Oblivious, he continued towards Mallow Street.

As he came to the door of the Bridge Club, the boy felt for his knife. Then, drawing a key from inside his hat, he disappeared inside. Shards of daylight filched through the keyhole as he mounted the dingy stairs to the room that ran the length of the building on the first floor. Inside, the candles flickered as he fell upon the bread and cheese on the oak table as if he hadn't eaten for a week. He drained a glass of port and poured himself another, this time methodically taking in the bouquet of the Douro.

The sound of the door to the street prompted him to jerk upright with his knife in hand. Steps hammered upwards as the amber flames danced in the grate, peppering the room with low light. Simmons took a deep breath and then relaxed as the dim shadow of a smaller, plumper and older man appeared in the doorway. He had a Scottish accent.

'Jesus. Are you all right, Will?'

Simmons nodded. 'Filthy is all.' He smiled. His voice was low, his accent dense as the marshy ground where he had been brought up by his mother's people – an Essex lad.

'Do you have it?' the gentleman asked.

Will reached into his inside pocket and brought out a block the size of a large brick, wrapped in linen. He was not an inquisitive fellow. In his business, those who pried stood a good chance of ending up dead. Still, he had taken a peek and had decided on balance that he'd best not speculate on why a block of chocolate was worth all this fuss. If the gentlemen wanted to ship the stuff over from the Americas and pay

11

him to transport it by hand to London, then that was their prerogative. The quality knew how to mind their business; he need not mind it for them. He laid the parcel on the table next to the cheese.

'Here it is.'

With deliberation, the man set a hardy ebony cane by one of the chairs. It was topped with a small silver fox's head, discreet but distinctive. He picked up the brick and turned it over. His eyes gleamed.

'Excellent. Well done, boy.'

'I'm afraid there's bad news, sir.'

'Was there much of a fight?' the man asked with a sigh.

Will shook his head and pulled out his knife, the sight of which answered the question – the blade was stained with a smear of dried blood.

'He was for thieving it. Fucking thief.'

'Why do they do it? We pay them well enough.'

Will didn't reply. There was no need. He had no scruples about killing the captains employed by the Old Street Bridge Club if they did not keep their bargain. So far, two had become too greedy – one last year and the other only a few days before. Will had stabbed both men to death without compunction.

'What we want is someone reliable.' The gentleman paused. 'Scum we can trust.'

'Like me, you mean?' Will chortled.

The gentleman smiled. The corners of his pale-blue eyes crinkled. It was not for nothing he was known as Charming Charlie Grant. He lit a candle, illuminating his immaculately chosen suit and the swathe of freckles that he was sure kept him looking young despite the sprinkling of grey overtaking his pale ginger hair.

'My dear boy . . .' His voice trailed. 'We cannot keep replacing captain after captain.'

'London isn't short of a captain or two. I'll ask around,' Will said breezily.

Charlie Grant shook his head. 'I think,' he said, 'that's where we've been going wrong. You're very efficient at disposing of our problems, but it's no use trying the same thing over and over and having the same trouble. We need to change.'

Before Grant could elaborate, the conversation was interrupted by the thump of the main door. The men's eyes met and Will reached for his knife. Grant stood up, cane in hand, seeming nonchalant but poised in case he had to fight. He placed himself in front of the table so that its contents couldn't be seen from the door. The gentlemen who entered were dapper.

'Fisher.' Grant nodded, relaxing. 'Hayward. You're early.'

'Later than you,' Fisher pointed out.

Hayward took a light from the fire, puffing on a thick cigar. 'Mr Simmons,' he said. 'You brought our parcel?'

Simmons nodded.

'Good,' Hayward continued smoothly as he settled into his chair. 'Drink?' he offered, his voice crisp with upper-class authority.

'I'm fine, thank you.'

Grant assumed a position in the centre. 'So, Will's view is that we are in need of a new captain. There has been a recurrence of the old trouble.'

'Yes, sir. I'll make some enquiries at Greenwich.'

The men moved, and Will sensed a ripple folding beneath the surface of the room. He realised that they had discussed this.

13

'The thing is, Simmons, you're a good man.' Hayward handed Will a glass, though he had declined.

'We liked your father,' Fisher continued seamlessly, 'and we like you.'

Simmons shifted. He hesitated before drinking. In general, the Old Street Bridge Club was a practical organisation and Will was wary of praise. He knew from experience, if you plan to kill a man it's easier if he isn't expecting it.

Charlie Grant laid his hand on Simmons'ss shoulder. He laughed. 'We're not after you, man. God, no. In fact,' he continued, 'we have a proposition. A promotion, you might say.'

Simmons hoped they weren't going to send him north. He'd never been to Scotland, but he knew the gentlemen had business there. The coastal towns of the East Neuk were as famous as those of Cornwall for assisting the representatives of gentlemen such as the Old Street Bridge Club to avoid His Majesty's Customs and Excise. God knew how many of these schemes the men had running. He'd heard rumours of Italian wine and treasures from India. For an English gentleman of both vision and means, the wide world lay open-handed.

'Where do you want me to go?' the boy asked.

'We're expanding,' Fisher replied. 'Why should we let these captains know, as we previously have done, that these small packages are so valuable? There's no need to alert anyone to the matter of our . . .' Here he hesitated. Even in their own company, the members of the Old Street Bridge Club were habitually circumspect. 'Little treasures. It only makes the captains wary. Naturally they wonder, and wondering makes a chap greedy. The source of our recent troubles – all that wondering. We are only additional income there for the

14

taking, or so they think. So we've decided to finance the whole trip. It'll make the fellows less suspicious.'

Simmons'ss mind boggled. They had been bringing over a block every six months – how were they going to find enough of the stuff to justify an entire vessel, and what made the chocolate so damn special, anyway? Charlie Grant was evidently enjoying reading the boy's expression.

'We'll charter a ship to bring over beans. Cacao. It's a compatible cargo and shouldn't arouse any suspicions. The chocolate market is growing in London. Two new manufactories this year, to say nothing of the apothecaries who trade in the stuff. A cargo of decent chocolate beans is worth more than a hold full of spirits and it's less likely to be pilfered. We'll bring it in at Cornwall, the way we've been doing with our other stock. You run it up to town and we'll sell it at a profit, and a good profit at that – enough to cut in the captain.' He paused for effect. 'The packet, of course, is different. It will come with you and will be between us alone. The captain will know nothing about it.'

'It'll come with me?'

'Aye.'

'You want me to . . .' Simmons hesitated as the enormity of what the gentlemen were suggesting dawned. He had never been beyond British waters except one brief visit to Ireland. Will was not a natural sailor. He had heaved up his guts from port to port. In fact, for some months after the trip he had had nightmares about sailing out of sight of the shore and woken in his box bed in a panic.

Grant hardly skipped a beat. 'That's right. The Brazils. You'll pick up the packet from our contact and charter a ship home. We need a captain who's a rogue but not an outright vagabond. You must find him.'

'We cannot keep up all this killing, m'boy,' Fisher said very definitely, as if he were discussing the management of fish stocks on his estate. 'You'll get caught sooner or later, Will, however good you are. And it's getting trickier. You'll have seen the fliers along the new docks offering rewards for information. We don't want to see you hung. That's no help to anybody.'

Charlie Grant put it delicately. 'This way, you go into business. It's a step up – your father would have liked that, wouldn't he?'

Simmons shrugged. His father had died three years before and had been a smuggler from the age of eleven. All his life he had had great respect for the trade of dodging excise. 'They might have the money, but we have the skill,' he had often said. The Old Street Bridge Club, however, was unaware of the revolutionary views of Mr Simmons Senior.

Charlie Grant continued. 'The captain will have no reason to suspect anything, so your undoubted skills with the knife will be spared. The cargo will run in your name. Triple our money, cut in the captain and the rest is yours. By my calculations you'll make a tidy sum, more than worth the effort, and you won't have to put up a penny. On top, we'll pay you the usual fee for bringing us what we're really after. If it works, instead of one brick of chocolate, we may ship half a dozen. The route hasn't been reliable enough to justify the risk till now, but you can change that, Will.'

Simmons blanched. It was a generous offer. 'I cannot sail,' he stammered.

Charlie Grant refilled the boy's glass and affected his most charming smile. 'Why there's nothing to it, my dear fellow. Others do the sailing. You merely sit aboard.'

16

Hayward took a small leather pouch from his pocket. It clinked as it landed squarely in Simmons'ss hand.

'And nothing to lead back to us,' Fisher said, his voice laden with threat. 'You must be sure of that.' Smuggling, after all, was a capital offence. 'We'll back you all the way, but if you shaft us—'

'Now, now, gentlemen.' Charlie Grant stepped in. 'We've been working with Will for a while. He knows the score. You'd never let us down, would you, Will? And Brazil, you lucky fellow – the doe-eyed beauties of Rio Grande do Norte. The dark-skinned lovelies of São Luís . . . Natal is a young fellow's paradise.'

The gentlemen laughed.

'You'll like it, really you will.' Hayward smiled.

Simmons felt a rush of anger. His eyes flashed. 'What if I don't want to?' he said.

The gentlemen looked momentarily nonplussed. Charlie Grant turned to fetch more port and Hayward shifted in his seat. Simmons didn't notice Fisher, who moved like lightning, cutting behind. The boy's reactions simply weren't fast enough as Fisher snared a vermillion silk cord round his neck. As Simmons struggled against the garrotte, Charlie Grant looked distressed. Hayward stared into the fire. Will's face was turning purple when his hand finally found his knife, but it was hopeless. Grant laconically disarmed him from a distance, bringing down the elegant walking stick mercilessly with a bone-shattering crash. Will wanted to cry out, but his scream died with a gurgle. Then, just as the boy thought he was done for, Fisher let him go and Will collapsed onto the thin boards, gasping for breath and expecting one of them to end him. The gentlemen,

17

however, returned calmly to their places as if nothing had happened.

Fisher lit a cigar. 'The Old Street Bridge Club doesn't brook argument on this kind of matter,' he said.

Charlie Grant offered Simmons a hand, hauling him to his feet. 'Really, my boy, we know what's best.'

Simmons spluttered. His hand was agony. He knew the gentlemen were vicious. You couldn't get to where they were in the trade and not spill a decent pool of blood. His heart sank as he put his good hand to his throat. *That must be how it feels,* he thought, *when a fellow swings.* At least he knew the men would be true to their word about the money. They might be dangerous old bastards, but they paid well. Charlie Grant turned over Simmons's knife in his hand. *That'd be irony all right,* Will's mind flashed, *to be stabbed with my own blade.*

'I'll give it a go,' he managed to get out.

Grant nodded. 'Good. You've been working with Pearson, haven't you? It's about time the lad was given more responsibility. He'll take over your current position.'

Simmons nodded reluctantly. Sam Pearson was nearly nineteen. A long-bodied, red-haired risk taker, he would relish the promotion. Solid in a fight and tricky enough for the job, his slow West Country accent belied a sharp mind, absolute loyalty and a ferocious disposition. He'd had also been stepping out with a girl from Budock Water. If he was planning to marry, the extra money might suit him.

'I'll talk to him.' He ran nervous fingers through his blond hair as he rose, bundling the money into his pocket. 'When I've sounded him out, I'll show him the ropes – the ones he doesn't know yet. Up this end of things.'

18

'Tell Pearson to call next week,' Fisher replied, as if he were issuing an invitation to dinner.

Will bid the gentlemen a dazed goodbye and shambled towards the door.

'Here,' Grant said, handing over the knife. 'It's dangerous out there.'

The men remained silent until they heard the boy's steady gait on the street. Hayward lit a cigar.

'Really. Doe-eyed beauties,' he said, eyeing Grant. 'Dark-skinned lovelies . . .'

'I had to encourage the lad.' Grant shrugged.

'Yes, indeed. I was only thinking of my wife.'

'Trouble, old man?'

'She thinks I have a mistress. She says I'm so very intent she can't imagine what else I'd be up to. She has a jealous nature.'

Fisher let out a crack of laughter like a whip. 'My dear fellow,' he said, 'I'm sure Mrs Fisher sighs with relief when I take it upon myself to dally elsewhere. Besides, better the ladies suspect that than the truth. Poor woman thinks, no doubt, that you fund her famous outfits from the proceeds of your land and some luck at the races. Buy jewellery – always my advice. Copious jewellery has kept Mrs Fisher happy for years. Indian rubies are all the rage. I'd find her a nice necklace, if I were you,' he said, folding the scarlet cord into his pocket.

Charlie Grant stood up. He found himself ill at ease on the subject of the opposite sex. He had other proclivities, but he didn't indulge them. His private life was a locked cupboard, its contents a mystery even to himself.

'Time for the off,' he announced. 'I'm glad we didn't have

to kill the boy. I've become fond of him. Fisher, would you?' He handed over the package.

'Leave it with me. I have a buyer.'

'And a cup of chocolate for breakfast, gentlemen,' Hayward slipped in slyly, ever the wag.

'I expect Simmons will come round,' Fisher mused.

Charlie Grant examined the silver head of his cane for damage. Only once before had they disposed of a courier. It had not been a pleasant business. Still, the Old Street Bridge Club's network of well-paid informants and contacts meant that they generally got what they wanted. Simmons had no chance of getting away, particularly if he wasn't prepared to get on a ship, and even then it was only a matter of alerting the right people, offering a reward and waiting. The Old Street Bridge Club indulged itself in the luxury of taking the long view. It was an institution in its third generation.

Fisher shrugged. 'He'll be fine. He may even come to like the life. He'll certainly like the additional funds. Sometimes these fellows simply need to be taken in hand.'

The others nodded and reached for their hats. Fisher scattered a pack of cards across the baize table. Grant dropped a couple of scoring cards on the floor. Then, leaving the candles and the fire alight, they left the fug of their offices and proceeded as usual through the needle-sharp winter air back to the safety of their well-aired West End beds.

2

Brazilian interior

Maria lingered amid the overgrown vegetation. One of the mules had become mired in mud. The men had been trying to save it for almost an hour. The poor animal was up to its flanks and already exhausted; its neck was a dark, glossy slick of sweat, its eyes flashing in terror. Maria sniffed. The jungle smelled of earth, plants and long-dead animals. Last month there had been flooding in these lowlands, but the water had subsided, leaving only dark ambient pools between which the men hacked a soggy path through the undergrowth. The sheer weight of the air muffled sound. It lay on the lungs like a sodden flannel, a tsunami of heat cut only by thick green foliage studded with poison. The minute you entered this place, everything you brought with you started to rot. Still, despite the difficult terrain, Maria had to admit the jungle had a strange if overwhelming beauty that seemed lost on da Couto, the gruff, dark-eyed diplomat who had been sent to accompany her.

Brazil had been more complicated than she had expected, to say nothing of the journey to get there – a jumble of shallow-bottomed boat trips up wide, muddy rivers and trains of dusty horses crossing parched desert. No sooner had she arrived than the nationalist uprising got underway, miring the country in a vicious civil war. In the upheaval, Rio's high society had welcomed Mrs Graham and in short order she had been introduced to the Empress. Her Majesty was an elegant and intelligent woman with an interest in botany. She was familiar with Maria's book about India and immediately asked the Englishwoman to become tutor to her daughter, Maria da Gloria, the Princess Royal. The heir to the throne was not long out of nappies. The Empress chose her words with care. It was, after all, a friendship born of only a few weeks' acquaintance. Still, she liked the look of this solid Englishwoman with impeccable manners, and she needed help.

'A lady such as yourself will endow my daughter with a restrained view of the world. I want her to see things. I want her to be educated, Mrs Graham.'

Even for royal ladies, an education beyond the simple matter of music and art was not a given.

Maria had nodded. 'Of course,' she said. 'I understand.'

The court had resented Maria's appointment. She was a foreigner after all, even if England was an ally. The Empress, however, ignored the murmurings and quickly Mrs Graham found herself fond of the little princess – a plump, smiling infant whose first words had been in English. They played hide-and-seek in the royal gardens and Maria started the princess's botanical education by making garlands of lawn daisies to wreath her little bed. Much to her mother's delight, Maria taught the little girl to lisp the Latin name of the pretty flowers: *Bellis perennis*.

'There is court etiquette of course,' Maria said to the Empress, 'and that must be observed, but I should hate the

22

princess to lose her early years. A happy childhood is an education in itself.'

It was an education that Maria's own childhood had lacked. Young Maria Dundas had been removed from her mother's care at a tender age. Mrs Dundas had been deemed unsuitable by the family, or at least not aristocratic enough for the responsibility of bringing up its next generation. She was erratic. Maria recalled the arguments, or what she had overheard of them. The marriage had been a love match, and when Captain Dundas's love had died he left for Bombay and entrusted his daughter to Lady Dundas, his haughty sister-in-law. She had proved a formidable guardian. Unpleasant and calculating. When Maria was twenty-three, at last old enough to do so, she had joined her father in India. She had been travelling ever since.

The Empress hugged her newly appointed governess and smiled. 'My daughter is in hands that are both safe and wise. I prayed for an upright woman. A good woman. And God has answered.'

In due course, Mrs Graham was given leave to return to London to buy books and materials for her new charge. She kissed the little girl goodbye as if she were a cousin or a niece. With no children of her own, the connection had been immediate. Maria had pointed out England on the globe in the schoolroom and the little one spun it round with her plump fingers. Maria told the girl that the most difficult part of her journey would be the crossing of the Atlantic. 'This part, the blue,' she said, pointing it out. 'Blue,' the little princess lisped. *Azul. Celeste.*

Now, covered in mud with the thick air pressing down on her, that conversation seemed a world away. And Maria

23

realised that she had miscalculated. The green was going to be far more difficult. It struck her as ironic that somewhere in her baggage there was a vial of scent – a royal parting gift that was composed of orchid oil and musk. It had been days since she had been able to wash, let alone preen herself with oils and unguents. *It will be a while yet,* she thought, *before fragrance becomes possible.*

The perfume was not the only royal gift in Maria's possession. She was also carrying a communiqué addressed to Admiral Cochrane, the Brazilian navy's commander – a renegade Englishman who had been a confidant of Maria's husband. Her orders from the Empress were clear.

'On your life,' Her Majesty had said as she handed over the missive, 'don't tell da Couto. The man has no subtlety, but he will get you there. You must hand this to Cochrane in person. Da Couto will take you cross-country – it is too dangerous by sea along this coast.'

Maria prided herself on being capable. The self-reliance born at least partly from the confined cruelty of the Oxfordshire boarding school to which Lady Dundas had banished her proved excellent preparation for lifelong travel in the world's far-flung reaches. Still, this journey had tested her. When they left the city the train of bearers had been fine, but now the jungle had swallowed their clean clothes and good manners. The men's skins were all shades of coffee from milky to espresso black, and they stank of mule shit and sweat. Many had their clothes reduced to tatters. Others had simply removed their apparel. In the oppressive heat, Mrs Graham could hardly blame them.

There were times over the last week, hacking through the vegetation, when she had wondered if the overgrown path wasn't more dangerous than going by sea – even if shipping

24

was under fire. There was little in the verdant undergrowth that didn't possess teeth. She quickly learned that the thin muddy rivers were stocked with piranha, that all manner of venomous snakes concealed themselves not only on the ground but twisted round tree branches too, and that the wild monkeys were, to say the least, delinquent. One chattered over her head as she stood by the muddy pool and she kept half an eye on it. Sometimes the monkeys attacked for no apparent reason. But they were not the worst of the jungle's trials. Many of the flowering plants were not only poisonous but also, if handled incorrectly, fatal. Worst of all, you couldn't pass water without breaking the flow, for there were flesh-eating insects waiting to use a hot stream of piss as a conduit into the human body. In short, the jungle was a hellhole. The difficult conditions were made more unpleasant by the company. If the jungle leeched energy out of you, Senhor da Couto would surely stifle any life force you had left.

The diplomat checked Mrs Graham's whereabouts from his vantage point. 'It's taking too long,' he said.

'I could help,' Maria offered.

Da Couto's thin mouth set in a cruel line that cut his face in two. He turned away. Assistance from a female was unwelcome. Maria watched as one of the men dropped a rope and da Couto's temper tipped over the edge. He pulled out his riding crop and laid furiously into the man's naked back, cursing in Portuguese. The switch cut tiny slashes in the man's skin and thin trickles of blood snaked down his dark flesh.

'Mr da Couto,' Maria objected. Such cruelty was pointless. 'Mr da Couto!'

He ignored her and continued to whip the slave as Maria interposed herself. The bearers looked on as da Couto caught the woman's arm with his lash. Then he froze, realising what he had done. Maria waved off the injured man and motioned for two of the others to fish the rope from the mud. Her skin stung, but the blow had drawn no blood through the cotton of her plain grey travelling dress. Her fingers felt weak as she flexed them. There would be a bruise.

'*¡Vuelva trabajar!*' she said to the men. Get back to work.

The bearers didn't move. Da Couto glowered. Sliding off the saddle, his black eyes still with fury, he dismounted and roughly grabbed her, his fingers pressing into the flesh of her arm. Maria's stomach turned over in shock, but she did not feel afraid. If anything, she relished the challenge. One of her earliest memories was of her father ordering a man beaten for stealing an apple from his ship's stores. That, however, had been justice. By contrast, da Couto was randomly brutal – a slave to his poor temper.

'You think because you have the Empress's ear . . .' da Couto snarled. 'You think because you are an English woman . . . But I am in charge.'

Maria's resolve was steely. It was like dealing with a feral dog or a poorly trained mount – she simply had to take control.

She cut him off. 'I think, Mr da Couto, that you are speaking in English, so, happily, none of these men know what we are saying. And I think what is important, sir, is that we get going again as quickly as we can.' She forced herself to smile and pat him conspiratorially on the arm. Da Couto gathered himself as he loosened his grip. The bearers stopped gawping. 'In the event, it's probably as well that you won't speak Portuguese to me, sir.'

In the beginning she had asked him to help her practise, but da Couto insisted on using his very formal English and simply pretended not to understand when she tried the vocabulary she had learned in Rio. As a result, the only new words Maria had picked up on this trip were curses used by the men. Alongside Portuguese, the bearers spoke a strange argot that she could hardly discern – a language of African descent mixed with something Hispanic. She was curious about what they discussed when they switched to this from Portuguese. She heard them at night in the absolute darkness, whispering in a pack before falling asleep – low words and sharp clicks. Maria had an ear for languages, but this was beyond her.

'You mustn't interfere,' da Couto snapped.

Maria smiled. 'There's enough danger here, sir, without making it worse for ourselves. We require the services of all these men.'

Da Couto's stony expression was hooded with menace. 'Wait over there. It will not be much longer.'

The thin cotton of Maria's dress chafed her damp skin as she moved to the other side of the pool. Not for the first time, she thought how pleasant it would be to return to England for a few weeks, where the weather at this time of year would be brisk and the dangers less visceral.

As the men fitted the ropes around the trapped animal, Maria flexed her ankles and her wrists, stretching her legs under the cover of her fitted dress. She had seen native women in India flexing gracefully like elegant statues in the privacy of their quarters. Saluting the sun, they called it – a mystery of the Orient. Now, lengthening her stomach like a reclining cat, she longed to bend down and touch the muddy ground. She would do so tonight, she decided, in the privacy of her tent and without the constraint of her bodice.

Da Couto circled the mud. The mule was bound in a thick

web of sodden ropes. Three more mules and a horse had been harnessed to pull it clear. The diplomat nodded curtly. On his signal, the cry went up and slaps of encouragement sounded on the animals' damp flanks as they moved forward to pull their trapped confederate free.

As the mule scrambled to safety, there was a sudden rumble of thunder and a flash of lightning and the air immediately felt clearer as huge drops of rain splashed onto the jungle floor. Where it hit the leaves, the sound amplified into a drum-like rhythm. The men cheered and three of them began to dance.

Maria turned her face upwards, her dark hair immediately glossy and her cheeks glowing. The path would become a morass in seconds. It was difficult to believe that she had thrown snowballs in Chile only a few months before and that her fingers had been nipped pink and painful with the cold. In the jungle, the mere memory melted as quickly as a cube of ice.

'Are you all right, madam?' Da Couto peered at her.

Twice in the last week Maria had woken in the night, imagining da Couto lingering outside her tent in the sticky darkness. Her eyes jerked to the holsters slung like saddlebags across her horse's back. In one she had a loaded gun, which by now would almost certainly be too damp to fire. In the other she kept an extra water bottle and a small flask of brandy for medical purposes. Over the years she had learned to stow her own supplies, just in case.

'I'm merely attending my manuscripts,' she said steadily. 'I have two books ready for publication. The papers must remain dry.'

As she spoke, huge drops of water ran down her neck, slipped under the thin dress and pooled in the small of her back.

'We will not be much longer.' Da Couto turned his horse.

Maria double checked the buckles and pulled a rug over the opening in the vain hope that it would keep the moisture at bay. At home, she knew, her manuscripts would be pored over. If Spain and Portugal loosened their grip on South America, there would be opportunities for British trade. Her publisher, John Murray, was a man who liked to bring valuable reports to London, and London invariably loved whatever he brought. He'd have her words typeset quickly and the books would be on sale in every bookshop in the country before she had time to resupply and return. She looked forward to remembering this whole experience from a very great distance. She would tell Murray about the impossible terrain and her malicious companion and they'd laugh about it.

'It was a trial,' she'd admit, 'but I got through it.'

She pulled herself smoothly into the saddle, her manners fitted round her like armour. Almost lazily, while Mrs Graham's back was turned, the diplomat raised his whip and struck one of the slaves.

'Mr da Couto. Really,' Maria scolded.

Da Couto said nothing, only motioned the bearer on his way as Mrs Graham nodded curtly that she was ready. Her hand moved without a thought to check the buckle on the small leather dispatch bag strapped to the saddle. Then she pushed a wet strand of hair away from her face and sat ramrod straight, mirroring the long-backed kapok trees – the tallest and most majestic of the jungle's botanical treasures.

'Madam, please, be careful,' the diplomat said without conviction.

Maria sighed. She reached out to touch a vivid orange flower that jutted towards her from a bush sprouting leaves so dark they seemed almost black. Only just in time she pulled her fingers back as she remembered that the jungle was not to be trusted. For a second, as she turned, Maria thought she saw da Couto glower in disappointment. His smooth facade dropped like a shadow.

No wonder he hates me, she thought as her horse walked on to join the others. *He thinks we come this way solely for my pleasure.*

3

England to Brazil

Will Simmons's trip did not start well. In fact, it exceeded the boy's expectations in its dreadfulness – far worse than the day he'd sailed a bumpy crossing to County Down. At least the passage to Ireland had been mercifully short. Now, for several days as the ship headed south, he vomited over the side, he vomited into a bucket and he vomited onto the deck. At night, between snatched bouts of sleep, he vomited over the edge of his hammock. A rope of sick unfurled from his insides, almost smothering him as it came out. Practically delirious, Will would have sworn he hadn't eaten as much in his whole life as came back up again. He lost all sense of time and place, engulfed in the aching nausea that prolonged day and night until each minute seemed like an hour. In short order, he prayed for death, despite not believing in the mercy of God.

Then, when the ship docked to take on supplies at Tenerife, the sickness abated. Will emerged into the sunshine looking like a pile of crumpled clothes with a pale head on top. His stomach felt as if it had been turned inside out. He had lost weight and felt woozy, but at least he was no longer retching.

He washed in a barrel of seawater to remove the stench and went ashore.

Abroad was a revelation. The boy from Cornwall marvelled at the lush plants and the plentiful baskets of oranges and bananas. He'd never seen sky so blue. The pristine whitewashed walls entranced him and the yucca plants were as strange as living sculptures. As Will walked the bone-dry streets, he relaxed in the heat and his left knee, which for two years had given him nothing but gyp in the damp English climate, moved as easily as if it were a rusty old lock greased with pig fat. At a dockside inn run by an Englishman, Will ravenously ate his first food in over a week and fell asleep in the sunshine listening to the man's daughters play the castanets.

When he set sail once more, he had to admit that the Old Street Bridge Club was right: once a fellow got used to it, travel was not as bad as he'd expected.

Crossing the Atlantic, the ship docked next at Trinidad, where a small block of chocolate was brought on board at Matelot with the rest of the supplies. Despite having delivered the gentlemen several blocks of cacao, Simmons had never tasted the drink. He took small beer at home – coffee being for gentlemen of business, tea for ladies and chocolate for the nobility. Here, the whole crew were fed the dark, warm drink, sharpened with a shot of rum. Not all of them liked it.

'It looks like shite,' the cabin boy hissed.

But the concoction certainly didn't taste like shite. Will smiled as he raised the pewter cup to his lips and the bubbles exploded on his tongue. The chocolate was rounded like port or brandy but satisfying like brose.

'I could grow fat on this.' Simmons grinned, his mouth alight, as he sat on a barrel.

'At home, they reserve it for Her Ladyship,' a toothless old sailor laughed, raising his tankard.

The daily chocolate left Will in high spirits, so that some days he believed he could wheel with the gulls that fished the foaming water close to shore. Now that he felt so free, it came to him that the corner of England which up till now had been his whole universe, was in fact only a tiny scrap of a boundless realm. The world was an enticing whore slowly opening her legs. Will listened eagerly to the stories told by the old sailors – tales of Chinese junks and polar frosts. Tales of Indian monsters, and herds of horses in the Americas that, if a man could only catch one, he could keep.

Best of all, here he was no greenhorn, no scum, no lowlife. While he travelled, he was a man of the world. All this time and he had never known. He wondered what the captains he'd negotiated with had thought of him – green as grass. No wonder they'd tried to cheat him. He'd thought a trip to Eel Pie House for a bit of fishing and a bland supper was a grand outing. *Not now*, he thought, *not now*.

Brazil came quickly. By the time they made harbour on the mainland at Natal, Will quit the ship a different fellow from the surly, pale-faced lad who had boarded at Portsmouth. His hair had lightened and his skin was golden. Things had shifted. The ship was heading south with the tide. Several of the sailors turned out to bid Simmons farewell. Below decks, he shook hands like a gentleman leaving his own wedding and said he hoped they'd meet again. Then, coming up on deck, he halted nervously at the top of the gangplank. The voyage had been a safe haven. The sailors were rough, but everyone was on the same side. On the alien dock that teemed before him, he would be alone thousands of miles from home.

'Go on, Will!' one of the men shouted from the wooden belly.

Simmons took a deep breath. His heart raced as he forced himself to smile. Then he steeled his guts and walked down the gangplank, away from everything and everyone that was familiar.

It was like diving deep underwater. Natal was heaving. The air was hot as an oven and the noise was overwhelming, but Will noticed nothing of that. When he surfaced, he was along the dock and, listen as he might, he couldn't make out one word of the King's English among the stevedores, the sailors with shore leave and the merchants touting for trade. He spun on his heels, taking in the incomprehensible bustle, surprised that from a distance he couldn't even see the vessel that had been his home all these weeks. *I must find the Bridge Club's man*, he thought to himself.

'Senhor Dourado?' he asked. 'Senhor Dourado?'

Someone must be acquainted with the fellow.

*

Captain James Henderson liked Natal, especially down here in the evening, with the ships creaking in the darkness. He spent a good deal of time up and down the coast of Brazil and the town was one of his favourite ports. Supplies were high, the people were if not always friendly at least reasonable, and Natal had managed to stay out of the fighting that was impeding trade further south. Tonight, Henderson cut a fine figure on the deserted moonlit dockside. His hair was dark and his skin was pale as wax. His eyes were a shade of blue so light they were almost transparent. They might have made him seem younger were it not for the shadow of his beard. He didn't look Brazilian. He wasn't. But he'd lived here for a long time.

34

The captain had spent a pleasant evening ashore – he had procured a fine dinner and a woman with whom he had swapped the generosity of her favours for the generosity of his wallet. Now one hostelry after another snuffed out its lights. Up an alleyway the sound of footsteps receded as the last straggle of sailors quit the dock. Far off there was a peel of laughter as two harlots shared a joke – a flirtatious, disembodied, comforting sound. Henderson was walking back to his ship when he came across the lad. It was evident the boy was English, because he was talking to himself in the middle of the cobbled quay.

'I thought they was all Indians,' he said, drunkenly, his voice laden with wonder. 'I could have swore it.'

Henderson grinned. The lad was perhaps ten years younger than he was. He was not badly dressed and carried a sailor's roll that looked brand new. He clearly hadn't been here long. This, the captain noted, might prove amusing. Henderson cleared his throat.

'Hardly see an Indian in these parts, old man.' His voice was clear, his English accent chiming like a cool glass of clean water. 'Seen plenty in the interior, all feathers and bare chests, but at the coast they're a rarity.'

The reply was unexpected. The boy started. He drew his knife as he spun round, squinting to make out the fellow in the low light. Two sailors passed, ignoring the drawn weapon. Henderson said nothing. On the tall side and well built, the captain could handle himself in a fight – he had the strong, slim shoulders of a fellow who threw a powerful punch, and he wasn't afraid. In fact, a small smile played at the corners of his mouth.

'You need to be desperate or crazy or both to go into the

35

jungle, and you seem neither. But that's where the Indians live, if you really want to see one.' His pale eyes remained calm as he appraised Simmons's blade.

Will stared as he tried to place Henderson's accent, which was London by way of Brazil and New York and well beyond the boy's experience. Henderson was a handsome man and he'd squared up like a gent.

'You won't need your knife, mate.' The captain coolly held out his hand as he stood the boy down. 'I was only being friendly. My name is Henderson.'

The boy considered a moment and stowed his weapon. 'Will Simmons.' He grasped Henderson's fingers. 'Sorry. It gave me a turn, hearing English.'

'Quite understandable,' the captain replied, still as polished granite, and better dressed.

Inclined to tarry and investigate this drunken, late-night orphan of the town, Henderson withdrew a pipe from his pocket, stuffed it with tobacco and set it alight. A comforting waft of sizzling toffee shag clouded around the men. It would have been nothing extraordinary at home, but here, on the deserted, late-night dock, it was like meeting a pale English shade. Simmons's mouth dropped.

'You're newly arrived? Where are you berthed, if you don't mind me enquiring?' Henderson asked.

'I took passage and the ship is gone.' Simmons stifled a hiccough. 'I'm here to transact some business. Do you know Senhor Dourado, sir? I've been looking for him for hours, but no one seems to speak English.'

Henderson drew on his pipe and left a long pause before he decided to answer. 'There's a local man of that name – a trader. He has a warehouse in that direction' – he gestured

36

– 'towards the end of the quay. You'd most likely catch him at home – he's not so present in his affairs. I'm sure he'll have men to look after his stock.'

'My business is with Dourado alone.'

Will sounded dramatic, but then he was young.

'If I were you I'd head to town tomorrow. There's a square.' The captain gestured in the opposite direction. 'That would be the place to ask. Most private householders are abed. Matters at the docks run late and even here they're fading. I'm sure Senhor Dourado will be at home in the morning.'

Simmons nodded. 'Thank you, Mr Henderson.'

'Captain,' Henderson corrected him, tipping his hat. 'I'll take my leave then. Goodnight.'

The captain tarried one last moment to take in the final details of Will's appearance. If the boy had business with Dourado then he was evidently up to something, but that was not Henderson's concern. Still, his curiosity was lighted. Will was fresh from England. Henderson had not seen London in a long time. It must be fifteen years at least. Simmons somehow brought the city to mind, but Henderson was unsure what, if anything, he wanted to say about it. With no words coming to mind, the captain raised his hand and made his way onto a small ship of shabby appearance. Two men on watch sprang to their feet.

'Did that ship cross from England?' Simmons said to the captain's departing back. He found the question had formed quite involuntarily.

Henderson knew that his vessel was unusual. Old-fashioned, even.

'The *Bittersweet*'s a beauty, isn't she?' he turned and leaned in conspiratorially. 'She handles a dream. She might be traditionally built, but she's shoaly as a stream. You can bring her in, you see, almost any bay at all.' He winked.

Simmons grinned in recognition and Henderson smiled back. *Ah,* the captain thought, *now I'm getting the measure of the fellow. He's a smuggler.*

'Puts me in mind of a caravel or a fluyt,' Will said.

Henderson shrugged. The *Bittersweet* was wider than a ship of the line, and shallow for a cargo vessel. She housed twenty men, at capacity. The design was less unusual in these parts than it was where Simmons had come from. Caravels, after all, were Portuguese. 'The Yankees love their morning chocolate.' He hovered comfortably at the top of the gangplank.

Simmons hoisted his roll over his shoulder. This had been a lucky encounter. The boy's rum-sodden mind focussed. Henderson not only spoke English but was also just the kind of fellow who might run the Bridge Club's return cargo – decent, but not too decent. Someone who paid his debts and had done no more jail time than was usual. Just like Mr Grant said. Will had not thought to look for a captain before he had secured the Bridge Club's supplier, but if the chance fell into his lap, he'd take it. Now he thought on it, the shabby old ship was perfect too – nothing flash, which meant it wouldn't attract the wrong kind of attention. He cleared his throat.

'I may have a proposition for you, Captain. I need to find this Dourado fellow. I'm in the market for some chocolate beans. I hear it is the crop of the continent. And then I shall have to transport it.'

Henderson leaned over the side. Cacao was his cargo of choice. He'd been running it since he was a nipper. 'Where do you want to bring it in?' the captain enquired, low.

'England, of course.' Simmons was green. To him, there was only one destination.

'Is there much trade in cacao over the Wash?'

'Yes, sir. And growing.'

The captain nodded. England to him meant London. He'd been brought up there. Somewhere in the murky recesses of his mind it was still home. He took off his hat and ran his fingers through his hair. Returning was an attractive idea. Still, to discuss the matter further in common hearing would be foolish. Brazil was more laid back than other territories, but smuggling was still a felony. Henderson was circumspect, weighing up the invitation before issuing it.

'Can I offer you a drink?' he asked after a short pause. 'I'm planning to eat a custard tart before retiring – you're on Portuguese territory and if there's one thing the Portuguese do to perfection it's a custard tart. *Pastéis de nata*, they call them. I prefer 'em sprinkled with cinnamon. Have you yet had the opportunity?'

The boy grinned. 'Not yet, but I'd be delighted,' he said as he stepped off the quay and followed the captain up the gangplank.

4

Lord Cochrane's private study, Recife

Angelino hovered by the door in case he was needed. His greying hair was slicked behind his ears and it was not without pleasure that he eavesdropped. The rumour was that this Englishwoman was Lord Cochrane's lover. To Angelino, this seemed unlikely. Lady Cochrane was both younger and more beautiful than Dona Graham. Besides, Her Ladyship was in close proximity, asleep upstairs, along from the nursery where her children slumbered. Still, Angelino wanted to see what His Lordship and the dark-eyed *dona* got up to, left alone in the cool of the evening. He set his eye to the well-crafted brass keyhole and drew the cool green room into focus, with its leather-bound books and its ormolu timepiece on the white marble mantle. The clock struck midnight. He put a hand to his crotch for comfort and tried to hear what was being discussed.

His Lordship was not in uniform. As head of the Brazilian navy, Admiral Cochrane allowed himself a degree of sartorial freedom and tonight he wore an elegant pair of pale-gold britches and a flamboyant green jacket that showed off his figure. Maria thought he looked very fine as he poured her a glass of red wine and then paced in front of the window, which lay open. Behind them, the sun had long since set over the ocean like an orange pool of melted lustre and now the darkness was peppered with shipboard lanterns that marked the outline of the harbour. Maria had known Admiral Cochrane for almost twenty years. They always spoke frankly to each other.

'Kitty finds the conditions difficult. She's looking forward to the end of the conflict,' Cochrane confided.

'I can hardly blame her, but heavens, Thomas, haven't you only just started?' Maria sipped the wine, her elegant wrists highlighted by long honey-coloured satin gloves.

It was a comfort to be back in civilisation. It had taken two baths and a full day of careful unpacking to remove the rainforest from Mrs Graham's person. Between these duties she had told Cochrane's children stories about the jungle and instructed the eldest in how to play cards. As well as doing her duty.

'Kitty and I visited the hospital this afternoon. It was not pleasant, poor souls.' Maria had seen such scenes before, but it hadn't inured her. On the crowded, under-equipped wards, the wounded were dying in droves, carried off by infection after the ravages of post-battle surgery. The sweet stench of gangrene had made both women retch as they donned aprons and rolled up their sleeves. It was Lady Cochrane's first experience of war. She had managed not to cry in front of the injured men – that was the main thing. The tears had only seeped out in the carriage home.

'We mustn't let the children see. Nor Thomas.' Kitty dried her eyes. 'I can't help but worry about it all,' she sniffed, confiding in Maria, for the state of the injured and battle-worn troops was not the only matter on Kitty Cochrane's mind.

41

The family was here because the admiral had been disgraced in London. 'It's Thomas's reputation. My father was cut dead when he had to leave. I never worry for my husband on a raid or in a battle. He cannot die, Maria, he will not, until he makes everyone proud once more. He thanked God when the uprising started – now he will be able to make his name again.'

Maria sympathised. A man could lose everything over a rumour. She was sure that the admiral had not done what they said – stock exchange fraud was hardly in his nature. But London was harsh if you landed on the wrong side of its good opinion and, for the time being, Cochrane was in disgrace. Maria laid her hand on Kitty's shoulder.

'He will be pardoned. People will petition for him. They must. Everyone will be in awe of his naval successes. Thomas is a marvel and England will want him back. It will take time, that's all.' A man, after all, might regain his lost reputation, particularly if he had talent.

The admiral took a sip of claret and settled into a leather armchair. 'The job has to be done,' he said. 'By hook or by crook, Brazil will be independent. It's best to be quick – it'll mean fewer casualties in the long run.'

'I know,' Maria said gravely, banishing the memory of the makeshift hospital with its livid flesh and raw suffering. Wallowing was no good to anyone and it wouldn't get her to London any quicker or, for that matter, back to Rio to take up her position. 'You've turned around the war in six weeks, Thomas. It is quite amazing. Their Majesties can be nothing less than delighted. However,' she admitted, 'I did not come here only to deliver Her Majesty's missive. I need your advice on how I am to get home.'

Cochrane put down his glass. 'Really you oughtn't to be

travelling, Maria. I can't imagine what they were thinking, sending you this way – apart from to deliver the dispatches. You are reckless, my dear. No ships are leaving for England – it will take a month at least for things to calm down. We can find you passage then.'

Maria shook her head. She had promised to return to the royal nursery as quickly as she could. Even in wartime she knew there was always a way. 'That's all very well, but I don't have a month. I need to get back to London.'

'London? My dear lady, at the moment I can't see with certainty how we'll get you out of Recife,' Cochrane replied. 'I can spare no resources. We may have won a battle, but that is not a victory in the war. I'm maligned enough at home without being the fellow who lost the precious Mrs Graham on the high seas by dispatching her inappropriately. Murray would never forgive me. Can't you wait?'

Maria laughed. 'Silly,' she teased. '"The precious Mrs Graham."'

The admiral, however, was adamant. What he did not tell her was that Lady Dundas had written to him. Given his state of social disgrace in England, the old harridan must have been desperate. But there were few Englishmen in South America and, for that matter, in Brazil, and they all knew each other. Given the tone of the letter, the admiral was not sure that Maria ought to return to London. Despite the fact that she had never liked her niece, it was clear Lady Dundas would do everything in her power to keep the poor woman there. Still, Maria was used to sticking to her guns. If Lady Dundas took her on, he'd like to see that battle. Maria regarded him coolly.

'Are you sure you want to go back?' he asked. 'When the

43

Brazilians sent instructions they did not include ferrying you across the water, my dear, and I'm stretched as it is.'

Maria took this in. 'I must,' she said firmly. With or without Cochrane's help, she was determined, but it would be easier with it.

The dispatch pouch lay open on the table. The Emperor of Brazil's instructions were clear. The fight was not yet over and, though it might take till Christmas, Cochrane must force the Portuguese ships off the coast and isolate Portuguese sympathisers on the mainland. The power of the entire fleet must be dedicated to the fight.

'Dear Lord,' Maria sighed good-naturedly, 'please don't say I must travel onwards through the jungle again.'

Cochrane smirked. His fingers darted to the folds of his carefully knotted gold silk cravat. 'I have heard,' he said, 'that everything there has teeth.'

Maria's eyes brightened. 'Even Senhor da Couto.' She leaned in. 'By the end he was set to finish me, I swear. I've never seen a man more eager to take his leave, and I myself have never been so relieved to be delivered safely by a guardian. Though I hesitate to call him that. The jungle was formidable and he was just as bad. If I make my way onwards by land, at least I will be on my own reconnaissance and I can choose my own compatriots.'

'It's a rich country, but it guards its treasures well.' Cochrane emptied his glass, thinking of his family home in coastal Fife, where the coal at Culross had to be ripped from thin seams under the cold grey firth. The Cochrane family employed an army of miners as strong as pit ponies and not much taller. Until recent generations, they had been serfs. The pale colours of Cochrane's homeland were a distant memory.

44

Maria was aware she was lucky to be able to go back. She had no wish to rub it in.

'The jungle is alive. It's dangerous as a living nightmare and brimful of hostility. I was bruised, but I always heal quickly. At least I'll sleep in a proper bed tonight.' She stretched beneath the long skirt, flexing her ankles, unseen.

Cochrane regarded her. Mrs Graham was certainly elegant. This evening one would scarcely believe she was a bluestocking, for she had happily abandoned her accustomed daywear, the ugly grey travelling dress, in favour of something more fashionable. She lounged on the little sofa dressed in pale swathes of cascading satin, a blue feather with a small gemstone-and-pearl clasp clipped into her dark hair. Through the study's atmosphere of musty paper and sealing wax, she smelled of orchids. The doctor at the hospital reported she had raised the men's spirits. There was something about Maria Graham that you could believe in – a slice of home. If not unique in her travelling, she was at least extraordinary. Not many women had the force of personality needed to make long journeys. Still fewer were such good company. She would bring him to the point, he supposed, one way or another.

'If there was a merchant ship, I'd happily take passage—' she started.

'Madam,' Cochrane cut in, 'I know there's little point in telling you what to do.'

Maria blushed. She folded her hands neatly in her lap. 'I only thought a merchant ship would—'

Cochrane put up his arm to cut her off. There was no measure to be gained in beating around the bush. He would simply tell her the truth. 'If it is a merchant ship you are considering, there are few such vessels and almost certainly

45

you will have difficulty in finding a vacant berth. In wartime, the goods that are most profitable are food and weapons, not travelling English ladies. Besides, in the current situation it cannot come as a shock to find that each and every one is captained by an opportunist. It is not quite like taking passage on a pirate vessel or a smuggling ship, but the truth is it's not far off. We've had to string up half a dozen renegades in the last week and that's after we'd offered them the chance to join us and been refused. You know I don't hold against trade, Maria. Gentlemen of business can be gentlemen nonetheless, but the kind of fellow who trades in these circumstances . . . I would not encourage you to put your life in such hands. I do not say this solely because you are a lady. I would advise a man the same, but there are some indignities to which a woman can be subjected and you would be at great risk. Especially if you were captured.'

Maria nodded. Cochrane's advice was genuine, unlike that of many men, who, it seemed, were simply vexed by a woman attempting anything other than a gentle afternoon ride. She had had to stand up to such things ever since age of eight, when matters had been decided against her mother. Everyone wanted to dictate to a girl she had realised as they chose her clothes and censored her reading matter before packing her off to that hateful school, miles away. At first she'd prayed she might be allowed to go with her father on his next commission – but to no avail. Then she told herself the restrictions would stop when she reached adulthood, but they didn't. Everyone wanted to dictate to a lady. Cochrane was a friend, though. He was telling her the truth as he saw it.

'I understand,' she said. 'It's only that da Couto chartered a ship.'

'A tub,' His Lordship objected. 'It was a fishing boat. And he was heading south – that is quite different. For an Atlantic crossing you need something seaworthy.'

She called his bluff. 'Oh, a fishing boat would be fine. At least it could get me part of the way. My only alternative is to head inland and north till I reach another port.'

'Da Couto was a fool.'

'Without question.' Maria's eyes danced. She stretched her neck like a swan. 'I can't tell you how relieved I am to be rid of him and instead to be in your capable hands.'

Cochrane sighed. The interior was far too dangerous and if he didn't step in he could see Maria was determined on some damn foolish course – chartering a skiff and getting into trouble. He raised his hands in surrender. 'You'll be the end of me. I'll be sending two ships up the coast in a few days. They'll be on reconnaissance and if they come across enemy vessels they will engage them. However, one of them could make a short detour to drop you somewhere less central to the resistance than Recife. Somewhere you'd stand a decent chance of finding safer passage.' Cochrane pulled a chart from his desk. 'I'll have to find somewhere they can set you ashore.' The admiral's finger landed on the map. 'Have you visited Natal? It's the state capital of Rio Grande do Norte and a decent size for a trading port.'

Maria shook her head.

'It's safe, or safe enough – it declared for the Emperor early and it's out of the general run of the fighting. All shipping has been curtailed, but you should more easily pick up passage from there to England. If nothing else, you will certainly find a berth to North America, where you can change vessels. It should keep you out of trouble.'

'Thank you.' Maria smiled. 'I'm not afraid of a spat, Lord Cochrane.'

Cochrane tapped the chart, pleased he'd found some kind of a solution. 'Quite,' he said.

Her delight seemed to brighten the candlelight. The admiral smiled. When Maria had first married Thomas Graham, the young captain had been impressed by his wife's mettle. He said she was as tough a woman as he had ever met and that was probably true. He had hoped to have sons, Cochrane expected. There was something indomitable about Maria – like Britannia. He'd heard that she kept her head during a Chilean earthquake the year before when men of greater age and experience had panicked. Afterwards she was discovered calmly taking notes, recording the way the land had risen, for publication, she said. 'We do not know nearly enough about these phenomena. And there is only one way to learn,' she had snapped, as her would-be rescuers attempted to remove her from the aftershocks.

'You women! Lady writers.' The admiral refilled his glass. 'Do you never think it would be easier to travel somewhere there isn't either a war or a hurricane? With a maid?'

Maria laughed. She was relaxed now she had found her route. 'I do not relish help, Lord Cochrane, either in my toilette or in my travels. But I'm glad of your offer. Natal will do very well, thank you.' She leaned over and kissed his cheek.

The admiral blushed. He rolled up the chart and took a long sip of wine. 'This is not to be part of your scribblings, dear lady. Please, for the sake of posterity, leave without my interference. By rights I should not be accommodating you. It will be our secret.' Cochrane returned to his seat. 'You have gone quite Brazilian,' he declared.

'Well, I shall miss the excellent coffee.' Maria grinned. 'I have become an aficionado. Do you imagine they might serve me in London's coffee houses when I get home?'

His Lordship hooted. This was what made Maria such sterling company. 'Next you'll be attempting to trade in stocks, madam, or take a seat at Westminster,' the admiral said indulgently.

Maria would support such advances, but she knew he was joking. 'I'm looking forward to riding in the park under the trees and, oddly, to an English pudding, boiled in a cloth and eaten with a spoon,' she said.

Cochrane's eyes stopped dancing. 'Yes. Of course,' he said, suddenly serious. The admiral missed England but he wouldn't admit it.

Maria bit her lip. She had not meant to sadden him. 'I'm sorry, Thomas,' she started, but Cochrane lifted his hand.

'I'd love that too,' he said. He pulled himself up. 'Well, we shall only have you for a few more days. Kitty and the children will be sad to see you go, my dear.'

'Only a few days?'

'Indeed. The surgeon assures me that the men who are going to die will have done so by the end of the week. I'm replacing their numbers with slaves – letting them work off their price. Along with their freedom, they shall have the first wages of their lives, and we shall be at full capacity. I've never had such eager conscripts, though now we must train them.'

'That must be why the men are calling you Papa Cochrane.'

'Are they?' Cochrane blanched, genuinely discomfited by the news. 'Good heavens, Kitty will be appalled. And you must promise me, Maria, not to do anything foolish. Rio Grande do Norte is the best I can manage – you must make your way carefully from there.'

49

Mrs Graham put out her hand and they shook upon it.

When Lord Cochrane called for Angelino, the footman came promptly. The admiral comforted himself that the quality of serving staff in Brazil was marvellous.

'Bring Mrs Graham a night light,' he instructed. 'I've work to do and she needs to get to bed.'

'Night night, Papa Cochrane,' Maria teased.

Walking along the corridor, Mrs Graham resolved to sit up late, watching the pan-tiled roofs of Recife against the mackerel sky. She was bound to miss the sky south of the equator when she made it home, but at least here was a night or two when she could curl up comfortably beside the window and enjoy it.

Angelino held open the bedroom door and lit the candles inside. A strange fellow: he kept peering at her. She dismissed him. 'That will be all.'

She must be careful. The Cochranes were people to whom she could admit her weaknesses, but respect for a lady was too easily lost. You could be yourself up a mountain or even in the jungle, but when you reached civilisation a lady was expected to simper and take the long route. Maria never could stand it for long.

Natal

Will Simmons tracked down Dourado the next day. As Henderson had advised, once away from the docks Will obtained directions to the merchant's house easily. Natal was a town of faded grandeur. The sun was still on the east side of noon and the day's heat was building in intensity. The air smelled so pervasively of baking that there was no telling from where it emanated. A small group of barefoot boys played half-heartedly with a rubber ball in the dust, staring with eyes as hard as diamonds. A baby cried from inside what appeared to be an abandoned building with boarded windows. Off the marketplace, broken-down carts strapped to thin mules ferried baskets of vegetables to the market square.

Not far on, Simmons stopped. He caught his breath before he knocked on the door of the tall, ornate building with shabby orange shutters. In England the home of a prosperous merchant would be crisp in appearance, everything shipshape, but here it was nebulous, the pale-pink stucco so muted that from a distance you might think the whole structure was a dream. It felt as if it were crumbling before his eyes, the paint peeling in long strips and the brasses mottled. Simmons was shown inside by a butler who opened the door as if startled that there was a visitor. Dressed in a gaudy brocade jacket, the man had skin as dark as a roasted coffee bean. Silently, he showed Simmons through the shady hallway. After the walk uphill, the cool of the house was a relief. Dourado sat in his study, resplendent on a red leather chair dotted with studs. A plump merchant in the middle years of life, he was evidently delighted by Simmons's arrival. Once their business was transacted, he invited Will to stay for port and biscuits.

Port had become a potent political symbol in Brazil, and Dourado refused to sell the supplies in his warehouse, aware that it might mark him as an unpatriotic recidivist. He was canny, for as the Brazilians claimed the land and the Portuguese drew back, men were hung for far less than a Portuguese taste in liquor. Still, it seemed a terrible shame to let the vintage casks go to waste, so Dourado marked them for his personal use and he was stolidly drinking his way through the entire stock. Simmons – English, newly arrived and therefore unoffended by the provenance of the proffered drink – was an unexpected connoisseur. He lapped up the ruby nectar, showing appreciation not only for the port itself but also admiring Dourado's antique glasses with barley-sugar stems, of which the older man was particularly proud.

Dourado refilled the glasses and decisively snapped a biscuit in two, causing his long lace cuffs to ripple. It was pleasant to have fresh company. Of late, Natal had come to a halt culturally. Even the opera house had lain empty for months. Nonetheless the town continued a hub for timber, rum, salt, tobacco, sugar and cacao beans – treasures from the plantations inland and the booty of the jungle, which sprawled to the south like a vast emerald pool into which Senhor Dourado and his like dipped occasionally for their profit, if not their pleasure. It was for reasons of profit that Dourado tarried in the slow, sleepy provinces rather than move south to the court. For the most part he was happy with his decision. Still, sometimes the company palled and he longed for Natal's happier days, before the war had broken out, when there had been a different concert every evening and an opera at the weekend.

'I've been expecting you,' he said.

Will shrugged. 'There was a problem with the last shipment. The captain proved unreliable. From now on you'll be dealing with me, if that's all right, sir? And if it turns out well, we may scale up. The gentlemen will be in touch.'

Dourado nodded. The Bridge Club, or as he knew them, *os ingleses* – the Englishmen – had been excellent customers for over ten years. They had sought him out, recommended by an acquaintance long since passed on. Dourado had no names or addresses for his London-based clients, but they paid in advance – a rarity in an untrusting world – and despite occasional changes to their timetable, *os ingleses* had proved largely reliable. For this, he afforded them a good price and regular service. The boy seemed fresh, unlike many of the captains who had arrived to pick up the biannual parcel. 'Will you stay for luncheon, Senhor Simmons?'

Simmons looked momentarily tempted but shook his head. He wasn't hungry. Natal had already supplied him amply this morning with hot doughnuts fried at the dock. Besides, he had another meeting. Henderson had promised to secure the boy a cargo of cacao beans on commission. Will had thought to buy the beans from Dourado at first, but Henderson swore he would find it cheaper and, after all, the more money Will made, the more he would keep. Dourado might supply the Old Street Bridge Club with their precious parcel, but they had left no instructions as to where Will was to procure the rest.

'I have to get back to the harbour,' he said dutifully. 'I'm sampling cacao.'

Dourado considered this. The old merchant's eyes were reptilian. One hand balanced on his belly, obscured by the frill of his cuff, while he sipped his drink with the other.

'I can supply you,' he offered with a slow, deliberate blink. 'You need only ask. My warehouse has a plentiful stock. Rum. Cacao. Sugar. Salt. Whatever you need.'

Simmons shook his head. 'Thank you,' he replied. 'I'll come back to you, if I may?'

It was most unlikely that Dourado would be able to match Henderson's deal. It transpired that the captain could source beans directly from the mountain farms. Henderson had agreed a flat fee for this service and hadn't been greedy, which boded well for negotiating the passage. Simmons would stick with that. It was clear the captain was an enthusiast. 'Occasionally they even send a bag or two of wild beans,' he had said, his eyes gleaming, for wild chocolate was a particular prize.

'Perhaps, with your permission, I might stay to dine on my next visit?' Simmons said courteously, turning to Senor Dourado and laying his empty glass on an inlaid side table. 'I shall no doubt be back in Natal later in the year and on that occasion I hope to remain longer. It would be a pleasure to break bread with you, sir.'

54

The merchant gave a mannered nod. His thin tongue flicked across his lips. He could wait. In fact, he'd enjoy it.

Will carefully stowed the block of chocolate in a long leather bag on his belt. In the heat, he had abandoned his English jacket with its useful pockets. 'It will not spoil?' he asked.

Dourado shook his head and showed not the slightest surprise. If the Englishmen chose not to tell their couriers the nature of the goods, which were frankly unspoilable, then he would not betray their confidence.

'No,' he promised, reaching out a cool hand and grasping Will's firmly. 'It is very . . . dense. I look forward, Mr Simmons, to seeing you again.'

★

Back on the quay, Captain Henderson had repaired to a bar. He dragged one of the chairs outside, where he could take advantage of the pleasant breeze off the ocean, and called for rum and a plate of fruit. The local custom was to siesta over the hottest part of the day, but since he'd arrived in Brazil as a child Henderson had never held with that. Instead he preferred a leisurely lunch and the opportunity to read. Now taking off his hat, he pulled his dark hair back from his face and settled to his meal. The mango was ripe, the fragrance mouth-wateringly sweet. On the dock, he watched a group of barefoot fishermen working in the sun repairing a jangada's sails. One of them was playing a drum, setting a rhythm reminiscent of the slave ships, upon which, no doubt, some of them had made their voyage to Brazil. The sail was white with mottled golden markings, faded by the sun. *They'll quit soon,* Henderson thought, settling in his chair. *Perhaps Will might be back by then.*

The captain liked the new arrival. The crew of the *Bittersweet* were a hand-to-mouth bunch with predictable rough pleasures, but Simmons had a real passion for travel. The Englishmen had stayed up late talking as the beeswax candles burned low and the cabin became scented with warm honey and spirits. As they talked, Henderson had been transfixed by the idea of a return to England. An excuse to go home and see what was there. Now the captain adeptly sliced the fruit on his plate and, with the busy dock moving behind him and the drumbeat measuring his thoughts, he wondered if London was the same as when he'd left. He slipped a slick morsel into his mouth and downed a shot of rum. He had not been home for more than ten years: in fact, now he came to count, it was nearer twenty.

The place still had a vague hold on him. He found the country of his birth difficult to remember with exactitude. If he tried, the small house near Covent Garden where he had resided swung into his mind's eye, a jagged array of half-recalled snippets in a cloud of confusion. The place had smelled of lavender and thyme, which fragranced the smooth satinwood drawers and the heavy damask pillows. He had been young then – a whippersnapper devoted to his mother. Afternoons, as the rain trickled down the window, he'd sneak into the kitchen for hot bread and a slice of cheese eaten with a glass of milk and a slug of brandy. Every morning a tutor gave him lessons in languages and mathematics, history and fine art. Once a week a dancing master arrived and the dining room was cleared so he could learn Scotch reels. Then in the evenings he'd read aloud by the fire as his mother wrote her journal. Mrs Henderson was an enthusiast who noted everything.

Henderson wondered if the house might still be there and, if so, who might live in it. Was it still a place of leather-bound books and butter toffees? Were the shops in Covent Garden as grand? Had the buildings on the fringes of Soho been completed? A pang stung his chest. He had not thought of the place for years. He was a man now – a captain and very far away.

When his mother died, it had been James who organised the burial despite his tender age. The family's solicitor wrote to the boy's father. Then the sole occupant of the house, or at least its sole master, the youngster, waited. The staff continued to do his bidding. The tutor arrived every morning. The dancing master came once a week. Money was released to cover the accounts. Apart from the absence of Mama, nothing changed.

'We must be patient, James,' the solicitor said when the boy visited him in his offices on Broad Street.

Yet while the tardy reply surely made not one jot of difference to the solicitor, James could not be patient. To him, his father's instructions meant everything, for the rest of his life hinged on them, and the truth was that he had no idea what might transpire. He remembered sitting, the clock ticking loudly in the drawing room, waiting to know. Waiting, in fact, to have something to do. Anything. Even just to eat dinner. One day he walked to the British Museum with his tutor. Thereafter he resolved to take a constitutional promenade every morning. He toured the park, fed the ducks and stared at the horses. Once he even flirted with a maid, carrying the girl's shopping basket to a house off Soho Square, not far from his own.

In time, his father sent instructions that the boy was to come to Brazil. The letter weighed heavily in James Henderson's young hands. He read it three times and sank onto the bottom step in the hallway. He had no idea how far Brazil was. He was only twelve years of age, and though he had the measure of a hundred yards or even a mile or two, five thousand miles was incomprehensible. However, still a child, he did as he was bid, leaving the solicitor to close up the household and forward the last of the family's English affairs while he took passage. A child travelling alone, he was older than the youngest of the crew, and set out in style, quite the gentleman. He carried with him a map of Brazil that he had found in a periodical. He studied the picture nightly.

'I'm looking forward to life in the colonies,' he remembered saying, envisioning a traditional plantation house, an abundance of household servants and a stable of horses, if not the searing heat and humidity, which came as a shock.

His family was respectable. His father owned a small plantation. Or at least that was what his mother had always believed. For all her reading, she had been naive and, worse, she had endowed her only son with the same malady. Even now, years later, he did not like to think of the disappointment that greeted him when he had disembarked.

Henderson poured another drink and tried not to brood. He was too old to go through all that again. He passed a hand over his rough chin and turned his attention to a fracas that was building at the quay. Something was going on. The dockside was as busy as ever, but people were showing no sign of quitting their employment for the slow afternoon hour or two that went with the sun. In fact, quite the reverse. Such a crowd was gathering that it blocked his view of the horizon.

Henderson craned, but he couldn't see what the fuss was about. The fishermen stood on tiptoes beside their raft, the drum abandoned and the patchy golden sail crumpled over the mast. Several self-important officials bustled out of their offices and a couple of messengers were sent into town to alert anyone well connected who might have an interest. Something was about to transpire.

Henderson stood up to check the *Bittersweet*. It seemed unaffected. The serving girl came with more rum in a pottery jug. 'You've got a nice face.' She winked brazenly.

Henderson smiled. Women liked it when he didn't shave. They liked a real man – grizzled but with the manners of a gentleman, or what they thought was a gentleman. Then he caught sight of the cause of the stir and he discounted any notion of an indulgent afternoon dallying upstairs. He nudged the girl to one side. 'Bring me coffee,' he said.

Standing up, he made out a ship in his line of vision, sailing towards the harbour. 'Well, I'll be blowed,' he breathed, for within a few hundred yards of the dock there was a frigate with both the British and Brazilian flags hoisted. Henderson pondered what that might mean. So far there had been no trouble at Natal and certainly no battleships this far north under any flag. No wonder the crowds were gathering.

The girl shrugged and shimmied back to the bar as the captain finished the last of his rum without taking his pale eyes off the incoming vessel. Was the war set to come this far north?

The British ship docked smartly, the familiar naval whistles prompting the crew like clockwork. A smooth-cheeked junior officer was dispatched ashore to settle the papers. The crowd obstructed the boy's progress and fired questions at him in Portuguese as he pushed his way through. His crewmates tarried on deck and appeared to feel no need to enquire about the crowd's intent or indeed communicate with them. It was very English. Henderson liked the coolness of it. Usually the stallholders would be plying their wares over the side, but everyone wanted to know what the ship was doing before trying to make a profit. Henderson strained to see as the ship's captain moved to greet a lady emerging from his cabin.

Henderson straightened. This was a strange development. Usually the presence of a woman wouldn't trouble him. Henderson was used to female attention. He was tall, strong, well dressed and capable, to say nothing of the fact that, while he wasn't rich, he certainly had money. The captain made no bones about it. He took female attention when he wanted it and ignored it when he didn't. But something about the woman on the British vessel caught his eye. The lady was immediately intriguing though, he had to admit, it couldn't have been her looks that caught his attention. Respectably dressed in a clean, well-made grey outfit, her dark-brown hair was smoothed into a tidy bun under a demure hat. She was in her thirties, petite and pale-skinned – nothing extraordinary, but nonetheless Henderson couldn't take his eyes off her. What was remarkable, it dawned on him, was her absolute lack of adornment. Women of all classes in the Brazils moved in a veritable swathe of flowers, wrapped themselves in brightly coloured shawls and cut back their clothes to show enticing strips of flesh, which, in most cases, was available for hire and, occasionally, to purchase outright. Apart from elderly widows, females here decorated themselves with diamanté, polished turquoise, dyed feathers, ribbons, amber beads and pearls. Respectable or not, they shimmered all day and all night. Not this one.

Even in the bright sunshine, she was so buttoned up that she might as well have been in uniform. Her cheeks were not rouged and her hair sported no oil. He couldn't see as much as a sliver of gold and not a single ribbon. What on earth was she doing here? In a single smooth movement she stretched like a long grey cat and twisted her wrists. Then she gave the naval captain a thin smile and tidied herself primly, as if that were needed. Finally, she raised a dark parasol. In all, if Henderson was honest, he found the woman's presence more perturbing than the warship.

When his coffee arrived, Henderson allowed the bitterness to sharpen his mind without taking his eyes off the deck. The woman had the deportment of a ballet dancer. She was moving towards the gangplank, her parasol casting an elegant shadow.

The crowd on the dock shifted as the British captain descended with the woman behind him. In their wake, two sailors carried a brown leather trunk and three smaller bags. They pushed through the gathering. As one man asked a question in Portuguese, the captain, his hand on his sword, answered staunchly that he was only seeing this lady safely settled then he would be on his way. The crowd continued to bark their concerns. It must be intimidating, Henderson thought, but the woman showed no sign of being cowed as the Brazilians fired questions like unrelenting cannon. What was happening at sea? What was the news? Without slowing, the captain calmly answered these enquiries. The rebels were routed in Recife and almost all of Bahia had fallen, though not yet Maranham. The ship would leave immediately.

'We have no orders for Natal,' he said.

The relief was palpable along the dock and the news spread.

61

The crush loosened. Several men peeled off into the bars. A woman let out a yawn and headed, no doubt, for a thin mattress in a shuttered dockside room. One or two people took off towards town to spread the tidings. *Bahia has fallen. The ship is leaving. It has no business here.*

With the mystery of the frigate's appearance solved, slowly the crowd backed off. A line of port officials shrugged and, slapping each other on the back, headed to the *taberna* for lunch. Vendors started to sell beads, cotton, knives and bananas to the crew. Three women dressed in lavishly ruffled red skirts flirted over the side and money changed hands. The captains of two or three vessels bought drinks from a stall and toasted each other. The fisherman by the jangada went back to the beat of his drum.

Meanwhile, the English officer and his grey lady strode towards in Henderson's direction, towards town. The woman's demeanour was impeccable, undisturbed except by one youngster who, transfixed by the captain's naval uniform, was running ahead, squeaking intermittently with excitement. This appeared to amuse her. Henderson saw a smirk flicker across her face. He laid a coin on the table to pay and, without really knowing why, stepped into the street as the English party passed.

'Might I be of assistance?' He doffed his hat. 'I know Natal and I'd happily help.'

They were striding at what could only be described as a military pace. The lady shook her head curtly. The English captain barked, 'Move along now, sir,' and strode faster. The woman kept up with him without turning a hair. Her eyes betrayed no shock at the sights of the quay as they unfolded – not the sweating deckhands, the prostitutes crowding the ship, the hubbub of stalls, including one where three slaves were for sale, their ankles manacled. She might as well have been walking through a country garden as she moved inexorably away from the water.

'Where are you going?' Henderson asked.

'We're fine, thank you, sir,' the English captain insisted. 'Please get out of the way.'

Henderson stopped, still-eyed, and stepped to the side. He was not a fellow who was generally dismissed. He considered following the officer and the lady as they turned towards town, but he thought better of it. The woman, he noted, was wearing a haunting orchid scent. It hung in the air, fresh among the fetid sweetness of the dockside. The atmosphere around her seemed cooler because of it. And he realised, though the captain was clearly not her husband, the woman was wearing something gold after all – a wedding ring. The disappointment that turned his stomach surprised him. He was a practical man, or at least he had been since he arrived in Brazil. Once he realised he was not the son of a respectable plantation owner, his expectations were quickly doused. His father put him to work running spirits north and sugar south (for that was how he had started) and ever since there had been no room in his life for dreams or fancy. He made excellent money. He had an education. He ran a tight ship. What more might he aspire to? Now this dowdy Englishwoman caught his imagination and for the life of him he couldn't understand why.

He stared after her as she disappeared around the corner like a shadow, the sailors struggling with her cases. A grin spread across Henderson's face as he strolled back to his chair to wait for Simmons.

'I wonder what your name is?' he said under his breath.

'Senhor?' the waitress asked.

'Rum. More rum.'

Perhaps it had simply been too long since he'd seen an Englishwoman.

★

The British ship set sail within two hours and the woman did not reappear on the dock to wave it off. Henderson was glad when Simmons arrived to distract him, and the two men drank, waiting for the samples of cacao to arrive. Time in the colonies was an elastic matter. Henderson didn't carry a timepiece. There was no point. Matters transpired at their own pace. In the shade, sheltered from the heat dripping like flame from the sky, several street children slept with a pack of mongrel dogs they had adopted.

'You missed it.' Henderson grinned. 'There was a frigate done up to the nines. Fifth class. She dropped into port and didn't even fully resupply.'

'But they wouldn't attack here?' Will asked.

Henderson shook his head. 'I can't see it. It's the state capital all right, but it's not nearly as strategically important as other towns on the coast. Besides, it was a royalist ship – Brazilian, not Portuguese – and Natal's Brazilian through and through. That's just the feeling up here.'

Will gulped his beer. Even warm, it was refreshing. 'It doesn't feel like a capital,' he said. 'I'd say it's more like a market town. In the provinces. Hereford. Somewhere like that.'

Henderson shrugged. He had never been to Hereford. What he knew was that Natal was always relaxed, like a loyal old retainer left in charge of a stately home, taking off his shoes, cooling his feet in His Lordship's fountain and enjoying the cellar. The architecture of the town was quite fine. The atmosphere was easy. There had been no fighting. 'All the action has been around Recife and Bahia. The court is further south – it's safe there.'

The revolution held allure. When the war started the captain had thought of presenting himself to Cochrane as a gentleman volunteer but, though he could sail, he had no military experience. Besides, however competent on the water, he doubted a smuggler and for that matter the son of a smuggler would be welcome at His Lordship's cabinet.

In time, the shadows lengthened and work resumed on the dock. A while after the clock tower struck five, a thin farmer emerged from the crowd wearing loose, homespun trousers and a dark-brown shirt that blended with his skin so exactly that the two were almost indistinguishable. As he leaned in to shake hands, Will caught a whiff of woodsmoke and beans. The man was clearly delighted to see Henderson. He clapped the captain on the back and bowed very low, his limbs like sticks and his black eyes small as pinheads and just as sharp.

'I came as soon as I could,' he said.

'There's no need to rush,' the captain assured him.

'Here?' he asked.

Henderson nodded. 'Just set up to one side.' He handed the farmer a drink.

The man downed the shot. Then he unpacked two small sacks of roasted beans, a pestle and mortar, and a chocolate pot for heating the drink. He set up his equipment on the cobbled quay, chattering in swift Portuguese, which Henderson intermittently translated as he lounged on the inn's veranda in a ragged patch of shade. The farmer set a fire in a small circle of stones. It was an intriguing ritual and the rhythm lulled any worries Simmons had about his lack of knowledge. In no time the chocolate paste was transferred into the whisking pot with a slug of hot water. The aroma that rose was extraordinary.

'Have you ever had it fresh?' Henderson asked.

Simmons shook his head. On board, the ship's cook had used block chocolate. This smelled different – strong, almost like coffee. The farmer tipped in raw sugar and added chilli powder from a flacon in his pocket. Then he poured.

Simmons coughed as the scent of chilli caught in his throat, but when he tasted it, it was like the chocolate melted into him. The boy could swear his senses were enhanced. He could see more clearly. Somewhere along the dock someone was playing a pipe. The music crept closer. Will felt his pulse race as if he might float to the sand dunes beyond the last jetty. Somehow the chocolate in his mouth had disappeared.

The native's tiny eyes sparkled. He laughed, revealing the even yellow teeth of a skeleton. Then the farmer held up a finger and proceeded to the next bag of beans.

Henderson said, 'That one was the cheaper of the two.'

Will tried to focus.

The captain continued smoothly. 'I don't remember chocolate being drunk widely at home. In fact, I don't remember it at all. I was young when I left.'

'New manufactories are on the rise,' Will garbled, the ideas coming together in his mind. 'They make a powder that is cheaper than the slabs. I haven't tried it.'

'What brought you, Mr Simmons, to the idea of importing the stuff?'

Simmons halted. He had no intention of telling Henderson

about the activities of the Old Street Bridge Club, but he had never thought to concoct a story that would make sense without them.

'Why should the toffs have it all?' he stumbled. 'I'm a businessman.' He ran his finger along the inside of the cup to pick up the remains of the chilli chocolate. 'All men should have cacao. And women too. It's on the rise and this stuff is delicious.' He blushed. 'Isn't it delicious?'

Henderson stopped. The boy was lying or at least concealing something. The only reason to continue after Trinidad, if chocolate was your game, was for the quality and Simmons had never tasted such fine chocolate before. So what was the boy doing here and why was he trying not to reveal it?

'Most enterprising.' Henderson let it pass.

Will smiled. 'I shall make more money from this than from what I was doing before.'

At least that was said with conviction.

The next beans were darker, but that meant little when it came to flavour. Simmons peered into the pot as if he were considering the world's mysteries while the farmer whisked so vigorously he must be surely be hurting his arm.

Would I run something of which I had no knowledge? the captain wondered.

He never had. It was the first principle his father had instilled. Still, Simmons was offering an excellent rate at no financial risk. Henderson was set to profit more than he would running the same cargo up the western seaboard to the burgeoning ports of Boston and New York. Perhaps, he mused, it was simply time to return to England. It would be interesting to see the place with adult eyes. He remembered little of London – only tiny details that intrigued him. Perhaps

67

something of his old life lingered. To know it as he knew Rio or Washington or New York suddenly appealed. He wondered why he hadn't thought of returning before.

The farmer held out the second sample.

Simmons sipped. 'Oh, I like this one.'

The man nodded, as if concurring that the boy had made an excellent decision. Then he barked some figures. Henderson cut in, speaking so swiftly that it was impossible to pick out individual words. The men argued solidly for the best part of five minutes, with the farmer looking as if he had been hit in the stomach and an expression on Henderson's face as if the man had uttered some dreadful obscenity. In the end they shook hands.

'Some of both. Sixty/forty,' Henderson announced, the deal done.

Simmons looked contented. He was enjoying himself so much that he no longer cared about making money. The coin he was spending wasn't his anyway. He was sure Henderson had driven a good-enough bargain. He picked up the pewter cup and licked it. There was something about drinking this thick liquor in the heat that made him feel languorous.

'And some wild beans?' The boy fancied himself a connoisseur.

Henderson entered into a fast-paced discussion that resulted in his hand being shaken.

'How long till we leave?' Simmons enquired.

Henderson thought he detected a crestfallen shadow pass across the boy's face when he assured him that with luck they could set sail in two days, maybe three. Then, the deal done, the men ordered rum.

'To London,' Henderson toasted, and Will clicked his

tankard as they settled contentedly to watch the sun sink below the horizon and the nightly promenade along the balmy dock of vagabonds, freshly arrived sailors and whores. The smell of roasting meat rose from the street stalls in a sizzle and a fiddle player begged for coin as he rasped a haunting melody. Life could not be more perfect.

6

Natal

Maria Graham woke early and was served breakfast in her room. The eggs came with a chilli condiment that set her mouth on fire. She downed her coffee to douse it and set off about her business.

By contrast, it was with a sore head that Captain Henderson emerged into the searing sunshine from the shadows of his cabin. The flat stench of stagnant seawater hit him in a wave as he perused the quay and remembered that although he had had a pleasant evening with Mr Simmons he had not elicited the information for which he had hoped. Henderson knew from experience, however, that when a man offered a portion of money up front it was expedient to respect his privacy.

With the *Bittersweet* set to depart, the crew were hard at work, scrubbing and waxing the surfaces and checking the ropes. Henderson's mate, Clarkson, was a reliable taskmaster. The captain strode across the deck and dipped his head into a barrel of tepid water. There was no breeze today. These places never changed. He ran a hand over his hair. He must, he knew, look a sight. In Brazil that didn't matter, but if he was going back to England he was damned if he'd arrive looking anything less than dapper.

Taking the matter of his sartorial propriety in hand, Henderson waved vaguely as he headed down the gangplank and across the dock, making for the city. There was a tailor near the market square who had a good reputation. The sun was almost at its height and Henderson kept to the sharp shadows between the bonds and dockside bars. The heat made the captain's skin prickle. Over the years he had never got used to the tropics. It was an inconvenient trait for a ship's captain in these parts. Still, from the shadows you could see more clearly.

The first he noticed of Mrs Graham was her fragrance – a light but lingering trail that rendered everything more vivid. Henderson's grogginess disappeared and he felt a remarkable sense of clarity. As he looked up he saw her coming from the direction of town, striding purposefully through the crowd, still wearing the same grey dress as the day before. The captain pulled back, letting her pass, glancing towards the commercial quarter and then over his shoulder at her receding figure. There was something about her. Something inexplicably important. He knew of a certainty that the tailor would simply have to wait. He must follow this woman and find out more. On the fringes of his cocked hat, his hair was tied in a ponytail, already almost dry in the sun. He ran a hand over the scrape of beard that grizzled his chin and wondered if he should have shaved. No. He was respectable enough. He fell into step.

Maria appeared at home amongst the hubbub. Henderson noticed she clasped her purse carefully, clearly aware that it was easy to have your pocketbook picked. He dodged through the throng, keeping her in sight as she inspected the ships, stopping at one vessel after another but setting off again almost immediately. Henderson hung back. As he passed he asked a Norwegian deckhand what the lady had wanted, but the man spoke neither English nor Portuguese. Henderson decided that keeping the woman's figure in sight was more pressing.

Ahead of him, Maria continued methodically making her way along the moorings. A shipment of sugar was being loaded, hoisted precariously with uneven ropes. She passed it and paused for only the merest second at the *Bittersweet*, then she shrugged her shoulders. This was Henderson's chance. He clutched nervously at his starched cuff.

'You do not rate the *Bittersweet*, madam?' He bowed.

Maria turned. She barely nodded, recognising him from the dock, the day before. The man who had accosted her. 'I expect she does not sail for England.'

'You are mistaken. We are for Falmouth, or very close, and after that I will sail up the Thames. I have a fancy for London. I lived there as a boy.' Her eyes, he noted, were so hazel they verged on green.

'And I suppose you are the captain of this vessel?'

'James Henderson, madam, at your service.'

'She seems a trifle light for the job, Captain Henderson.'

'She handles a dream, Mrs . . .'

'Graham.'

Maria considered a moment. Unlike Henderson, she was solely focussed on her passage. She knew there would be no British naval vessels at Natal, but she had hoped to find a decent passage. The *Bittersweet* was a tub compared with any other ship she had sailed on, and it had to cross the

72

Atlantic, which was no millpond, as Cochrane had pointed out. For a start, the body of the boat lay peculiarly low in the water for a ship she estimated to be of some ninety feet. For another thing, it was very old-fashioned. The deck looked like a Portuguese caravel or perhaps a Dutch fluyt, the like of which had not been seen in His Majesty's navy or indeed any other since the days of Lord Nelson's grandfather, and Lord Nelson had been dead for almost twenty years. Maria had promised Cochrane to be careful – this was exactly the kind of fellow he had implored her to avoid. He seemed too keen, for a start, and his manner was a trifle familiar.

'Thank you for your kindness, Captain Henderson, I may come back to you.'

Henderson persisted. 'There are not many, Mrs Graham.' He sounded a good deal more confident than he felt. He now wished he had shaved.

'Many of what, sir?'

'Ships bound for England. Mostly from Natal, vessels sail south for either the capital or the whaling, or north for the Americas. Anyone going west normally makes for Lisbon, although at the moment that route is not much in use. There are few of us English here and we are very far from home.'

Mrs Graham perused him coldly. She did not relish being herded into making a decision, or the sense of foregone conclusion that emanated from Henderson's person. There was something of the rough dandy about this man and she didn't like that either. He had not shaved.

'As I said, Captain Henderson, I may come back to you. Thank you for your kindness. Good day.' She turned away.

Henderson felt as if he had been slapped in the face. He stood on the dock, reeling. Women generally accommodated him, particularly if he tried to be charming and engage them in conversation. 'Oh.' The word popped out of his mouth like a button off a fat man's waistcoat.

Seemingly unaware of his continued presence, Mrs Graham disappeared onto a Danish merchant vessel as the captain collected himself. A flash of her grey dress passed above his head. He drew himself up. He was certainly not going to stand here, staring after her. Gathering his wits, he set off in the direction of the tailor's, though as he strode up the hill he could not stop running over the conversation. The exchange might have gone better, he realised drily, though he was unsure exactly how. She had seemed to expect something from him – something else.

A block from the old concert hall he turned down a side street past a stall selling fresh pastries and honeyed nuts. The journey to England would take six weeks at least, and although he would arrive in summertime he judged it best to pick up a warm scarf and some thicker vestments. The captain's birthday was in June, but he recalled one year when he was five or six shivering in the cold as his birthday cake had been cut. His mother had drawn the scene in her journal. The motley collection of woollen items he wore on his regular trips to American cities would never do for the English capital. To stroll around Mayfair in sartorial disarray would be an insult to his entire upbringing.

At the tailor's door, Henderson hovered, finding himself reluctant to enter. The spectre of Mrs Graham lingered in his mind's eye. Perhaps she had rejected him because he looked unkempt. Ladies, he dimly recalled, were particular about a chap's appearance. Given the look of most sailors on the quay, he knew he was a veritable Beau Brummell, but still.

In the sunshine on the doorstep, a grey cat was asleep. Its tail flickered.

'I shouldn't have let her get away,' he muttered.

With consternation, he noted it felt as if he might never have a chance to redeem himself. What if their few words this morning turned out to be the only chance he had to speak to Mrs Graham? This was an unpleasant sensation. Henderson glanced back down the hill in the direction of the docks and worried that she had found passage on another ship. Then he worried that she had returned to the *Bittersweet* and he had not been there.

The captain fished in his pocket, took out his pipe and lit up, leaning against the wall as the wisps of smoke curled round him. He had not met a lady in several years – the women on the docks were of a different mettle. The Dutch woman in Washington to whom he frequently sold his cargo might have been a lady once, but Mrs Graham was another thing altogether. She was a study in restraint. The only showy thing about her was that perfume. Its richness reminded him of marzipan. He tried to imagine he was still English – fresh off the ship and brimful of manners. A gentleman. What would he have done? He had been better then.

On a whim he knocked out his pipe against the door frame and turned back to the square. There was nothing for it but to make enquiries about where the English *dona* was staying. He dodged between the shadows cast by tall palms over the stalls that peppered the marketplace. A small crowd of dark women thronged around a barrel of olive oil and an argument was taking place between two men in front of a wheel of cheese. After three attempts, Henderson was directed to a *conselho* by a girl selling leather belts and drawstring purses.

'The new Englishwoman lodges there.' She gestured. 'Grey dress.' She mimed Mrs Graham's bun with a flick of her fingers. 'Yes. That way.'

It was a Brazilian house. Further up the hill there was a scattering of premises inhabited by British merchants. These did not have the quality of crumbling paint that characterised even the most respectable Brazilian street. Henderson did not see any of the English socially, and only occasionally for trade. He could not say if that was because he avoided them or they avoided him. It was interesting that Mrs Graham had not chosen to stay among her own kind – a good sign, he thought.

Small birds swooped from the roof as he rapped at the door. Their trajectories seemed suicidal as they dived through the intense blue horizon, whizzing like bullets past the thin gutters and pulling up impossibly only seconds before crashing onto the cobbles.

'I would like to leave a message for the English *dona*,' Henderson said when the housemaid answered. 'Bring me a pen and ink. Bring some paper. I must write a note.'

★

Later, much calmer, having visited the tailor and eaten a light meal standing up at an open-fronted stall, Henderson returned to his cabin. For some hours now he had been wondering if his phrasing had been correct. Miles away, he jumped at an unexpected and rapid knock on his door that recalled his attention to business. Henderson caught his breath and only let it go when Simmons appeared smiling in the door frame. This, the captain realised, was probably timely.

Will had clearly had a good day. The scent of strong spirits

76

preceded him, but he was not rolling drunk and his golden skin was highlighted pink in places where he had sat in the sunshine. 'I heard there's a fight with good odds tonight,' he said. 'Beyond the beach. Bare-knuckle.' Simmons nodded at the freshly delivered top-hat case on the captain's table. 'That's fancy,' he commented.

'London,' Henderson said by way of explanation. 'Help yourself to a drink.'

The youngster poured himself a brandy. 'You're going up west when we get in then? A silk topper and all. Captain Henderson, are you, by any chance, a toff?' he teased.

Henderson shook his head sadly. 'I would like to visit the place that was my family home in Soho. I don't know if I'll pass for a gentleman.'

Simmons flopped into a chair, set to tarry. 'Well, you've got the hat. They'll like that. And if you're to pass for a nob you'll have to be clean-shaven. That's the fashion. London's changing. Everyone says so. They call it development – new docks in the East End. I'd recommend you fetch yourself a decent blade, Captain. A fella needs protection, gentleman or not. London's a hard place. What was it like when you were there?'

Henderson smiled apologetically. He didn't say that he remembered very little except for his mother and she, most certainly, was gone. He had taken fencing lessons, but the purpose of these had never been clear. Still, a wave of nostalgia washed over him for the way he imagined his childhood home.

'I'm curious to see it,' he admitted. 'And if I need a blade, I'll take your advice.'

Simmons nodded. He fanned himself with a small piece of card with tattered edges that he drew from his pocket. 'When we get in I'll show you the other side of the city, where the toffs don't go, or at least not many. We can visit the Rose Tavern.'

Henderson laughed. 'The Rose Tavern? There must be hundreds of those. Run by Mrs Smith no doubt. Off the high street.'

'Off Old Street – I have friends opposite. Investors. You turn down Mallow Street . . . Mallow Street, mind—'

'I won't stay long.' Henderson cut in. 'I just want to see it again. See how it feels.'

'Cold and bloody wet,' Simmons joked. 'I won't be staying. Next time I was thinking I might come by way of New York. I'd like to see it.'

Henderson shrugged. 'New York is a small place. Not exotic. And if you don't like the cold, I'd avoid their winter. In January the Hudson is even greyer than the Thames.' The captain perked up. 'This fight you mentioned – I know the place.' It would do him good to take his mind off Mrs Graham. The woman had been haunting him.

Will sprang to his feet. 'Lead on,' he said.

The moon was low but not full. The men set out along the dock in conversation. As they dropped onto the dark beach, Simmons declared, 'There can be no better place in the world than this.'

Henderson had to agree. The beach was beautiful. The stars lit the sand and balmy air rode in as the waves washed up on paradise. A few hundred yards ahead, a glow in the sky radiated from the spot where the fight was set to start. Some of the crowd carried torches. The sound of a woman busking floated towards them and the smell of frying pastries wafted on a cinnamon cloud. Two boys with a black dog on a tether shared a sausage. Further up, where the sand gave way to scrub and clustered palm trees, the sound of laughter floated across as ramshackle spectators wandered onto the beach from between the trees. Reaching the gathering, Henderson realised there must be a couple of hundred people. The ring was marked with a square of stakes roped at right angles, and the crowd milled round, eating, drinking and making bets. Two huge black men sat in opposite corners. Their skin was oiled so it shone in the flickering lamps, which threw grotesque shadows on the uneven sand.

Simmons licked his lips. He loved a ruck. Henderson eyed the fighters. He was at home here. The captain was solid enough to make a showing, should he ever be tempted into the ring.

One of the black men was bigger than the other, but not so much bigger that the smaller man might not make up for it by sheer determination when his blood was up. The fight would come to that. As one of them turned, Henderson made out a sequence of scars on the man's back. He had been flogged viciously, and not long ago.

'Are they freed men?' he asked one of the bookmakers.

The man nodded curtly as he picked his teeth with a sliver of bone. Behind him, a black-eyed Negro woman hovered as if she was tethered to him.

Will decided to cut the chit-chat. 'Three to one.' He held up his fingers and pointed to the fighter on the left.

The bookmaker took the money and passed Simmons a scrap of cork marked with an indistinct scrawl. The woman's eyes shone as she watched the cash change hands.

'You?' Simmons asked.

'I never gamble,' Henderson said. 'These fights are fixed.'

Will shrugged. He didn't want to believe it. Besides, even if it was fixed, he could still win.

The crowd jostled, finding their places. Henderson was about to mention they might have a passenger on the voyage home. A lady. Then an old man rang a bell and everyone turned to watch. *I can tell him later,* he thought.

There was a moment of calm as the crowd's attention focussed. The bell rang once more and the fighters started pounding. One man dodged a blow and landed a sound punch to the other's face, then jumped out of the way so that the retaliation missed. The crowd exploded. It was an exciting start.

'He's a regular Mendoza, straight off,' Simmons shouted, excited, as the man hopped backwards and forwards so his opponent couldn't land a punch. 'Look at him.'

'He'll get tired in no time,' Henderson replied.

Prizefighting could go on for hours. It was simply a matter of how long the men lasted. These two were chasing each other round the ring like whippets on a track. It was exciting, but it couldn't last.

After a minute or two, Henderson turned to talk to Simmons, but the space beside him was vacant and he noticed his friend was over to the side, no longer watching the fight. The woman with the black eyes leaned sinuously towards him as she whispered into his ear. Simmons curled his hand lasciviously around her waist. Henderson grinned.

The first fighter's face was swelling and a thick trickle of blood snaked down his dark skin, but he started to land his punches. Henderson caught the whiff of sweat and the salty tang of blood on the heavy night air. It was like watching two dogs, or perhaps two bullocks.

80

'You're missing it,' Henderson shouted as he glanced towards Will, but Simmons was no longer anywhere to be seen. Always wary, the captain checked the whereabouts of the bookmaker. He was right beside the ring, shouting encouragement to the first fighter in heavily accented Portuguese. The woman was gone. Henderson grinned once more.

The boxer's strategy was having an effect now. The dancing fighter slowed and took an uppercut to the chest that left him heaving while the other boxed his ears. The dancer let out an animal sound and the crowd jeered. The two boys strained to hold on to their dog, which was barking and pulling on the lead. It seemed as if the whole crowd moved behind the slow boxer as he went in for the kill. The other man was strong, though, and took the blows. He even landed a couple of solid punches. Both men had swollen lips and eyes, blood streaked their chests, and they were panting hard. But the second fighter just kept landing punch after punch.

'Go on!' Henderson bayed.

The big man pounded on, but the second fighter stood there like a statue after all his dancing and took blow after blow. Above the crowd Henderson could swear he heard a sharp crack, a broken rib likely, and then the huge man keeled over like a felled oak. A flurry of sand rolled to the edge of the ring. Everyone stared. The fighter stopped in confusion, as if he hadn't expected it so early. Then he nodded, slowly raising his arm in victory as the crowd screamed. Half a dozen spectators ran into the ring. The old man dodged the jubilant bodies and tried to revive the unconscious fighter by pouring a bucket of seawater over his head as the prizewinner took a lap of honour. Three girls, no more than thirteen, flung streams of fuchsia at the victor's feet, baring their breasts wantonly in their excitement as the fighter turned to check his mate, who was still on the ground. Clearly this was not the way it normally worked. The prizewinner looked bemused. The crowd hesitated, the cheers dying down. All at once, everyone's attention was focussed on the unconscious man.

The old man shoved the fighter's shoulder and then slapped him – a sharp crack in the silence. Time froze. A wave broke on the balmy black beach. The old man listened to the chest. Then he put his hand beneath the fighter's nose. People held their breath. Once more he slapped the man, this time harder. There was no movement. The old man looked up. He shrugged.

'*Il es morte*,' the cry started.

A quiet mixture of panic and excitement flowed across the crowd. A woman flung herself onto the dead fighter's body, howling and gulping the air like sweet wine. The prizewinner stared in shock at what he had done, his face carved out of rock.

'*Il es morte. Il es morte.*' The phrase became an anguished babble, everyone on a knife edge of shock and glee. The prizewinner's eyes were wide as he crossed the ring and gently shoved his opponent with his foot.

'Ade.' He called the man's name. 'Ade?'

His lip quivered.

And then, slowly, the dead man moved. He pushed off the howling female on his chest and sat up straight, like a golem brought to life. The prizewinner grinned and flung his arms around the fellow. The crowd went wild. The dead man raised his hand and they cheered till their lungs were fit to burst. The second fighter's face betrayed his relief. Everyone was laughing. Strangers flung their arms around each other.

Women screamed for joy and splashed in the surf. Spirits were higher than when the fight had been won.

'Ade! Ade!' they chanted, fists punching the air.

Four men hoisted the resurrected corpse onto their shoulders and paraded along the beach.

Henderson smiled. It made a charming show. He backed off and sat on one of the dunes. A second later, Simmons came to join him.

'I had me a negress,' he said proudly. 'Did that one win then?'

'No. Strangely, he's the loser. They thought he was dead.' Henderson laughed.

'In that case, I tripled my money.'

Simmons headed into the crowd to find the bookmaker.

'Ade! Ade!' everyone was shouting.

The second fighter had been escorted away, taking his prize money and leaving the crowd dancing like lunatics under the dark sky.

'Three to one.' Simmons motioned at the man with the bone toothpick.

The fellow's smile disappeared. He cocked his head to one side, a tiny slick of sweat above his upper lip. '*Que?*' he said.

'My bet. Three to one.' Simmons fished the scrap of cork out of his pocket.

'Ade.' The man pointed and then shook his head to communicate that the fighter now jubilantly playing in the surf had not won the fight.

'I bet on the other one.' Simmons grinned.

The bookmaker moved quickly, but not quickly enough to fox Simmons. The Brazilian's blade of best English steel flashed in the low light. If he had expected this to warn off the white man, he was mistaken. In one deft move, Simmons cut in, competently grabbing the fellow's forearm and wrestling him to the ground, where the boy held the knife at the man's jugular, his face sharp.

'*Meu dinheiro,*' Simmons insisted. My money.

Henderson grinned. Simmons had only been here a couple of days, but he'd picked up the important words.

'You better pay.' He leaned in, adding his translation skills to the threat just to be clear. '*Você tem que pagar.*'

The bookmaker held up his hands in surrender. He reached into his pouch and took out a few coins, his eyes betraying his terror.

Simmons nodded, pocketed the money and backed off. '*Obrigado,*' he said. Thanks.

It was on the tip of Henderson's tongue to say what a formidable team they made as Simmons turned to walk back along the beach with his winnings. It was pleasant to be surprised by someone – perhaps in Simmons's speed there lay a clue to why he had lied yesterday about his business arrangements. In any case, the boy's skills with the blade belied his easy manner. But before Henderson could ask where he'd learned to fight like that, the black-eyed girl Simmons had just had in the sand dunes appeared and rushed into his arms.

Will froze with his mouth open. Henderson smiled at the girl, and then, with a dull ache in his chest, he realised what she'd done as Will Simmons fell onto the sand, a stream of blood pooling beside him.

'Jesus.' Henderson reeled in shock just long enough to allow the bookmaker to grab back the money with one hand and take hold of the girl with the other. She gave a snake-like smile as she stuck her bloody knife into her belt, and in a flash the couple disappeared into the darkness.

Henderson knelt, pulling Simmons into his arms.

'Shit,' Will whispered.

'I'll get you back to the *Bittersweet*.' Henderson tried to lift his friend, but Simmons let out a sigh more terrifying than any injured howl.

Men were running up the beach joyfully shouting '*Ade vivo*' as Will Simmons's breath grew wheezy.

'Take it back to them in London.' He spat the words with difficulty. 'Ask for the gentlemen at the Rose. Give them everything, you understand? I have the key. In my hat. The Old Street Bridge . . .'

'Hush, none of that.' Henderson quietened the boy.

He lifted Will and turned to walk back along the sand. On the *Bittersweet*, Big Al Thatcher had sewn up many a barbarous slash and cut on a bare wooden slab in the galley. He was a solid Yorkshireman and he'd sort this out. Not every knife wound was mortal. But after only a few steps, Henderson realised it was no good. The crowd on the beach was screaming, dancing and singing in celebration, but the boy wasn't breathing. James Henderson was carrying a corpse.

Natal

Maria had no intention of unpacking. The lodgings were clean and well kept, but she knew she wouldn't be staying long. The captain to whom Cochrane had entrusted her safety had offered to secure her passage before he left. Now it occurred to her perhaps on this occasion it would have been easier to let him. It was too late now. This was her second day at port and she had yet to find a suitable ship on which to travel, nor direct passage, except with Captain Henderson, whose vessel she judged as suspect as his person. Aside from the *Bittersweet*, there were two ships bound for Africa, but they were set for Calicut thereafter and there was no saying when a suitable passage might arrive on the Ivory Coast to take her north to Europe. Plucky though she was, Maria knew her odds in all things were better from the dark continent of South America than the one that lay opposite. On the upside, from Natal it was an easy matter to get to the northern states – anywhere from Trinidad to Boston or New York, from where she could find an Atlantic passage with relative ease. This, however, would potentially add weeks to her voyage, and a deal of

86

expense. It was infinitely preferable to find a direct berth.

She pored over the maps, trying to calculate, as Thomas would have done. It came to this – she had two choices. One was to make for Trinidad and hope to find a ship to take her east (a reasonable proposition, but slower), the other was to hazard a passage with Captain Henderson, which, if it came off, would see her in Piccadilly delivering her manuscripts to John Murray inside of six weeks, perhaps seven. She pondered the possibility – weighing up Thomas Cochrane's undoubted horror at the cut of Henderson's vessel and the discomfort she felt at Henderson's eagerness to engage her interest when he had pushed her to embark with him on the dock. Gentlemen did not behave that way. But, she reasoned, he had written then, afterwards. *Madam,* the letter had started, *I hope I have not discomforted you. I apologise if this is the case.*

That night, after dinner was served on the heavy mahogany dining table on the first floor of her lodgings, the landlady, festooned in jewellery of bright Vauxhall glass, brought tisane to Maria's chamber. Mrs Graham sipped alone, sitting at the window, an Englishwoman on her travels, watching the line of pale-pink buildings that snaked towards the square, their carved buff gables cutting into the starry velvet sky. Maria was accustomed to summing up new places, and in her estimation Natal was a quiet trading town like an assortment of others up and down the coast. The faded buildings were attractive, but there was nothing much of interest to fill them in the way of commercial goods or ideas. Put plainly, Natal was a backwater. The smell of baking wafted across the warm air from a hundred ovens. It was a familiar fragrance, redolent with rosemary. Maria reached for a small biscuit.

Sweet as honeycomb, it melted in her mouth. She nibbled, leafing through her journal. She had sketched as she made her way across the country – a sedan chair in Bahia and a picture of slaves dragging a hogshead in Pernambuco. Each image brought back a memory. She felt strangely hungry. *I ate scarcely an hour ago. I cannot have an appetite,* she chided herself.

The food had been dreadful on her passage from Recife – cornbread and unseasoned meat. She had been tempted to take to the galley if only to find a few flakes of salt or crumbs of pepper or chilli (which no ship in the Southern parts could possibly lack). A little spice would have made a world of difference. However, when it came to it, even the great Maria Graham did not dare to openly criticise a ship's cook. In her experience they were formidable men and quite capable of not only holding a grudge but acting upon one too. The food in the *conselho* was far better. She had enjoyed a satisfying if spicy breakfast and a more than adequate dinner of soup, fried fish and roasted vegetables. The tisane and biscuits were soothing, but she felt a curl in her stomach. *Perhaps it is this uncertainty,* she thought. *The conundrum of what to do.*

After Captain Henderson's letter had arrived the day before, Maria asked some locals for references and it transpired that Henderson was well known at the port as a competent captain. However, as far as anyone knew he had not made an Atlantic crossing. He seemed a decent enough fellow of his type – a small-time trader, she guessed – but the ship was hardly inspiring and the whole situation was just what Cochrane had warned her against. Maria didn't fear the sea but, as taught by her father, she respected its power. In her experience the ocean had no intent to drown travellers. The Atlantic was merely a highway and fatalities were surprisingly rare, though, in high storms and with bad navigation, they did happen. She had spent a good deal of her life on board ships and prided herself on being able to judge a captain's ability. A lot depended on the measure of the man. So far, she'd describe Henderson as steady, if perhaps one for the ladies – which might be put down to his rough good looks and even his confidence. If not young, he was younger than she was. He had clearly been brought up in the colonies, for which allowances had to be made. *He seems able and he's certainly honest,* she thought. *He said his was the only ship and he was right.*

Henderson's note lay in her lap and she read it again. *I shall render you my own cabin, madam,* he promised, *should you choose to trust yourself to my stewardship.* It was well phrased, she thought, and he wrote with a fair hand. By all accounts he knew the shores of the eastern seaboard. She examined the narrative style – formal and a little old-fashioned, she decided. With a smile, she wondered what John Murray would make of it. The thought of seeing her old friend again was what made her keenest to return to London, and not only because he would buy her manuscripts. Murray had been Maria's mentor since she had started to write. In the beginning, he had found her editorial work where she had honed her skills.

'You are quite mad, girl,' Lady Dundas had declared with disdain. 'This is tantamount to employment. No lady in our family has ever worked.'

Maria folded Henderson's letter carefully. Perhaps she had misjudged him simply because he was eager. There was no crime in that, but at sea she would have no defence from his eagerness and it was plain he was no gentleman – not really. Her mind flashed back to the jungle and, with a smile, she recognised the poor man couldn't be a worse ordeal than da Couto, and she'd managed that.

I might ask to inspect this cabin of his, she thought.

Below her, the street was deserted. A snatch of carefree laughter wafted into the night.

'I should read before retiring,' she said out loud.

There was a book by the bed. Maria hesitated as her limbs sank into the soft cushions. The trip through the jungle had left her exhausted and she had been rushing for the week or two since – helping at the naval hospital, sitting up late with the Cochranes at night and playing with the children early. Downstairs, the grandfather clock in the hall chimed ten. Maria shifted and at last, and with her head resting on a pillow embroidered by the landlady's daughter, the renowned Mrs Graham was overtaken by sleep.

*

The next morning, fully refreshed and with her toilette settled, Mrs Graham hoisted her parasol to protect her skin from the brazen sun and made for the docks. It was early, but she was glad to see Captain Henderson was already at work, overseeing the loading of his cargo. Maria settled to wait in the shade. There was little purpose in disturbing a man when he was busy. She enjoyed the sights and sounds of the dockside – ports were places of freedom. From above, she could hear a sailor in an upper room, whining as he had a tattoo cut into his arm. Two street children loitered by a warehouse, hoping to snatch whatever might drop from the bundles that were delivered, or to pick a pocket if a rich and careless enough prize happened their way. A pig wearing a collar wandered along the cobblestones, and to one side three sailors ate steaming doughnuts, watching her as she sat patiently while Henderson's cacao beans were hoisted, the dust from the sacks peppering the hot air. The captain was squabbling with the thin farmer who had delivered his goods. They were shouting in Portuguese so fluent that Maria could not follow the words.

Henderson, however, appeared ill at ease. He evidently did not notice her. Eventually the farmer relented and the men shook hands, though the captain was still not willing. He handed over some money and raised his hands as if he had surrendered.

'I don't know what to do,' he said, slowly enough for Maria to translate. 'I have no need of it now.'

'You will take it north and sell it,' the farmer replied, waving him off. 'It's top quality.'

Then, with his purse of coins in hand, the little man walked away as the captain shouted to his crew to load the beans. Henderson seemed different from the last time Maria had seen him – he was agitated and less jovial. However, if he really hadn't wanted to accept the delivery she didn't suppose he would have. He was twice the size of the little farmer, for a start. Observing him now, there was something about the captain that reminded Mrs Graham of a black dog, the kind of animal that could fight to the death but instead might make a good-natured and solid companion. Maria stopped. If the captain was in poor humour, perhaps this wasn't the moment. Still, she had her business to attend to. She had decided to investigate the *Bittersweet*. If he was loading, she might not have long.

'Captain Henderson.' She moved forward, trying out his name.

He looked up as if he was coming out of a dream. 'Oh. Good morning.'

'Are you set to sail? Do you still have a berth for London?'

Henderson paused. Then he bowed his head. 'I'm sorry. I'm no longer for London, madam. There's no need.'

Maria hovered. This was entirely unexpected. He had been so eager. If she had been concerned that he had designs on her, the worry evaporated.

'But I have a need,' she insisted. 'I must get home. And I'm afraid you were quite right. Natal enjoys little regular passage to and from England. I'm relying on you – on what you said yesterday. Your letter.'

Henderson peered at her, as if he was looking for some hidden intent.

'I wondered,' Maria continued smoothly, 'if I might look at the cabin?'

His eyes showed no objection, so she turned smartly and boarded, with him trailing behind, too troubled, it would seem, to reply.

'She looks less strange from the deck, doesn't she?' Maria smiled. 'The *Bittersweet* is a most unusual vessel. At first I thought her Chinese, she is so low and flat. Have you seen a sampan, Captain? I have only had the pleasure of inspecting a drawing, but the style is similar. There is also something of the galleon about the *Bittersweet*, don't you think?'

Henderson said nothing, but he motioned Mrs Graham ahead. She strode confidently into his cabin. It was strange – he had not anticipated what it would feel like to have a lady aboard. She seemed contented and with her she brought an air of purpose and calm. He was certainly enjoying that.

The cabin was larger than she expected and better fitted. A finely carved oak table at one end was covered with charts. Against one of the panelled walls there was a well-made cabinet containing decanted port and brandy, and on the other there were shelves and two fitted trunks.

'I'm keen to get home. Will you help me?' she asked. 'In your letter, you see . . .' She scrambled in her bag.

Henderson tried to remember what he'd written. Dealing with Simmons's body had pushed everything out of his mind. The lack of care shown by the authorities for a sailor killed in a brawl did not surprise him, but the amount of money in the boy's effects certainly had, alongside the key in his hat and the oddly bound bar of chocolate, ready to be grated and added to hot water or milk to make a drink, which, no doubt, would taste rather musty, given the chocolate's poor quality. Whoever Simmons's associates were at Old Street Bridge, he would send on the effects from the north. Plenty ships left from New York for London. Given the money involved, he had decided he would take the balance of the arrangement fee he'd agreed with Will and something in addition for executing the matter. Then he would wash his hands. London had been a foolish idea, best abandoned. Now the contents of his letter to Mrs Graham came back in a flood. He'd been tremendously courteous, he recalled. He noticed that he felt calmer now she was here, still in that grey dress with her dowdy hat, the air around her redolent with orchid oil. Perhaps all women in England had this effect. Perhaps they all smelled of flowers and exuded a calm and measured purpose. He couldn't remember.

'I am afraid my plans have changed, madam,' he repeated.

'An acquaintance died last night unexpectedly. It was for his sake that I was to go to London.'

'For his sake? You do not fancy seeing London yourself? You mentioned you had an interest . . .'

Henderson looked flustered. 'Indeed, but it was business that took me there.'

'What is your cargo?'

'Cacao. We sail with the tide for New England.'

'And there is no need of cacao in England proper? Come, sir.'

Henderson dropped onto one of the wooden chairs. He took off his hat and laid it on the table, passing a hand through his hair. 'I hear there is demand. England loves its exotic foodstuffs, so they say. Simmons told me they are making cacao into a powder. But I do not know what this cargo is worth there.'

'I have seen the powder.' Maria's tone was enthusiastic. 'It is manufactured with a press. A most ingenious advance. Captain Henderson, I shall speak frankly. I'm in great need of returning to London. I have two manuscripts to deliver to my publisher and supplies to locate for the Imperial Emperor. I have been engaged, you see, as tutor to Princess Maria da Gloria. I will be no trouble, I promise. In fact I shall have to work during most of my passage – making a fair copy of my terrible scrawl. You have changed your plans once. I hate to trouble you, but might you change them again? This cabin will do nicely. I would be terribly grateful and I can pay. It may not be the full commission you had hoped for from your friend, but it is something. It would greatly oblige me.'

Henderson sat frozen in the chair. A vision of the little house in Soho flickered across his mind's eye, his mother at a desk, writing in her journal, with hazy sunlight streaming through the morning windows. This woman inhabited a world he had once thought his own – a world of publishers and reliable suppliers. A London that was confident and competent amid its grey, puddle-strewn streets. Was it possible that it was still there?

'It will be summer in England—' he hazarded.

'That is no guarantee of the weather.' Maria cut in with a smile. 'Still, it will be pleasant to see the trees in Regent's Park. That is always a pleasure. Even in the rain.'

'Regent's Park. Yes.' Henderson nodded slowly as he realised he wanted to see it.

Will's death had shaken him. The boy's prone body had lain below deck all night. It had been pronounced bad luck by the men, though Henderson never held with such superstition. The last thing Will had asked, however, was that Henderson deliver his effects. The captain now realised, it was as if Mrs Graham were his conscience. The spectre of London brightened a little and he imagined meeting fellows like himself, briskly walking down rainy Pall Mall. She had rallied him to go forward and greet them.

'Why not?' he said, his eyes distant. 'I shall look forward to seeing it.' He smiled. 'In the meantime, should I arrange for your baggage to be brought aboard, Mrs Graham? You will, of course, have my cabin. We'll arrange our affairs as soon as the cargo is loaded.'

Maria sat down. She gave small smile as her hands folded neatly in her lap. The *Bittersweet* might be old-fashioned, but Cochrane could not be too displeased with her decision, surely. The cabin was well appointed and the place was ship-shape. The men loading the beans were working together.

95

The ropes were properly coiled, the sails tied with precision. The place was spotless, which she hadn't expected. It was all in order. Better than that, if she was truthful. And the captain seemed changed. Today he was quite serious.

'Thank you,' she said simply. 'This table is perfect for writing. It will do very well.'

8

On board the Bittersweet

Sun on sail across blue water, Henderson kept his distance. Will Simmons's death had been a watershed of sorts, and now Mrs Graham was aboard, intruding on her felt as if he was taking advantage. Mostly he was taken up in the difficult matter of planning the Atlantic route. This kept him at his desk till late each evening, setting his charts on the makeshift slanted table in the tight, dark cabin into which he had moved. He worked long hours from these cramped quarters, no larger than a store cupboard and lit by two dim candle lamps. They would travel first to Trinidad, resupply and then turn eastwards for England. Upon occasion on this first leg, when the captain tried to approach the lady on deck, he felt awkward. He found he could think of nothing to say, so he stood with his mind racing, tongue-tied and cursing inwardly. On the other hand, when he was not in her company he thought of little else and had to draw his mind purposefully back to his charts. After his first attempts to engage her in conversation, he simply kept to his cabin, and when he surfaced to find Mrs Graham strolling on deck between the coils of rope, the cleats and the great sails, he nodded a stiff good morning. The whiff of orchids comforted him long after she had swept off to continue copying her manuscript.

As the outline of Natal faded into the misty line where the ocean met the sky, he admired the cut of her figure as she receded down the deck in the tidy grey dress, her hair clasped at the nape of her neck. It was as if she was a dream, like London, which he could not entirely grasp and of which he was not worthy. He wanted to be part of it but had forgotten how. It seemed extraordinary and strange that this paragon among women had condescended to travel on his ship. In fact, she'd insisted upon it. Her presence was at once otherworldly and familiar, none of which explained why his brain ceased to function when he was in her company. It was troubling.

She approached the captain one morning. 'Is there a service?'

The bright sunshine made her squint. Henderson looked bemused. His shadow elongated on the boards and, behind him, the rigging cast a spider's web on the shimmering water.

'It's Sunday,' she pointed out. 'A service would be customary.'

The captain smiled shyly. 'Oh no,' he said. 'If the men wish to pray, of course, they can.'

No Sunday service, she noted. This made Henderson more interesting, although it would have been the height of rudeness to enquire on the subject of his personal religious devotion. Most captains were concerned with the crew's spiritual needs as much as their physical discipline. Henderson appeared to occupy himself with neither. It was a marked difference from every ship she'd travelled on, though, as she observed it, the *Bittersweet* seemed to function – better than that, it was well run.

'Do you never punish the men?' she found herself asking.

Henderson stared, her assumption crossing his mind in a flash. 'You think because I don't force them to pray or brandish the nine-tails that I'll never control them?'

Maria felt her cheeks flush. It sounded as if she was hoping for a da Couto – that she preferred a brute. 'Sir, I admire the trust you place in your crew . . .' she started.

Henderson laughed. The pink curl of his mouth was joyful and he was so swept up that he continued without thinking. 'There's no need to take back what you said. You're entitled to your opinion and you've seen it work differently. But I run this ship. If I need to punish someone I do so, but I will not fuel the place on daily beatings, petty rules and superstition. My crew deserves better.'

Behind them, Maria noticed two of the men listening. He might not say much, but Captain Henderson was to the point when he did speak.

'I meant no offence,' she said.

'None taken, ma'am.'

From his tone she could tell he meant that, and that was unusual too. Normally if a man's ideas were questioned he became surly.

As she walked away, Henderson cursed himself for being so strident. Mrs Graham hovered at the prow. Behind her, terns and petrels swooped for fish in the surf. The captain peered as she moved, just for a moment, as if she was flying with them long and lean, stretching over the side like a figurehead ready to dive. There was something fluid about Maria Graham. Something out and out elegant. As she returned to her cabin, he was still staring. She raised her hand, as if surprised to see him. Then she glided back to work.

After that, between cabin and deck, Mrs Graham relaxed into a comfortable rhythm. For her it was a luxury to be alone and for that reason the ship quickly came to feel like home. Between reviewing what she'd written on the history of the Chilean War of Independence, she continued to watch Henderson, who might be silent but was certainly competent. In Maria's view (and she gave some time to this), he would not have cut the mustard as a captain in the Royal Navy. The navy accepted eccentrics, but British captains were mostly conventional men. Convention was a quality that Henderson appeared to lack entirely. Nonetheless, the captain's approach to his crew was unexpectedly enlightened. Yes, that was the word.

Maria's father and her husband had both been naval men. Shipboard life had been familiar since her childhood. It had occurred to her many times that on board it didn't matter where you were coming from or where you were heading. Each voyage had its own charisma. Like writing a book – word by word – or crossing a country – step by step – each minute had to be lived moment by moment. If you strove to arrive, it felt twice as long. Being at sea, after all, was constructive. Once you set sail you were, by definition, going somewhere. 'A journey is an achievement, Maria, just as much as a mathematical proof,' her father always said.

In this manner, a tacit arrangement emerged between Maria and the captain, so that between Natal and Trinidad they sailed as if on sister ships bound in the same direction, hardly saying a word. Most days, for hours, Maria buried herself in her manuscripts. In the warm patch of light by the cabin's glass, she stretched corsetless every morning, bending in the Indian fashion, breathing deeply. The dry warmth, she noticed, gave her greater flexibility, and the sun felt good on her skin. Sometimes she lost track of her thoughts and that was the most pleasant feeling of all, bringing with it a stillness that usually came only with deep sleep.

When she made her needs known, the cabin boy provided – cleaning the room and airing the linen. He delivered food from the galley and a pewter jug of hot water for the wash-stand. The boy was no more than twelve years. His skin was the same colour as the dark wood of the cabin and he wore a grave expression, as if he had never smiled and never would. Maria showed him her drawings. Over two years she had built up quite a collection – the church at Valparaíso, dragon trees, strange jungle plants, the boats in the harbour at Bahia and the palace at Rio. The boy's dark eyes grew wide, drinking in the details like dry earth sucks in water. She described the strange cattle, the royal palace's huge kitchens and the long hallways studded with crystal chandeliers and embellished with marble. He eyed her books suspiciously.

'How did you learn to read?' he asked.

Maria's heart dropped. Her mother had taught her in the years before she was taken from her daughter. Maria remembered sitting in the nursery. Later, Miss Bright, her schoolteacher in Oxford, had slipped volumes secretly into her hand – Shakespeare and Ovid, matters that should be beyond the scope of a little girl. Maria had drunk them. The England of her childhood was cold and disapproving. School had been a grey cage and her aunt's home, where she spent the holidays, a golden prison. Books had been her best escape.

'I learned at school,' she said. 'I can teach you, if you like. This is A,' she sounded, drawing the letter.

The boy copied her. After that, each morning he learned as

101

she sat on a barrel in the sunshine and drew on the deck with chalk. As Henderson passed them, he nodded silently.

Why, he is a man of no words at all, she thought to herself.

As a result, it came as a surprise to Mrs Graham when the captain gave a businesslike rap on her cabin door one afternoon and informed her the port of San Fernando was in sight. She fixed her hat in place with a silver pin, checked her grey skirts and quit the cabin for the sunny deck. Shielded in the shadow of the sails, Maria watched the lush island of Trinidad come into focus. The salty sea air rippled with the sweet scent of sugar.

'There are plantations?' she asked.

Henderson nodded.

'Poor souls.'

'Sugar and cacao. They have a deal of coffee as well.'

'Do you always carry chocolate, Captain?'

It was a fair question. Henderson paused. 'I buy and sell what I know,' he said. 'I used to load rum and sugar, but chocolate is popular and not everyone knows what they're buying, so I have an advantage. I spent some time on a plantation as a child. My father lodged there – the woman . . .' Here he hesitated, for the arrangement was as far from respectable London as he could imagine. '. . . was an excellent cook.'

Maria nodded. The food aboard the *Bittersweet* was certainly a cut above the usual shipboard fare. She had come to look forward to the hot chocolate delivered to her cabin in the morning, sweet and spiced, and the fresh cornbread that went alongside it still warm on the plate. The wine for dinner varied according to the dish and was well chosen. Fresh fish was grilled and served with lime. There were plenty of times she had been reduced, of necessity, to ship's biscuits and dried meat on a voyage. Some seagoing men didn't mind that, but she guessed Henderson would. Maria was sure the captain had a hand in the menu, which bore the mark of a more cultivated taste than that of a ship's cook. After her unaccountable hunger in Natal, her appetite aboard the *Bittersweet* was sated.

The sunshine baked the dock and Maria sighed. She was becoming tired of the endless good weather, the fly-ridden, sweaty docks, barefoot brown children playing in the dust, picking pockets where they could, the tangle of ships with palm trees behind, the sailors at port and their relentless drinking. She longed for a moment of proper English coldness. It would be pleasant to sit in a house overlooking a London street, taking tea and scones and watching the world pass the window. There was something restful in being served by pale-skinned, well-fed staff with a distant air. She imagined the touch of ice on her skin and the invigorating freshness of a bright but cold morning. All the civilisation of England. It would feel good not to be under an obligation to observe everything so keenly. *Perhaps I am homesick at last,* she mused. London was coming, with its bittersweet expectations of her. She glanced sideways at the captain and wondered if he felt that way too.

As the men brought the *Bittersweet* to anchor in a well-practised routine of sail and rigging, Maria noticed a fellow burst out of an open-fronted rum stall on the quay and wave enthusiastically. Blond, he wore a wrinkled pale-linen suit with a white cravat and an eccentric hat made of woven rushes, some of which were still green. The gangplank was lowered and the gentleman bounded aboard, carrying a bottle of rum. He bowed very low when he saw Maria, enquiring firstly in Portuguese, and then English with a Scandinavian accent, what she was doing there.

103

A grin broke on Henderson's face. He took the rum and managed the introductions. 'This is Thys Bagdorf,' he said. 'Mrs Maria Graham.'

'I sell James beans from my family's plantation.' Thys beamed and held out his hand.

'Not today, I'm afraid,' the captain replied.

Thys took the rejection in his stride. 'You will know what you missed, my friend. This year's crop is excellent. What have you got in your hold?' he asked.

'Cacao. It was bought by someone else on commission in Brazil. I'm delivering it, and Mrs Graham, to London.'

Thys bowed again. 'I had intended to drink this bottle with you, James. But now you have a lady on board you must both come to dinner.'

'I have to check my charts for the crossing,' Henderson protested. 'We will only be here a day. On the return, Thys—'

'No. Come tonight,' Thys pushed. 'My sister is at home. I shall invite one of the other captains and you can discuss your route. It will be your last society for weeks, will it not?'

'I was hoping to find something to read,' Maria admitted.

It was unlikely there was a bookshop in San Fernando and certainly nothing in English. It had occurred to her that at this rate she'd finish her writing halfway to London and be left without occupation and no one to talk to but the cabin boy.

Thys boomed, 'We have English books – there are even some novels if your taste runs to it. Ladies always prefer a novel. The famous Miss Austen has reached us even here, though I have not read her work myself. *Emma*, isn't it?'

Maria blanched. Novels were too frothy – she might enjoy one if she was unwell, but scientific journals were far more appealing. 'Thank you,' she said. 'And if you had anything botanical I would be particularly interested.'

Thys was bluff. 'No matter. You shall borrow whatever you like. I insist. Come at nine o'clock.'

At the mizzen, Henderson heard one of the men quip – something about a lady with a book. There was a ripple of lurid laughter like a pot of paint spilling over onto the boards. A steely glance was enough to stop its path, and it was as well he was unshaven, for, he realised, he was blushing.

Maria had not noticed. She waved at the top of the gang-plank as Thys quit the ship.

That afternoon, the lady loitered on deck and watched the trade on the quay. There seemed more slaves here than at other ports. Ships spewed the men onto the dockside, weak and in chains. It turned her stomach.

Well before the sun sank, Mrs Graham retired to her cabin and laid out her evening dress. Through the glass, the sky was streaked with thick orange bolts. She lit the candles and closed the shutters. The thud of water on the boat's side beat an inconstant rhythm.

The cabin remained peppered with Henderson's belongings. His new lodging was too small to accommodate everything and he had abandoned his charts of the southern waters on the heavy wooden shelves. A brass model of the solar system had pride of place, similar, she noted, to one her father had owned, though, unlike her father, Captain Henderson's effects didn't appear to tally with his personality. The orrery seemed too highbrow. Captain Dundas had used his as a gentleman's conversation piece. Henderson, to date, had displayed little such interest.

Maria set the metronome in motion. It ticked in time with

her thoughts. The captain bemused her. He was tidy, well dressed, competent and, most of all, silent. By the cabin boy's account he was also brave, and there was a roughness about him that suggested that might be true. By contrast, he was unexpectedly cosmopolitan. He loved food and drink, though he showed no sign of being either a glutton or a drunkard. On the evidence of the voyage alone, she would have considered him simply very private and perhaps shy, but he had pursued her with such vigour before they set sail.

There were two leather chests beneath the shelving and, her curiosity piqued, Maria decided to explore. She might at least uncover a looking glass, for there was no mirror in which she might dress her hair. That, she told herself, was what she was going to do – find a glass. Her heart quickened as she stood before the hinged brass handle and she hesitated only a moment. As she opened the lid, she was hit by a wave of dust, which forced her to draw back. Then, as it settled, she peered inside. On top there were old clothes and, after digging through those, a sheaf of notes, written, she realised, by a child. These included Latin declensions, mathematical calculations and a poorly executed pencil drawing of a cat sitting on a velvet cushion beside a rain-spotted window. No glass came to hand, so she moved on. The second trunk was not so dusty or so full. Inside, there was a pouch of coins, a lading notice from Natal and a parcel wrapped in linen. She lifted it up and stretched inside to peer right down to the bottom of the trunk. *How like a man to have nothing useful stowed away,* she thought. The boat rocked suddenly and she lost her footing, dropping the linen parcel, which split open. A large shard of something brown fell out. *Chocolate*, she thought. *How odd.* Now she thought on it, it seemed an extraordinary item to find stowed in the captain's cabin. The hold was full of cacao beans and the cook had copious chocolate in the galley. Perhaps this bar was of exceptional quality. She picked it up and sniffed the freshly shorn edge. The block released a musty aroma, confirming, even with her limited expertise, this wasn't of the best – in fact, quite the reverse.

Then, as she retrieved the broken piece, Maria noticed something glinting within it. A seam of brightness that she couldn't quite make out. Her curiosity piqued, she fetched her toilette case and extracted a silver sharp used for cleaning nails. She sat down at the table to examine her discovery, halting only momentarily to overcome her natural respect for property that was not, after all, hers. Still, it was intriguing. Pulling the candle towards her, she carefully bored a hole near the edge of the chocolate, as she had seen done to check freshness and quality. The sharp hit something solid.

Like a hound to the chase, Maria dug further. Whatever was inside was a good deal harder than a stray bean or a cluster of cacao nibs. She continued to dig in the light, carefully placing the dark shavings onto a piece of paper like a surgeon dissecting a corpse. In a minute, she had prised a small rough stone, the size of a misshapen apricot, from the interior. Her heart racing, she picked it up and held the stone to the light. She was no expert, but she was sure it was an uncut gem, its milky, uneven surface streaked with cacao. Scrambling, she searched her jewellery case and brought out her hairpin capped with a jaunty blue feather, a scatter of pearls and a small, bright diamond. Then, holding the stone steady, she drew the diamond across it. It left a thin line, a mere graze. Maria put it down. It couldn't be an uncut diamond then, but nor was it glass. The colour was very light – perhaps it was topaz.

Maria sank back in the dark leather chair, suddenly breathless. The captain had a secret and she had found it. The man was a riddle, but she hadn't expected this. She steeled herself, drilling six more holes in quick succession into the chocolate bar. Natural uncut gemstones peppered the bar like shot. They varied in colour, but already she counted two emeralds and something that might be a diamond – smaller than the others but very dense and, if it was what she suspected, surely worth hundreds. The hairpin could not graze it. She drilled one last time and hit again. Carefully, she widened the hole and angled the candle lamp. The hidden matter glowed gold. The metronome halted.

The only rational explanation was that Henderson was smuggling these items or, at the very least, that they were stolen. Horrified, Maria's hand rose involuntarily to cover her mouth. She lost track of time, but it could only have been a minute or two later when a knock on the cabin door startled her.

'Wait,' she called, bundling the block into its linen and covering it with a stack of papers. Then, with shaking fingers, she called out to enter and felt palpably relieved when it was only the cabin boy with a steaming jug. She hurried him away, turning the key in the door as he went. Then she directed herself to her toilette.

Thinking all the while, Maria washed her skin with a muslin cloth, though her gaze kept returning to the illicit gems hidden on her writing desk as she slipped out of her grey day dress and into the sky-blue satin evening gown with her pale-gold gloves. She twisted her hair into an elegant coil held in place by the hairpin. A dab of orchid oil finished her preparations.

Whatever was she going to do? There was still quarter of an hour before she must leave.

Perplexed, with her hands neatly folded in her lap, Maria sat at the desk regarding the bar. She ran through everything she knew of Henderson. Her mind kept racing ahead and she had to pull it back, like a runaway pony. Potentially this was a risky situation. There was no saying what a smuggler or a thief might do if she unmasked him, and yet the captain was certainly not a heartless monster, even if he might be breaking the law. For a start, he'd been genuinely upset by the death of his friend in Natal. The fellow they had met today, Thys, seemed thoroughly respectable and delighted to see Henderson. The crew followed Henderson's orders to the letter and not because he was a bully. Everything pointed to a genuine, hard-earned respect and a sense of decency. Was he a gentleman pirate? No, not a gentleman, but maybe a pirate or a highwayman.

Maria was a member of London's elite, but she took people as she found them. It often horrified the English community that she spent her time with local farmers and horse traders, eccentrics and mystics, but she valued expertise over convention and had long believed if you were going to make discoveries in the world you must first quit your Englishness and open your eyes. But still, hidden gemstones were beyond the pale. A bolt out of the tropical blue sky. This was smuggling. She stowed one of the stones in her purse, as proof, should she need it.

When the knock came, Maria's hands fluttered like tiny birds. She quelled them and then rose to let him in, studying the captain carefully as he bowed and crossed the threshold. His face was rugged but not unkind. Still, she could not bring herself to level such a terrible accusation. Smugglers were brutal felons as low as bandits, their bodies strung up at ports across the burgeoning Empire. Might he harm her if she challenged him? She was aboard his ship and in his care.

Henderson had dressed for dinner. He smiled, waiting for her, his eyes pale-aquamarine pools. 'The cabin feels lighter filled with your things. It smells better too,' he said with a smile.

Bravely, she held out her arm. 'Dinner,' she announced carefully. 'I should like to see the plantation.'

The evening's entertainment would afford her time, at least, to try to read him.

9

San Fernando

At the gangplank, there was a jaunting carriage with two chestnut horses and a rough-looking coachman in shirtsleeves who, from his patchy appearance, must have shaved with a blunt razor. Henderson helped Maria into her seat and positioned himself opposite. The carriage was barely upholstered, the seats not only hard but, in places, jagged too.

Maria did not meet the captain's eyes as they rode in silence through colourful evening scenes on the island's busy streets. Small boys were selling slick slices of red and orange melon on the corners. At first the cobblestones were deafening, but at least the roar of the wheels covered the lack of conversation, each bump magnified by the threadbare upholstery as Maria studied Henderson surreptitiously, searching for signs of criminality. All week, as she had wondered about the captain, this possibility had never occurred to her. A smuggler. She looked back over the passage from Natal and scared herself, wondering what else might have been going on aboard the *Bittersweet*, right under her nose.

The earthen track was a relief when it came. The lights from the houses and taverns gave way to darkness and a thin moon rolled into view, scarcely illuminating the byways. The movement provided a light breeze that cut through the muggy air as they reached the higher ground. The carriage's single lamp seemed insignificant in the face of such huge darkness. It cast a pale glow that scarcely reached the corners of the carriage. Henderson's cheekbones were a sheer drop.

Surely he wouldn't harm me, she thought.

He was such a tangle of contradictions it was hard to tell. At first she had judged him a man for the ladies – the way he had immediately fallen in step with her when she arrived in Natal, accosting her on the dockside and soliciting her attention. But aboard, he kept to himself, a mixture of reserve and open-minded ideas. *He has been quite admirable,* she thought. But then there were the stones. Was he all seeming and no being, like an illusionist's shade, dodging between different versions of himself?

Off the main road, the carriage climbed a rocky path, jarring from side to side. Henderson and Maria held on to thin leather straps fixed inside the door and apologetically jerked too close and then too far away.

'You will bruise,' he said. 'We must return to port in a better vehicle.'

The musky scent of pipe smoke wafted towards her as she brushed against his jacket. Her heart lurched. She almost said something, but the words were too difficult to form. *Are you a criminal, sir? A smuggler?* How could she even ask? The sound of tree frogs pulsed. She could hear them outside, now the cobbles had been replaced by softer earth. The noise needled her as she realised she had to know, else how could she return to the ship?

And then, before she could blurt it out, the ground levelled and the carriage drew up at a white wooden veranda that lunged out of the blackness. The world that had been hurtling past came to a sharp stop. Lamps were set at intervals along the planking, and two servants, or perhaps house slaves, emerged to greet them with Thys Bagdorf shortly behind, tonight in another pale-linen suit and immaculate white cravat. He wore an apricot flower in his buttonhole – a blooming cactus.

'Welcome,' Thys boomed, his blond locks flashing in the lamplight.

Henderson bounded down, clapping his friend on the back.

Thys bowed and presented Maria with a pale lily. 'For your hair.'

As Maria curtsied, there was a swish of satin. Then, to the sound of heels on wood, their host led them through the reception hall into an elegant drawing room garlanded with ginger lilies against a backdrop of pale-blue wallpaper. Such light after the darkness was splendour, the candles spreading their glow like liquid gold. Nature was tamed here. Inside, a pretty blonde woman sat on a wooden sofa sipping a gargantuan glass of pale liquid. It looked like a small bucket in her pretty hands.

'Mrs Graham, Captain Henderson, may I present my sister, Miss Ramona Bagdorf.'

Miss Bagdorf rose and curtsied. A butler appeared with a tray. Maria found it difficult to focus on the beautiful room and the unexpected company. She felt out of her depth, as if she were swimming in the candlelight, with her feet off the ground.

Thys was bluff. 'Captain Ebberhardt could not join us, but he kindly wrote instructions. He makes the Atlantic crossing frequently – most recently to and from Amsterdam.

Meantime, we must toast your voyage and safe return.' He raised his glass.

The liquid glimmered. Maria's eyes were drawn to Henderson's as she tried to second-guess him.

'I'm excited to see London,' the captain admitted, his tone almost boyish.

Thys was adept at managing society. 'Poor Mrs Graham. You are only permitted one day in beautiful Trinidad, it seems.'

'I must return to England,' Maria admitted. That was the truth of the matter. She cast around, passing the baton of conversation. 'Miss Bagdorf, how have you taken to the island? Have you been here long?'

Ramona nodded. 'I arrived last year,' she said in perfect English. 'At first there were terrible storms, but now the weather has settled. Thys bought me a horse.'

Thys shifted on his feet. 'My sister, Mrs Graham, is most unconventional. The other day I caught sight of her and, I confess, she was not sitting side-saddle but was mounted astride like a gentleman. She has been riding this way for some time, I understand.'

Ramona had the grace to look sheepish.

'My goodness. Where do you ride in this fashion, Miss Bagdorf?' Maria knew there were some rules she could break and others that were simply impossible. In all her travels, she had never ridden in such a manner. Society's judgement could not be avoided should such a shocking story seep out. Miss Bagdorf was clearly an Amazon. Next the girl would be wearing pantaloons.

Ramona maintained her composure. 'Most ladies might find it unsuitable, madam, but I was making my way across the highlands when I realised that riding to the side inhibits me.'

'Bravo!' Henderson saluted. 'Why not? Such stuffy traditions should be challenged.'

Miss Bagdorf blushed so that even her lips seemed flushed. She was a girl ripe for the picking. 'Trinidad is a jewel,' she said simply. 'I'm collecting recipes – we shall try some tonight. Soon Thys is sending me to London, where our Aunt Birgette is indisposed. I am to be her companion. Captain Henderson, I understand you have an eye for cacao?'

Henderson blustered a rebuttal, but Thys cut in.

'The best, James, don't deny it. I keep only the cream of my crop for you. There is no point in trying to sell you anything else.'

Maria watched as Henderson brushed away the compliment.

Dinner was a feast piled high with prawns, roasted plantain and spiced chicken, and then soft cheese and honey with bread so fresh it was difficult to stop eating. It was clear Miss Bagdorf preferred life away from the reserved behaviour of genteel Copenhagen. Her mother's *brunsviger* was abandoned for the food of slaves and the vigour of riding freely across the irrepressible landscape of the tropics.

'I like to eat with my hands,' the girl confessed. 'This food was made for that.'

Thys laughed. 'Our clothes, however, were not,' he quipped.

Maria laid down her cutlery and picked up a roasted chicken leg. Henderson regarded her carefully and followed suit.

'It tastes different, don't you think?' Ramona chattered.

'Next you will call the slaves to sing at the table,' Thys scolded.

A sliver of chicken skin fell from Maria's fingers onto her gown. She brushed it away.

'See,' Thys said.

Maria moved her arm and snagged her knife on the button of her glove. In a flash, Henderson leaned over and caught the blade in mid-air. It twirled between his fingers and he presented it back to her, the ivory handle foremost. Ramona clapped.

'Thank you,' said Maria, and told herself there was no reason the captain shouldn't be handy with a blade. *I have worked myself to high doh.* Even his smile seemed ominous. *Smuggler. Criminal. Thief.*

After dinner, the company played bridge. The captain was adept at finessing his hand and his prospects of winning were impossible to read from his expression. Maria was not surprised. *Perhaps he never shows himself,* she thought. *Perhaps below the surface there is only a void.* But that made no sense. There must be something. No man was good or bad all through.

'You mentioned you might return to London, Miss Bagdorf?' Maria enquired.

Thys cut in. 'We are waiting for word.'

'Perhaps I could travel with you, Captain?' Ramona's eyes slid across Henderson's wide shoulders. She clearly did not share Maria's reservations about her handsome dinner guest.

'We leave tomorrow morning. If you wish a cabin aboard the *Bittersweet*, you must pack immediately,' Henderson teased.

And Miss Bagdorf, seemingly unperturbed by this, played two trumps.

Long after midnight, they sipped pink demitasses of coffee

poured from a tall silver pot until at last the candles guttered and the plate of thin biscuits was finished. A moth fluttered across the room. It sank to the floor and still Maria had not concluded. It seemed too normal here. As the last flame disappeared, the party was left in darkness.

'Is the tax high on candlewax? I shall bring you contraband, Thys,' Henderson joked.

Was that an admission?

Thys laughed. 'Don't replace the lights,' he instructed the footman. 'Fetch lamps and the carriage. I have something to show you.' A dark figure, he jumped to his feet. Miss Bagdorf scooped up her wrap and, checking Henderson was following, reached for Maria's arm as the group headed into the tropical night.

'I have no idea of the time,' Maria noted. 'You don't keep a clock on the mantel.'

Ramona laughed. 'It's after sunset and before dawn,' she squealed, flinging herself onto the plump leather seat of her brother's open carriage. 'We have no need of more accurate timing than that. Sit next to me, Mrs Graham.' She held out a hand, kid gloves to her elbow.

Thys drove the horses – two bays. They headed away from the house and down a narrow road, no more than a track, through the dark foliage. The air was scented with tropical flowers and hops that bespoke an estate brewery. When the carriage stopped, Maria could hear running water, the hoots of night owls and the steady rhythm of the grass, creaking with insects. Half mesmerised, she wanted to stay and listen, but Thys hurried them on. Henderson handed her down. Slowly, in the dark, the little party followed Thys's lantern down the hill, a ramble in the pitch. Cacao pods jutted into the dim light, flashes of vivid leaves cutting towards them. He stopped at a small stream, his lamp glimmering over the black water.

'The river is sweet, isn't it?' Ramona turned, her hair so glossy it could be wet.

Behind them they couldn't see much – a tendril or two and the stream skipping over the edge and dropping into utter blackness. Thys doused his lamp.

'It's a waterfall,' Ramona announced.

'Come.' Her brother motioned as he clambered over the rocks. 'Follow me.'

Maria waved off Henderson's arm and fell into step, her eyes adjusting.

Over the drop, a luminous pond lay below them like a pale magic lantern. It was as if the moon had plummeted into the water and smashed open. Engulfed in darkness, with only a scatter of stars above, the place felt like a bright secret – something ancient and precious. Maria had never seen anything like it – a secret lake of light. The surface was opal. It put Maria in mind of a necklace she had seen once in Hatton Garden. She had been twenty-three and Lady Dundas had dangled the bauble between her fingers.

'Stay in London and I'll buy it for you,' she said.

Maria had been breathless – the way it held the light was hypnotic. But she was set on Bombay.

'Whatever would a girl like you do with jewellery?' her aunt taunted when Maria had turned down her admittedly generous offer. 'A dowdy bluestocking. Really.'

The lake was bigger than any opal and brighter too.

'What is it?' she asked, wide-eyed.

'I don't know,' Thys admitted. 'It started a few days ago. The slaves say it's a gift from the angels. They've been singing

118

devotional songs. I doubt the angels, myself. There will prove a more earthly explanation.'

Ramona sat on the edge of a flat stone, her slim ankles outlined in the light. 'Whatever caused it, it's magical,' she proclaimed. 'Don't you think so, Captain?'

Henderson did not reply and the girl looked chastened.

Maria squinted at the rocky path. The luminescence lit the uneven surface with an eerie blue that reflected the water. 'We must take a sample,' she declared. 'The Royal Society.'

'I'll fetch it.' Henderson stepped in. 'It's too dangerous for you to go down in the dark.'

Maria looked at her pale-stockinged feet encased in little more than slippers and was about to object, but Henderson had already started. He clambered down the rock face and stripped off his jacket, pulling back his shirtsleeves. Ramona peered over the edge, transfixed. She breathed something low in Danish. Henderson knocked out his snuff box and rinsed it in the pool. Then the captain reached into the illuminated water and, using his handkerchief as a makeshift net, scooped up the light, emptying it into the box as well he could. It took a few tries before he was satisfied. From above, the party watched as the glowing water swirled around his arm and lit the handkerchief like a bright star. Maria was spellbound as he folded the material and put the lid back on the little horn box. Where the water splashed onto the stone the drops darkened at once, as if a candle had been blown. Maria longed to see her own skin lit by the eerie light. Without a word, she slipped off her pumps.

'Mrs Graham,' Thys called, but he was too late.

The rocks were steep and grit caught Maria's stockings. It got between her toes. At the bottom, Captain Henderson caught her hand and held her steady, guiding her to an even section of the rocks.

'For the Royal Society.' He handed her the box. 'You are quite indefatigable, madam, if you don't mind me saying.'

'If I were less than indefatigable I'd be disappointed, Captain Henderson.'

The captain smiled indulgently as Maria removed her long gloves and leaned over the pool. She slipped her hand through the cool water, her slim fingers trailing a fairy stream.

'It feels like water,' she said.

Above, they could hear Thys remonstrating with his sister as she climbed over the top, now the way had proved safe for a lady. Henderson stepped backwards to aid Miss Bagdorf's descent, but the rocks were wet now. He slipped and landed solidly in the pool.

'Look. Now you're soaked, and Mrs Graham too,' Thys called down. 'Ramona! Don't go any further.'

Henderson stood up, the water illuminating his legs as if they were rooted. He took a bow. His teeth glowed as he laughed. Between his lips they formed an otherworldly translucent flash of white as Ramona arrived at the pool's side.

Maria shrugged. In such tropical conditions, water was hardly life-threatening. In many ways, the shower had been refreshing. She sat amiably on the edge, dangling her stock-inged feet like a curious child.

'What do you think causes it?' Ramona breathed.

'It can only be some kind of fish.' Maria smiled. 'Or a vege-table. Something very tiny for which great men will require a microscope. The sample will interest them in London. I wonder where it gets the light, for nothing can come of nothing. Isn't that the way? I can write and let you know what the gentlemen make of it. Scientifically speaking.'

Ramona held out a hand towards Henderson. 'We need to get you to dry land, Captain. You look quite sinister lit up like that.'

Instead of accepting the girl's help, Henderson reached down. He scooped a handful of bright water and tossed it into the blackness in the women's direction. Ramona squealed.

He mimicked Maria. '*It will greatly interest them in London. Greatly.* Maria, it's a miracle. It defies Raphael. It defies Gainsborough.'

His teeth, Maria noticed, seemed suddenly very sharp.

'Woman, you might never see anything so beautiful. It's angel water. And all you can think of is science.'

Maria couldn't help but smile, though she was aware the little gemstone was still in her purse.

If only science was all that was on my mind, she thought.

San Fernando

Dawn broke as Henderson and Mrs Graham climbed into a carriage and started the bumpy journey back to town. In London, it was common to live late like this, but it had been a while since she had done so. The rising sun revealed the extent of the hills, tinged by the verdant foliage of the plantation, so lush that it encroached on the track. A work party of slaves was already in the fields, a huge bare-chested overseer whipping one unfortunate. Maria had been patted dry, but one or two locks of hair had escaped Ramona's attentions and now and then a plump drop of water seeped out.

'Tired?' Henderson asked.

Maria shook her head. She didn't want to return to the ship without voicing her concerns, but here in the carriage they were alone. That made it more dangerous, for the captain was twice her size, but now was the time. She took a deep breath and gathered the words. *I must make it sound casual.*

'I have something to admit, Captain. It may make you cross.'

Henderson took off his hat. His ponytail was bound with a thin chocolate-coloured ribbon. He smiled. 'Madam?'

Her heart lurched. If he was guilty, might he throw her from the carriage?

'I was curious about the chocolate bar I found in one of the trunks in your cabin. It was wrong of me, but I have found your secret,' she said. It felt like jumping off the edge of a cliff. She was falling, falling.

Henderson's demeanour betrayed nothing. 'What do you mean?' he asked.

'I found your hidden cache.' She reached into her purse and pulled out the little rock. 'In the chocolate bar in your trunk.'

'Well, I'll be.' Henderson held up the stone to the low, early morning light that lit the carriage window. 'What were you doing rooting around in my old trunk?'

Maria's eyes dropped to the carriage floor. 'I was searching for a glass,' she said. 'To dress my hair.'

'Really?' He did not believe her. 'When?'

'Before we left the ship. I dropped the bar. It broke and I found this stone. It's a most disconcerting haul.' She chose her words carefully.

Henderson remained as relaxed as he'd been sitting on the Bagdorfs' long settees. 'The sneaky devil.' The captain smiled. 'This was in that old cacao brick? The Spaniards used to do it this way. The churchmen. To avoid duty to the Crown. I had no idea anyone was still employing the technique.'

Maria's limbs flooded with relief. Involuntarily, she beamed. He had not known. 'So these goods are not yours?' she breathed.

'That musty old chocolate belonged to Will – the English boy who died in Natal. He asked me to deliver it with his last breath. I couldn't understand why he prized such poor-quality goods. I assumed he was referring to his other possessions. Now, well, no wonder it was on his mind. And I had half an idea to send it to the galley for the crew's use.' Henderson chortled. 'My men are honest enough, but the cook would have been off at the first port. He's a Yorkshireman and canny. Who would blame him?'

'So you will pay the duty, Captain? You will turn it over?'

Henderson looked up. The pearls in Mrs Graham's hairpiece glowed white. The edge of the feather was quivering with the movement of the carriage as she regarded him intently, the colour of her eyes picked out by her dress. It was pleasant to see her impassioned about something, even if it was only the extent of duty due to His Majesty's coffers. But, as it turned out, that didn't mean he was prepared to lie.

'I shall deliver this block to Will's business partners, Mrs Graham, and what they do with it is their business. That's what I was asked to do, and I'm no thief. I will charge them for the privilege.'

Maria pulled herself up. 'You are a smuggler, sir, if you avoid the king's due. You forget I am on a mission for the Emperor of Brazil. My father and my husband were captains in His Majesty's navy. There is no question. The duty must be paid.' Henderson's eyes flashed, but now she'd started Maria found she couldn't hold back. 'The very definition of a gentleman is that he does the right thing by his king and his country.'

'Plenty of gentlemen would take goods such as these and run,' Henderson said flatly.

Maria shook her head. 'It is insupportable.'

The captain's voice grew hard. 'As insupportable as rooting in a gentleman's possessions, madam? For a glass, indeed.

You need only have asked for one. Tell me, what gives you the right to dictate to me, and in that tone?'

He was angry, but Maria held her nerve. 'Because I am right, sir,' she said calmly. 'And you know it.'

Henderson slumped in his seat. There was the nub. She probably was right, damn her – acting as his conscience once more, calling him to decency. The captain's heart sank. The truth was that he wanted this life. A woman like Maria. Dinner with friends. To be a gentleman. He realised in a flash that that was why he was returning to London. It was what had attracted him to her in the first place – not only her beauty but also her innate respectability. She was everything good he associated with being British, and he was not worthy of her any more than he was worthy of London. He couldn't simply put on a fancy coat and change everything. Outside, the tropical fields flashed past, but all he could think of was England.

He nodded. 'You have the truth of it. And it's brave of you to say.'

All his childhood, Henderson had lived in ignorance. Growing up, he had thought his mother was a lady, but she had no idea of the true nature of her life. Not even of her own husband. She was a fool who had been hoodwinked by a fine set of clothes. Henderson found her letters when his father died. She had adored the old man, writing to him all the detail of her measured English life. She prattled about new plantings in London's parks and repairs to the family's battered carriage, with its old-fashioned perch seat, as if these might concern him. Never once had she asked why her husband insisted she couldn't come to Brazil. The old man must have loved her, yet he had lied to his wife since the day they met.

125

It felt as if she'd have entirely evaporated if she found out the truth. She was an honest woman, Henderson berated himself, and he had turned out to be more of his father than of his London side. Else how could he have fallen so far?

Mrs Graham, her hands curled patiently in her lap, was waiting for him to speak. The satin of her evening gown caught the dawn light. She was an image of everything he longed for. She had seen him for what he was and, perhaps unexpectedly, the captain found he wasn't happy to dissemble. *That's why I have not been able speak the whole voyage,* he realised. *I don't want to be like him. I don't want to lie.* He cleared his throat.

'I can assure you, you are in no danger, madam. You're at liberty to disembark the *Bittersweet* if the arrangement does not meet with your approval.'

'How could I approve?'

'You have never bypassed official channels? In all your travels? Not once?'

Maria shifted. Of course she had. 'Never merely to make money,' she said. 'Forgive me.'

The captain considered. It was true that Will's business partners would pay because he had discovered their secret. Will had said so – but money wasn't the only matter. Henderson took a deep breath. 'You must leave this to me. It's not your business and is only mine by circumstance. You have no right to tell me what to do.'

He paused. If he wanted to be different from his father, then he must behave differently. He must be honest about his occupation. Henderson's stomach turned.

'I'm afraid it will disappoint you, madam,' he continued, 'but I must admit to being a habitual smuggler. It's how I make my living, and my father before me.'

Henderson waited for a puff of smoke and a whiff of sulphur, for Maria to shout or cast herself dramatically onto the track, for the carriage to become dim and the sky to cave in, the fields folding over, green on blue. Instead, his admission hung in the air.

'I see,' Maria replied calmly. 'That was not apparent.'

The captain had been enormously frank. More frank, she realised, than any man she'd ever had to deal with. She had not expected this. In her mind, if he was a smuggler he was all but evil, yet the man before her was both eloquent and thoughtful.

'You must consider what you want to do,' he said.

'I worried you might harm me.'

'Mrs Graham.' His tone was impassioned. 'You must know that I would never harm you. On that, I give you my word.'

And, with the early morning light flooding through the thin glass, she believed him.

As the carriage rolled down the hill, Maria sat back. She was glad she'd spoken and now her body felt heavy with exhaustion. She liked Captain Henderson, despite the fact he was in the wrong. This realisation did not perplex her as much as it ought to.

'Does the capital penalty not concern you?' she asked.

Henderson sat forward. 'That I should swing for it?' No one had ever spoken to him this way.

Maria nodded.

'I suppose not. That is only in English territories. In the northern states, the penalty is a term in prison.'

She lifted her feet to stretch her ankles. Did the captain care so little for himself? 'Don't you want something better?'

Her tone was intense. Unable to form an answer, Henderson

turned to the horizon. Outside the window, the sun was up.

Maria yawned. For once this had not been the usual battle about her role and what she might and mightn't do. It made a change. Suddenly she felt exhausted. The fact Henderson was a smuggler was no longer an occasion for terror. She had learned something new, she thought – about herself as well as him. If she had been out of her depth all evening, her feet now touched the ground.

When the captain looked round, Mrs Graham's eyes were closing. He took the opportunity to study her face. She was calm in repose and her breath was shallow as she drifted into sleep, her figure small in the seat, her skin white, in contrast to the dark leather. Her curled fingers were encased in pale-gold satin. They twitched as she slumbered. The sight felt too intimate and he looked away, grave-faced. He was certain she would never forgive him.

*

Coming into the city, the smell of the morning's ovens was on the air. Whooping, a street urchin ran barefoot beside the carriage wheels. As they hit the rough cobbles, Captain Henderson watched over Maria Graham, anxious as a new father in case the noise woke her as the bright townhouses jolted by. As the lady slept, Henderson considered that they could drink coffee and watch the docks spring to life. He tarried for a moment before discounting the idea. She looked too peaceful, for one thing. For another, he was loathe to disturb her and perhaps bring about her early departure from the *Bittersweet*.

As the carriage drew up on the dock, he didn't hesitate to lift her prone body aboard. The orchid scent lay heavy on his chest. Maria's arm flopped and her hair came loose, unravelling like a sheet of dark silk that folded over the sleeve of his jacket. The men on deck stood to attention. One nipped ahead and opened the door to the cabin.

'Nice night, sir?' He grinned, eyes bright.

'Don't be cheeky,' Henderson snapped.

Carefully, the captain laid Maria on the bed. The shutters were still closed and light pierced the edges of the wood, casting bright stripes along the cabin floor. Henderson deposited Maria's velvet evening purse on the bedside and loitered, unwilling to leave. He cast his eye across the papers scattered over the tabletop. She had been making a fair copy of her work. The sheaf was piled untidily. Maria's handwriting wasn't as neat as might be expected and the papers weren't absolutely in order. On top was her account of the Palace of St Cristóvão. He drew a finger along a line of script, as if to absorb her words. Then, regarding Will Simmons's chocolate slab, he removed a small knife from inside his jacket to extend Maria's exploration. At the far end he cut away a thick chunk, exposing a roughly formed bar of yellow gold. She'd been right – it was a regular treasure trove. Careful not to disturb her, he secreted the bar, the shavings and the scatter of gemstones in his pocket. The larger stones would make a couple of carats each when they were cut. He'd lock it away in his cabin, he decided. Then he'd need to think.

Outside, Henderson repaired to the open-fronted bar where Thys had been drinking the day before. It was a cut above the usual. In one corner he found three copies of the *Daily Courant*, eighteen months out of date. He ordered rum and sat looking onto the *Bittersweet*'s mooring as he examined the monochrome engravings. He took in London's tall buildings, the fashionable ladies and the gentlemen in their top hats. He didn't recognise the politicians, the doyennes of society or even the king. Could the city really be his home? It felt that way.

The landlord, an ex-slave, towered above the table. 'More rum, sir?'

Henderson shook his head. 'I'm looking for a ship with a berth suitable for a lady. Bound for England,' he enquired.

'Your ship is for London, I heard.'

'Do you know of any other?'

The man didn't move an inch. 'The ones flying the Jack is the ones to enquire at. Seems that way to me.'

'The traffic is fine?'

'Traffic, sir?'

'To and from England. There is a regular flow?'

'Oh yes, sir. As much as any place across the big water.'

The captain paid and took a stroll along the dock. Staring up at his own ship, he watched an open-topped terracotta bowl of thick bright blood being delivered to the galley by a half-naked child. There would be black sausage tonight to sate the men's appetites.

Further along, three ships sported the Union Jack. He enquired of the sailors on the dockside where they were headed – two ships, it transpired, were bound for the Americas, while only one was on its way east. The *Jury* was a respectable enough vessel – a merchant ship run by a captain who had quit the Bombay Marine. It was to set sail by the end of the week, loaded with sugar and bound for Portsmouth. Henderson loitered. He did not want Maria to board it.

The captain wandered back to the *Bittersweet*. Crossing the Atlantic, there would be plenty of time to investigate the

130

secrets of the chocolate bar and try to figure out the cut of Will Simmons's jib. The dead boy had seemed callow, but now there was a whiff of the mastermind about him. Might he have been up to anything else? Was everything and everyone different in London? Perhaps the city would transform Henderson too. The gemstones would certainly be more valuable there.

Striding aboard, the captain summoned the mate. Clarkson was famously lucky at cards, which Henderson put down to his wry expression. Whether he was dealt a good hand or bad, he always looked convivial.

'We can cast off in half an hour or slightly less,' the man said. 'The tide is turning. It's favourable weather too, breezy enough.'

Henderson lifted his hat and ran a hand through his hair. 'Half an hour?' he asked.

'Yes, sir. If it pleases you. You said you wanted a quick turnaround. I had the cannon cleaned and shot prepared. In case there might be trouble. Pirates.'

Henderson's eyes moved in the direction of Maria's cabin. He had a sudden longing to breathe in her scent, gulping it down like a glass of Tempranillo, swimming in it like a hidden pool. He endeavoured to control himself.

'Has Mrs Graham stirred?' he asked.

'No sir, not as far as I know.'

He motioned the mate to follow him along the deck, looking down the dock at the *Jury* and peering out to sea. Then, with the other man waiting, he quietly recapped the route he'd plotted.

'The *Bittersweet* is smaller but she's faster,' he mused. 'We'll get there more than a week before they do. Perhaps even longer. The *Jury* is loaded to the gunwales. She's heavier by at least half again. We'll beat her to port, no doubt about it.'

'Beat whom, sir?' Clarkson enquired, smiling no more and no less than usual.

The captain took a deep breath. 'Set sail, Mr Clarkson,' Henderson instructed. 'Quietly.'

'Quietly?'

'The lady is asleep.'

Clarkson looked uncharacteristically bemused, but the captain ignored him. The crossing would take more than a month, and perhaps half that again if the weather were against them. But any ship would face the same conditions and the *Bittersweet* would have several days' march on the *Jury*, on top of what she could make up along the way.

'Gentleman be damned. I am her quickest way there. Raise the anchor and cast off,' he said, disappearing into his cabin.

Inside, instead of looking at the chart or lingering on what Mrs Graham's view might be of the ship's departure, Captain Henderson removed the brick of cacao from its hiding place. As he chopped into the chocolate, he wondered how many gems and how much gold was in there. His heart was racing.

11

On board the Bittersweet

Maria turned over slowly. Her mouth felt dry and her arm lolled over the edge of the bedclothes. She focussed on the shady outline of the decanter that sat on the table, its dark contents shifting from side to side. Then she noticed the petticoat she had left on the chair was also swaying in the shadows. The tide must be high. She hesitated, waiting for the familiar thud of dockside water against the frame of the ship, but nothing came. She hauled her legs over the side of the bed, rising to open the shutters. As the warm light flooded in, she gasped, for there was no question that the *Bittersweet* was at sea. An unobstructed blue vista stretched before her. Sinking into a chair, she lifted the discarded linen that had swaddled the smuggled chocolate. The bar and the booty embedded within it were gone. There was no way to tell what time it was, but the light in the cabin had the feel of a Caribbean late afternoon. Mrs Graham felt in a state of abject disarray. Her stomach growled as she poured a tot of wine, sipped it and then set the pewter cup to one side. Carefully, she removed her hairpin and drew off her gloves, her eyes drawn to the porthole.

'We are at sea,' she intoned as her mind flashed through the possibilities.

She had never said she wanted to leave the *Bittersweet* – she hadn't reasoned her way through that argument yet. The truth was she wasn't sure whether she was judging the captain too harshly. There was something about him – something that might never work out, like an equation that could not be solved. Now, however, she had no choice as to her passage and she certainly minded that. Maria surveyed the desk. The journal of her voyage to Brazil was all but finished and she would move on to Murray's Chilean book next, but she was so vexed she could scarcely imagine being able to concentrate. The captain might at least have consulted her. She looked out of the window once more. There were no seabirds – he must have cast off hours ago. It was an outrage.

She splashed her face with cold water and drew the grey dress from the trunk, changing quickly and pinning her hat in place. Then, not even checking her appearance in the reflection of the porthole, before she stepped out of the cabin into the sunshine.

On deck, Henderson was nowhere to be seen. Two of the sailors doffed their caps and wished her a good afternoon. The ship's sails were full and the *Bittersweet* glided along at a clip – there was no sight of land on any side, only the Atlantic and the sky, clear as crystal. The men were coiling rope, the smell of wax and sea spray seeping towards her from their direction. The ship had the habitual feel of the first day of a long voyage – she recognised it from every vessel she'd ever set sail on. The crew were smart to their orders, supplies were high in all things, optimism included, and full wages were due at their destination.

'Where is the captain?' she asked.

'In his cabin, ma'am.'

Maria stretched her fingers like a concert pianist about to take the stage. The joints clicked as she headed across the deck. She knocked smartly and entered without waiting.

Henderson was squashed inside, sitting at his desk with a chart before him and a small tankard of port in place of the inkwell. He had washed, shaved and changed, and looked annoyingly fresh.

'We are at sea, sir,' Maria stated flatly.

The captain sprang to his feet, knocking over an empty cup and propelling two of his papers to the floor.

'The tide was with us and I checked at the dock,' he said. 'There was no ship for London for another week or so. I took the decision on your behalf.'

'You didn't think to wake me?'

'I did. Of course. But you were tired and you seemed so peaceful. I know how keen you are to make time.'

Maria sighed. Henderson reeled. The cast of her eyes was like a punch in the face. He couldn't blame her.

'First it transpires you are a smuggler, and now a kidnapper,' Maria said simply. 'I don't wish to be churlish, Captain Henderson. Those around you say you are a man to be trusted. You garner respect from your crew and yet when it comes to—'

'I know. I know.' He gestured half in apology, half in explanation. His actions had been weighing on his conscience. 'I cannot say how sorry I am, Mrs Graham. I find myself, when it comes to your person, I find myself . . . in difficulty.'

'My person?'

He looked sheepish, but he had brought it up now. 'Yes,

madam. You are so admirable. It seems that in your presence I am seldom myself. I wanted to keep you in company.'

Maria laid her hand on her stomach. The cabin was tiny and she was jammed against the desk. Henderson was no more than a few inches away, the familiar scent of tobacco smoke emanating from him. It felt comforting. Strangely, however, that annoyed her more. She felt as if she was being unreasonable, though she was sure she had the high ground. No one had used this excuse before. Not even her late husband.

'If you expect to flatter me into condoning your actions, Captain, I assure you that won't work.'

'Oh no,' Henderson insisted. 'I know what I am and I hope I have been clear about it. I'm not trying to flatter you, Mrs Graham, I'm only offering an explanation.'

He did not turn away. It was just like yesterday – eye to eye, absolute honesty and no backing down. There was something of the prizefighter about Captain Henderson.

Maria had often observed that a person's true nature was only apparent *in extremis*. This conversation felt like a head-to-head bout, or at least like a high-stakes game of cards. She'd travelled in the company of many men who would have liked to have set off without her permission, organise her lodgings and curtail her plans. Their interference, however kindly meant, had never felt so personal. Captain Henderson was disarming, not least because he was so frank.

'I pride myself on making my own decisions, sir,' she said. 'I do not welcome gentlemen making them for me.'

Henderson nodded sharply. 'You are quite right.' He bowed as far as the space in the cabin would permit him. 'It was selfish of me not to consult you. Might you forgive me, Mrs Graham?'

Maria sighed. There was no course of action but to abide

by what he'd done. They were at sea now. 'When do you expect to arrive in England?

'That will depend on the weather. It will take a month at the minimum and most likely a week or two more. We're reliant, as I'm sure you are aware, on the winds, though at this time of year there should be nothing untoward. We'll go as quickly as we can. There was no ship to get you to England faster. I trusted I was doing the right thing.'

'You cannot have been sure, sir.'

'No.'

Mrs Graham paused. Had he been less apologetic, she would have fought harder. It was difficult not to forgive someone so apparently decent. Still, it irked her. She was bound for home on a smuggling vessel, however appealing the man at the helm.

'There is nothing to be done.' She nodded curtly, her eyes still hard as she swept out of the cabin, taking some of the light, it seemed, with her.

Henderson sank back into his seat. He felt like a heel – the worst kind of cad – and yet the night before, they had chatted like old friends at dinner. He had teased her and she had laughed. He opened the desk drawer to reveal his haul from mining the chocolate bar. There was a pirate's treasure trove of gemstones and three small bars of gold that were pleasingly weighty. He touched the nearest one for luck and then jumped as a second knock rapped at the door. Thinking it was Mrs Graham returning, he shot to his feet like a guilty schoolboy and slammed the drawer shut.

The door opened to reveal Big Al Thatcher, the ship's cook, whose skills extended to minor surgery. The *Bittersweet*'s crew did not run to a ship's doctor.

'Pressed neck of pork tonight, sir?' the old cook asked, his accent as fresh as if he had left York only the week before. 'We have cream and I thought I'd try a sauce. A sweet Madeira? With ginger?'

Henderson nodded. 'The Spanish white we picked up in Natal will complement it nicely,' he mused. 'We'll need something full-flavoured. Have a table set for Mrs Graham and I to eat together, would you?'

Big Al's long face twitched. The *Bittersweet* rarely afforded passage to guests and certainly not to ladies. He felt out of his depth cooking for the quality, never mind setting table. Under Henderson's tutelage, his culinary repertoire had expanded from the simple home cooking upon which he prided himself to a small array of fancy sauces and prime cuts. Now it seemed tables required to be set.

'Where would you like to eat, sir?'

The captain thought for a moment. Given Mrs Graham's annoyance, he could hardly arrange dinner in the woman's cabin and then invite himself for a meal, though the captain's cabin, which she now inhabited, was the usual place to eat.

'On deck,' he tried.

Big Al looked momentarily dubious. 'We have cheese to finish, if a picnic is what you desire,' he offered.

'Yes,' Henderson chimed. 'A picnic. Exactly. Port with cheese and some fruit.'

'I loaded fresh figs, sir. And we have some exotics.'

'Very good. Have the cabin boy invite Mrs Graham. Dinner on deck. Yes.'

★

The stars were breathtaking. Maria would miss that about the tropics. In her memory, London was invariably foggy, and even when the fog abated, the city was peppered with too many gaslights to allow the constellations their glory. At night the skies were a uniform dun brown over the sprawl. It was, her father said, the price London paid for being the biggest and best city in the world. As a child, Captain Dundas had taught her the names of the stars, mapping the constellations with ditties that aided memory. At her family home, many a night in his long absences, she crept from her bed, sneaking to the chilly window with a blanket wrapped around her shoulders, to watch the moon wane and the stars trace their passage, ever mindful that thousands of miles away they were shining down on her father's ship.

Later, after she left England, the stars stayed with her, their positions varying – cold companions whether they were viewed from a campfire in Khandesh, a nunnery in Umbria or the top of a Chilean mountain. They proved comforting when a journey was arduous or Maria found herself in danger. This dinner was a good way, if unconventional, for Captain Henderson to say he was sorry – these were the last few weeks after all they might dine al fresco, before the constellations were masked by the cloudy skies of Northern Europe. South of the equator, the night sky swirled as the ship cut through the surf, providing a stunning backdrop.

The ship continued to make way and the sound of singing wafted from below deck as the men diced. One or two would lose their wages before they earned them. Others would emerge on the dock like millionaires at the other end of the trip. The candles flickered in the breeze between the oil lamps illuminating the small dining table set with two wooden chairs.

At first, Maria had worried that they would quarrel again, but the captain's company had been convivial over dinner. The food had been delicious and now she settled against a tapestry pillow and decided to make the best of the voyage.

'Who made this cushion?' she enquired.

Henderson shrugged. 'The soft furnishings came with the ship,' he said. 'There are not many and they are rarely used.'

'And this ship was your father's?'

'Yes.'

'You owe your father a debt of gratitude then. What was he like?'

Henderson faltered. 'He was a smuggler like me. He'd been away from England the better part of forty years by the time he died in Brazil. My mother had only two visits from him, both brief.'

'Henderson is a Scottish name, like Graham, which was my late husband's, or Dundas, which is my own.'

'Indeed. I have no idea where my father was born. He met my mother in London and married her there, and now they are both dead so I have no means to find out. Neither of them talked a great deal about themselves. The old man was dashing, or so my mother said. She met him at a ball in Knightsbridge.'

'He was a gentleman, then?'

'She believed so.'

'But you doubt it.'

'He had charm. And he had money. People spend more time on social niceties than I expect such matters merit. We all wish to be part of that club. I admit that I should like it.' Henderson's stomach lurched. The words felt raw, but he continued. 'As a boy I considered it my birthright. I was

140

brought up a gentleman, but I found another way. Part of me still misses what I left behind. I love the London I remember. I have no idea if it is still there or, indeed, if it ever was more than my own childish fancy.'

Maria sipped her wine. She was tutor to the heir of the Brazilian throne so she could hardly deny that social niceties were important, and yet she did not like to feel snobbish nor unkind. She'd always been considered a poor relation – her aunt still baulked at her literary attempts. The family's disapproval of everything about Maria seeped across the wide ocean no matter how far she travelled. Lady Dundas had wanted to control her marriage, her education, her wardrobe and, she thought with a twist, the mother from whose care they had removed her. Throughout, Maria had proved troublesome. She'd swapped an opal necklace for the starlit seas and still she was never considered good enough, no matter her distinguished reviews.

'A man is generally judged on his merits,' she said. 'And his actions.'

Henderson shook his head. They both knew that wasn't true. Not entirely.

'We are all somebody's child,' he observed.

She nodded. 'The child of our most prosperous parent, and his family.'

Henderson sliced a mango. The fragrance perfumed the night air. Maria lifted a sliver of cheese.

'It's the custom to drink coffee,' the captain said. 'Perhaps while we're waiting you might like to take a turn about the deck?'

The sound of the ship cutting through the water carried over the side, the constant wash and slap a steady rhythm.

The sails creaked. It felt like only the two of them on board as they walked towards the prow into the velvet darkness. The satin of Maria's gown was smooth against her skin, the slight breeze forcing it against her body.

'I'm learning Portuguese from the cabin boy,' she admitted. 'I shall need it for my new commission.'

She was acutely aware that her fingers were trembling, but she tried to ignore them. It crossed her mind that she remained slightly afraid of Henderson. This was confusing, for she also enjoyed his company. He was confident, for a man who could not hope for the support of society.

'Ah, the cabin boy?' he said. 'Now that one is a finer lad than he should be. I found him in New York. He was half-dead, beaten and abandoned just off the quay. He'd have died if I'd left him, for winter was coming. I worried that if such treatment was all he'd known, he would be vicious, but he has blossomed.'

'You took him in?'

'We needed a cabin boy, and had he not been a good one we'd have set him ashore. Do not think me a bleeding heart, Mrs Graham. I've left a man half-dead more than once. I've hanged a man for insubordination. When I was younger, I had a temper.'

'The boy's Portuguese is good.'

'He has a facility for languages. He spoke English already and some Dutch, but he's picked up the Hispanic tongues. They are common at port and we have three Brazilian sailors on board. We had seven, but the war for independence put paid to four. Those left aboard are not patriots.'

'You know your crew. Not every captain could name his sailors' politics.'

'I run this ship.'

142

'Still . . .' Maria did not continue. Many captains all but ignored the seamen except to see that adequate orders were barked in their direction.

Captain Henderson shrugged. He lifted his glass and smiled. Maria fought the warmth she felt towards him. After she had challenged him that afternoon, she noticed a change – a shiver down her spine and a jump in her stomach. The man was an odd mixture of comfort and danger. Staring northwards now, she thought of John Murray's drawing room. Who was the toast of London these days? Who was Murray inviting to his famous salon? The greatest minds in the world. Wits and intellectuals – members of the Royal Society and hot-blooded young poets mingling over a glass of German wine. Not one of those firebrands had ever made her feel this way. When she had left the captain's cabin that afternoon, it took her five minutes to recover her equilibrium and, she realised, not all of her anger. When he had told her about his profession, she had been disarmed. When he set sail without consulting her, she'd pulsed with fury. Now she felt moved.

It was a new experience. Her late husband had never turned her stomach to jelly. Thomas Graham had been a competent naval officer and her closest friend, but he had never made her blush. Surely this was the behaviour of a foolish girl in a novel, not the widely admired Mrs Graham. The captain was, at a guess, five years younger than she was, and a felon.

She turned her gaze westward and, reaching into the satin bag dangling from her waistband, pulled out a small fan that she snapped open in an effort to cool down. Looking back, if she was honest, these feelings had turned in her belly in the carriage as they'd rattled up to the Bagdorf plantation. Now, she realised, if she attempted to rein in the feeling, it only became stronger, like some kind of alchemical reaction. Maria watched Captain Henderson brush a lock of hair from his face. So far he had admitted to being a smuggler and then he had effectively kidnapped her. Was this childish spellbound fixation in fact some kind of fear over what he might do next?

'Madam . . .' Henderson started.

In a rush, she wondered if the captain might be about to propose something indecent and, worse, that if he did, if she would consider it.

'I am of the view we should dine outside every night.' He motioned her back to the table.

Maria realised that she was almost disappointed. *The silence was easier to cope with,* she thought. *How will I make it through a whole month of this?*

'Thank you, I should enjoy that.' She gave a slim smile. 'I fear it is time to retire.'

Henderson gave a curt nod. 'I will see you to your cabin.'

'No need,' she murmured, giving a little dip, hardly a curtsy at all. It was time to call a halt.

The captain bowed and watched her figure disappear into the darkness. He lingered a while until, smiling, he dragged his attention to business. He had his starlight duties to attend. Many calculations could only be carried out at night. Henderson called the cabin boy to clear the table and then he turned to his sextant on the bridge. From a height, he noticed the boy steal a sliver of cheese, ramming it into the pocket of his breeches as he collected the plates.

'Hey!' Henderson called down. 'Thatcher will give you a ship's biscuit if you're hungry.'

'Yes, sir.' The boy kept his head low, like the dog he was.

'Put it back.'

The child's dark fingers fished out the cheese and laid it on the pewter. He started to pile the tableware.

Long after midnight, the deck was balmy and silent. Two men kept the night watch while everyone else slept. Late, the captain hovered outside Maria's cabin, making his final round. There was no noise from within, and if there was a light inside it was too dim to show round the frame. He waited, wondering how long it was decent for a woman to be widowed before she could remarry. The wooden door seemed like the entrance to a different world – not an imaginary past, but a possible future. Something real. He leaned opposite, his back to the planking, and regarded it for a long time. Perhaps, Henderson considered, if he wasn't respectable he might at least find himself worthy of Mrs Graham's attention, and that of London too. For the first time, he saw a path of his own, not a legacy passed on from his father or the trail of disappointment bequeathed by his mother's expectations. Instead, here in the dark passageway was something new. Now he had sight of it, might he find his way in the world with no shame?

12

On board the Bittersweet

The next day, Mrs Graham did not emerge from her cabin and Captain Henderson kept to himself. At four bells of the afternoon, he sent a message once more inviting the lady to dine with him, and she agreed.

Then, early in the evening, Big Al Thatcher was distracted by some merriment among the crew – an argument over a game of dice. A scuffle broke out, opponents tumbling across the boards. A punch was laid with a sharp crack and, at once, the cook left his station and went on deck to put money on which man would win. A shilling, which he lost in two minutes flat. As it transpired, however, those two minutes were enough. As he turned back to work, Thatcher discovered the galley was engulfed in smoke. A greasy bundle of rags was aflame and had spread to the day's cornbread, which had ignited with vigour. The cook tried to beat out the blaze. He poured a bucket of wine over the base, which dampened it, but still flames leaped upwards. The wooden frame of the galley started to kindle, the stores showed signs of smouldering, and smoke began to pour across the deck. Maria emerged on deck in her evening attire just as two men jumped overboard in panic, grabbing a barrel each to keep them afloat. Several of the crew were screaming. Taken aback only momentarily by this mayhem, she quickly took in the crisis, calculating quickly how far they must be from shore. It was too long a distance to furnish hope of easy rescue.

She hovered, unsure what to do, as Henderson emerged from his cabin. He didn't hesitate, calling the men to order.

'Fetch buckets,' he instructed Clarkson. 'Anything that will hold seawater.'

Clarkson brought what he could – half barrels, washing bowls, pewter tankards and zinc buckets. Henderson formed the crew into a chain to draw seawater over the side. There was a strong smell of melting butter and burning ham. The men were coughing as the dark cloud belched thickly across deck. Maria took her place in line.

'There's no need, ma'am,' Clarkson said.

'I want to help,' she insisted. 'I need something to do.'

The work was hard. Maria's dress was soaked in an instant, flecks of charcoal staining the satin, but she persisted. The constant flow of water brought things under control impressively quickly. Al Thatcher and Henderson stood to the fore, dousing the flames until the deck drew back into view. The men were a raggle-taggle bunch, smeared by the smoke. Those nearest the flaming kitchen were found with their eyes streaming. The sound of coughing echoed round the deck in between the low murmur of conversation as the men assessed the damaged and apportioned the blame. Henderson stripped off his sopping greatcoat and ordered the cabin boy to beat out the last of the smoke, which had dwindled till it was mere steam. Inside, the galley was crusted in blackness. The boy moved like a smudge across it.

One of the sailors had been badly burnt – a livid stamp on his right arm as if his skin was embossed. He crouched, whimpering. Big Al Thatcher bundled him below decks, assuring Henderson that as long as infection didn't set in, the fellow would be fine in a day or two. 'He will keep the limb,' he said. 'But it may scar.'

'We must tack,' Henderson ordered Clarkson. 'We have two men overboard. Cowards, both of them.'

Clarkson took command. Such manoeuvres were tricky. A man had to look sharp – the mainsheet could cut off your head and the ropes could hang you. Accidents were not as rare as they should be, especially after a night on the rum or if a sailor's nerves were on edge. The *Bittersweet* turned, however, without incident and Clarkson scooped the shamefaced deserters out of the surf as the crew jeered. Maria hung back, watching.

Henderson waited by the mizzen. He inspected the miscreants with his arms crossed. Through the material of his shirt, Maria noticed a long scar on his arm. There was, she realised, a lot she didn't know about this man, and she felt what was set to happen now might reveal some of it. The crew fell silent, anticipating the captain's pronouncement. The unlucky two knew to cower before Henderson struck out, his fist like lightning. The captain was strong. In only a second or two, both men went down.

'You don't abandon ship unless on my command,' Henderson spat. 'You don't shit till I tell you. Understand?'

The men were shaking now, cowering.

'Bloody cowards,' Henderson sneered, nodding at Clarkson, who handed him a whip.

Maria looked away. The sound of it was bad enough. Far off, she could swear she spotted a porpoise. Her stomach turned.

148

The smoke had sickened her and the pitiful screaming was worse. The damp material at her wrist rubbed the skin pink.

When the whipping was over, she turned again. The men were bloody, their crewmates still looking on, unforgiving. It was they, after all, who had been abandoned.

'Half rations for a week?' Clarkson asked, and Henderson nodded.

The men disappeared below deck, flanked by the bo'sun. The captain seemed so mild sometimes, almost milky. Many officers doled out discipline by proxy, but when it came to it, Captain Henderson did what was required himself. He caught her eye and nodded. She nodded back. She should have gone back to her cabin, she realised. That would have been more seemly. The crew dispersed and Henderson turned to inspect the damage to the fabric of the vessel, issuing orders to the ship's carpenter. Even the sea breeze couldn't blow away the smell of smoke. Maria hovered by the galley. A ragged puddle of light seeped in where the side had burned through.

'I'll square it off, sir. It'll be good as new,' the carpenter swore. 'A porthole, eh?'

'Bad show, Thatcher,' the captain pronounced.

The cook had seen to the injured man and was squaring up now he was back on deck. 'I deserve a punishment, sir.'

Henderson laid a hand on his shoulder.

'Just be careful, man,' he said. 'You have one of the most dangerous jobs on the ship. A moment's inattention is all it takes. That fellow's injuries are punishment – every time you see them, you'll remember. Don't let it happen again.'

Maria hung back as the cook wiped his huge hands on his smoke-stained semmit. The captain had the measure of him, and it took half an hour for him to regain enough spirit to go back to work, taking stock of his supplies. In the galley, the stove required mending, and the fish caught that afternoon was burnt to a cinder along with the entire supply of cheese, which although melted to a crisp remained edible and unexpectedly delicious. The butter was ruined. A small urn of milk had been used to douse the flames and now there was a sour odour where it had singed the deck. The drum of ship's biscuits in current use had not been ruined beyond serving, but they tasted of the fire.

Maria withdrew to her cabin and patted her hair dry. She aired her evening gown, which dried almost instantly in front of the open window. The smoke had left a grey swirl on the fabric, but it would rinse away. She washed her hands and face and then curled up and watched the sky darken through the glass as she replayed the panic, the punishment and the cook's tortured expression when the captain forgave him. From the deck, the sounds of repair floated down – wood being hammered into place and men hauling barrels.

An hour later, when the boy announced that Henderson's invitation to dinner still stood, Maria found herself eager to join him. She wanted to talk. Outside, the deck was deserted now and Henderson stood as she approached the depleted table. Instead of fish, fresh vegetables and wine, Thatcher had prepared chocolate with brandy and a plate of the crisped cheese. It was late and the stars were out.

'Elegant enough,' Maria said, gracefully sinking into her seat.

The men had been issued with rum and hard tack. It had been pronounced that the galley would scrub up, and Clarkson was fixing the oven, though it might take a day or two. Supplies would run low the rest of the trip and they would be reliant on fishing, but they would survive.

'Some evening,' she said.

'I apologise.'

'What for?'

'That you had to see it and that you were put in danger. I promised you would come to no harm. We're only two days out of Trinidad and you might have died. We might all have.'

Maria nursed the warm drink in her hand. This chocolate was different from the morning confection – less sweet and as thick as posset, so that it slipped slowly over the lip of the cup as she tipped it into her mouth. The taste was extraordinary – startlingly rich. It lay satisfyingly in her stomach. From below, a melancholy song floated up on the evening air and she floated with it, leaning back to watch the stars swirling. It was always the same in a crisis – the ship you were travelling on became the centre of the world.

'We'd have been in trouble had the flames spread,' Henderson said.

He had changed his clothes, but there were smudges of soot on his face.

'You were admirable, Captain.' She looked him in the eye. 'I've seen men in battle. I've been on a ship under fire, but today you saved our lives. In such hot weather, the wood above the line must be dry as kindling. Had you not been so timeous . . .'

'Were you afraid?' he asked.

Maria lifted a shard of cheese. It was an odd texture, but melting had intensified the flavour. 'There was no time for fear.' She shrugged. 'I heard shouting, but you had the men in order very quickly.'

'There was a lot of smoke,' he said.

'It passed through my mind that we were too far out to row back to Trinidad and we'd have been down on our luck had we to abandon the ship.'

The captain regarded her. 'You look very nice.' He smiled.

Maria passed a hand over her skirts. In the low light, perhaps the marks left by the smoke looked like a pattern. No one ever commented on her appearance. Certainly not to say she looked nice. Thomas never had. 'For a royal governess, you mean? On a boat. After a fire.'

Henderson stopped, suddenly serious. It seemed strange she did not know. That she put herself down so. What had she been used to? He lay down his pewter cup and paused before leaning across the table and pulling Maria towards him. She could smell the ash on his hair. He slipped his arm around her waist and drew her close as he kissed her. Her body suddenly liquid, she found that she kissed him back with an insistent rhythm. It was like flying.

When they pulled apart, she was breathless, her lips felt swollen, and it took a moment to understand what she'd done. Henderson's eyes slid over her and she felt a warm wave of desire break across her body, followed swiftly by anger that advanced like a starched sheet. Drawing back her hand, she slapped him hard and scooped up her things, turning to leave. It was the worst kind of insult.

Henderson interposed himself. 'A woman. You look very nice for a woman, Maria.'

Before she could reason, Maria kicked him hard in the shins. 'Damn you,' she hissed. 'I am a lady.'

Henderson laughed out loud. 'You look very nice for a lady too.'

She took in a sharp breath. This man was a kidnapper, a liar, a smuggler, a criminal and now a predator. What on earth had she been thinking? She should have got off the ship when she had the chance. Her cheek stung where his beard had scraped her. It fired her fury, but before she could spit a riposte, the cabin boy crossed the deck carrying an additional pot of hot chocolate from the galley. She froze while he poured. What she wanted to say should not be voiced in front of a member of the crew, even in temper. At least it gave her a moment to think. Henderson smirked. As the boy retreated, he got in first, damn him.

'I should not have kissed you. I apologise. My blood is up after the fire and, madam, I must confess, I grow very fond of you. I was fond of you from the beginning.'

'You need not be,' Maria spat. 'I am years your senior and a widow. There is nothing worthwhile in this. You cannot take advantage and then simply apologise. You must decide to behave better, sir.'

Henderson bit his lip. 'You feel like I do. I know it.'

This incensed her. How dare he? 'How you feel is irrelevant, sir. And how I feel is none of your business. You have insulted me.'

'I admire you, madam. A kiss is not an insult.'

'Where I come from it is.'

And there it was. London.

The world Henderson longed for. The place Maria belonged.

The captain sank back in his chair. 'I'm sorry. I behaved out of turn,' he stumbled, trying to explain. 'I don't understand the terms – that is to say, I'm not used to this. But I give you my word, I'll not touch you again. I will behave better, just as you ask.'

Maria faltered. Her hands flew to her hair, to check that something at least was in place. 'Well then.'

'My intentions . . .' he started. 'Only, I have so enjoyed your company, you see, and—'

She cut him dead. 'I have enjoyed your company too, Captain Henderson. Do you think you might be able to ignore this rash gesture? Do you imagine tomorrow we might dine and talk once more of botany and astronomy, and you will behave like a gentleman?'

And there it was. *Like a gentleman.*

Henderson sighed. He solemnly gave his word. He shook her hand. He bowed. Abashed, he caught a flash of slim ankle as she returned to her cabin and felt guilty. When she disappeared inside, he called for brandy.

13

On board the Bittersweet

Maria lay on the bed, wakeful. The flame guttered. Most voyages left ample time to consider. On this journey, she realised, she would have more to consider than most. The ceiling was pine, the wood knotted and stained. She followed the ingrained lines, thinking about what had happened. She had quite lost herself. Did other couples feel such astonishing passion? It was outrageous. She turned, disquieted, recalling a glance she had seen in Recife between Admiral Cochrane and his wife, which she now understood differently. Yes, it dawned on her – Cochrane and Kitty were in love. It was a feeling contrary to the friendship she had felt for her own dear Thomas. She must be careful. This was surely a kind of madness inside marriage, never mind out of it, and Henderson was entirely unsuitable.

It occurred to her that the tiny dot that would mark the *Bittersweet* on any map as they travelled north could not represent the significance of what she felt. She had seen ancient maps about goodness, French maps about love – perhaps there should be a map that showed importance. A private document. The cold blue of social importance – the royal household. The London to which she must return, lit by the practical green of those who brought money. And then there were the sunny orange fires of desire that shone here, aboard the ship. Her heart weakened as she realised there was another map – a shameful chart of other people's expectations and of currency lost. Maria knew her own mind, but she was also aware that that didn't matter as much as how other people saw her, even if she knew of a certainty that those people were wrong. A woman could lose everything over a misapprehension. London was unforgiving in such matters. And in this case, not only her personal reputation but also her professional judgement were at stake – both fragile shells easily crushed. There was an undeniable chemistry between her and Henderson. Nothing came of nothing. On her map he would appear orange as fire, like a beacon, and she a watery red, bounded in shame. Overwhelmed by it. She had wandered across the globe for years, believing herself free, and now she realised that all the while she had been constrained. She longed to wheel like a gull. To be at liberty.

Maria's fingers traced the outline of her lips, her mind wandering as the candle burned out at last and the cabin plunged into darkness. She lay for a long time, listening to the creaking of the boards. She was still trembling, or at least it felt that way when, still torn, she finally drifted into fitful sleep.

*

The next morning, she woke thinking of her book before she remembered what had transpired. The sun slipped its fingers below the shutters and she squirmed. It would be easier never see him again. On shore, that was exactly what she'd do. But she was not ashore. Her stomach fluttered. Perhaps this cabin would become her cell. Perhaps she ought to simply stay here. The boy knocked on the door, bringing her morning chocolate and a jug of warmed seawater in which she might wash.

'*Toca aquí*,' she said. Put it there.

Things seemed normal and yet somehow the world had changed. As she washed, she let the water drip, listening to its splash in the hammered-metal bowl. A line of sunlight cut through the cabin.

That day, her diligent copying was abandoned and Maria stayed inside. She sat by the window, watching the waves and bathing in the light. All travellers know how to wait. It was something of which Maria had never written, but a good deal of what she did involved simply passing time. Waiting for the weather to be right, for a ship to sail or another to arrive. Waiting for permission, for a guide, waiting to see if there might be a storm or if a horse would become available to hire. Now the day passed slowly. Each creak at the cabin door stopped her heart. The boy came late in the afternoon and announced the captain's invitation to dinner. Maria hesitated.

'You aren't hungry, miss?' the boy questioned.

Hunger was not the appetite that was on her mind. And yet if she did not go out to him, perhaps he would call on her here.

'Are you unwell?' the boy hazarded. 'You haven't taken a turn about the deck today.'

'I'm fine.' Maria relented. 'I'll come at the usual time. And tomorrow, I promise, you can read to me. You must practise.'

Deciding not to dress in her fancy gown, she sat thinking until the sun sank. She must try to be sensible, she told herself. She must try not to overreact. When the bell sounded on deck, and with all things well considered, she quit her cabin wearing her grey travelling attire.

The table was set as it had been before and Henderson was waiting under the scatter of stars. He rose as she appeared, her candle lamp in hand.

'You have come for dinner?' he asked.

She put down the night light. 'I did not want to wear anything more formal . . .'

'You think it was the dress?'

She cast her eyes downward. This was humiliating. There was no hiding from him. He was too direct, used to this, perhaps, whereas she felt awkward – a novice even at her age.

'Please.' He pulled out her chair. 'Even if it vexes you, I must apologise again.' A small jug of chocolate was already on the table. 'I had Thatcher make this. I thought you might like to try it. I only ever drink a tot now and then. It's strong, but I like it.'

'No wine tonight?'

Henderson poured the chocolate. 'I shall call for wine if you like. In the meantime, I propose a toast.' He smiled. 'To the rest of the voyage. In company.'

Had he truly regretted it, then? Maria followed the captain's lead and downed the shot. After only the merest pause, the inside of her mouth grew fiery. She coughed.

'This helps,' Henderson said, and passed her a slice of orange.

It did. The fire was doused and what remained was a curious feeling of being very alive with only a twinge of the regret that had taken hold of her belly. She caught his glance. 'You cannot look at me like that, Captain.'

Had she not been fired up on chilli, she might not have voiced it, but then, it seemed, Henderson appreciated directness. If it was such an effective weapon in his arsenal, perhaps she should employ it in hers.

'I shall try not to.' He did not even deny it.

'We must be friends,' she stated calmly. 'This will pass. We must eat together as friends.'

The captain was bluff. 'The galley is mostly repaired, but we have caught no fish today. It will take a real friend to eat what Thatcher has made. He has a store of dried cod for such occasions. Sadly, it escaped the fire. The Portuguese like it, but I admit I do not.'

'Do you never simply go through the motions?'

'On these occasions, certainly, I pretend. I make-believe it is not dinner time but the hour to break my fast and I have him griddle cornbread.'

'We shall breakfast together, then?'

'It is my favourite meal. Since I was a child.'

'Little boys can be strange.'

Henderson laughed.

It occurred to Maria that the captain seemed to draw back any veil. He revealed things. As Henderson leaned in, Maria calmed herself. He did not realise his effect, the smell of the pipe tobacco and the urge she had to touch his hair. It was a compelling form of torture. She thought of her schoolmistresses, her aunt, her cousins – the look on their faces if they knew of this.

Henderson smiled. 'In my first year in Brazil I almost blew up my father's storehouse trying to make a string of firecrackers from vinegar, brown paper and gunpowder. I manufactured them in my bedchamber. I was not a happy child. What I was thinking, I cannot say.'

'So you are by nature a scientist,' Maria countered, for at least they were talking. 'It's a sign of intelligence.'

159

'May you only sire boys, Mrs Graham. It seems you will forgive them anything.'

Maria flinched only an instant, but he saw it.

'Do you want sons?' His voice was searching.

Maria shook her head. He had done it again. Still, she decided to make the admission. 'No. Not that.'

Children would have changed everything. Everyone expected that she and Thomas had been disappointed, but for Maria her childlessness was a relief. As a mother, Murray would not have published her. The few ladies on his roll were unmarried or so elderly their children were grown. Had Maria had sons, her education would have come to far less.

Besides, that side of marriage had not been a pleasure for either herself or her husband. They had abandoned it early in their relationship, for it had only made them quarrel. They settled instead into the affectionate intimacy of holding hands, arms wrapped around each other, warm in sleep but never going further. Thomas was a different man to James Henderson. He had been smooth, gentle and inoffensive. A gentleman. Still, she had been fond of him. Many in society had noted the closeness of the Grahams, but no one guessed that, despite loving each other, their friendship masked a lack, an utter lack, she realised now, of passionate intimacy. Before, she had not even thought of it as a secret. Now it seemed shameful, her childlessness the proof that this woman who had done so much was inexperienced. This, she told herself, was not what mattered. And yet.

'You have a great mind, Maria,' her father, Captain Dundas, had said, putting an arm around his daughter. He had come home from a voyage – nine months in India – and

160

suddenly she was a lady. 'You must use what you have learned.'

If she had not had children, she told herself, at least she had written books. Words were a reliable escape from the sadness of being sequestered at boarding school or the heaviness of a dull voyage. It was no surprise that she had written two books in two years when she was mourning poor Thomas.

'You're so direct,' she said. 'In a way, you remind me of my father.'

'Was he an ogre?'

'Not at all. I was fond of him.'

This was an understatement. With a stab, Maria remembered how lonely she had felt when her father went to sea, two years at a stretch sometimes. She recalled the joy of his return – sitting by the window of her aunt's house as he told her about his adventures, pressing her fingers to the glass so she could feel the chill as he told her about the searing heat of India and Africa and the islands that floated between, neither one place nor the other.

'The world is everything, Maria,' he swore.

Had he known about this feeling that was as large as a continent?

The boy arrived with a warm loaf and a bottle of wine. He set them on the table.

'We should eat.' Maria tore a chunk of bread and Henderson poured.

'More cacao,' he told the boy, who disappeared into the galley.

'With every meal?' Maria teased.

'Perhaps not every meal.' Henderson smiled. 'Do you mind?'

'The chocolate we talked of at home – the powder made by a press. This tastes so much nicer.'

'Good.'

They set to eating. Maria was glad she had stuck to the grey. It sent a clear message that she wished she might take to heart. She flung herself into the diversion and Henderson did not press his advantage. Instead, he talked about cacao, describing its outlandish appearance, the cracking of the pods when they were ripe, and how the beans might be roasted and winnowed, the nibs removed. Maria fetched her sketches from the Brazilian highlands and, with the bread finished, they pored over them as he identified the wild and cultivated cacao and she showed him the most unusual flowers she had come across during her stay. Vivid Amaranthaceae and elegant orchids vied for attention with canna lilies. She wished she had drawn more.

With Henderson, there was an extra dimension to mere conversation, and if a door had been opened into a forbidden room, neither stepped through, though they both hovered at the entrance in plain sight.

'These bromeliads are like jewels.' Henderson studied her sketchbook. The leaves hung heavy, lapidary as rubies. 'You would suit such finery.'

Maria's heart fluttered. The opal necklet she had once, only once, allowed herself to covet flickered across her mind's eye. She folded the sketchbook closed and affected to stretch her arms. 'It's late,' she said.

'Let me escort you to your cabin.'

He lifted a lamp high and the shadow stroked her shoulders. He had never before restrained himself like this. Her perfume lingered and he followed its trail.

'Goodnight.' He bowed.

Maria did not speak.

As the door closed, Henderson found he couldn't move. The world stopped without her. He dimmed the candle lamp as he hovered, for he did not want a line of light to betray him. The thin passageway held his attention, each sight of the threshold a silent prayer, a symbol of wanting more. The voyage, he realised, was time out from the world, and every moment the captain stood there on the cusp, it was as if his feet were burning indents in the wooden planks. He remembered a quote from Samuel Johnson, a man redolent of London. He had not thought of it in years. When making your choice in life, do not neglect to live.

*

As the stars fell into place along the *Bittersweet*'s course, this spot became a place of pilgrimage for Henderson on his nightly rounds. He loitered outside Maria's cabin every evening after she retired. Dinner after dinner as the ship's supplies dwindled to the last of the lemons. Some days there was fresh fish and others only cornbread or rice. The cook flavoured the chocolate with cinnamon and long curls of orange. Night after night. For Henderson, the closed cabin door punctuated the sunny days, long dinners, close conversation, checking the men, plotting the chart and keeping the log.

'It cannot be far,' Maria said at last, and he fetched the chart to show her.

There was a nip in the air now, an undercurrent. And as the weeks passed, Henderson kept his promise. He had not touched her, but the conversation had become gradually more intimate. Maria admitted the punishments she'd suffered for not behaving as her aunt wished. She spoke of her early propensity for botany and how shocked her family had been at her desire to travel and her decision to write. Henderson talked of his shame when he met his father for the first time. Small remembrances. Secrets shared.

'I had not realised we were so close to England,' she said, her head bent over as she read the chart and her finger traced the last few inches.

Henderson rolled up the parchment.

'It will not be long,' he said.

Piccadilly

John Murray, the capital's most celebrated publisher, crossed Piccadilly set to visit his tailor on Jermyn Street. Mrs Murray had suggested his waistcoat was old-fashioned and he knew from experience that he must act timeously upon such a pronouncement.

'Something grey, sir – the colour of your hair – would be more distinguished,' she insisted.

Murray, friend and advisor to such notables as Lord Byron and Johann Wolfgang von Goethe, to say nothing of the distinguished lady authors who placed their literary work in his care – the sadly deceased Jane Austen as well as the celebrated Mrs Maria Graham – always took his wife's advice in sartorial matters.

The early summer fog was so thick today that even the sounds of horses' hooves were muffled and a fellow would be lucky to recognise his own mother should he come upon her. In these circumstances, how Lady Dundas, Maria's aunt, picked out Murray's figure in the gloom was a mystery.

'Mr Murray,' her voice chimed, instantly so compelling that the publisher stood to attention as the venerable lady materialised next to him. Attired as always in the height of fashion, her outfit dripped fox-fur trim and seed pearls. Beside her stood Georgiana Graham, Maria's sister-in-law and doyenne of St James's. 'This is terribly fortunate,' Lady Dundas drawled. 'I was only just saying to Miss Graham, we could expect you to have news of Maria. Do you know where on earth the girl is? I declare I can hardly keep up with her.'

Murray bowed.

'The last I heard, madam, she had moved from her year's residence in Chile and was settled in Rio de Janeiro.'

Georgiana clutched the ribbons of her drawstring bag as tightly as she pursed her lips. 'Writing a book, no doubt.'

'I certainly hope so.'

'How very French,' Miss Graham managed, with only the hint of a sneer.

Murray drew up his shoulders. Maria was a friend and a favourite as well as one of his stable of authors. While not entirely in favour of, as his wife put it, those ghastly females who wish representation in the House, the publisher was certainly fair-minded about the fairer sex. Maria's decisions had not quite scandalised London, but almost – the attitude of her family didn't help and he felt his blood rise as he stood up for her.

'Your niece has the happy knack of combining commend-able notices with a prose style that is a pleasure to read,' he said smoothly. 'She sent me a few botanical sketches last year, which I passed to Sir William Hooker when he visited recently at Kew. He was most impressed. She has a keen scientific intellect as well as a winning way with words. Mrs Graham is a credit to you, ladies – to your family, indeed to your entire sex.'

Lady Dundas looked most discomfited by this news. 'Maria is a widow and we had hoped she might come home,' she said sadly.

Miss Graham cut in. 'I have raised a memorial to my late brother. I visit it every day and yet Maria as his wife has not even seen it.'

'When she comes home I am sure she will be delighted,' Murray lied.

'And when, sir, might that be?'

Murray shrugged his shoulders. So many of his authors were abroad. The storerooms at the publisher's house on Albemarle Street were chock-full of their correspondence and journals. Byron insisted on dispatching boxes of artefacts he bought on his way across Europe, including several bulky paintings and curiosities. He had also deposited a shocking memoir that Murray was holding – although noble, the boy was sometimes beyond the pale. Mrs Murray bemoaned the space that such rigorous record-keeping required.

'We shall run out of storage for our wines, sir,' she insisted, but Murray was adamant. The correspondence must be preserved.

'Even the notes of no consequence?' Mrs Murray pushed him. 'Those promising to visit soon or simply sending birthday wishes?'

'Yes, yes, my dear.' Murray was immoveable. 'One never knows what may later be of interest. Papa always said . . .'

Mrs Murray cast her eyes heavenwards. She was sure her son, John, would not take his father's system of administration so seriously and she saw no reason why her husband should so respect his own father's wishes.

'Many of the correspondents from your father's day are

deceased,' she pointed out. 'What use can their letters possibly be?'

Murray worried that in his absence his wife might rummage. He had left instructions with the household staff that should such an occurrence take place, they were to fetch him immediately and delay Mrs Murray for as long as they could.

The wily old publisher bowed very low.

'I expect Mrs Graham will come home when she's ready, ladies. Grief takes us all differently and Mrs Graham has important work to do.'

Georgiana's lips let out a puff of air, as if to blow the words Murray had uttered clean away. For women such as Lady Dundas and her protégée, there was only one way to behave. Maria, who, in Murray's view, showed absolute restraint, had edged beyond the cusp of her family's expectations.

'Heaven knows what she will get up to next.' Lady Dundas, exasperated, took her leave by bobbing a half-curtsey and clasping Miss Graham's arm.

Murray fervently hoped what the girl would get up to would be some writing.

'Well, London awaits.' He bowed and stood back to let the ladies pass.

As they disappeared into the fog, he sighed with relief. He didn't envy Maria her position. Then, shrugging off the exchange, he continued towards St James's Place and the comfortingly male preserve of his tailor.

15

On board the Bittersweet

That evening aboard the *Bittersweet*, Captain Henderson and Mrs Graham removed their dining arrangements to the cabin as the northern air proved too bracing to dine on deck, even now, in spring. There had been showers on and off all day.

'Invigorating enough, sir,' Clarkson had commented.

Come nightfall, the watch wore greatcoats.

Henderson hovered in the doorway before he knocked.

'Come in,' she said.

The cabin boy had set the table and brought extra lamps. The room smelled of honey and violets. As Maria rose, there was the merest whiff of orchid. She nodded. 'I removed my papers.'

Henderson smiled as she wrapped a shawl round her slim shoulders. He admired her lack of artifice. The grey dress had become somehow more intriguing than any amount of ostrich feathers and crimson silk. It was odd being inside. It felt more private, more contained. When he placed his chair next to hers, she jumped.

'I made a promise,' he said.

Her eyes were always so serious when he spoke that he came

to consider carefully everything he said. No one had listened to him like that since those lost London days. Sometimes Mrs Graham was like a bird that might at any moment take flight. He wanted to put her at ease. The captain had never felt such tenderness.

'You have been browsing.' He indicated the books piled to one side.

Maria nodded. 'With my work finished, I thought to read.'

She now regretted neglecting to take advantage of the Bagdorfs' library before she left Trinidad. Now even the frothy novels Thys had offered held an allure. She might even be prepared to try Miss Austen's dreadful *Pride and Prejudice* – a book she had always avoided, considering it little more than gossip written for the libraries of spoilt young ladies. Mr Murray had offered her a copy on several occasions and she had declined even him. Until now.

Henderson picked up a volume with Maria's name tooled in gold on the spine. She blushed. 'One of your own? May I borrow it?'

She acquiesced.

That night, dinner over, the captain taught Maria to play poker, a game he had picked up on a trip to New Orleans the year before. She was not, he noted, adept at bluffing. She knew that this would be another scandal, yet she indulged it. What would London think? Maria tried not to concern herself. But what, oh what, of London? It was now only days away.

Late, when the captain retired to his cabin, he opened her *Journal of a Residence in India*. The book disarmed him. On its pages, Captain Dundas, Maria's father, sprang to life about his business as Maria explored shrines, temples and palaces.

170

She had literary talent – he could taste the turmeric on the air and feel the violent release of the monsoon as the streets of Bombay turned to mud. He was filled suddenly with awe at her abilities. She had missed nothing, from the sizzle of a morning chapatti to the indulgence of a cow wandering freely, knocking over market stalls and sending sari-bound women scuttling to the chink of their cheap jewellery as they hurried out of the way.

He lingered over the passages where her father appeared, accompanying her on an elephant ride during which the animal almost ran amok, and introducing his daughter to his officers, one of whom she was later to marry. In the passages that contained Captain Dundas, Maria seemed eager, finally spending time with her father after years of study in England, for which she did not fully express her distaste. Henderson saw now that behind the steady eyes of the grown woman there was a girl keen to please the man who had been missing for much of her young life. She was kept away from everything she loved, he understood at last. *Just like me.*

Henderson leaned his head against the cabin's wooden wall as he put down the book. Outside, the slow sunrise was dawning. The cabin boy knocked and delivered a morning tot of rum. 'Sir.'

The captain rubbed his eyes and knocked back the spirit. He ran his hand across the roughness of his chin. Later he would shave.

'Not far now, sir.' The cabin boy was excited.

The men had told him about England and Mrs Graham had taught him his letters. Reading was an effort, but each day it became easier and the child felt invincible in anticipation of a new world.

'Three days or so.' Henderson's eyes fell to his chart as he waved the boy away.

Three days, he thought, and she'd be gone. The captain hardened his resolve. He must ask her soon, though it might break the spell. He must pluck up his courage. He would do it tonight.

★

Up early, washed and dressed, Maria raised aloft her dark waxed parasol to protect her skin from the fine rain that spread like filigree over the deck. The air already felt like England. The crew no longer worked topless and had assembled a jumble of cotton shirts and loosely knitted vests as the ship sailed northwards. Today, four of the men were fishing over the side. Two were tending lines and two more were trawling. Their attention was focussed on the choppy water. The men ate only ship's biscuits when the fishing failed.

'Grey,' one commented, gesturing in the direction of the sky. An overcast vista boded well for a decent catch.

Maria loitered out of their line of sight and took a seat on a barrel. With London so close, she found she had mixed feelings. She told herself that she was looking forward to it, and tried not to think too clearly about leaving the *Bittersweet* or, more specifically, Captain Henderson. The voyage had provided respite from the judgements of England's capital city and the expectations of Rio. Onboard this strange-looking vessel, Maria could be herself.

Carefree, she decided to tarry and eavesdrop. There was little other occupation and she anticipated it might be fun. She shifted inside her bodice, lengthening her spine as she

172

settled. At the other end of the deck Clarkson stood at the wheel, while around his feet two sailors scrubbed the boards. For a long time, the party of fishermen behind her were silent. One knocked out his pipe and lit it. The sound of puffing ensued. Maria smiled. The cool air was refreshing and the smell of kindling shag was pleasant. Soon she would go inside and read. The cabin boy passed with a bucket of slops and nodded a greeting. Then there was a whoop and what sounded like a scuffle as the nets were hauled up and the catch landed on deck. A slosh of water cascaded across the boards. Maria lifted her feet.

'That's a fine 'un,' a voice declared as he put an end to the fish's flapping with a cosh.

'Big Al'll be delighted. There's more there than the captain and his lady can eat,' a second voice said.

Yet another man chimed in. 'You think they really eat in there? God knows what they're up to.'

Maria started. Her blood ran cold, as if of a sudden she had woken up. She cast her gaze up at Clarkson, but he was too far off and hadn't heard. *God knows what they're up to.* She felt a rush of fury. How dare these men presume? The chorus of lewd laughter horrified her, as, out of sight, the sailor's voice continued lascivious, rich with innuendo.

'Night after night. That Mrs Graham's a fine-looking little hen.'

Maria squinted around the side of the barrel to see a man whose fingertips had been slashed making a bawdy gesture, his voice a stern whisper.

'And who can blame the captain? She was a married woman and comely. She must've been missing the hot and the hand of a real man to scratch her itch.'

173

The men laughed uproariously again as they worked the nets.

Maria recoiled in horror. She felt quite nauseous. How could she have been stupid enough to believe the *Bittersweet* was different from everywhere else? Henderson's easy manner had lulled her, she realised. She had indulged herself foolishly and let down her guard. She had opened herself to derision. Her fingers were quivering with humiliation. The shame of it! Had she been asleep all this time? They thought her nothing but a floozy. A tawdry whore! She fumbled to her feet and, almost crouching so Clarkson would not see her face, she stole to her cabin, her eyes awash with tears. The whole ship had been laughing at her. They were laughing now.

Inside, pacing in panic, she tried to block out the echo of the sailor's jeers by reciting poetry – Byron's *Childe Harold* (which Murray had sent to her the year before), Keats's 'Ode to Autumn' and stanzas about Greece by Miss Elizabeth Barrett, memorised from a periodical. Maria did not aspire to the modern ideals of the Romantics. She was a pragmatist, but now the words poured out – an accustomed escape. It was no use – she couldn't stop thinking about the man's ribald fingers flashing together. She couldn't stop pacing unless it was to fall to her knees. She eyed the cabin door with suspicion. *How dare they,* she thought. And the rest of the day she didn't step across the threshold. She doubted she might ever do so again.

As night fell, Maria's shame did not diminish. On this tiny ship on the wide ocean there had been little that she could not discuss with Captain Henderson, from the cultivation of cacao to the frequently horrifying stories of some of the crew – where they had come from and what they had done. Thatcher had lost the family alehouse in Bridlington to gambling debts before he came to sea, and Clarkson's wife had sold him to the press gang when he was only twenty, for she was, he told the captain, a right besom who had taken a dislike to him after four years of marriage.

Tonight, though, as the captain arrived and they took their seats, Maria found she could not mention what she had heard on deck. It was too fresh a bruise. It ached as she sat in her grey dress beside him. The candlelight passed its honeyed glow across her countenance. Inside, she squirmed with discomfort. Oblivious, Henderson was in a good mood. He poured the wine and grinned as he talked about mapping their course. His charts, it seemed, were accurate and they were making good way. He had enjoyed her book.

As they moved on to discuss botany – the differences between those hardy specimens that could withstand the sea air and the hundreds lost in transit each year, the despair of England's horticulturalists – Maria could only think of the men beyond the door. The crew presuming that James was tupping her like some thrupenny whore.

'Might you join the Society?' she questioned, distracted, trying not to show her shame. If she sent him away, she'd have to give an explanation, and that was something she certainly could not bear.

Henderson gave a non-committal shrug. The Royal Horticultural Society was the province of gentlemen. A fellow needed a proposer and a seconder. He'd have to be a publisher of pamphlets at least.

'You can apply to speak,' she suggested. 'They would be

most interested in your botanical knowledge. "The Taming of the Cacao Bean" – I can hear it now. Few will know the exact differences between wild and plantation-farmed. London welcomes new minds.'

'Perhaps.'

Maria searched the cabin boy's face as he brought a dish ready to serve. The boy put a tankard of white wine between them and made a curious little bow. A low curl of mortification unfolded in her belly as he retreated and closed the cabin door. Did the child think so little of her too? Had he heard the men talking? Henderson sat back. The candlelight flickered so there was a moment of darkness – a mere blink. Maria fingered her cutlery. Her heart was pounding and she found herself trying not to look at the bed. Perhaps she should call the boy back. It might feel safer. Henderson put his hand on her arm.

'Are you all right?'

She pulled back, nodding. He had not come so close since the day he kissed her. She could smell the soap on his skin – a hint of nutmeg and blackberry that sneaked in below the familiar musk of pipe tobacco. Her fingers fluttered. These moments left her wary of her own behaviour and yet she sought them out. The shame.

'Mrs Graham,' the captain said, 'it seems to me that when this voyage is over I shall miss having dinner with you. These weeks have been a golden time.'

'Yes,' Maria mumbled.

'I have something to ask. I have wanted to ask for some weeks now, almost since I first saw you.'

Maria panicked. Here it came. Here. Her heart beat so fiercely she could scarcely believe it was not visible. Her mind

176

raced. Had it all been leading to this? Had he apologised for kissing her only to propose something worse? How would she resist him when her own body rebelled against her better judgement? London would scorn her. London would know. And the men. With the sound of lewd laughter ringing in her ears, she jerked back her chair and pulled her wrap around her shoulders like armour. The rights of marriage were reserved for marriage. That was true blue, but if he asked her, is that what she would reply?

'I can't. Please,' she implored. 'It's not possible, James, however much I might wish it.'

The captain took his time. 'Everything is possible,' he said steadily. 'We are free people, both you and I, but I have no wish to upset you.'

'I'm not upset.' Her voice avowed otherwise.

'I thought we were friends.'

'Yes. Friends.'

'So marriage is impossible?'

Maria started. She had not expected that. 'Marriage,' she said, 'would be out of the question as well.'

'As well as what?'

Her eyes fell to the bed.

He laughed, his voice booming. 'Did you think . . . Oh, Maria.' He reached for her hand but caught it only fleetingly. 'But you are a lady, remember?'

A line of fire coursed through her blood. She had to drag her gaze away. They had all been right about her, it seemed. Her school. Her aunt. The gentlemen who scorned her work. The officers who tried to take charge of her lodgings. The men on deck.

Henderson continued. 'My dear, are you simply afraid of

that? It is bound to be the easy thing between us. It will be different to what has gone before.'

Maria drew herself up. She felt appalled that he had laughed. Was she nothing but a joke on the *Bittersweet*? Her cheeks burned. 'I was married for over ten years to Captain Graham,' she managed.

'And still it scares you?'

It was as if he could see through her. She could traverse the Amazon, ride a camel, hike the Chilean highlands and calculate the force of an earthquake, but she was afraid of this, this tawdry and mundane thing that most women took in their stride. A tear strayed down her cheek. She brushed it away angrily. How had she avoided it for years with Thomas and yet suddenly she felt compelled towards this man – a person totally unsuitable? A person she had met on the dockside – someone completely unconnected to her life. A smuggler. A kidnapper. A liar. They had not one single acquaintance in common. He was without a home or a family. And yet he was fascinating. The most interesting man she'd ever met. He meant far more to her than the polite acquaintance she was pretending. She had been punished all her life for taking risks she could justify, but this, she knew, would put her beyond the pale. The infamy! How could she have let herself get into this position?

'I will not marry you, Captain Henderson.' It was with a great effort that she kept her voice low.

'Is it my station?' he replied. 'I'm set to change, Maria. I'll find a respectable profession. Not only for your sake but for mine too. I've been considering it.'

Maria didn't trust herself to speak. She knew these vague promises meant nothing in London. In matters of propriety, the real world only took into account what was here, not what might come. It was difficult enough to defend her right to travel independently, to write what she pleased, to have her opinions valued on a par even with more poorly educated men. She had fought hard for these privileges. How could he even ask her? If she married James Henderson, she'd lose all respect and, with it, everything she'd worked for since she first set ink to paper and posted a tentative manuscript to Murray. Her mind raced. The bed was bad enough. The thought of losing control was horrifying, but if the *Bittersweet*'s crew considered her nothing more than a smutty joke, nothing was surer than that London would think worse. She imagined the gossip – leaving with one husband and arriving home with a lesser man. The city would squeal with delight and never take her seriously again.

'I'm sorry,' she said quietly, desperate, her hand held out as if to hold him off. 'You must leave.'

Henderson took in the words. He did not object, only got up slowly, his eyes raw. 'Please forget I distressed you with the idea,' he said as he bowed, then crossed the threshold and firmly closed the door.

Maria could not believe he had gone. It seemed too quick and now too quiet. She stared horrified at the remains of the meal, as if the abandoned plates and unserved fish were carnage after a battle. For an instant she almost ran after James Henderson, but if she did so, what could she say? She had never believed in the blousy love of poets. She had mocked Lady Caroline Lamb when the girl made a fool of herself over Byron. Now she thought she might read a hundred novels and perhaps even cry at the stories. She tried to imagine what Murray would advise (if, indeed, she could ever voice her shameful concerns to such an august friend). She pictured the old publisher's grey-haired head cocked to one side as he considered the implications. Worse, she pictured the reaction of her father – his memory desecrated. He had wanted her to be a lady.

Even if she returned with Henderson to Brazil, the captain would not be welcomed at court. The Brazilians were every bit as exacting as the British when it came to hierarchy. She knew what da Couto would make of such a match – it would delight him – and da Couto would not be alone. Her position would be terminated immediately and Her Majesty would be right to do so. She was above this.

And yet Maria felt what could only be described as a longing amidst the shame. She wished she didn't care what others thought. She worried that the gnawing sensation in her belly might never cease. Would she die in her dotage still wanting him? Wondering? The thought sent her into a terrified frenzy, as if she was out of her depth in treacherous water, kicking for her life. Instead of stretching, which she feared might make the feeling larger, longer and harder to bear, she curled up into a tiny ball on the wide wooden boards and sobbed quietly. It had all been leading to this. Of course it had.

Outside, Henderson hovered. He leaned against the wooden planks opposite the door, the taste of sour wine growing in his gullet. He had misjudged the situation and, worse, he had misjudged Mrs Graham. No sound emanated from the room. He stood back.

'I am nothing,' he whispered.

The captain froze for some time in silence and confusion. It took determination to turn away, but as he swung towards his cabin he found he was limping, as if the wound was physical.

His feet ached. Nothing made sense tonight. He slapped his leg in annoyance, drew himself up and disappeared in the direction of his charts. Why would she want him? It was a foolish idea. He had nothing worthwhile to offer a woman of quality. He must turn his attention to business. What had he been thinking?

16

Cornwall, three days later

Close to the coastline it was blustery tonight, the waves whipping up a summer storm. The *Bittersweet* pitched and rolled in the dark, the fierce weather sweeping across the deck in a vengeful spray. These waters were dangerous, home to diseases that would send a shiver down any sailor's spine – the Dogger Bank itch, it was said, made you peel off the skin between your own fingers. Henderson tried to focus. There were sinister reefs hidden, deathly shards of rock just beneath the surface, and, in conditions such as these, without detailed knowledge of the safest passage, it was risky. That was why the stretch was popular with smugglers – you had to know your way.

Will had pointed out this part of the coast on the chart. All those weeks ago under the burning Brazilian sun, he had scattered the names of safe villages carelessly into the conversation as if he were strewing raisins through a bannock bun.

'The gobblers try,' he had said, 'but mostly we win the toss. Still, it's a different game from my father's day.'

'Do you mean the customs men?' Henderson asked.

'Aye. Time was they only came on land, but now they've

formed a sea patrol. I have a cousin with a three-masted lugger at Ringstead Beach. He's found it hard. They're like sharks following a trail of fresh blood. Of late he's been going the other direction – running cider to Dieppe. It's enough to turn a man to real crime.' Will grinned. 'They need to think of that. Cornwall is a smuggler's paradise. They'll never subdue her. The Cornish would die before they set their livings aside. England'll hang you, see, for a rabbit or a loaf of bread, never mind a shipment of rum.'

Lubricated by a good half-bottle of caninha, Will had spoken of hidden alleyways to fool the excisemen and of false cellars in tiny cottages that could store as much as a Whitechapel bond. Most of the contraband disappeared close to where it was brought in, he said. Barrels of genever at two shillings and sixpence a keg and Roscoff brandy, worth more, for it was a gentleman's tipple. Only the cream went to London – rare items like the chocolate beans in the *Bittersweet*'s hold, red wine from fancy French chateaux and the occasional ship-ment of Indian embroidered cloth. This was not Henderson's concern, Will insisted, the beans already had a buyer – he need not worry on that account.

Tonight, however, even making shore was not certain. Henderson couldn't remember the name of the place Will said he lived, though he was sure this was the right stretch. He checked for a funt – a warning light – in case the gobblers were close, but the choppy sea was only briefly illuminated by the moon breaking through the clouds.

Over the days since he had declared himself, he had tried to speak further with Maria, but she would brook no conversa-tion and he had no wish to force her. As a result, Mrs Graham had eaten alone in her cabin, and enquiring of the cabin boy as to her health or, indeed, the state of her mind had yielded little information. If nothing else, the boy had proved himself loyal. This storm at least gave the captain more time in the lady's proximity if not her company. After the beans were landed, they would both face London. The big city loomed in Henderson's imagination, a slushy grey apparition far more terrifying than the jagged rocks and raw weather. His palms felt sticky at the thought of what he might find – the ghosts of his childhood and those of the life he might have had haunted the fringes like Judgement Day. To explore it with Maria would be comforting, though he knew that was an illusion. She would be off immediately the *Bittersweet* moored. He did not want to think about it.

Fortified by hot port and swaddled in all his woollen clothing at once, Henderson directed the dark scramble of men to weigh anchor. Then he sent Clarkson ashore in a rowing boat with three men to see the lie of the land. Henderson lit his pipe and watched as the little boat made the beach, Clarkson's lantern disappearing in a jerky motion across the crest at the top of the sand. The second in command was an able nego-tiator who always appeared friendly, even when a knife was drawn. He was accustomed to being prepared for anything, ever since his wife's skulduggery with the press gang. He'd been told to use Will's name to secure assistance – to knock up the first cottage and see if anyone knew to expect a friend of Will Simmons. That was the way of a fraternity held together by its secrets. The right name was a password.

Henderson ran a hand over the stubble on his chin and made a mental note that he must be clean-shaven for the capital and must change into the suit he'd had fitted in Natal. He had no reputation here, but that meant he might make a new one, and London would welcome him the better for a proper cravat.

As the first pale light of a grey dawn stole across the horizon like a watermark, Clarkson's lamp appeared once more on the shore and slowly the black smudge of the rowing boat made its way towards the *Bittersweet* with, Henderson noticed, an extra man on board. Clarkson was the first back on deck. His breath smelled of small beer – no surprise, for while Englishmen abroad never claimed to miss their families, Henderson had heard every member of his crew bemoan the lack of good ale. Nowhere brewed the same from the Brazils up to the Hudson, from New York to Calicut. It was something in the English water, something in the Kentish hops – a taste of home that was impossible to reproduce.

The mate hauled the others onto the deck.

'Captain,' he announced, 'this is Sam Pearson. He knew Will Simmons.'

Sam was a thin, red-haired lad who unfurled over the side as if he were a tent going up. His skin glowed almost translucent in the dawning light, peppered with wide pale freckles.

'Will's dead?' he asked immediately.

Henderson nodded. 'He was stabbed.'

Sam's eyes swung to port, as if he might jump overboard if the captain's answers did not meet with his approval. After all, he only had the crew's word for what had happened to his friend, and pirates were not unknown along the coast.

'The man must've been fast with a blade,' Sam commented warily. 'Will could fight.'

'It was a woman,' Henderson explained. 'She put him off his guard. There was an argument over a bet. I'm sorry. There was nothing I could do.'

185

'You buried him?'

Henderson nodded in confirmation. 'In Brazil. Hallowed ground. I have Will's things below. You can deliver his possessions to his family.'

'I'll tell his sisters. They're the only family he has,' Sam said solemnly.

From the galley, a steam of hot bread hit the air as Big Al started work for the day, but the seamen ignored the tantalising smell. They were paid when the cargo was landed.

'So,' said Henderson, 'will you guide us in?'

'Yes, sir. There's a safe bay half an hour on and there'll be men ready to ferry the beans. I sent word. I'll show the way.'

The boy spoke with a thick accent that made him sound slow, but there was no question he knew what he was doing. Smuggling here was a businesslike affair and Sam, like Will, seemed competent.

'We can't sink it, can we?' the boy asked.

'No. The beans can't be soaked. They're easily tainted. Is that the usual way?'

'Yes, sir. Mostly we run spirits. Best way is to sink 'em and bring up the barrels later. A ship acts like a beacon for the Preventatives, but sink the cargo and you can fetch it at your leisure off a rowing boat.'

Henderson mused that English excisemen must be more efficient than the Yankees. On his trips north, he simply unloaded. There were hardly any excise fellows on the Hudson or the Charles, and those there were could be paid off easily. The spirit of the Americas was one of the right to trade and the place was simply too vast to patrol effectively.

'You don't just bribe 'em?'

Sam's face lit up. 'My father talks of those days, sir. Not

186

any more. Sometimes we get into a right scrap. There's been a couple of deaths of late.'

'All right.' Henderson put up his hand. 'No need to go into that.' It would only spook the men. 'You show us where to go, Sam,' he said, and at his signal the *Bittersweet* raised anchor, the crew ready to bring her home.

The boy pointed the direction. On the horizon, gulls were flirting with the slate-grey surf. 'We need to keep west until we're beyond the point.'

Henderson nodded to Clarkson to follow these instructions.

'Good. If we have half an hour, there's private business we can see to, you and I,' the captain said.

Downstairs in the cramped cabin, Henderson turned up the tallow lamps. Vague spectres leapt upwards, playing along the dark walls. This early in the morning was a time of indistinct shadows, inside and out. Sam loitered.

'You'll require paying, Mr Pearson? We must come to terms.'

At close proximity, Henderson realised Pearson's body was so thin it looked as if his clothes were holding him up. His trousers were stiff with dirt and his woollen sweater smelled no better. The boy smiled, revealing a set of ivory teeth like pianoforte keys.

'This is Will's cargo? The one he set out to fetch?' he asked.

Henderson nodded.

'They pay me for that. I don't need nothing from you, Captain. I got my instructions. What arrangement did you make with Will? I'll see it's honoured, for surely it's us should be paying you.'

Henderson allowed his eyes to betray nothing. 'We had no time to make proper arrangements, or at least nothing in detail. I have taken my arrangement fee already, but I shall expect a decent cut in addition.'

Sam nodded. 'We need to offload the beans here. The lads will see them safely away and I'll make sure you're paid. It's Will's cargo and there's them who's expecting it. What are your plans in England?'

'I had thought to go to London for a few weeks.'

Sam adopted a sage expression, as if London was his second home. 'I'll come with you and see you right, then, sir. The money's in London. Isn't that always the way?'

The boy's eyes were unclouded by deception, blue as a fresh stream in summer. Still, he was asking a good deal. Few captains would turn over their cargo without seeing money up front. Henderson weighed a brass compass in his hand. The light from the porthole barely illuminated the ruffled blanket on the bed. Despite the lamp, Pearson's pale face was mostly in shade.

'You want me to hand over the goods?' the captain asked. 'Without agreeing a price?'

Sam stood stock-still. There was nothing shifty about him.

'There's no other way, sir. We didn't know you was coming. We didn't know what had happened to Will – that's a change of circumstances all right. The gentlemen pay their debts. They'll give you a price that's more than fair, I'd stake my life on it.'

'Which gentlemen?'

'Why them's we work for, Will and I,' Sam said, slowing as the sentence progressed and it occurred to him that perhaps he shouldn't tell the captain about his employers.

Henderson paused. Sam hadn't mentioned the block of chocolate. He reasoned that, at least, would stand surety

188

alongside the arrangement fee, if his instincts about trusting the lad were mistaken. The gold and precious stones were worth more than the rest of the shipment put together, and a good deal easier to smuggle ashore.

'You expect plenty, Mr Pearson,' the captain said. 'See that you merit it. And I'll take you on your oath. You've staked your life, boy.'

Sam nodded gravely. 'Aye aye, sir. Once we're done here, we can sail east, cut up the Thames and dock at Greenwich. I'm quite the London lad these days. I'll keep you right.'

Henderson waited. Still the boy didn't allude to anything other than the beans.

'We should get back on deck,' the captain said, glad this was happening early. Mrs Graham never quit her cabin before mid-morning and did not break her fast until the men were halfway through the first shift of the day. With luck, the unloading would be over before she woke and he could cast off for the wide mouth of the Thames Estuary without setting her ashore. It would give them another day together, perhaps two if the storms continued. He wanted to mend the offence he'd caused, or at least win the chance to apologise.

On deck, a sheet of drizzle swept down from the dawning sky, punctuated by a bustle of dark clouds. The crew were soaked to the skin, working the ropes as the *Bittersweet* lurched through the surf. The only whisper of Sam's cove was a sharp bristle of trees like a ragged beard on the horizon. Nature had hidden the shelter well.

'The Hollow,' he breathed. 'You have to take her wide. You can't see the reef, but it's there.'

Henderson nodded and the ship moved. At the farthest point, anchored rowing boats appeared, bobbing to one side of a makeshift stone jetty. It was a clever little cove.

Henderson passed the brass quickly to Sam. One of the boats was floating upside down, the underside slung with barnacles and a slimy string of ochre seaweed. The jetty was deserted, the shoreline unpunctuated by a single helper. The cottages on the harbour shed dark, thin wisps of smoke skywards. Gulls were interspersed between the chimneys. The boy examined the scene carefully.

'Should there be men?' Henderson asked.

Sam nodded. 'If they've gone, there's a reason,' he said. 'And if there's no one there, or no one showing, something's wrong.'

There was no sign of excisemen on the horizon, but only a fool wouldn't listen to a man familiar with the ground.

'About, Mr Clarkson,' the captain barked.

As the ship heaved to, Henderson checked the cabin boy had kept his footing on lookout halfway up the mast. The boy saluted, the dark nubs in his mouth clearly on view and his eyes alight. He loved a bit of action. The *Bittersweet* arched back towards the open water, avoiding the reef.

'Keep an eye out,' Henderson directed.

'Out to sea, sir,' Sam suggested. 'South, I'd say. We can try again later. After dark, we might hazard unloading straight into the village.'

Henderson said nothing. He shifted his weight. The horizon remained clear, but still, what might happen if they were caught? He found himself considering Mrs Graham's position and suddenly it was as if a page had turned. He loosened the woollen scarf around his neck. This didn't feel right any more and he was uneasy, as if wearing another man's clothes. It was an extraordinary feeling. A moment of revelation.

He had thought to change his life by marrying and then altering his ways, but it occurred to him now to ask, why not the other way around? There was no need to visit London before he made good on his resolutions. Suddenly he realised that he could do what was needed immediately. It was a tantalising prospect – he might step ashore an honest man. He glanced in the direction of the ever-closed door to Maria's cabin as the shore receded. To bring Mrs Graham into this was quite wrong, he reasoned, and if they were caught, that would be unavoidable. He watched Clarkson wrangling the men. In Trinidad, Maria had asked if the penalties made him afraid. The truth was, it had never been a consideration before, but now he wondered how many of his men might swing if things went wrong today.

'Once we're a way out, see the men are fed, including Mr Pearson,' he instructed the mate, 'then bear west. They'll have trouble following us that way. And keep me informed.'

'Aye aye, sir.'

Sam hovered as the crew swung into action. Eyes burning, he watched the *Bittersweet* as it tacked in a different direction to the one he had advised.

'Come on, lad.' Clarkson pulled the boy's arm. 'We'll get something in your belly, shall we?'

The boy turned to remonstrate with the captain, but he was gone.

For once, outside Maria's cabin, Henderson didn't hesitate. Decisive, he knocked and entered. The shutters were closed and the room felt sequestered by the heavy silence of sleep, the air thick with it. On the table, the remains of dinner had been swept one way and another during manoeuvres. A splash of red wine trickled across the surface where it had spilled, and a scrap of bread lay torn and uneaten, rolling across a stray piece of paper upon which Mrs Graham had scrawled notes. On the other side of the room, Maria turned under a thin sheet and sat up, blearily.

'James?'

The captain steeled himself. If he intended to change, he should simply do so. This, he realised, was the nature of being a man. He crossed to open the shutters and Mrs Graham scuttled to cover herself, pulling a wrap around the shoulders of her white lawn nightgown. Her hair was down and she twisted it into a bun, checking her appearance with fluttering fingers. He had never intruded like this before. What did Henderson intend bursting in this way?

'If you give me a few minutes, sir . . .' She was flustered, trying to read him.

Henderson pulled up a chair. 'My apologies, but there's no time. You said you'd tried that cocoa powder. What was it like?' he demanded.

Straight as Britannia, Maria stared at him blankly. 'It's not as good as the cocoa aboard ship.' She glanced hopefully towards the door, as if at the very mention of cocoa, breakfast might be served.

'Simmons said the cocoa trade was booming. So who makes it, Mrs Graham?

Maria sank back against the pillows. Henderson was perplexing sometimes. Of all the reasons he might have burst in here, this line of questioning had not been on her horizon. 'Who makes cocoa?' she repeated.

The captain nodded sharply.

'Well, several manufactories. Fry's is the largest, as I recall, but any apothecary might set up in the trade. The Quakers excel in such matters.'

'Religious men?'

Maria shrugged her shoulders. 'I don't see . . .'

'So I could simply put the goods into bond, sell them to a manufactory and pay the duty?' the captain said, this revolutionary thought only now coming to him as a real possibility.

Maria smiled in a thin line that spread across her face like a low sunrise. 'You wish to pay the king's due, Captain Henderson?'

'I think I may. Do you know where they are based?'

'Fry's? Bristol, I think. I can't be sure. But I recall that it is Bristol. How strange. From a packet of lozenges – Fry's of Bristol. That's what it said.'

'The beans are of excellent quality,' Henderson murmured. 'There is no reason the trade wouldn't pay a true price.'

'Well,' Maria chipped in, 'they are men of conscience but men of business too and they will know the value of the thing. They must get their beans from somewhere. There is a coach from Bristol to London. The Bristol Rocket. It would see me in Piccadilly by next week. We must be close now.' She sounded excited.

'You have reformed me, madam.' Henderson nodded brusquely and rose, scraping the chair across the boards.

But Mrs Graham had not finished. She could not let it go. 'The other night, James,' she started.

'Please don't trouble yourself.'

A low flush crept across her face.

'I have no wish to embarrass you,' he said. 'I know I'm not respectable. Goodness and badness, respectability and otherwise, are complex matters. I had hoped you would forgive my

193

complexities. I understand that you cannot and I am sorry for troubling you.'

He turned, but Maria caught his hand. She wanted to explain. She had been thinking of it for days. Now she ignored the pang in her stomach – the ignominy of it. The air of urgency about Henderson made it easier, somehow, to speak.

'The thing is that I value my reputation.' Her tone was pressing. 'Everything I have strived for depends upon the respectability you consider so unimportant. My whole career, my life, can turn on a rumour. No matter what you or I might want, the stakes are too high.' Her words hung in the air.

He might have retrieved those stakes, but Henderson had no intention of talking. If they discussed the matter, it would make no sense. He wanted to marry her. He'd made that plain. What could be more respectable? Her fingers were soft in his palm. In a rush, he bent towards her. They kissed, lightly at first but then with increasing passion. He didn't register the knock on the door and only sprang back as it opened. Horrified, Maria couldn't bring her eyes to meet his, let alone the mate's, who had edged into the cabin.

'Sir,' Clarkson said. 'They have spotted us.'

'Who?' Maria's voice sounded distant.

'There's a cutter and a barque,' Clarkson continued.

'I'm coming.' Henderson waved the man away. 'I'm sorry,' he said.

Maria pushed her hair behind her ear. Whatever had caused this confusion aboard had at least made it easier to speak.

'No good can come of such passion,' she said quietly. 'I have to get back to London . . .'

The ship veered. The captain stepped backwards.

'What is happening?' Maria asked as she almost tipped over.

'Get dressed, Mrs Graham.' Henderson turned.

The least he could do was make sure, if the *Bittersweet* was boarded, that Mrs Graham was not in a state of undress. As it was, once she understood their predicament, she might never forgive him. He must try somehow to avert the crisis. As he left she was already out of bed, heading for her grey dress.

On deck, Henderson put the glass to his eye. His line of vision was partly obscured by a shroud of low cloud, but you could make out the ships nonetheless. The wind was whipping up the water.

He motioned to Sam Pearson. 'Is that the Preventative waterguard?'

Sam nodded. 'Yes. Pirate ships don't come so close nor look so vicious. You don't want them to catch sight of me, sir. They know most of the ships working the trade hereabouts and most of the fellows who crew them. They don't know who you is, but if they see me, they'll tumble pretty quick. My hair, you see. I should put on a cap.'

'Mr Clarkson will stow you below decks, Mr Pearson.' The captain's orders took on a naval air and the boy responded with a cheeky salute.

From high above, the cabin boy let out a whistle to show the ships were making ground. Henderson barked orders, sending the *Bittersweet*'s crew scuttling. Their best chance was open water.

When Maria came on deck, her grey dress camouflaged her against the sky and the motion of the ship almost upended her in the commotion. Her hair tumbled around her shoulders, out of place immediately, the little hat she had carefully pinned in place almost obscured. She was instantly soaked. The black waxed parasol was nowhere to be seen, but it would not have survived the wind. It swept across the captain's mind that if the situation wasn't so dangerous, it might be comic. What had he been thinking, putting a respectable woman in this position? She had been right.

Sam Pearson took a cap from one of the crew to cover his bright hair and refused to be stowed. He had a sense that the captain was not going to keep their bargain and he fought his way back to confront him. The ship was broadly heading back towards the Atlantic.

'Where are you up to?' he glowered.

'Change of plan, boy,' Henderson announced. 'It needn't worry you.'

'But . . .' Sam's voice trailed as he stared in the direction of the village.

'If we get through this, we'll put you off at Bristol. Work the passage and we'll settle up afterwards, fair and square.'

'You won't get the goods in at Bristol. There's bondsmen and harbourmasters. They'll cop you for sure.'

'You need to get below,' Henderson said firmly.

'I shan't.' Pearson scorned him. 'This isn't right. We had a deal.'

One or two of the sailors dallied, curious as to what might transpire. No one ever questioned the captain's judgement. Not above decks or below. That was mutiny on a calm day, never mind when the ship was cutting through a storm and being pursued. Sam's fists were clenched as a crowd formed round him.

'The gentlemen won't like this,' he insisted. 'It's their cargo and you can't . . .'

Henderson's eyes flashed a glance as sharp as a razor, but Sam ignored it.

'You're as good as thieving,' the boy continued in outrage.

'I'll repay the capital plus interest, being a cut of the profits. But I'm determined on doing what's right, Mr Pearson. Call it a change of heart. I'll be paying the duty due, and beyond that we shall make a deal. You must settle now.'

Sam had no intention of it. 'It ain't your cargo,' he spat.

The boy launched himself at Henderson, who dodged the attack, landing a sharp right uppercut that sent Sam reeling. Four of the men rushed forward, but the captain waved them off. Anyone left on deck stopped what they were doing. Everyone was watching. Maria found herself transfixed, the men crowding around her, jostling to get a look as Henderson hovered over the boy and punched him in the stomach like a piston. The boy might have been thin, but he put in a good show. Still, the captain was stronger and it didn't take long before, plucky or not, the youngster folded. Henderson pulled Sam Pearson to his feet, propping him against the mizzen.

'Never question me on my own ship,' he snarled. 'We'll cut a deal. Perhaps not the one you want, but things have changed. That happens at sea.'

Sam's breathing was constrained. 'They won't have it,' he wheezed.

Henderson shrugged. 'Like it or lump it, and be thankful I'm not throwing you overboard. Search the boy for weapons and confine him below, Mr Clarkson.'

197

'You'll wish the customs men had got you by the time the gentlemen are done,' Sam spat over his shoulder, his voice as ominous as a witch's curse.

Henderson addressed the crew. 'Any more of you?'

Matters had changed, after all. There was silence. Not one of the men met the captain's eye.

'Get on then.'

'How long will it take to reach Bristol?' Maria enquired coolly, as the men dispersed.

'There was nothing else I could do.' Henderson's tone was insistent.

She nodded curtly. He was right. 'Your eyes turned quite devilish.'

'Maria, are you flirting with me?'

'I've never seen you so passionate.'

'Oh, you have.'

Henderson took the eyeglass from his pocket. The weather was covering their path as the ship zigzagged out to sea. The going was choppy. Maria had not flinched at the pursuit. Her nerve was impressive.

'Keep up the speed,' he shouted 'They can't follow us if they can't see.'

'Shall I prepare to open fire, sir?' Clarkson asked.

Henderson paused. He stared at Mrs Graham as if he was contemplating an excellent vintage or an inspiring view. If he was going to do this, he must do it now.

'Sir,' Clarkson pushed.

'I will not fire on His Majesty's Customs,' Henderson said. 'We shall outrun them if we can and explain ourselves if not.'

The mate took a moment to take this in. His blunt fingers scratched his filthy hair, but he never looked anything less

198

than jovial. 'Aye aye, Captain,' he barked, and the *Bittersweet* swung for cover into the last of the storm.

Maria flopped onto a barrel. She folded her hands primly in her lap. It would seem Henderson had the makings of a gentleman, albeit a gentleman in trade. He wouldn't be the first to fight his way to respectability. *Good for him,* she thought. As the sailor with the injured fingers passed her, she glared his way. Then she steeled herself and wondered how long it would take her to get to London. The world was waiting and she must attend her business. She must.

17

Bristol docks, two days later

Young Richard Fry's agile fingers served him well, though not with the ladies, for in that regard Richard's conquests were naive in nature. He had indulged in a stolen kiss when the opportunity arose, but he'd never had to tackle an obstacle such as a corset. All the sons of chocolate manufacturer Joseph Fry had been brought up to save themselves for marriage, and though he was a hot-blooded young buck of only seventeen years, Mr Fry's youngest certainly intended that. That said, his attention was sometimes diverted by the plump haunches of Mary Hewson, a worker at his father's factory. Mary was a pretty girl – blonde, rosy-cheeked and, like all Fry employees, well fed. The family treated their workers better than many treated their personal servants and had been shocked when the newspapers brought to light the case of a maid in one of England's stately homes who had been found dead in her bed. The girl had perished from lack of sustenance and the family's doctor had felt the need to release the shameful secret as a matter of conscience. Mrs Fry led a time of family thoughtfulness, inciting her sons to pray for the soul of the poor creature. Around the country, employers stipulated that cake and cheese must be served in the servants' hall. The hoi polloi, seldom seen below stairs, inspected their scrawny employees and adjusted housekeeping budgets marginally upwards. Fry's finest cocoa had benefited – sales were higher than usual for the time of year. However, the Frys were good people and could say quite honestly that they would have preferred the poor maid had survived.

Young Richard found himself drawn to such stories of poverty and cruelty for reasons that were not apparent to his family. Safe in his parents' comfortable, middle-class home, surrounded by the twin tenets of Moderation and Temperance, the boy seemed very much like his brothers, although Mrs Fry had noted her son's predilection for anticipation. Richard was always the last to finish dinner and the slowest to dress. Mrs Fry privately worried that her youngest son took too much pleasure in all things. Though, strictly speaking, there was no sin in Richard's lingering, it played on her mind.

Mr Fry had noticed more. In his view, the boy was like a puppy still to be trusted off the lead. He had no idea what his son might do, but he looked forward to finding out. Secretly he hoped Richard might prove an adventurer, though that would horrify Mrs Fry, who kept her boys close, hand-reared like lapdogs. Mr Fry suspected that what Richard needed was a stretch – something to form him. He had recently decided he would think upon it and come up with something suitable.

None of them had any idea that Richard was running well ahead of his father and already pursuing a secret life of his own. Had Joseph Fry realised where the boy was really spending his time, he'd have been horrified. Bristol harbour housed a long line of bonds, warehouses and businesses that straggled along the water. Richard liked coming close to

201

what he thought of as 'real life' – those people living in abject misery who made up half the population of England's great nation. He regularly set out to investigate this underworld and, indeed, to master it.

He bought a set of clothes from a pawnbroker. He rubbed dirt about his person and tousled his hair, adding some goose fat nicked from a pot in the pantry, so his well-kept locks hung in limp strands like those of a pauper, a stranger to Mrs Fry's glycerine soap and the cleansing effects of warm water. And day on day, thus arrayed, he set off. The dirtier he looked the more it seemed he might penetrate the intriguing nooks and alleyways, the dead ends and back rooms where men gathered to throw dice. He learned to blend in among the tavern whores. He watched as thin children scavenged the middens and fished forlornly by the stinking pontoons. He became accustomed to the packed public houses with working men oozing out of every window like yellowing sausage meat. He delighted in such desperation. Quickly, he'd torn extra holes in his trousers, for at the start he had not been nearly ragged enough. Coming from the respectability of the Fry household, it had been easy to underestimate the worst of the poverty.

The first time he tasted alcohol, the boy retched, but he quickly learned it was possible to grow accustomed to practically anything. After only a week or two he could withstand the stink of the hide vats overflowing with piss, and face a hearty working man's breakfast despite the miasma. In fact, he was drawn back often to fit in among the tanners, innkeepers and ne'er-do-wells, and the girls selling stolen snuff, moonshine and themselves from dingy rooms by the river.

Most of all, Richard learned to take chances, and that

thrilled him more than anything. Here, at the bottom of the heap, all life was a wager. Unlike his mother or, indeed, his brothers, the boy was not a reformer. He did not seek to uncover vice to encourage its reparation or indeed to help. Instead, he treated the intentions of others as an intriguing puzzle that he might outwit. Therein lay the game and, for that matter, the profit. Richard Fry liked to win far more than he liked to evangelise, and he sought knowledge more than he sought to use it for good.

The boy had learned a great deal about sleight of hand from the men who touted card tricks on the dock. Gambling was a sin spoken against often in the Fry household (as much as the sin of drunkenness). There were, as far as he could make out, two sorts of gaming man. 'Find the lady. We'll play for the fun of it, shall we?' Conmen, every one.

And then there were those who indulged in private matches of stakes up to a shilling. The first time he sat at the table – or, if he recalled correctly, it was a barrel-top – Richard could not have been happier were he betting ten guineas a time at a club on the Strand. Here, his family name could buy him nothing. He had to prove his worth. And he did. He fought when he had to. Not the boxing matches or fencing classes of a gentleman but the deadly, frantic lashing, the whatever-it-takes scrabbling in the filth, rolling, still fighting into the stinking water. The I'd-rather-die-than-lose mantra of shanty men who might die any minute. He wore his bruises with pride, though at home he had to explain them away as sporting injuries – a spot of wrestling or a fall sustained out riding. When he was cut, he doctored himself. Slowly, scarred but quick-fingered, Richard Fry found satisfaction. He might have been born a gentleman but he could make his way among the ragged and the desperate. He understood how things worked. He could win.

In truth, this was not a million miles from the underbelly of the Fry's business. Deceit was part of manufacturing chocolate, although the Quakers did not admit it. Old Mr Fry, like many of his competitors, employed fellows they hesitated to call spies to fall into conversation with workers at rival factories and procure the recipes of the most popular lozenges, jellies and chocolate confections. Culinary turncoats were paid plenty, but they required coaxing. The Frys had a reputation for innovation. Fry's history was littered with delicious, innovative fancy goods. Richard's grandfather had initiated the use of the steam engine, first at his apothecary shop and later in the factory. The machine had exponentially speeded up production of their most successful product to date – Fry's Finest Cocoa. Many an apothecary making cocoa in his back room would have given his right hand to be initiated into the mysteries of the locked third-floor kitchens at the Fry manufactory, which was in the charge of Richard's stolid elder brother Francis, also head spymaster for the family business. Francis was adept at winkling out secrets be they guarded by Menier in Paris or the more recently opened business run by the Rowntree family further north. It was not for nothing that the Fry's enterprise was the largest and most successful in England and that Richard was a fellow with a curious mind – it might bode well for his future in the chocolate trade if only he were to direct his curiosity the right way.

The day the *Bittersweet* docked in Bristol, Richard had sneaked out for the afternoon. He diced for almost an hour till the table dried. Then he set off towards the dock, where his gentlemen's clothes were secreted in a barrel. While he enjoyed the hearty unravelling of an evening in Bristol's less salubrious quarter, this was not a pleasure he might afford himself tonight. This evening, the Frys would attend a recital. The thought gave him a thrill. If the respectable doyennes only knew how he'd passed his afternoon, they'd be horrified. He was cutting it fine. He'd have to scrub himself raw to remove the smell of poverty in time for dinner.

Richard barrelled down the alleyway. Three stevedores walked together in a clutch and he stiffened to fight them if he had to, but the men passed, speaking English peppered with Gaelic. As he cut into his hiding place, he wasn't looking where he was going and collided with an oncomer. Instinctively he pulled up his fists.

'You need to mind where you're going, friend,' he snarled, his accent not displaying the usual well-educated vowel sounds of a chap who routinely read Homer and debated the finer points of the Bible with his relations.

The man looked up and for a split second there was the possibility that things might turn nasty. Then recognition lit in the fellow's eyes.

'Richard? What are you doing in that get-up?' Francis asked his younger brother.

'What are you doing here?' Richard parried.

'There's a ship docked with a new supply,' Francis said. 'Cacao beans. They're the best I've seen in a while. The bondsman tipped me off and I came to have a look on the sly. Richard, you're filthy.'

Richard's eyes burned. In all the years, he'd never been caught, though once he'd had to hide behind a water butt as his father passed in a carriage.

'What kind of beans?' he enquired, for if a fellow wanted

to distract a member of the Fry family, asking a chocolate-related question was the quickest way to do so.

Francis's mouth split in an easy grin. 'There's even some wild. Brazilian criollo, mostly. The ship set sail from Natal. Thank God it docked here, not London. I haven't seen it before – a scruffy old barque – but they must know what they're doing. It's a godsend. There's been too much forastero of late. If we can strike a deal, here will lie our remedy.'

Traffic from the Brazils had been inconsistent because of the war, with most beans loading from Trinidad. The top end had been hard to come by.

'The captain has asked about us, of course,' Francis continued. 'It was the first thing he said. The bondsman put him off till tomorrow, so I thought I'd sneak down and see. Father will be delighted. What are you doing here, boy?'

Richard shrugged. He felt like a child caught at midnight in the pantry, jam smeared across his lips. 'A man's conscience is his own,' he intoned. It was a family phrase.

Francis giggled. 'Well, that may be, but a gentleman's toilette is the business of those around him.' He wrapped an arm around his younger brother's shoulders. 'I'll walk with you,' he offered. 'If Mother catches you looking like that, she'll faint.'

★

Henderson wondered if his father had not meant to lead the life of a respectable planter but the complexity of the lading papers required to pay duty had driven him to a life of smuggling. The captain had been in the office of the bonded warehouse for at least an hour. Progress was inhibited by the fact that the clerk was drunk. The only reason Henderson continued to listen to the fat old sot was that he was talking about the Frys. He appeared enamoured of the entire family.

'Very generous,' he slurred, rubbing his swollen red nose. 'Old Mr Fry was very kind when my wife passed away. They's fair-minded, they is, the Frys. The boys an' all.'

Despite his inebriation, the fellow wouldn't make a stab at how the illustrious chocolate maker might view a shipment of several tonnes of cacao of Brazilian origin except to repeat that Mr Fry was a generous personage, 'wunnerful' if ever there was a crisis, but would not inspect the shipment until tomorrow at the earliest.

Henderson paced. This was taking too long. Maria had started packing when he left the ship and quite beside that there were the men to consider. The *Bittersweet*'s crew were restless.

'Sir,' he said, 'might I induce you—'

The clerk hiccupped loudly. 'Aw,' he said, and hiccupped again.

The captain's temper was wearing thin. 'I should like to dismiss my crew, sir. It is getting late and I have matters to attend.'

'I seen one of your fellows off the ship like a shot.' The drunkard's eyes were suddenly hard. 'Going by that, the rest might not even be aboard when you get back.'

Henderson paused. The man in question was Sam Pearson, whose hot temper had not abated for the duration of the trip. The captain had no desire to explain the boy's behaviour, but if his departure had been noticed, he would have to say something. Such ill discipline reflected badly. He held an impassive expression, as if he were holding a better hand.

'A passenger. I expect he wanted to see to his business. As do we all, sir.'

The drunkard's thick fingers sorted clumsily through the papers as if they were made of strips of leather. The smell of stale spirits hung like a cloud. Henderson craned to stare out of the grubby window in the direction of his ship. The afternoon sky was grey outside the casement. It folded over the city like a pewter roof. Now Henderson had docked, he was nervous – not of this simpleton, but of what might transpire. The terms of honest trade were unfamiliar and he had yet to settle into them. He had calculated a price for the beans – a minimum amount – but he had no idea if it was reasonable. Like all luxuries, the duty on chocolate was high and he needed to take that into account. Different commodities had different values in different ports. A good price in New York might be of the middling sort in Bristol or vice versa. It was a comfort that Will had been cheerful about the cargo's value in English waters. Still, Henderson would need his wits to determine what the best price was here and achieve it. Before he had buttoned his lip and descended into what felt like a protracted and furious sulk below deck, Sam swore the gentlemen he worked for were reasonable, which was promising, and this fellow in the bond clearly admired Mr Fry's personal qualities, which was promising again. But would it come off? The one thing (in fact, the main thing) about smuggling was that it afforded large margins. Henderson was accustomed to clear profit, and plenty of it. How paying duty and dealing with legitimate men of business might affect that, he had yet to figure.

The warehouseman reached for a small brass stamp on a piece of twine. He inked it and pressed the face onto each page of Henderson's papers. Then he held the sheaf towards the captain. 'Good day, sir.'

On board the crew waited, the deck in order. Clarkson had

begun to resupply. Despite the prospect of fresh meat, the men were expectant, like greyhounds about to be let loose for a run, a flash of teeth and a tensing of muscle. Tomorrow, Big Al Thatcher would have his work cut out. The men got into fights routinely and it was a surety that more than one would return with slashed skin and a dose of the pox. The captain lifted the lading papers high.

'Off you go,' he said.

The men cheered and crowded to disembark. Tonight, the *Bittersweet* would be left with a skeleton crew, chosen by ballot.

Henderson loitered on deck. He regarded the lading papers in his hand. *Well, it's too late now,* he thought. Here he was, a respectable merchant, his fortunes in the hands of the unknown Mr Fry. He tucked the evidence into his pocket and was drawn to more pressing business by the sound of Maria's trunk being hauled on deck by two of men remaining. She was leaving. He stood in her open door, watching as she hugged the wet-cheeked cabin boy and gave him three leather-bound books she had put aside.

'You must practise your reading,' she said gently. The books were worth a year's wages.

'I promise,' the child whispered.

'Here.' She thrust some coins into his palm. 'You have looked after me so well. Thank you.'

Henderson knocked on the door frame and the boy let go of Maria's skirts and skulked into the hallway.

'Come in,' Maria said as she pulled a dark woollen cape over her shoulders.

Henderson's things had been returned to the cabin. They lay forlornly to one side.

'I had hoped we might have dinner. I hoped you might wait for me to sell my cargo and afford me the pleasure of sailing you up the Thames,' he said.

Maria looked at her feet. She had a great deal to do and she felt in the humour for none of it. Somehow, the trip to the capital hung heavily now – a list of tiresome things that ought to be a pleasure. She wanted to tell Henderson that she wished things might be different, but, doing that, she would open the floodgate to a conversation in which she could not possibly indulge.

Henderson moved forwards and Mrs Graham jumped back with her hands before her.

'I'm sorry,' she said. 'We cannot—'

'Maria, is this because I kissed you?' he asked. It had been weighing on his mind. The question cut through the cabin like a knife. Her eyes betrayed her nervousness. There seemed no trace of the girl who had wheeled with the terns.

'They are waiting for me in London. It will be quicker to take the coach. I am charged on behalf of a princess. I have a commitment to London's greatest publisher.'

There was no measure in arguing, but he wanted to try. 'I wager you have feelings for me, madam. I know it. My offer stands.'

Maria's flexed her ankles beneath her skirts. 'I can't and I won't, sir. The stakes are too high.'

Henderson looked at his feet. He had pushed her to come aboard and he had as good as kidnapped her to make her stay, but the lady had every right to her wishes.

'We shall be friends,' she said. 'I hope to be of use to you, sir.'

'I'll organise a cab. Might I accompany you to the staging post?'

Maria nodded. 'I should like that.'

The rain was spitting and the air was edged pleasantly with cold. The cloud brightened as Mrs Graham stood on the dock, her trunk and the three leather bags coming down behind her, her feet on solid ground for the first time in weeks. Perhaps she might feel more herself in this weather, on English soil. It had been a long while.

She delighted in the chill on her skin. 'I dreamed of this in the jungle, and now it seems so strange.'

She breathed in, taking in the scent of the Fry manufactory, which was nearby. People strolled the streets by the tall building simply to enjoy in the scent on the air. The chocolate beans gave off an exotic richness before they were cooled and sent for winnowing. The smell was reputed to be a more tempting than baking bread.

Henderson handed her up. The driver had a vile running sore on his face. When he smiled, it looked eerie, like a shifting porthole that looked inside the man's body. Henderson tried to ignore it. Had English summers always been like this? He couldn't remember. 'The staging post,' the captain ordered and slid onto the seat opposite Maria.

Bristol town was close to the harbour. They trotted through the first streets, built of brick, until they passed a fine square that seemed constructed of Portland stone but might only be stucco. Some of the houses looked as grand as those in Bath, or at least the pictures Henderson had seen of them. Along the concourse there was a run of shops with canopies over the doorways. The driver shouted the sights as they passed them. 'Along there's the Corn Exchange.' His voice was sing-song. 'And we're coming to the Theatre Royal.'

Maria found herself having to hold back from observing

211

everything as if she might have to write an account of her arrival – a succession of first impressions of this alternately grand and shabby provincial town, and a description of the afflicted driver for colour.

I'm in England now, she scolded herself. *Everyone knows what it's like.*

The cabman continued. 'King Street. Very famous,' he said, without declaring why.

The stage left from an inn near the theatre, but the day's coach was already gone. The courtyard would not have been out of place in the countryside – a shock after the sophisticated crescents of fine houses they had passed. A scatter of chickens pecked at the muddy ground, avoiding the wide hoofs of a piebald carthorse. At the door, two men haggled over a cask of spirits – an unexpected delivery of rum. Maria widened her shoulders. This movement caught the attention of one of the men. He put up his hand to halt the conversation and both fellows stood back to regard these new, well-dressed customers as they enquired about travelling to London.

'The Rocket is gone. It leaves at four o'clock, madam.' The man spoke in a West Country accent so thick that Henderson and Mrs Graham had to concentrate to follow it. 'That's every day 'cept Sunday, of course.'

Henderson puffed. The man wouldn't know four o'clock if it slapped him in the face. Such timetables were hit-and-miss affairs. The coach, like every one in the country, went when it was ready or when it was full. Still, there was nothing to be done. Maria, meanwhile, peered inside the hostelry and evidently liked what she saw. The place was tidy and a pleasant smell of roasting meat emanated from the kitchens. The clientele looked reasonably respectable. There were no

212

rolling drunks or prostitutes, or at least none that might be obviously identified.

Maria oversaw the taking down of her trunk, tipped the cabman without staring at his deformity and then made sure her things were properly in the care of the inn's boy – a muscle-bound fourteen-year-old whose clothes were clean, if ragged at the edges.

'I'll take a room,' she said, dealing with the man in the doorway. 'And I'll try again tomorrow.' She spoke slowly so he would take note. 'The Rocket leaves tomorrow, does it?'

The man nodded. 'Yes'm,' he said. 'Four o'clock. We got a nice enough room, if it pleases you. We've had fine ladies stay before. I'll send your bags up, shall I? And if you want a box for the theatre tonight, you let me know.'

Henderson bit his lip. She might have decided to return to the *Bittersweet*. Mrs Graham was drawing a line. He felt a glimmer of panic he'd experienced on the dusty streets of Natal when he'd thought he might not speak to her again. Behind him, the clouds parted and the sun shone through. Matters in the courtyard seemed to pick up pace as a pretty serving girl crossed the cobbles and a boy tending one of the horses laid into his work, showing off for her benefit.

Maria turned. 'I might like to walk. It's been some time and I saw some parkland near the crescent. We have a fine spell, if cloudy. Will you take a turn with me, Captain, and perhaps if it is not too much to ask, you might join me for dinner?'

Henderson beamed. He bowed and held out his arm. 'A promenade,' he declared.

Maria laughed. 'Well, we have been aboard the *Bittersweet* and, fine vessel though she is and though the vista be excellent, she is two minutes in one direction and less than a minute in the other. It's not much of a stretch.'

Henderson nodded. At least it was something.

It was not the general habit in Bristol to promenade in the afternoon or early evening. Such practices were dangerously continental and could be unpleasant when the weather was inclement. The rain earlier had been only a spit. After the biting cold and high storms of April, the oncoming summer was welcome to many in the city, though to those returning from the tropics, the thin sunshine felt brisk where it broke through. Still, there were some ladies and gentlemen in the park clustered under umbrellas. The complexion of the hoi polloi was universally pale compared with Henderson's and Maria's. It was almost impossible not to pick up some colour on deck, and though Henderson's visage had seemed pale in Natal, it was clear in this company that he was well travelled. Two of the women on the other side of the lawn looked like ghosts, the captain observed, and walked with their eyes cast skywards, cutting grand, if distracted, figures as they hurtled along.

Behind them, the curved terraces of high houses reached over the trees, as if the buildings stood on tiptoes to maintain a view of the park. From the side streets, the occasional tinkle of a service bell fetched across the grass as a door opened at the haberdashery and a lady strolled inside past the piles of straw hats and piece goods. In the park, the blossom was out, the young leaves were bright and along the boundary there was a swathe of newly planted ash trees. Church bells struck six o'clock – time for evensong.

'I feel like breaking into a run,' Maria said. 'There's so much space.'

Henderson smiled. 'But you won't. It would be most unladylike.'

Maria laid her hand on his arm. 'Of course not.'

'Does one never get to do what one wishes in polite society?' he tried.

Maria rolled her eyes. She hoped the captain wasn't going to be tiresome, not least because she found him difficult to resist. It was easier now off the *Bittersweet*, and she hoped it would be easier still in London. It was important to get back to normal.

'It is my wish to deliver my manuscripts. It is my wish to gather materials for my new charge . . .' she started. 'When I get to London—'

'These are paper wishes, Maria. Insubstantial. Fleeting. They cannot drive you.'

She ignored him. 'I shall see old friends. I shall be welcomed by old friends,' she said pointedly. 'I hope that perhaps there will be news of the war in the broadsheets. When we left, Cochrane was close to victory. I hope he has achieved it. These wishes are not paper, James. They are important. They are the work of our nation.'

'I'm going to miss you, and you shall miss me too, I wager. We are flesh and blood, not merely some kind of legacy.'

'You're confident, sir.'

'Not at all. I am half-terrified. I have lading papers, Maria. I have fiscal responsibilities. I have a profit to make. But still, I shall miss you. Every day. And I know you will feel the same.'

'You, sir, shall find another lady. A far more suitable lady than an old widow like me.'

'A lady who doesn't care about my station?'

'Your station is changing, is it not? Come now, let us part friends.'

Henderson nodded. 'Friends,' he said, with no edge to his tone, and then without warning he grabbed her by the waist and waltzed along the path.

Her heart was racing. She dropped her head so that it touched his shoulder. Somehow that gave her strength. People stared momentarily at this high-spirited display, but they soon turned back to their conversations. Maria couldn't berate him. It wasn't in her. She wished sometimes she might behave more like a man.

'Really,' she managed to get out.

Henderson dropped her hands and held her eyes with his own as he bowed. 'Forgive me.'

'You can't continue to do whatever you want and simply say sorry afterwards, James. Honestly, did they teach you nothing about decorum in the colonies?'

They turned to walk back in the general direction of the inn. Her fingers were butterflies that could not find somewhere to light. She wondered if it had been a good idea to invite him to dine. She felt light-headed despite the fresh air and had to drag her attention back to the manuscripts secreted in her bags and to the necessity of the Empress's shopping. She was used to partings, but this was difficult. Henderson, however, did not push his advantage.

'I wager they'll have lamb. It's the perfect time of year for English lamb and we shall find a decent French red here – why, the coast is only a whisper away. No one makes gravy like the English. I had not thought of it, but there will be proper English pudding. Treacle pudding, Maria.'

A sly smile split Maria's lips. He was not trying to ruin her. She must simply be careful and keep control of her feelings. At the least, the food would be a distraction.

'Mrs Maria Graham invites you to a very English dinner, sir.' She curtseyed.

'Excuse me.'

The voice came from behind and the tone was authoritative. As they turned, an older gentleman in a pale frock coat bowed. Two younger men stood behind him on the path. One seemed somehow too pink; his hair was slightly wet where it protruded from his top hat. The older youth had an easy air. The old man smiled.

'Excuse me, madam. Did you say Mrs Maria Graham?'

'Yes.'

'Here in Bristol?'

'Yes.'

'The scholar?'

Maria nodded.

The gentleman beamed. 'Oh, I beg of you, where is she? I should like very much to meet the lady. I am a great admirer.'

Maria stood straighter. 'I am she,' she announced.

The man looked flustered. His nimble fingers played on his walking cane as if the breeze had caught them. 'Mrs Maria Graham, the author?' he hazarded, as if it were not possible.

'Yes.'

Captain Henderson hooted. 'This gentleman finds you too pretty, Maria, to be a bluestocking. And far too young, I'll warrant.'

'Oh no. No. Certainly not,' the old man insisted, his cheeks already rosy but growing substantially more so. 'I have admired your work, madam. *A Residence in India*? *Three Months Passed in the Mountains East of Rome*? Marvellous. Why, it is quite as if I was travelling in such exotic locations myself. You have a wonderful eye. Given the maturity of your

217

prose, I had thought you might be of more advanced years, that is all.'

'Indeed.'

'I must know what brings you to Bristol, if it is not too impertinent a question. And, of course, if I might be of any assistance.'

Maria curtseyed. 'I'm on my way to London. Lately arrived from the Americas.'

'Another book, I'll be bound.' The old fellow chortled. His sons looked embarrassed at this familiarity. One hopped from one foot to the other and the other stared into the distance. Maria took the intrusion in good grace.

'If John Murray will take my manuscripts, then yes. Two books. A residence in Chile and a voyage to Brazil.'

'Capital. Brazil.' The old man clapped delightedly and the loose ends of his pale-blue cravat bounced against his waistcoat. 'Mr Murray. Now there is an exceptionally interesting fellow and I can hardly think of a subject that would hold my attention better. Well, if you are in Bristol this evening, I must invite you and your husband to a recital and dinner. We are to have Beethoven's new sonata for the pianoforte.'

'Well, I don't know . . .' Maria started.

'I shan't hear a refusal,' the old man insisted, his cheeks now glowing with excitement and his lips peppered with spittle. 'Why I shan't be forgiven if I don't bring you. And quite right too. You must inveigle your wife, sir, to grace us with her company.'

'I am Captain Henderson.' He bowed and took up the old fellow's idiom so successfully that Maria regarded him with surprise. 'Mrs Graham, sadly, is not my wife, but I'm sure that she would be honoured to attend. We were to dine alone,

218

but what of it? Mrs Graham has had no other company all the long trip from Brazil and neither of us has any acquaintances in Bristol. The invitation is most kind. What is your name, sir? I shall be pleased to make your acquaintance.'

'Where are my manners? My name is Joseph Fry. At your service.'

Both Maria and Henderson regarded each other plainly. It flashed through Henderson's mind that surely this could not be the fellow of whom he had spent the afternoon being so wary.

'Mr Joseph Fry the manufacturer of cocoa?' Maria asked.

'Indeed. My sons will be delighted to make your acquaintance, madam. Mrs Maria Graham. In Bristol. Who would have thought? A published author of such renown. Richard! Francis! You must be aware of Mrs Graham's work?'

The young men bowed. They looked, Henderson thought, like plain enough lads. English through and through, and the greener for it. Such boys, working in a family business, must lack a sense of adventure, he thought. If they were brought up here, what could they have experienced? A smile broke out on his face. For years he had done business with the sharp-eyed burghers of North America. He had scrambled for every penny. Mr Fry was of a different mettle, and his sons too. Doing business with gentlemen felt easy already. Perhaps he had belonged in England all along, Henderson observed, as the younger boy kissed Maria's gloved fingers. The older one merely bowed and kept his distance.

'My wife and my other son are waiting at the concert, which is at the home of a dear friend of the family, Mrs Falconer. Do you object to music?'

Both Henderson and Mrs Graham affirmed they did not.

'But we aren't dressed for dinner,' Mrs Graham said.

'Pah. To have a mind such as yours at the dinner table, madam, one cares little about evening dress. It is mere convention.'

'If you insist.'

'I certainly do,' Fry fussed. 'Come along. We are almost late on account of Richard. He is, it seems, most particular about his toilette. And that has, of course, ended luckily for us. My guess is they will hold the commencement of Herr Beethoven's sonata until our arrival.'

'I hear your cocoa, sir, is excellent. Mrs Graham recommended it only the other day,' Henderson said.

'Well, well. How kind. You shall see us forgiven for our tardiness, Mrs Graham,' Mr Fry insisted, now striding with his silver-topped cane in hand, ushering them towards the park's gates. 'And that is very fortunate. Isn't this nice?'

18

Bristol

The drawing room sported a carved mantle of green Carrara marble and the long windows looked westwards so as the sun dropped from the sky every last beam of cold light was on show. The women were decked in velvet and satin, each curl in place as they listened to the piano. The men stood, their clothes darker and their hair powdered. Richard Fry longed to pick the pockets of the worthies at these events, but though he knew how to effect such a crime, he restrained himself as the mournful sonata (number 31, his mother hissed) got underway. Instead, the boy's attention was taken up by the butler's shoes, the amount of rouge worn by the three ladies of marriageable age, and the noting of a tiny mouse, dead but unattended by the waiting staff, where the skirting met the floor.

Mrs Graham perched on a chaise upholstered in lavender velvet. Captain Henderson's hand, she became aware, was a mere inch from her shoulder. Joseph Fry hovered nearby.

As darkness settled over Bristol like glossy tar and the Avon was shrouded in black almost in time to the music, the glow from the candelabras made the small glasses of Madeira that had been distributed shine like topaz. It had been a while since the captain had needed a fire and the flaming logs in the grate intrigued him. He settled to listen. For Henderson, the music was simply a hymn to Maria and to this as well – this grand occasion of coming home. He had never been invited to a recital. The ease with which Fry had extended his invitation and the delight of the hostess at meeting Maria, an unexpected guest of honour, was full of promise. It was exactly what he had hoped of England. The world he had left behind was, it seemed, quite as he imagined it.

At dinner, the long mahogany table stretched from one end of the house to the other, decked with glittering tableware. Henderson was seated next to Mrs Fry on one side and a young lady so shy she could barely bring herself to speak on the other. The girl's mother glared, silently lashing blushes out of the child, whose cheeks reflected the vermillion dining room walls.

'Don't concern yourself,' Henderson whispered. 'Conversation can be overrated.'

This at least made the child relax and Henderson turned his attentions to Mrs Fry, who was concerned by the tardiness of her male relations and the ins and outs of morality. She scarcely drew breath as she ranged between these subjects.

'I have no idea, Captain, where the Fry gentlemen get to. One hesitates of course to act the harridan, but they hold up everything. Why, even when we are to meet.' Here she lowered her voice in the manner of someone whispering on stage. 'For we are Friends, you see. Quakers. And tonight – a social engagement with such dear acquaintances. The Fry gentlemen are perpetually half an hour late. The music was wonderful, wasn't it? Many of my husband's brethren don't hold with the playing of music. Are you a gentleman of conscience, Captain?' Mrs Fry did not pause for a reply. 'For I can understand why the playing of instruments may seem sinful and yet there is such beauty in it. I myself liked to sing hymns when I was a girl. Of course, I do not drink. That is beyond the pale.' She sniffed, eyeing Henderson's wine glass. 'Intemperance,' she spat, 'is a sin.' Here Mrs Fry left a short pause, but it was so unexpected that Henderson had not enough time to gather his thoughts. He sneaked a sideways glance at the silent girl, who was engaged in buttering a piece of bread. 'You see, sir,' Mrs Fry continued, 'there are so many pitfalls . . .'

The table was decked with food. Tureens of creams and consommé were laid alongside an elaborately decorated poached fish, roasted meat and boiled calf's tongue, a simple garden salad and creamed carrots. Rolls baked in the shape of diamonds, glistening pats of pale butter, jellied apples, lemon mousse and a pudding gorged with raisins rose above marzipan fancies and a vat of custard topped with butter-scotch. The simple courses served on board the *Bittersweet* paled in the face of this sculpted array. On the other side of the table, Henderson watched Maria in the candlelight, as beautiful as she was every night. A goddess to be worshipped. Would she cut him dead if she met him at a gathering such as this in London? Without Maria, might Captain Henderson hope for an invitation? He paused briefly to assess his chances and then turned his attention back to the food until his hand came to rest on his stomach.

Smooth as silk, the ladies retired in a cloud of perfume and chatter, into the candle-strewn drawing room. As the door closed, there was a moment of absolute silence that lay like a blanket over the gentlemen. Tobacco, a snuff mill, two decanters of port and three more of gem-like cordials were fetched by the butler and two footmen. The table breathed out and a burst of conversation followed, an octave lower than that which had accompanied dinner. Cigars were passed. A fug gathered.

'Captain Henderson,' Mr Fry exclaimed. 'You have not been home for some time?'

Henderson rolled a cigar expertly between his fingers. He belonged here; he felt it. 'I have been in the Americas, sir,' he declared.

'Brazil, eh?'

'Indeed. Venezuela. The Guianas. And, along the eastern coast. Trinidad. Boston. New York.'

'And what do you think of our erstwhile colonies?'

'They are managing well enough without His Majesty. I hope it is not treason to say so. They are provincial, of course, but prospering. New York has grown in the last year, quite substantially.'

'The colonies trouble me.' Fry swept aside the Declaration of Independence and lumped the Americas together with other British possessions worldwide. 'They continue to employ the evil practice of slavery. I am a man and your brother. That is my motto. And still our navy captures ships cargoed with men. There are too many who are happy to benefit from such wickedness. It is shameful, is it not?'

There was a general murmur of assent. The Frys and their ilk were Whigs and abolitionists. Good men. Henderson nodded. It was his own inclination, even if he was not fully educated in its precepts. English politics were far distant.

'Yes,' the captain chimed. 'Though I know a few abroad who think it is their right to own the person of another man or woman, I do not condone the trade or its practices. Still, I cannot understand how the world will set itself if it were to cease.'

'Better, I'll warrant,' Joseph Fry insisted. 'It is unconscionable for such evil to continue. Thou shalt not labour on the Sabbath. Do they think of that as they enjoin their human possessions to work all hours? Why, even Reeves here, whose family made its fortune in sugar, has quit. The last man among us, and we are proud of him. If we cannot endure it at home, why must we bear the practice abroad? What is wrong in England must be wrong the world wide.'

Reeves sipped his wine. He was dressed like a fop with a powdered wig that sent up puffs of chalk when he moved. 'We sold our plantations. But it is not as simple a question as you'd like, Fry. Not every slave wants to be free. Not every master is the fiend you'd paint him. And prices will rise as a consequence of the ban. We are out of it and I am glad. It was far-sighted of my father. He is a gentleman of conscience and could bear it no longer.'

Richard Fry, drinking mint cordial the colour of emerald, cut in. 'I say let the prices rise. This is a matter of conscience alone. We must make the change and see how the world falls.'

'Easy for you,' Reeves replied. 'But how do you know where your beans come from? If slavery is abandoned, the prices of exports will rise, Richard, and will you choose the more expensive cargo?'

Richard looked as if he might spring to his feet. 'We cannot audit every shipment. We can only trust the word of those with whom we trade. Chocolate is an expensive commodity.

Sugar too. And by our industry, we hope to bring it to many whose conditions are not a great deal better than those indentured on the other side of the ocean. Did the story of that poor starving maid not send a shiver through you? What kind of people are we if we do not feed our own? Fry's cocoa should be for everyone. And as you know, prices have fallen this year – sugar and cocoa are down.'

'The price has fallen only because production is up. Costs have certainly not fallen on plantations where they do not indulge in slave labour,' Reeves snapped. 'Besides, chocolate is a luxury too good for most. My kitchen maid can have milk. Chocolate is for my wife on a Sunday. You are the latest of us returned from the colonies – what's your view, Captain Henderson?'

Henderson took a sip of port. He considered. 'I know of no cacao plantations that do not use slaves,' he said slowly. 'But there are few British plantations in Brazil where I trade. And in Trinidad, where we docked en route, slavery is widespread. I agree that each fellow's case is different. Some use their slaves more kindly than others. But that does not make the principle right. And if prices rise to take into account a labourer's wage, I cannot see how the common man will be able to afford chocolate. It is difficult to farm.'

'See.' Reeves was triumphant. 'It is an impossibility Fry. You cannot have your cake and eat it. You cannot abolish slavery and provide cheap, nourishing food.'

Joseph Fry, ever the patriarch, stepped in to smooth matters. He was a nice old duffer, even if the business he engaged in could be cut-throat. 'Dear me,' he said. 'There must be a way we can have both morality and a profit. We are masters of invention and must shape the world. This is England.'

Henderson took his chance. 'I hear you have a new

machine,' he ventured. 'Perhaps that is what you are referring to? A press?'

Fry laughed without sounding amused. 'News travels far. The machine is of Dutch invention and it makes dutched cocoa – a nutritious food and, in time, we hope, increasingly affordable. Fry's has no outlets in South America, sir, nor in New York. Where did you hear of it?'

'Mrs Graham told me.'

'And the press interests her?'

'Indeed. Mrs Graham has many scientific interests – both botanical and in industry.'

'Well, you must bring the lady to see it. Tomorrow. Fry's is at your service.'

Henderson noticed the Fry boys baulk at this generous offer, but neither uttered a word against their father. 'It would be my pleasure,' he smiled.

The dinner party broke up after midnight. The Frys, horrified that Maria was staying at a common tavern, tried to induce her to accept their hospitality. Henderson watched as she batted away their kindnesses like flies. He felt a proud familiarity in her independence.

Later, they sat in the carriage in silence as it rumbled through the dark streets. Maria shivered in the cold. Henderson offered his coat, but she refused, staring at the glossy cobblestones, slick with rain. When the cab came to a halt at the tavern doorway, the inn was dark save for a boy with a candle, ready to show the lady inside. Through the open door, a lick of flame glowed from the grate as the captain handed her down.

Maria bid him goodnight. 'It was pleasant to be in company with you.'

227

Henderson offered to inspect the room she had been allocated, but Maria would have none of it.

'If it is unsuitable . . . Your safety depends, madam . . .' His voice trailed.

'It will not be unsuitable, James,' she insisted with finality. 'I am always safe.'

He wondered under what circumstances she might accept help or advice. And yet, she lingered a moment in the chill.

'Goodnight,' she said.

'I shall come for you in the morning. To say goodbye. I wondered tonight about your views on plantation slaves. We have never discussed . . .'

Maria put a steady hand on his arm as she turned. This was difficult enough.

'Tomorrow,' she told him.

He hovered as the light receded, her slender figure disappearing inside. Stepping backwards, he waited for illumination at the window, but then realised that the wooden shutters were closed. A raven peered down from the roof, as if guarding the doorway.

'This is foolish,' he muttered as he took his place again and ordered the driver back to the docks, but as the carriage trundled towards the road he saw a slice of orange light from an upstairs room cut into the darkness. He smiled. It was a small victory. She had forsaken the fire to open the shutter and check he was gone.

19

Bristol

The captain was woken by the sound of two men vomiting on deck. He called for water to wash. It took longer than usual to arrive, for even the cabin boy was suffering the effects of the first night ashore. The boy's fingers were blunt and his footfall heavy. Henderson dismissed him, then shaved and dressed, choosing his new suit and struggling to fix his cravat the way he'd seen the gentlemen wearing theirs at dinner. The attire was not entirely comfortable. Still, he breakfasted feeling quite the dandy. It crossed his mind that Maria had been right. He ought to buy a looking glass, for he wanted to check his appearance more closely than was possible in the narrow reflection he could make out in the small panes of glass to the rear of the cabin. Finally he strode on deck to issue instructions. Viewed in the bright morning light, the crew were in a dreadful state.

As the bells of St Nicholas struck nine, it was Henderson's intention to leave the men to their recovery and spend the day with Maria. He wanted to be waiting when she rose for breakfast, but he was halted by a movement from the direction of the warehouse. It was, by any reckoning, early for a gentleman to be abroad and yet accompanying the bondsman were two figures which, Henderson squinted, seemed familiar. As they approached, they proved to be that of Mr Fry and his youngest son, Richard. Fry raised his arm in greeting. Henderson returned a nod. This would be first then, selling the beans.

'Aha,' Fry said as he came up the gangplank, unsmiling and with his dark greatcoat flapping in his stride. 'This is felicitous, is it not, Captain Henderson?'

'Indeed, sir.'

Richard hovered behind his father as he looked over the *Bittersweet*. Grey, wide-eyed, lean and very English in the morning light, the lad seemed here under sufferance and had the look of a glistening stickleback, hungry for a jaunt upriver. Mr Fry, a jolly bundle the night before, had hardened his resolve overnight. Purple veins stood out on his cheeks and he did not crack a smile. The visitors inspected the deck and eyed the men, taking in the details of life aboard. About the ship, evidence of intemperance abounded – empty barrels stacked ready to go ashore and the stink of stale alcohol hanging around the crew. Captain Henderson had to admit that the *Bittersweet* was not at her best, but then she had not expected visitors. He reminded himself that Fry's approval of the cargo was all that mattered. The old man was attending the rigging with a detached air.

'You crossed the Atlantic Ocean in this vessel? With Mrs Graham aboard?' His voice was flat.

'Yes. My ship may be old-fashioned and on the small side for modern tastes, but she's strong. I'm sure Mrs Graham would have preferred a naval escort, but Brazil is at war and traffic is severely curtailed. We made our way well enough.'

'I'm informed you are cargoed with cacao beans, sir.'

'Bought in the Brazils, Mr Fry. You are about your business early this morning. I thought to call on you later to discuss the matter.'

Fry paused momentarily. 'The early bird, sir, catches the worm.'

'You are most welcome.' Henderson's low bow did not appear to soften Mr Fry's demeanour.

'So, it would appear that you know your chocolate?'

Henderson nodded. 'I hope so. I was brought up, in part, on a plantation and I have been trading in beans ever since. I had not thought to vex you, sir, but can I assume you're here to buy?'

'You asked for me, Captain. Of course I'm here to buy. I'm interested in your cargo, but I'm also bemused at why you didn't mention the matter yesterday evening.'

Henderson felt chastened. 'Business did not seem a suitable topic at a social occasion.'

Fry weighed this up and appeared to accept it. 'I see. You had best show me what you've got.'

'Would you like to sample? We have two varieties of culti-vated beans and three sacks of wild cacao, which is becoming rarer by the year. I always sample by taste – it is the only reliable means, in my experience.'

'Wild beans?' Fry's eyes sparkled despite himself. 'I'm captivated,' he said drily.

They removed to the cabin. Mr Fry made himself comfort-able at the table, but the young lad hovered, peering at a pile of the captain's possessions, which had not yet been sorted after Mrs Graham's departure. Richard's gaze fell on the orrery. His expression did not change.

'The men went ashore last night for the first time in some

231

weeks.' The captain felt he had to excuse the state of his crew. 'They are a rough lot, but they work hard. Might I offer you a brandy while we wait?'

Neither of the Frys indulged, both being Quakers, and upon enquiry it transpired there was no cordial aboard.

'The chocolate will suffice,' Mr Fry declared.

'And after, I was set to call on Mrs Graham and bring her to see your famous press.'

'When I offered that, I had no idea you were a chocolate man,' Mr Fry said with candour. 'I was under the impression your interest was purely scientific. I'm afraid, in the circumstances, I must withdraw the invitation.'

Henderson nodded. 'I do not manufacture chocolate, sir. I should make that plain.'

Fry nodded. Still, no one in the trade would be admitted. The press had been constructed from a design that Francis had procured – that is to say, stolen. Fry had employed three Scottish engineers to build it. However, he wasn't here to discuss the blasted machinery. Mr Fry turned his attention to the business in hand.

'We are glad you docked in Bristol in any case, Captain Henderson. Most of our cargo comes in at Deptford.'

'Well, I hoped to sell to you straight off, sir, so it made best sense to port here. It was Mrs Graham's suggestion. I hope you will appreciate the quality of the shipment.'

'Mrs Graham suggested selling the cargo to Fry's?'

'Your name went before you. Mrs Graham had enjoyed some your lozenges.'

Fry perused the captain carefully, distracted only when Big Al Thatcher entered the room ready to prepare the chocolate. He settled to watch as the cabin filled with a scent redolent

232

of burning sunshine and tropical colour. As Big Al Thatcher whisked the drink, the captain sat back.

'Have you visited the plantations?' he enquired.

Fry shook his head without taking his eyes from the preparation. 'My father was an apothecary, Captain Henderson. That is how I came to the business. Cacao has tremendous health benefits, not least in providing an alternative to alcohol for the working classes. The machine in which you have shown an interest will make that possible. At least I hope it will.'

'A worthy aim, and profitable, I'm sure.'

'Quite apart from the issue of slavery, to which you know we are opposed, the duty makes it almost impossible to bring cocoa within reach of the lower classes. The rate is too high.'

'The government may yet be induced to drop it—' Richard said, stopping sharply as his father's eyes came to rest upon him.

'The duty must be paid,' Mr Fry said, his tone absolute. 'The pressing matter is that slavery must be abolished. We shall see what transpires after that.'

Three small pewter cups were set out for each of the men and the Frys drank. The atmosphere loosened. Richard finished each cup slowly, savouring every sip with his eyes closed. In the meantime, a tiny murmur of appreciation escaped Mr Fry's lips. Henderson waited before he spoke.

'It's good quality, is it not? Small increments in the quality of the beans make a huge difference, though I imagine not all palates are as sensitive as yours.'

'Our customers benefit from our good taste,' Mr Fry replied. 'There is no doubt, as you say, these beans are wonderful. And so we come to talk of money.'

Big Al was sent away. Richard Fry leaned over the table to replace his cup. He almost seemed angry that the cargo was as good as promised. His father waved him off.

'What price had you in mind?' Fry started.

'What offer did you hope to make?'

Fry smiled. 'Well, if that is the way it is to be, I have a question. Why don't you want to bring this shipment to auction? Or is that on the advice of Mrs Graham as well? Do you conduct all your business according to a woman's wishes?'

Henderson laid his hands on the table. 'I admit I had not considered going to auction. I'm accustomed in the Americas to dealing with a single buyer. Your name came up. If it is your advice to take the cargo to London and offer it at auction, then I shall. I'm bound to visit the city for a week or two. But I'm offering the cargo, here, before I go. That, sir, is a courtesy, honestly extended. I hoped the shipment would appeal to you.'

'We use forastero for the cocoa powder, mixed with some trinitario. You are quite right – these beans are special. Less and less comes to us from the far south, Captain. There is a limited market for the best. The navy buys from Trinidad directly – not Brazilian beans. These are top end, but we have customers who prefer to buy quality. While we endeavour to bring our products within the reach of all, some of what we produce will always be for those with more money and, indeed, better taste.'

'That business pays well, I hear.'

'Prices for cacao are coming down, as you heard last night, but I'd wager you'll make a profit and so shall we.'

Henderson stiffened.

'For these beans I will offer one hundred shillings a tonne. It's a fair price,' Fry said.

In America, this would be an astounding figure. Still, the captain did not immediately accept it. Having come all this way, he wanted the best price in this market, here at the mouth of the Avon, not on the Hudson. He watched Richard's face. The boy was clearly annoyed with his father and thought the old man had started too high. This was only the beginning of the negotiation, but it was a good indication. Fry, a better card player than his son, betrayed nothing. *So the old man is wily,* Henderson thought. He cleared his throat.

'I don't want to be greedy, sir, but there are three sacks of wild beans. They do not come to a tonne, or anywhere near it, and they must have a separate value. The rest of the shipment is of excellent quality. One hundred shillings is a fairish price, I agree, but on the slim side, even with prices dropping. This cargo is special. You're buying without competition and you'd need to be more generous to secure the deal. At auction, I warrant, as you suggest, the price would go higher. Might I counter?'

Fry nodded.

'One hundred and forty shillings a tonne, and six guineas for each sack of wild – they are small sacks, but the beans are rare. I was lucky to secure them. Plantations are taking over the land. Wild cacao is a delicacy your customers will enjoy and, more importantly, one they will procure nowhere else but Fry's.'

'Six guineas a sack?' Richard sounded incredulous.

Henderson ignored the interruption. 'Wild beans are not tended by slaves, sir. That is the nature of wildness. For customers of refined sensibilities, serving this cacao will render the confection not only a drink but also a statement of intent. If I remember correctly from the talk at dinner last night, it is an intention much admired. This chocolate has not been tainted by the sweat of slaves. You can sell it as such.'

'Freedom chocolate?' Mr Fry mused.

'To inspire a fairer trade.'

Fry laughed. 'You are out of the usual run of captains, Mr Henderson. We are not generally tutored in how to sell our produce. Though, mark you, it is an extraordinary idea. One might even say a revolutionary idea. Albeit for a very special kind of customer.'

'I think only of the feelings, particularly of women, sir. Ladies are soft-hearted and yet they love their morning chocolate. When you offer something special, it comes with an individual price. A cabochon diamond, a bolt of finest silk or chocolate that can be guaranteed not to cause a moment's moral discomfort. It is a rarity.'

A smile spread across even Richard's face. 'We can produce a special packet,' he intoned.

'Fry's Wild Reserve?' Henderson offered.

'We shall sell our first to Reeves.' Richard's voice was slow. 'After what he said last night, let's see if he will bankroll his principles.'

Mr Fry pushed back from the table. 'It's an intriguing idea,' he admitted.

'Wild cacao is left for the poor to scavenge, there's so little of it. The man who sold it to me knows I like the taste. Most traders would not even be offered it. This is a unique opportunity, gentlemen.'

Fry waited. Then he put out his hand. 'All right. Six guineas a sack of wild, and one hundred and twenty-five shillings a tonne for the rest. That way, you have a deal,' he said.

Henderson looked him in the eye as the men shook on it.

'You are a gentleman of grand ideas, Captain Henderson,'

Fry observed. 'You seemed slippery. But I see now you are an idealist, and that is to be admired.'

'Sir.' Henderson bowed. 'I'll warrant you've met many men more slippery than I.'

As they rose, the captain's mind was already buzzing. This was over six times more than he'd ever made in an American port. The money was genuinely good, even given the excise. Will Simmons had been right. The British market was ripe. The boy was a genius. A speculator. Had he lived, he would have been a rich man.

'It's good to do business with you, sir,' Fry said as he turned to leave. 'If you come this way again . . .'

The thought had occurred already to the captain. 'Perhaps next time I shall bring something of lower quality,' he suggested. 'Your aim, sir, of chocolate for the masses, is highly commendable. It is a long voyage, though, and I must do the best for myself.'

'Trinidad, of course, is closer,' Fry mused. 'And there are always forastero beans.' He sounded quite mournful.

'Had these been forastero of good quality, how much would you have paid?'

'Seventy-five shillings a tonne. Perhaps slightly less. Richard is right. The prices are dropping.'

'I might devalue my cargo, simply in the time it takes to cross the ocean.'

Fry shook his head. 'Prices in England will always rise ahead of prices in the colonies. There is no harm in poorer beans if I can sell one thousand men forastero, albeit cheaper – that will be where the greatest profit lies.'

'*The Wealth of Nations*.' Henderson named Adam Smith's influential economic treatise.

Fry nodded. 'We can only hope that Mr Smith is correct in his beliefs and that the widest market will be most beneficial. Now, having tasted the merchandise, I should like to inspect it, if you please.'

After some time in the hold, Mr Fry left the dockside. His men were instructed to carefully offload the *Bittersweet*'s cargo. The bondsman took orders and the Frys took their leave. As they did so, Richard grasped his father's arm.

'I want to watch him,' he said.

Fry patted his son's hand and took his seat in the cab as the door closed. The boy was always straining at the leash. 'Do you consider Captain Henderson dangerous or merely interesting, Richard?'

'Francis does it, Father. Francis watches for you.'

'Francis watches when there is a matter of business to assess. This man has sold us all his goods. Is it simply that you find working in the manufactory tiresome?'

Richard almost stamped his foot. 'You think I can't do it.'

'Do you believe it may be of profit?'

Richard nodded. 'In my gut.'

The feeling twisted as surely as if the captain had a loaded die or a hidden ace up his sleeve. Henderson had bested old man Fry – six guineas a sack was a crazy amount for wild beans that cost nothing to grow.

Mr Fry stroked his chin. Perhaps it was a good idea to give Richard a run. It might get this restlessness out of his system. 'Perhaps it's time you struck out on your own.' He pushed down the window and beckoned to the captain, who was seeing them off from the foot of the gangplank. 'Might you have a free berth on your trip to London, Captain?' he asked.

'Richard wishes to visit his cousins in Marylebone. If you can accommodate him, I will gladly pay his passage.'

Henderson bowed. 'It would be an honour.' He smiled. 'We will make way once we are unloaded.'

Fry waved his hand regally. 'Most obliged.' He tapped his stick on the roof to set the cab in motion, leaving his son to oversee the transportation of his latest purchase.

*

Maria broke her fast in her room and dressed. It was strange to be so steady after the constant movement of the ship, and to be so far from Henderson. For weeks now they had moved around each other as if in orbit. This morning, she realised she had no idea of his whereabouts. The stage was not due for hours. She peered out of the window onto the cobbles. At least it was dry and bright. The weather in England was so changeable. She felt tremendously English, taking an interest again in rain clouds and breaks of blue sky – abroad, things were predictable and people only noted the extremes: the earthquakes and the thunderstorms. Because of her long shipboard confinement and the brisk sunshine, it was difficult to keep to her room. Her journey to London would take two days at least, and quite probably three. For much of that time she would be confined to a carriage. She tried not to think of the *Bittersweet*.

Maria had formulated her plan. First she would visit Thomas's family in Mayfair, where she would lodge, and then Murray. She must also visit her aunt and, more pleasantly, one or two of her favourite booksellers. Maria could get any editions she desired from Murray, but she had a fondness for bookshops, bar one. Mr Thompson, off the Strand, had made it clear that he did not approve of ladies writing, especially about serious matters. He refused to stock her titles. Mr Bromer and Mr Thin were kinder, more enlightened gentlemen. She would take the prestigious business of the young princess's education to their establishments and buy leather-bound editions for the court schoolroom. Her Imperial Highness had given Maria a letter of introduction to a London bank that would secure more than adequate funds for everything the princess might require.

Maria wondered what changes the last three years had wrought on the capital. London was in a constant state of flux – new buildings and, she had heard, a horse-drawn tram in the West End. She longed to see it, and to read the latest proofs. The capital was girded in scientific advances. She looked forward to discussing them. Still, as well as moving towards these wonders, she was also moving away from something. Maria stretched, raising her hands high and then pushing them as low again. *Highs and lows,* she thought. There was no argument against the fact that becoming Mrs Henderson was out of the question. And yet the thought of the captain warmed her cheeks. She checked the cobbles once more. Three black men were transporting barrels on a wagon. Maria smiled. It was pleasant to know here, at least, all men were free. And what, she wondered, of the women? *I am free,* she told herself, though she knew it wasn't entirely true.

Finding her cape, she set out for the park. Being able to stride out still felt like a luxury. She was unhindered by the footmen walking the lapdogs of the fashionable, almost the only other occupants of the wide green spaces so early in the day, bar one or two prompt gentlemen riders. She considered extending an early call to Mrs Fry or, indeed, Mrs Falconer, the hostess from the evening before, but Maria was not really interested in society and she feared that instead of speeding the time towards her departure, such an activity might make it drag. Besides, calling at such an early hour would only disturb the ladies. She did not wish to visit the Fry factory without Henderson. That would feel like a betrayal. Instead, she cut out of the park and picked a path along the fine terraces, following the line of the rooftops and peeking into the long windows to catch sight of the Indian cabinets, sculpted Chinese dragons and elegant palms in the more fashionable upstairs drawing rooms.

Maria had never had a drawing room of her own. In Italy she had rented a house, but nothing in it had been of her own choosing. Likewise in Chile and in Brazil. Since she and Thomas married, the couple had moved almost constantly. She had followed him from ship to ship, writing one book after another. As she swung back past the theatre where the playbills were being pasted for the evening's performance of *The Prince of Homburg*, it struck her suddenly that she had been in perpetual motion for years now, always missing the next play, the upcoming concert and news of her friends. Apart from her books, she had not amassed even commonplace possessions – pieces of furniture or paintings. To own a painting and to have it with her would be a pleasant extravagance, she realised. It was one that up till now she had not missed. A flutter of melancholy turned her stomach. Had she been running from something all these years, scattering her opportunities to stay in one place and establish something real and lasting? Her mother had tended a garden and Maria had never appreciated that

– the art of making plans and growing them to fruition. She made friends wherever she went, or, rather, acquaintances, but the people in her life came and went – few of them were constant. To know somewhere or someone completely was rare. Instead she chose the constant stimulation of different cultures and the kaleidoscope of company that went with them. Is that what was troubling her? A picture of Captain Henderson's cabin and his long box bed flashed across her mind's eye, the sight of it a humiliation. *What on earth is wrong with me?* she thought. *Will I never be content?* Surely she had everything that any woman of sense might desire. London feted her. She had friends. She had family. She had reviews.

That afternoon, Henderson did not arrive. Time dragged until it was too late to go anywhere or to see anything. She tried not to linger by the window, so, almost at four of the clock, the sound of his steps in the hallway came as a welcome surprise. She curtseyed as he entered and he immediately apologised, bowing very low.

'I wish you would allow me to take you to London, Maria. There is still time to change your mind.'

Mrs Graham drew herself up. It was going to be difficult whenever they did this. It might as well be now. 'I have matters to attend.'

'The post is an arduous way to travel – far worse even than the *Bittersweet*.'

She liked that he kept his sense of humour.

The boy had come for her trunk and the bags already. The coach was downstairs, the first set of horses harnessed in place. There wasn't long. Maria did not look at him.

'Will you avoid me in London, Mrs Graham?'

'I will not see you in London, Captain Henderson, or at least I doubt it. A lady cannot call—'

He cut in. 'I could call on you.'

She nodded. 'If you do, I will receive you gladly. If I can be of any help . . .'

'Are you sure?' he asked.

She nodded, but offered no address, time or definite arrangement.

He paused. 'I shall accompany you down.'

In the yard, two girls leaned against the side of a cart, lazily watching the coach loading. One dandled the other's fingers flirtatiously in her own. The boy from the inn had loaded the bags and now sat crouched on a stool, cleaning a leather apron with a brush. Maria checked to see if Henderson noticed the vignette, but his eyes stayed on her. He kissed her hand as he handed her up. A man and a woman in the carriage shifted as she found her place. Maria wished she had removed her glove. Her heart was pounding with the terror of never seeing him again, of making a mistake. Maria Graham did not make mistakes. She could not afford them. She peered down, feeling as she had when she was a child and her father left on a voyage. She felt unaccountably alone, although this time she was the one leaving.

'Goodbye then,' he said. 'I shall call on you in town.'

'For London, Miss? Charing Cross?' the coachman asked as he slammed the door.

She lifted a hand to wave, but Henderson's figure was obliterated by muddy glass. The coachman mounted and the carriage moved off. The female passenger smiled apologetically.

'It's a long journey,' she observed. 'Three days, the fellow said.'

Maria nodded. It felt like one of the longest journeys she would ever undertake. *I'm doing the right thing,* she repeated to herself silently, and dragged her attention away from the vague receding figure still waving from the inn's gatepost.

Long after the coach had disappeared round a faraway corner, Henderson stood in the eye of the courtyard.

'Goodbye, Maria,' he murmured. 'I shall see you there.'

20

On board the Bittersweet

The night before the Thames came into view, the captain perched by the prow, waiting for the first sight of the city to appear over the horizon. He couldn't sleep. Here it was – the city of his childhood. He did not want to miss his first glimpse. In the dark, he remembered his mother taking his hand, helping him to walk downstairs in his new shoes when he was very small. He visualised the chimneys belching smoke into the snowy sky, a line across the slate roofs he could see from his nursery window all those years ago.

Installed in the second cabin, Fry had been observing Henderson these last days. The boy was adept at gaming, and after his first night aboard Clarkson reported he had won at crown and anchor, fleecing several of the men. Henderson had taken the boy aside as the mate looked on, breakfast cooling on the plates sent from the galley.

'It's not right, Richard. Mr Clarkson says you have talent, but we don't gamble with the men. If they end up owing you money . . .'

'People are never just taken as they are,' Richard spat, hard-eyed.

245

The captain stood up to him. 'You're not in need of the money.'

'No. It's the skill I enjoy.'

Clarkson crossed his arms, as if he were the boy's nanny. The mate had grown fond of Fry already – the boy was eager to learn, if a touch difficult. He clearly had talent, but it wasn't obvious yet where that talent lay, beyond the gaming table. 'A boy of seventeen making his own way is mostly just lucky,' he said. 'But you've a way with the dice, that I'll admit.'

'Plenty boys are married at seventeen. My cousin is married,' Fry sulked.

The captain, observing this exchange, gave a wry grin. He wasn't sure if his amusement was at Fry's surly manner or Clarkson clucking like a mother hen.

'My brothers make their way,' the boy objected.

'Your brothers? Is that what this is about?' the captain said. 'What made you want to come aboard, Richard? The post is a quicker way to town. I am happy to afford you passage, but I'm curious.'

Fry paused and drew up his courage. Things had changed since he left Bristol. Though he'd engaged in laying wagers, in only a few hours on the *Bittersweet* he had found something that intrigued him even more than the fall of the dice. Clarkson and his crew were tough – a breed of men he hadn't exactly encountered among the poverty-stricken slums. They worked as a team under the captain, who engendered a flinty respect. The crew told tales about how Henderson had brought down one man or another, or saved the ship by navigating through a storm. Fry's fascination in these heroes of the wide world was crystallising now, and he decided to admit it. He rolled the words around his mouth as if they were a slowly melting bonbon. 'I wanted to see

246

what you were up to, Captain Henderson. I had a feeling about the *Bittersweet*. I came to search it out, and I was right.'

Henderson removed his hat and scratched his head. 'A feeling about what? You can't make decisions on superstitions and hocus-pocus, Fry. London is a big city and it will hold its own dangers. You know that, don't you?'

Richard laconically raised a fist. 'I can punch,' he said. 'I've fought my way out of trouble before.'

'No more gambling with the men, son,' Henderson ordered. 'And your fists won't do. London's the biggest city in the world. Fetch Mr Fry a knife, Mr Clarkson. That at least will be a start.'

'Yes sir.'

Clarkson disappeared below decks, and Henderson put his hand on Fry's shoulder and leaned in. He felt, if not paternal, at least fraternal.

'It must be boring, I suppose,' he said kindly. 'I was twelve when I left home for Brazil and it was too soon, in truth, but I was summoned. Still, I can imagine the lack of spice, if it gets later and a chap has some pluck. You look like you could punch like a rocket, but you need experience. You don't want to get killed on account of curiosity.'

Understanding flooded Fry's eyes. 'Do you think that's what it is?' he whispered. 'Curiosity? I don't want to be a fop. It's easy for a chap to appear simple. Like Reeves and all his sugar money. He knows nothing about the real world. I want something to do – not just do-gooding but something that earns respect.'

'I tell you what.' Henderson drew a pack of cards from his pocket. 'I'll teach you a game I learned last year in America. They call it poker. At least it'll keep you away from my men.'

Fry nodded as Clarkson reappeared and gave the boy the weapon he'd retrieved from below decks. 'The blade could do with sharpening, Mr Fry, but it's good enough. I can have one of the crew see to it for you,' the mate offered.

'No,' the captain interceded, laying the cards to one side. If Fry wanted experience, then best give it to him. 'That's not what Mr Fry is after, is it, Richard? Take him down and show him how to keen it himself, Clarkson.'

Richard's eyes had burned with delight and later they stayed up late discussing the merits of the five-card trick and arm-wrestling like junior officers in His Majesty's senior service.

Now, almost at London, sleepless and settled in his place in the ship's pecking order, the boy joined Henderson at the prow.

'Not far to go.' Fry shivered, leaning over the side to see the movement of the water. The misty air curled off the surface. It was so cold he could see his breath.

'We could do with some chocolate to perk us up, eh?' The captain was cheery.

From the galley they could hear Thatcher snoring, his hammock strung across the room.

'A chap requires an edible chocolate block in situations such as these.' Henderson smiled. 'Something to be eaten straight from the pocket by a working man about his business. Wouldn't that be the thing?'

'That's an extraordinary idea.' Richard's mind whirred. 'The bar would need to be soft. Perhaps the consistency of a slice of cheese. And we'd need to add sugar.' Fry's stomach growled as he imagined the rich taste of melting chocolate slipping down his gullet. Why had no one thought of it before? The recipe would be worth a fortune. For an instant, Richard missed his brother. 'Delicious to eat,' he whispered.

The captain certainly had some stimulating ideas.

After sun up, the *Bittersweet* banked up the Thames. The state of the river left Henderson open-mouthed. The water was fetid through Tilbury, North Fleet and Grays, green where it wasn't brown, a mass of sewage and discarded rubbish. At low tide, pockmarked children picked their way through the mudflats, looking for shellfish, poking the ground with twigs as thin as their grubby legs. At Deptford, when the men spotted the first corpse, an eerie silence descended. Time slowed. The crew kept about their business, all eyes to the deck, stolidly ignoring the bodies of dead smugglers and pirates hanged at Execution Dock. One man, untarred, at Rainham Marsh was almost covered in gulls. He must have been freshly sentenced – the soft parts of his body easy pickings.

Henderson removed his hat but refused to avert his gaze. He was no coward. 'There is no shame, lads,' Henderson called. 'Poor buggers. It's a good thing we're a merchant vessel, eh?'

A burst of bile-yellow ragwort poured out of cracks in the brickwork and fissures in the mud as a growing flotilla of bargemen, armed to the teeth, every one as violent as a South Seas pirate, called out their wares. 'Take you up the Thames, guvnor. As far as Shoreditch for tuppence. I'm robbing myself. Sixpence to Chelsea.' Business was brisk. The waterway, after all, was safer than the shore. A fog hung heavily in the morning air, blackened by the soot of a thousand chimneys. Two long-dead horses, putrid and bloated, were caught in abandoned netting that staked them to the shore. Rooks and crows cawed over the carrion, the black birds seen off periodically by cloud-white gulls with beaks like golden razors.

As the river curled back on itself, Henderson remembered the house where he grew up near Covent Garden, with its genteel cornicing strung like lace around the drawing room ceiling. There had been dancing classes, private gardens and flocks of scrawny sparrows along the road on Soho Square. It had been refined. Clean. Ordered. Not like this.

He decided to dock at Greenwich, as Sam Pearson had suggested. From the water, there was sight of not one church but two, the long grey spires reaching above the rooftops. Not that the place seemed set to be a centre of spiritual delights – there were plenty of hostelries to keep the men supplied. The stink of the river was almost overcome now by the waft of baking pies, sold from open-fronted stalls along the main street. Music emanated from public houses and further along a girl played a tin pipe and danced a jig for ha'pennies between tomcatting with anyone who would pay her – a whore to be had standing up.

Most of the crew were given shore leave immediately. Clarkson set a rota detailing work for the remaining men. Once dismissed, Big Al Thatcher moved so quickly you'd think he was jumping ship in broad daylight. Taking no chances, he stowed an eight-inch blade in his belt and disappeared into the maze to visit his sister, who kept a draper's shop two hours' walk along the water. 'I'll be a right surprise,' he beamed. 'That is if she's still there and with the same fella. She's always been flighty, our Jenny.'

Henderson hesitated. He stared at the grand stone Naval College that overlooked the Thames like a white-haired judge. The focus of his expectation had been on arriving, but now he was here, he felt unsure. He was in funds, though he had to repay Will's investors, but with Sam gone he had not a single name nor address. He would have to make enquiries. Perhaps, he reasoned, he might visit the tavern off Old Street that Simmons had mentioned. The Rose, wasn't it? Mallow Street? From memory, the investors were in the proximity of Old Street Bridge. It should be easy enough to find.

'Welcome to London,' he said to Fry, who was surveying the stretch of sailmakers, smithies, cutlers, chandlers and carpentry workshops. 'You'll stay out of trouble, I hope,' Henderson charged him as he fitted his hat in place and tried to get used to the extra foot in height.

'Where are you going, Captain?'

Henderson smiled. 'Home, I hope.'

Fry hovered on deck, mumbling something about cousins in Marylebone as Henderson readied himself. Here it was. London. His London. Leaving the boy to his business and the ship to Clarkson's care, he stowed a vicious flick knife with a serrated blade in his inside pocket and engaged a bargeman. He wanted to explore.

In a dream, Henderson alighted further west, at the City, and surrendered himself with only the vaguest notion of his course. St Paul's was clearly visible beyond the rooftops, and as he set off towards town, London opened like a book – a familiar illustrated tale. The captain disappeared into her, one of thousands, well enough dressed, with just enough purpose. The capital swallowed such fellows at the rate of hundreds a week.

At first, the streets were thin and the company mixed.

'Got a shilling?' a woman called, the smell of gin on her breath. 'A shilling if you want a good time?'

And then, suddenly, around a corner, there was a pristine church. Two gentlemen, starched and pressed within an inch of their lives and heavily armed with pistols, disappeared down an alleyway from which, Henderson feared, they would never emerge so clean.

He set his course north and west. It did not take long for the streets to become more regular and the buildings more stately. As he passed a lady outside a shop clutching a small box of purchases, he wondered what his mother's life had been like. She must have known people – other women living in London – though he scarcely remembered callers and certainly no friends. It seemed that apart from her maternal duties, she had lived a solitary existence, for there were few places she would have been able to visit alone.

Enthused, he cut up the Strand and tried not to stare at the women. There was something elegant about English style, but, still, no woman could best Maria. The London ladies' carefully matched gloves, scarves and hats felt like a form of manipulation – really, had some of these women taken into account the colour of their carriage when they dressed?

Entering the square at Covent Garden, his stomach turned over. Fly-posters for the Covent Garden Theatre were pasted over the walls; jumbled, tattered papers were everywhere. The paving stones were crammed with costermongers selling flowers and live birds, brushes and cutlery. Dimly lit under the colonnade, the shops were obscured by two men juggling knives and shouting showily in Italian. The atmosphere had the air of a social occasion and yet it was not the city he remembered. He had not yet, it seemed, come home.

Construction was underway and Henderson did not recognise the streets that led away from the market. Wooden scaffolding wobbled precariously over the facades. Things had changed in twenty years. Henderson stopped a gentleman, asked directions to Soho Square, and was waved northwards. 'Walk towards Charing Cross. Then turn up Frith Street,' the man instructed with a low bow. 'Don't go any other way.'

He was close now. Would the house still be there? The captain picked up his pace.

Frith Street was wider than he remembered. At the open door of one residence, it became plain it was a bawdy house and, now he came to notice, there were two such establishments at least. He was sure they had not been here when he was a child. Two slatterns slipped, giggling, into a carriage, and Henderson glimpsed a flash of a glass-eyed drunkard holding out his arms for one woman to the left and the other to the right.

And, suddenly, there it was. The familiar little brick-built house – only three storeys – facing straight onto the street. Just as he had left it. Henderson stopped opposite. There was a thin coating of mud on the stones. Looking up, there was no light in the windows. Overhead, a pigeon fluttered, landed on the roof and preened itself.

'Well, I'll be,' Henderson breathed.

This had been worth the weeks on board, the risk of taking the journey. He smiled like a lunatic at the wrought iron at the windows and the carving over the dull black door below the fanlight. Number 22. With time suspended, he lifted the brass knocker and rapped twice. He had to see it properly – he had to go inside.

After a moment, there was the sound of scuffling and a maid opened up.

'Sir.' She curtseyed. 'Yes? Sir?'

Henderson was unsure what to say. 'Might I ask, please, who lives here?' he managed.

'Why, Mr and Mrs Elmore, sir.'

'Are they in?'

The maid glanced over her shoulder. Then she shook her head. She considered for a second and then blurted, 'There's no one but me, sir. Cook's gone to inspect the new bakehouse and the butler is on an errand.' The girl closed her mouth with a snap.

The captain paused. 'My name is Henderson,' he said. 'I used to live in this house when I was a boy. I'd very much like to see it again.'

The maid looked perturbed. 'Oh, sir,' she said. 'That can't be proper.'

Henderson did not argue. Instead, he reached into his pocket and extracted a shilling. 'I beg your discretion,' he insisted. 'It was my family home.'

She hesitated, sizing him up, but he seemed like a gentleman, so she took the coin. 'You'd best be quick,' she said.

It smelled different. That was the first thing. It was clean and well kept, but it smelled of wood, he thought, and chicken stock from the kitchen. The front room was painted pale pink and contained a pianoforte. The hallway was papered pleasantly in cream and brown. There was a painting of the seashore mounted over a chiffonier. The shape, however, was familiar. And the light. It trickled downstairs from the cupola, leaving a familiar pattern of shadows that cut cleanly over the thin burgundy carpet. He recalled the rooms exactly like this, only larger and painted in shades of green. Henderson ran his hand over the carved banister and decided to go up.

'Sir,' the maid objected, following in his wake like a wraith.

On the first floor, upstairs in the hallway, he could have sworn there was a ghost, a whisper of his mother. Had she

254

sat there sometimes, writing her journal? Perhaps she had been scribbling that absurd correspondence that his father had treasured, concerned with household accounts, James's progress in mathematics and what was playing at the opera. She had signed each with her devotions. Yes. Henderson remembered, there had been a chair and a small table with a sloped writing box topped with dark leather – just the kind that Maria had with a brass lock and fitted inkwell. The paper was thick, creamy and came carefully cut to the size of his mother's choosing, with sticks of sealing wax the colour of blood.

Ahead of him, the girl fussed, opening shutters and picking her mistress's linen from the floor, but that hardly mattered. It was here. The centre of everything.

'Home,' Henderson whispered.

It was a strange and impossible sensation, like seeing two houses at once. The captain half expected to come across himself, eleven years of age and rattling down the stairs after a night spent on the lumpy mattress his mother had installed in the old nursery. Suddenly, he realised that the *Bittersweet* counted for nothing. He belonged here. In London. In a house such as this. It might not be his inheritance, but it certainly felt like his destiny. His legacy, perhaps. He had been torn away too soon. Perhaps the contents of the bar of chocolate and the profits of his lucky cargo might let him stay. Not here, of course, but somewhere similar. He had a chance to rediscover what he'd lost. A home. A sense of being English. And then there was Maria's way. The lecture at the Royal Society and the blandishments that went with it. His views on the cocoa bean and its cultivation. Acceptance. Being part of the greatest city in the world and the great nation to which it belonged. He had gone astray, and it was time to put things right.

'Well, well,' the captain sighed, handing over another sixpence as he bounded downstairs two at a time and into the street, where he turned back in the direction of Charing Cross Road. He had been right to come back. London was still here, and he would be part of it. Somehow, the chocolate would manage it. This was where he belonged.

21

On the road to town

It took Sam Pearson a week to reach the city on foot. He had
left his purse at home before the *Bittersweet* took off, so he
had no other means to find his way to London. At first, his
temper fired the journey. The first day he must have walked
twenty-eight miles, easily, in fury at his treatment on the
Bittersweet. But even as the injustice of his confinement wore
off, he continued to hit the road hard. After all, the gentlemen
of the Old Street Bridge Club required news. Rightfully, the
shipment Henderson had sold belonged to them. As a result,
Sam walked every hour he wasn't sleeping and hitched a lift
more than thirty miles from Bracknell to Collingwood in a
single morning by sheer luck when he offered to help loading
and unloading a wagon.

Coming towards London, he didn't eat much. Closer to the
city, contrarily, it got more difficult to find food and farmers
were less likely to barter an hour or two's work for some supper.
No matter. Starting early, up at four before the sun, he headed
for Old Street, with his feet aching and his stomach howling as
the city grew up around him. Walking through Notting Hill, he
was careful to stay north of Kensington, so he came in on the

right road. Miles on, towards Mallow Street, as the bells sounded ten of the clock, every step felt like it was taking too long, until at last he arrived at the mud-spattered front door where he fumbled with the key he always kept in his pocket, and mounted the stairs.

In the dingy club room, Sam fell on the remnants of food on the table like the ravening pauper he was. He picked up a wedge of cheese and ate it in swift, efficient bites, downing porter from a pewter tankard, though it had gone flat. The bells sounded towards the docks. When he'd done, Sam Pearson settled to wait, his belly stretched like a drum, crumbs all down his semmit. The gentlemen wouldn't arrive until late – that was their way. He worried what they might say, but Henderson's treachery wasn't Sam's fault. He'd come to tell them, hadn't he? Sam wondered fleetingly what they'd reckon to Will. It was Will who should be here. Sadness settled in his chest as he stretched out on the floorboards, his flash of red hair to one side. Outside, the sun was shining, and behind the shuttered window, Sam Pearson slept without dreaming.

*

He woke with a piercing pain in his leg, sharp as a crocodile's tooth. A dense shadow hovered over him like a malignant presence. The shadow quickly brought down a poker once more, this time onto his knee. Sam screamed. He rolled over, but the injury stung and he couldn't get to his feet from the shock of it.

'It's me, sir,' he insisted. 'It's Sam.' He cowered.

There was a hesitation.

The voice spoke. 'You broke in. Get on your way, you filthy sack of bones.'

The voice belonged to a woman. Sam tried to focus. Was it a sprite? Some kind of evil banshee? Then his eyes adjusted and Mrs Wylie backed off, brandishing the poker.

'I could fetch my husband,' she warned. 'Mr Wylie used to wrestle at Tyburn. He was All London Champion. He'd squash a piece of nothing like you as if you were a insect.'

Titus Wylie had never been inside the Old Street Bridge Club. One of the unwritten rules was that Mrs Wylie alone should undertake the responsibilities of readying the room. However, she was sure the seriousness of the situation might now merit his admission.

Sam put up his hand. He grabbed one of the chairs and hauled himself painfully onto his feet. 'Please,' he said. 'You don't understand. They are expecting me. The gentlemen.'

'Pah!' said Mrs Wylie. 'I can smell you from here. Vagrant!' she roared. 'The idea that my gentlemen would be expecting a stinking scrap of a fellow like you—'

'No. Ma'am, really they are. Look, they gave me a key.' Sam reached into his pocket slowly, so as not to alarm the woman. He drew out the front-door key. 'I'm waiting to attend their business.'

'Waiting to pilfer whatever you can, more like.'

'I ate what was left of the cheese. They feed you if you want, the gentlemen. I came a long way with news on an empty purse and I was hungry. Once when I was here, they gave me and my friend a whole pie. They don't mind.'

Mrs Wylie's eyes fell to the card table. What kind of business might a stinking homeless ne'er-do-well have to conduct with the players of bridge? Still, it appeared the boy did have a key. She decided to have a better look at him and, to this end, she edged towards the window and let loose the catch on the shutters. A stream of dusty afternoon light filtered through the filth-caked window. Sam squinted.

'I ain't seen you before,' she said doubtfully.

'I seen you,' Sam assured her. 'You serve over the road. I generally have a half at the Rose after I've done my business. You keep a fine cellar.'

Mrs Wylie lowered the poker and glanced at the basket she had left by the table. It contained a few bottles, a loaf of fresh bread, some pungent cheese and a ham.

'Well,' she said. 'I can't have you thieving from my gentlemen. You'll finish at the end of a rope, boy. Them giving's different from you taking. Don't you know that?'

'I've eaten now,' said Sam. 'There'll be no trouble.'

'You've got news, did you say?' Mrs Wylie enquired.

Sam nodded stoutly. 'Yes'm,' he said.

Mrs Wylie waited.

'You do what you do for the gentlemen, and I do different, ma'am.' Sam's voice was steady. He limped slightly as he moved further into the body of the room and heaved himself into one of the chairs. 'You got a good arm on you, I'll say that.'

Mrs Wylie turned. She cleaned the glasses with a crumpled rag that hung at her waist, then she lined up the empty bottles and gathered the cards and fallen score sheets.

'It's fresh, this bread. Don't touch it.'

On her way out, she picked up the chamber pot.

'Do you want something hot for your knee?' she asked. 'I can do you a compress for tuppence. I'll be back directly once I've got rid of the soil.'

Sam shook his head. 'I'll be fine,' he said.

★

It was dark when Sam woke next. The door opened with a creak and he was dozing in the chair.

'Sam?' Charlie Grant lit a candle. 'Is that you? We expected you days ago.'

Sam tried to spring to his feet, but his injured knee had swollen and instead he hobbled.

'What happened to you, boy?'

Sam looked sheepish. 'It was the woman who provisions the place. She thought I had broken in.'

Grant chuckled and put his cane to one side. 'A veritable Amazon, our Mrs Wylie,' he said. 'And she is curious now, no doubt. I'm sure Hayward might take a look at you. He studied medicine in his youth. Well – where's Will? Is there news of the cargo?'

'I come with news all right, sir, but I'm afraid it is not good.'

Grant put the candle to the fire, which was laid ready in the grate. He lit two oil lamps. 'What matters is the goods,' he observed. 'Are the goods secure, Sam?'

Sam shook his head. 'No, sir,' he admitted.

Grant's face froze. He turned. 'None of it?'

'Will Simmons died in Brazil, sir. The captain of the ship took everything. I tried to get him to land your cargo, but he wouldn't. He took the shipment to a bond in Bristol. He paid the excise.'

Grant's face scarcely moved, save one eyebrow, which arched. 'He took everything?' Grant paused menacingly, then folded into one of the wing-backed chairs by the fire. 'Is the captain not aware that Will's goods were backed by investors?'

Sam nodded. 'I told him. He says he'll pay you, sir – split the profits and all. But he's a slippery bastard. When I told him the goods wasn't his to make a decision on, he beat me and locked me in the hold. I got off as soon as I could. He docked at Bristol but claimed he was coming to London. He wants to see it, I heard them say. I don't know how much he sold our beans for. He's a bad 'un all right.'

'Well, that will never do, Sam,' Grant said bluntly. 'For the goods most certainly are not his to sell. Did he mention anything else?'

'Something else?'

'A bar of chocolate that Will was carrying in addition to the cargo?'

Sam considered a moment. 'No,' he said. 'Only the beans, Mr Grant.'

'Who is he?'

'Name of Henderson, sir. It's an odd ship – the *Bittersweet* – out of Brazil. Foreign-looking. He's got a woman on board.'

Charlie Grant half shrugged. Women were largely immaterial.

'A lady, I mean, sir.'

'I see.' Grant leaned forward. He ignored the sour smell emanating from Sam. The boy had clearly not washed in some time. 'Tell me everything you know. Start at the beginning and leave out no detail.'

Sam nodded. His eyes fell to the bottle of port Mrs Wylie had left on the table. 'Should we not wait for the others?' he asked.

Grant's face changed. The grip on the fox-headed ebony cane he favoured as a weapon tightened so that his knuckles turned white. Then he drew the stick slowly upwards and poked Sam where his leg was most swollen. The boy winced.

'You do what I tell you or I'll fix your other knee,' Grant hissed. 'Now tell me everything, boy. Every single bloody detail. Now.'

22

Further to the west

Henderson strolled up Piccadilly as the light faded and the bells struck eight. Outside the grand houses, lamps were being lit, throwing dim shadows along the stone and brick frontages. The pale evening fog was heavier here than further downstream. It settled over the city, curling up the river and into town, its tendrils nestling around the buildings and seeping into Henderson's clothes. Gentlemen in evening dress strolled past purposefully, and now and then a big-wheeled carriage rumbled by. At least it wasn't cold. He'd expected worse. The captain lit his pipe and stopped at Albemarle Street, making sure the shag caught light.

'Number 50,' he murmured.

The residence of John Murray – a tall house of Portland stone, its slate roof all but obscured by the fog. Henderson looked up. The curtains were drawn, but along the rims of the windows a line of warm light framed the glass and, if he was not mistaken, a shadow passed – someone was inside. Henderson puffed meditatively. It was late to make a call uninvited and he had no cards, but perhaps a mention of Maria might serve that function. He hoped she might even be inside. When she had talked of Murray's salon her eyes had lit up – something that had not transpired, he noticed, when they had discussed her marriage. It seemed that Albemarle Street was the centre of things.

He crossed the road and knocked. A tall butler opened the door and peered into the darkness.

'Captain Henderson for John Murray.'

The man hovered, the hallway behind him lit by two ornately detailed candelabra that, it occurred to the captain, must be French.

'Is Mr Murray expecting you, sir?'

'No,' Henderson admitted. 'Mrs Graham suggested I call. Is he in?'

'I will enquire.'

The door closed and Henderson drew deeply on his pipe. The fog was growing thicker so that the fanlight over the door became only a vague blotch of obscured yellow. On the street behind him, he could hear footsteps ringing on the stone. He caught sight of an indistinct outline now and then, of men passing or a message boy scurrying along, mumbling under his breath. Henderson collected his thoughts.

Maria had intimated that Murray would be interested in his botanical knowledge. To this end, the captain decided he would offer the publisher a treatise on the cultivation of the cacao bean. Henderson had hardly put pen to paper since his teenage years. The letter he had written to Maria in Natal was his first missive in a long time. Still, that had been successful and Maria was right – over the years he had amassed a great deal of botanical information. He need only apply himself to write it down. It shouldn't be too tiresome an exercise, especially if it got him what he wanted.

The captain knocked out his pipe and put it in his pocket, ready to enter. The door opened again, this time with a creak.

'Sir?' the butler enquired, the yellow light not illuminating as far as the edge of the step where Henderson was hovering.

'I'm here.'

'Mr Murray will see you. Come in.'

Inside, unexpectedly, it felt like hallowed ground. The hallway had an air of reverence. Murray, after all, published the nation's cognoscenti. The most august writers in the world had passed through this entrance and been ushered upstairs. No wonder it was grand, the staircase rising in an elegant sweep, skirted by its banister and set about with ornate wooden newel posts. The house smelled of leather bindings and melting butter. Henderson tried not to think of the poetry of Lord Byron or, indeed, any other famous Murray author, as the butler led him upstairs. Surely if Maria could manage to be part of this world, so could he.

Miraculously, it seemed, the door at the end of the landing opened onto a high-ceilinged, opulent yellow drawing room where an old man in evening dress rose to greet the captain as if it was a dream. The warm light burst in sharp contrast to the dim fog outside and immediately made everything so vivid that it was almost shocking. Henderson took in the huge oil portrait over the mantelpiece and a wall of leather-bound books before which a walnut desk was covered with manuscripts that practically dripped onto the Oriental carpet. Henderson had the sensation that he was struggling to breathe – almost as if he was drowning, not in water but in a strange mixture of ink, tradition and good manners.

'Captain Henderson is it?' The man stepped forward. 'I am John Murray, sir. This is my wife.'

Henderson bowed. 'James Henderson,' he intoned, moving his attention to the woman – grey-haired and, like her husband, well dressed and unassuming. It would appear that the couple were spending the evening alone. 'I'm sorry to call so late.'

'But you have news of Mrs Graham?'

Henderson shifted. 'I had hoped, sir, she might be here.'

'Here?' Murray was mystified. 'You mean in my house?'

Mrs Murray shifted in her seat.

'Yes. I parted from Mrs Graham in Bristol five days ago. She had expected to make London before me and declared she would come to you directly.'

'She is in England?' Murray's smile was warmer than the fire that crackled in the grate. 'You are a friend of Mrs Graham, then, sir?'

Henderson nodded. 'I captained the ship which brought her home.'

'Captain, you must sit down. This is capital news, isn't it, my dear? Would you like something to drink, sir? A brandy? A glass of port?'

Henderson paused. 'A brandy,' he said, unsteadily.

'Please sit,' Murray insisted, indicating a wide sofa with ochre cushions and gilded wooden arms that, the captain supposed, could not possibly be comfortable.

'She should be here,' the captain repeated, all thought of chocolate beans, recognition at the Royal Society or, indeed, writing a book suddenly evaporating. 'I don't understand. She was determined on London and quit Bristol by carriage. She has been working on two manuscripts.'

'Two?' Murray's face lit up. 'She did it then. Brazil and

266

Chile. She wrote it was her intention, but she has them completed, eh? Well, well.'

'You don't understand, sir. Five days is too long from Bristol. I sailed into London. Mrs Graham left before me by coach. She should have arrived.'

Murray handed him a tumbler filled with amber brandy and settled next to his wife, who shielded her face from the fire with her fan as she perused the captain silently. The publisher did not appear anxious and continued with jollity. 'We can only surmise that there has been some kind of delay.'

Henderson sipped. The journey from Bristol to the capital was one hundred and twenty miles by his reckoning, and the road was not especially hazardous. Such an itinerary could be completed in one day, if driven hard with a horse and a determined rider. Passenger coaches generally took it easier, for they were concerned with comfort. The Bristol Rocket stopped overnight twice before rolling into the centre of town. That Mrs Graham had not arrived ahead of the *Bittersweet* was inconceivable. Henderson gulped the brandy.

'Do you happen to know, sir, where the Bristol coach stages to? I mean, where its journey ends?'

The old man considered carefully. Though there were several coaching inns less than a mile from where he was now sitting, John Murray rarely left the capital. Still, he dispatched boxes of books to literary establishments all over the country. That, however, involved knowing how to leave London, not how to arrive.

'The Golden Cross is the inn in these parts. It's at Charing Cross – anyone will point it out. London is not short of coaching inns, Captain Henderson. The most famous is in Islington, but that is the wrong part of town. I imagine that coming from the west into the centre it must be the Golden Cross,' Murray decided. 'However, I shouldn't exert yourself, my dear fellow. Maria is famously unassailable. I doubt any harm has come to her on a journey from Bristol. The coach will have a broken wheel. It is not uncommon. Or perhaps she has run into good company. Let's hope that, shall we?'

Henderson laid down his glass. 'I will feel better for checking.' He rose.

Mrs Murray nodded and Mr Murray sprang to his feet more quickly than might be expected of a gentleman of his age. He looked perplexed. The captain was a curious fellow. A day or two in a matter of travel was nothing. Though perhaps the truth was that he was not comfortable in the company of a publisher – Murray knew the milieu of silver-spooned artists and scientists in his salon was not to everyone's taste, and despite the fact Henderson had called when the Murrays were alone, Albemarle Street had become quite famous. The captain might be intimidated.

'Man of action, eh? Well, thank you for bringing the news that Mrs Graham is close. I shall alert my print men to be ready and of course we shall look forward to seeing her, as well as having the honour of setting her books. You might have stayed to dinner, you know. We shall have guests shortly.'

Henderson shook his head. Many in London society might have paid highly for this offer. It was exactly what he had hoped for when he was standing on the doorstep. 'Thank you, sir.' He bowed. 'Perhaps on another occasion.'

Back on the street, Henderson stumbled once or twice without a night light and soon fell into step up Piccadilly behind some gentlemen who were better supplied. At Charing Cross, the Golden Cross was easy to locate – from it, a rumble of laughter and another of discord seeped into the dank air. The lights were so low that the sign swinging over the doorway was indistinguishable.

'The Bristol coach?' Henderson enquired of a man standing outside. 'The Rocket?'

The fellow shrugged and waved towards the busy interior.

Inside, the Golden Cross did not live up to its name, being neither golden nor, in any respect, holy. The packed wooden tables were a far cry from John Murray's drawing room. Peppered with candle stubs, the air was lit with low, grey light. Across the room, wormwood ale came in bashed tankards served on trays by grubby serving girls.

'A penny a pint. Purl. A penny a pint,' they shouted, dodging between the tables.

There was a low stink of vomit emanating from one side in a waft. On one table a woman was reading cards for a coin, and on another a man with a long needle was piercing the ear of a young boy, who was slapped so hard when he cried that he fell onto the floor – a mixture of sawdust, body fluids and beaten earth.

'The Bristol coach?' Henderson asked one of the serving girls.

'Doesn't leave till tomorrow, sir. At two of the afternoon.'

'The incoming.' Henderson grabbed her arm. 'Has one of the coaches not arrived?'

The girl shook herself free, slopping the pale liquid over her tray onto the floor. Without hesitation, she stamped hard on the captain's foot. 'Fuck off,' she spat, turning tail. 'Don't touch me.'

Henderson reeled, but didn't follow her. Instead, he continued to the dark courtyard at the rear. The stables were closed, the horses fed and the coaches housed, but there was a group of boys playing dice on a broken barrel below the hayloft.

'Have you any idea what's happened to the Bristol coach?'

'Came in at lunchtime, guvnor,' one of the boys replied – the leader of the group.

'Have they all arrived this week as expected?'

The boy stared. 'A coach got robbed all right. It was held up near White Waltham. That's what they're saying.'

Henderson took a shilling from his pocket. He held it up. 'If you know anything else,' he said, 'you'll have this. I'm looking for a lady.'

'A shilling?' The boy laughed, and his fellows abandoned the dice and lined up behind him, all eyes on the coin, as if they were spellbound. 'I heard information was golden. That's what I heard,' the child said with a cheeky smile. 'Got any more?' He held out his hand.

'A shilling's enough.' Henderson voice was calm.

The boy stopped, as if unsure what to do in the face of such a rebuttal. His foot kicked the dried mud meditatively and he chewed his lip without taking his eyes off the coin. 'Two shillings,' he tried.

Henderson grabbed him by the collar. 'Do you want the shilling or not? I can ask the innkeeper and the odds are I'll pay him nothing. It's your decision.'

The boy sighed. 'They took the mail and the baggage, but a lady had a go at them. Plucky bird. They struck her, course. She's in the inn at White Waltham. She had a shock, see, cos ladies ain't used to a beating.'

Henderson tossed the coin towards the boy, who caught it smartly.

'I want to hire a horse overnight.'

'Now, guvnor, this time of night, that'll cost you.'

The captain laughed. 'You'll be a millionaire by the time you're twelve, son. I'll give you three shillings. That's fair. And I want a horse that can travel in the dark at a gallop to White Waltham. There's an extra sixpence in it if you can get me on the road inside of ten minutes.'

★

Towards the outskirts of the city, the fog dissipated. A sliver of moon lit the Berkshire road indistinctly. Now after ten, it was getting late and the roadside houses had doused their lanterns. Farmers rose early and did not burn the midnight oil, for that cost hard money. Outside the raucous life of London, England mostly slept when it got dark. Rooks infested the trees. A fox ran from a thicket, a green-eyed flash of danger.

Henderson steeled himself. It was another forty miles to the village. Albion, the horse the boy had supplied, was sturdy enough for an animal that was let by the hour. The saddle and bridle, however, were of poor quality. The captain's main concern was navigation. At the inn he'd found a chap who drove the mail post. For another shilling, the fellow explained the route, which sounded simple, but missing a turn in the dark would be an easy mistake, and on land, unlike at sea, a traveller couldn't manoeuvre instantly. If Henderson missed the road or turned the wrong way, he'd have to retrace his steps or hope the route provided an alternative turn-off. Signposting was erratic at best, though the captain's knowledge of the stars would help. The Plough was clear here, which made finding the North Star easy. The captain geed up his mount. 'Go on, Albion,' he urged.

271

Henderson had last ridden the year before with Thys Bagdorf. The men had taken a trip to the Trinidadian highlands. At the time, he'd found it exhilarating to be in the saddle. Riding had dissipated the overwhelming heat, especially when they had cantered where the undergrowth allowed it. After weeks aboard ship, it was a welcome blast of freedom. Now Henderson's face felt cold, his nose had started to run and he hoped the bridle would hold out till he got to the inn.

Along the road, he had no idea there were so many little villages and farms. Brazil was covered in impenetrable jungle or huge plantations and a man could travel for days without seeing anyone. England was different. The market gardens on the way out of London were no more than a few acres each, and villages were peppered along the road like shot. Between the settlements, the ghostly landscape called his childhood nightmares to come and fetch him.

After two hours, Henderson came to Bracknell Forest, which he recognised by a mature oak tree slung about with white ribbons made from torn sheets. It was a local custom, the mail post driver said when he had issued direction, started by the villagers at Bray, but he didn't know why. The tree loomed out of the blackness, the strips floating eerily in the night breeze. Albion started, but Henderson held the horse in check, though his heart leaped. It was easy to get rattled in the pitch.

'Now, now,' he soothed. 'We're close, girl. Very close.'

He clapped his hands to warm them. It was only three miles now, but it felt like twenty and the road was not even. At least the moon was at its height, which made it easier to navigate the potholes. The last stretch, there was not a single house until finally the village appeared out of the darkness and

Henderson pulled up at the inn – a low brick building with a half-timbered upper floor and, swinging over the door, a sign with an eerie painting of the oak tree hung with white linen.

Through cracks in the shutters and from the light seeping underneath, the captain was gratified to see the flicker of a low fire and that there were candles alight. He slipped out of the saddle and, holding the bridle in one hand, pounded the door with his other. Then he pounded again. At length, the latch clicked and two men, one of them clearly roused from slumber, stood in front of him.

'What do you want?' the older man demanded gruffly. In his hand he held a cumbersome cudgel, ready for action.

'Is this White Waltham?'

'Of course it is.'

'I'm looking for the woman who was hurt when the stage was robbed.'

The older man looked at the younger, but neither of them moved. Henderson was glad he had his pocketknife. They looked like thugs, though that wasn't uncommon in an innkeeper and his boy. Besides, he had roused them close to midnight.

'I've come to make sure the lady is all right,' the captain pressed.

The innkeeper relented slowly. 'Take the gentleman's horse, Robbie. Come in, sir.'

Inside, it smelled of tobacco and roasted meat. The room stretched back, a labyrinth of snug corners with smoke-darkened, rough-hewn pillars obscuring the corners. The floor was uneven, though it held the heat from the fire, so it was warmer inside than out – not always a given in a hostelry, especially at night. Henderson felt a wave of relief.

'You'll be needing a room,' the older man said.

'Indeed.'

'Which is half a crown.'

Henderson handed over a coin. 'I must see the woman straight away. Is she all right?'

The man examined the silver, then slipped it into a leather purse on his belt. 'She got a fright but she's right enough now. Eleanor,' the fellow roared.

Almost instantly, a tiny serving girl shot from behind the bar, where she must have been sleeping. She smoothed her apron, her shoulders practically up to her ears, for the call had startled her. The girl's hands were raw, as if she had been scrubbing pots, and her hair fell almost to her waist in a thin straggle of an indeterminate colour. 'Yes, Uncle,' she squeaked.

'This gentleman wants to see the lady who was hurt.'

Though the girl seemed frightened, she still voiced her objection. 'But she is abed, Uncle. All the guests is.'

The innkeeper loomed over his niece, as if he there was a chance he might bare his teeth and bite off her head. Henderson was a paying customer and a gentleman. He could have whatever he wanted.

'Take me to her.' Henderson stepped in. 'She'll be pleased, I promise. I've come to help.'

The girl's eyes moved slowly over the captain's boots, as if she was evaluating the validity of this statement by the quality of the leather. Then she bobbed a curtsey and picked up a candle, slipping past her uncle as if she expected a passing blow, which happily did not transpire.

Henderson followed her up a dark wooden staircase against the end wall. On the upper floor, off a landing, there were private bedrooms. The girl stopped outside one of them, the light from the candle pooling as she knocked quietly on the door. Her pink hand was tiny. She moved to knock again, but Henderson stepped in.

'It's fine. You can go now,' he said. 'I'll come down later and you can show me my quarters.'

The child hesitated but didn't argue. She handed over the light, bobbed a curtsey and disappeared along the corridor in the dark. Henderson knocked again, harder. There was no reply. He turned the iron handle.

'Maria, are you all right?' he said as he stepped inside.

The room was small and, as far as he could make out, was mostly furnished with a thin mattress that was raised from the floor on a makeshift wooden base. Around it, a scattering of straw covered the bare boards on all sides. Henderson leaned down and shook the sleeping figure under the covers gently. 'Maria, wake up.'

The woman stirred, pulling away from his touch. Her face was in the shadows. 'Augustus?' she said sleepily.

'It's James.' The captain gratefully pressed her hand to his lips. 'I came directly I heard. I knew you'd been too long and there must be trouble.'

The hand was pulled back smartly and the woman sat bolt upright. Her vague outline seemed somehow wrong. Henderson moved the candle closer and realised his mistake too late as a high-pitched scream emanated from the woman's lips. He fell back. This room, now he came to think on it, didn't smell right. There was not a drop of orchid oil. If anything, it smelled of musty vegetables.

'Help,' the woman screamed. 'For God's sake. Mercy.'

'Madam,' he objected. 'Please. There has been a dreadful misunderstanding—'

Before the sentence could be finished, however, Henderson found himself pushed against the open door by a bulky man who appeared from further along the hallway, bounding in his direction like a huge lolloping guard dog. The captain dropped the candle, which snuffed out, leaving the room once more in darkness. It flashed through Henderson's mind that the fellow downstairs had a cudgel and that if he came to the woman's aid it would be difficult to fight him off.

'What the hell are you doing in my sister's room?' the man sneered, spitting into Henderson's face.

It was so dark that the captain could barely make out the fellow's features. 'It's a mistake. I'm looking for the lady who was hurt when the stage was robbed.'

The fellow didn't listen. He held the captain by the neck, his grip tightening. 'Some mistake,' he spat as Henderson tried to push him off. 'It sounds to me as if you are trying to press an advantage. Did you assume my sister was unprotected?'

'I'm looking for someone else. I don't care about your sister. Truly.'

The grip tightened further and, realising there was no other way, the captain brought up his knee sharply. The man let fly a yelp and fell. Henderson blundered onto the landing in the pitch. He was about to make for the stairs when there was a sudden crack. A door opened and Maria appeared, holding a lamp. She glided along the boards in a white nightgown. Her feet were bare.

'James? Whatever is going on?' she asked as she pushed past the captain and looked into the bedroom.

The man on the floor was moaning and the woman had got out of bed to attend him.

'Maria,' the lady said, 'help me with Augustus. The brute! The brute!'

'What have you done?' Maria turned on Captain Henderson. 'I came to help. You were hurt . . .'

Maria's eyes hardened. 'I'm not hurt. Don't be ridiculous.'

Maria stooped to help Augustus to his feet and stationed him at the end of his sister's bed.

'Mrs Graham, do you know this man?' Augustus managed to get out. 'He kneed me in the stomach.'

Henderson knew this to be untrue. He had kneed the fellow lower than that.

'James, you can't go around breaking into a lady's bedroom. Poor Miss Calcott must have had the fright of her life. I hope you've apologised.'

'It was an honest mistake,' Henderson mumbled.

Maria corrected him. 'It was not. You went to the wrong room, but you intended to disturb me in the night, I expect. Breaking into a lady's bedroom – I can think of little more perturbing. What on earth were you thinking?'

Henderson's blood was up. 'I was thinking, Mrs Graham, that you might require assistance. I rode three hours straight in the dark on account of the thought.'

'I came to my sister's assistance, sir.' Augustus got to his feet. 'And I shall take the ladies back to London tomorrow without any help from you.'

'Is this your brother, Maria? Thank God you've recovered.'

Maria baulked. Henderson's familiarity was beyond the pale. Could he not see that? If he cared for her at all, he must be more careful.

'There is absolutely nothing wrong with me,' she said firmly. 'Mr Calcott is not my brother. I don't need an escort and I certainly don't need some kind of saviour. It's quite idiotic.'

'But you challenged highway thieves. You were beaten.'

'Well, there you have a sum of half the story. And though it's none of your business, Miss Calcott also took the public stage from Bristol. When we were held up, I did challenge the highwaymen. I secured my manuscripts when they stole the rest of the luggage. Such papers have no value, except to myself and Mr Murray, and in that matter the men were quite reasonable. However, Miss Calcott, realising my success, decided to try her luck at rescuing a painting in the same fashion. A painting by Augustus, actually, who is her brother, and that did have a value.'

'Brigands,' Augustus spat.

Miss Calcott sank onto the edge of the bed, as if unable to stay on her feet as a result of the mere memory of what had transpired during the robbery.

'I can't imagine what you were thinking when you set out on this, this . . . imposition,' Maria berated Henderson. Her temper flared. How could he be so foolish?

Henderson felt himself deflate. 'But you could have continued to London on another stage – you're two days late at a minimum, and Murray is expecting you. If there's nothing wrong, why didn't you simply carry on into the city? There have been other coaches.'

Maria enunciated clearly, as if she were speaking to a simpleton. 'I stayed to look after Miss Calcott, who, like me, was travelling alone. We sent a message to Augustus, who arrived this afternoon to take her back to town. He has kindly offered to escort me as well, so I don't need to try my luck again on the public stage.'

'I thought—' Henderson started.

278

'What you thought is crystal clear, but it certainly isn't your place, James. It doesn't work this way,' she hissed. 'And that you don't understand that is, frankly, most ill advised. Now please, gentlemen, I will attend to Miss Calcott.'

Dismissed, Augustus limped into the hallway. Henderson followed, looking so diminished that his erstwhile opponent took pity on him.

'Come along,' the fellow said. 'Why don't we have a nightcap? They'll get you a room, I expect.'

Downstairs, if the innkeeper had heard the fracas above him he showed no sign. He sat by the fire picking his teeth until, at Mr Calcott's invocation, he fetched some scalded brandy. In the light, Henderson weighed up his opposition. Calcott was sturdy and in his early forties. He wore britches and a loose shirt. His hair was in a state of disarray, which he attempted to remedy by pushing his hand over it.

He introduced himself. 'Augustus Calcott.'

'James Henderson.' The captain shook hands and slumped into his chair.

'How do you know Mrs Graham?'

Henderson laughed. 'I captained her crossing,' he explained. 'From Brazil.'

Calcott nodded sagely. 'I see,' he said, his eyes sharp. 'I expect a fellow could be filled by admiration for her very easily. It must happen all the time. She's a remarkable woman. My sister and I owe her debt of gratitude. She interposed her body, you know, when the brute struck. She told him that was enough.'

Henderson nodded. Of course she had. 'I was only trying to help,' he said weakly. 'I worried she had come to harm.'

Calcott took his place at the other side of the fire. His

auburn hair had resisted his ministrations and flopped across his face. 'She's right, though, isn't she? It isn't your place.'

The innkeeper returned with two tankards.

'I made 'em sweet, gentlemen,' he said. 'Now, if there's anything else, just shout on little Eleanor. She's behind the bar. I'm off to bed. There's a free room, sir, at the end of the corridor. The only one we have left, as it happens.'

Henderson took a deep draw on the brandy as the innkeeper retreated. After the long ride, the hot, sweet drink tasted delicious. He needed something to pick him up. He had been humiliated, and he felt it.

'Quite a ride in the dark, I imagine,' Calcott said jovially. 'Not sure I'd risk it. You were lucky, old man. The robbers are still out there, you know.'

Henderson rallied. He might have been proved foolish, but he wasn't a coward. 'A man on a horse doesn't carry much. From their point of view, it's probably best to wait till daylight and pick on a fancy coach. I take it you have a fancy coach, Mr Calcott?'

Calcott laughed. 'You like her, don't you?' He drank deeply. 'Well, she'll never forgive you for this. You made her look ridiculous.'

Henderson's stomach turned. The fellow was quite right. He wasn't on board the ship now, with only the crew to notice. Maria had been furious. He'd made a serious error of judgement.

★

Aboard the *Bittersweet*, long past midnight, the lamps strung on deck shifted in the swell. Three men had fallen asleep aft and one of them was quietly snoring. In the gloom, Clarkson was showing Richard Fry how to throw a knife, spinning the sharp point towards a target. Richard's face displayed a beatific expression as the blade sailed through the air and embedded itself deep in the side of a wooden barrel marked with chalk.

'That barrel is about the size of a man's body,' Clarkson pointed out. 'If you can hit it, then you can land a fellow. Kill him stone dead,' he said pleasantly, retrieving the knife and handing it over. 'Go on, have a try.'

Richard tried not to imagine what his mother would make of the exercise, though the spectre of her disapproval pleased him tremendously. He found his balance and eyed the barrel, drawing the knife back over his shoulder before letting it fly.

'That's a good shot,' Clarkson said delightedly as the tip found its mark.

The boy as good as beamed. Fry let the knife fly a second time and grinned when it embedded itself more deeply. 'Practice makes perfect, eh?'

A balmy breeze shifted the lamps. Two sailors took their places on watch, nodding at Clarkson as they passed.

'Shore leave tomorrow, Sandy,' the mate said cheerily to one of them. 'You going to find yourself a woman?'

The other sailor laughed as his fellow squirmed. Almost six foot tall and wiry, Sandy could climb the rigging like a monkey, but he was shy with the girls. He took up his position overlooking the dockside without gracing the company with an answer.

Richard leaned against one of the barrels stacked at the mizzen.

'And you, sir,' Clarkson enquired. 'Will you be leaving us soon?'

Fry shrugged. He didn't want to. He was supposed to

visit the Gowers, his cousins who resided across town in Marylebone, a far more respectable parish than Greenwich. Their home was a pleasant place, but the boy had not come to make social calls and small talk. The rough conversation below decks and the opportunity to see up close how the crew lived was far more compelling. He liked this side of the big city. It was sophisticated, even if it was rough. During the daytime, you could hear French spoken where the immigrants gathered. Jews spoke Spanish on the market stalls and he'd caught snatches of Gaelic where the ragged, stinking Irish picked up what work they could, mostly in the building trade or as stevedores, unloading cargo if they were lucky. In the evening, he'd heard you could find a whore talk in whichever tongue you wanted. Even Latin, if you were so inclined. Richard was not a papist, but he was still intrigued. He let the knife fly once more and again it found its mark.

'Have you ever killed a man, Mr Clarkson?'

Clarkson crossed his arms. 'Hardly a man on board hasn't,' he admitted with a shrug. 'Travelling's rough. One voyage last year, we lost two men in separate brawls – one tavern or another. They get fired up on rum, see. You need to practise.' He nodded at the pockmarked barrel. 'That is, if you're considering going to sea.'

Richard's interest wasn't in seafaring. He was playing at being a sailor, but he'd die at home in his bed, he was sure. The thing was, he wanted to taste real life – the livid scars and the thick-fingered competence of the crew had given him a flavour for it. Like a child with a new toy, he didn't want to quit the ship before he'd heard every story.

'Do you think the captain might take me with him on his errand? Do you know where he's gone?'

'That'd be his lookout. He's the captain,' Clarkson said.

The mate was sociable, But he was unlikely to confide in this scrap of a lad. Fry launched the knife at the barrel once more.

'I'm getting the hang of it,' he said. 'It's all in the balance.'

Back at the inn

In White Waltham, the atmosphere the next morning over breakfast was strained. Maria wouldn't look Henderson in the eye and, having spent the rest of the night considering the captain's actions, she remained fuming. The party sat in silence over a table laid with bread, cooked ham and warm ale. Augustus alone was bluff, checking outside and reporting that it was a fine June morning.

'Let's get you back to Kensington,' he said to his sister, gently placing a long woollen wrap around her shoulders. As their heads moved together, Henderson noticed a striking family resemblance – hazel eyes, dark auburn hair and a complexion that particularly suited green. 'If we start now we should make it home for a late luncheon.'

There was, of course, no luggage. Maria only had her papers, which lay on the table, and the clothes she had been wearing for some days – the grey travelling dress and short black boots. Augustus tipped generously on the ladies' behalf, for the inn had hired them linens.

'Did you save both manuscripts then?' Henderson tried.

Maria nodded. 'And the letter of introduction to the bank.'

She smiled. 'The fellow who robbed us couldn't read. He didn't know the difference.'

'Capital, isn't it?' said Augustus. 'And, madam, you must allow me, in gratitude for what you did, to replace one of your lost outfits at our expense. An evening dress, perhaps? Miss Calcott uses a wonderful dressmaker not far from us at the Gravel Pits. I know it doesn't sound promising, but they have tremendous satins. It would be my pleasure to arrange a fitting and, if you will permit me, to pick a colour.'

Henderson turned, expecting Maria to object. 'Mrs Graham is very independent, sir,' he said.

'I'd be delighted.' Maria smiled. 'How very kind of you, Augustus.'

There was an awkward silence. Maria eyed the captain, her gaze unfaltering. This prompted the Calcotts to rise and see the carriage was brought round. They had a coachman, who had slept in the stable and was now readying the horses.

'Augustus says you'll never forgive me,' the captain admitted when they'd gone.

Maria stared blankly. 'You mentioned last night that Murray was expecting me. How do you know, Captain Henderson?'

'I paid a visit. We docked at Greenwich two days ago. I thought you would be in town and I half hoped to find you there.'

'You went looking for me at Mr Murray's Albemarle Street address?'

'Yes. You said I might call on you and I had hoped to engage Mr Murray in conversation about botanical concerns. It occurred to me I might write something. A book perhaps. About chocolate.'

Maria's eyes hardened further. 'You have no sense of etiquette, do you?'

285

'I left England when I was twelve years of age.'

'Please don't call for me at John Murray's offices again. The permission to call on a lady is at her own address, Captain Henderson, not that of her friends, or her publisher. Once, you promised not to harm me. I want to be clear that this is harm, sir. Going there. Coming here.' There were tears in her eyes. 'You stand to ruin my reputation in London before I even return.'

'If I was wrong, I'm sorry, but—'

Maria cut in savagely. 'Of course it was wrong, James. Don't you understand? I trade upon my reputation. It's almost as if you wish I'd found trouble and that only you would be able to remedy. If you continue the same way, people will talk. When you call for me at John Murray's, it smacks of the lapdog, James. It reeks of an illicit affair and they will sniff that out. Can't you see that your uncalled-for intrusion last night would have been the end of me in normal circumstances? And how would you replace the life I have? Publication? Respect? My own money? No – you'd have me marry a reformed smuggler. A liaison from which neither of us could possibly benefit. You must be sensible. If you disgrace me, I lose everything. If you disgrace me, how can I help you rise? How quickly might we both tire of that? I want the best for both of us, and your reckless behaviour will give it to neither. I'm lucky the Calcotts are so decent. They've promised not to breathe a word. They are acquainted with my aunt, of course.'

Henderson sprang to his feet. 'But . . .' The word hung in the air.

Maria hoisted the manuscripts into the crook of her arm,

the way a mother holds a baby. 'I've had enough of your buts and whys and wherefores. No apologies are acceptable. You presume too much. Good day, Captain Henderson.' Her eyes flashed as she crossed to the door.

Henderson's temper flared. She really was the most infuriating woman. He brought down his hand on the table as Maria's figure disappeared. Petulantly, he finished his ale, listening to the sound of the traces being threaded on the Calcott carriage and the clinking of the brasses as the horses stamped. Augustus put his head round the door.

'Goodbye, old man,' he said, raising his hand in salute. 'Don't worry, I'll get the ladies home.'

Henderson grunted. The carriage pulled away and the captain called for his horse. He must return to the *Bittersweet*, pick up the spoils of his cargo and seek out Will Simmons's partners. There was a great deal to figure out and no point in trying to assuage Maria when she was in such a temper. He had meant no harm.

Albion almost sighed when she was turned towards London. She sneezed and the stable boy laughed. Henderson paid his account – a bucket of oats and the stabling. Then he clicked the reins. Back on the road, it felt as if it was really summer, and the low heat was reliably set for the day. By daylight the road was pleasant, and Henderson rode the horse hard for a couple of hours, taking in the green lush countryside as it merged into the city. England was undeniably beautiful. Here, nature smiled at you rather than trying to catch a fellow out. There was a fresh scent on the air from the orchards. The captain tried not to dwell on Maria – the sweep of her dress as she left the inn and the finality of her warning, like a lid snapping shut. He did not allow himself the sneaking suspicion he had – that however much he loved her, she might be right.

With the easy road and pleasant weather, the captain was in town in three hours. At Charing Cross, Henderson returned Albion. The boy from the night before was mucking out the stalls and begging small change of gentlemen as they left their horses. The captain tossed the child sixpence, for he'd kept his word – the horse had been a godsend. 'Give her a carrot,' he said.

Out on the street, he bought a chicken pie to eat on his way and headed for the river – it was the quickest route back to Greenwich. The bustle of London felt like coming home, the bright streets familiar with their colourful costermongers and shops with displays on the pavement. He had even begun to recognise the look of the cutpurses that loitered in the shadows, round corners and in doorways. London was a city of layers – bright, brash buildings cheek by jowl with the shifting, shifty alleyways behind. Two separate cities. A fellow could disappear into either easily, or rise above them, he supposed. The streets were busy and filthy and alive, the sweepers hard at work, clearing a path for the carriages that were heading to Leicester Fields for an afternoon's entertainment.

It would take half an hour to Greenwich – London's size was part of the city's glamour, but that also meant constant journeying. As he stepped off the rowing boat at the dock, the captain smiled. Clarkson had been as efficient as ever and, ahead of him, the *Bittersweet* was looking shipshape – she'd had a lick of paint and Henderson could smell fresh wood shavings as he strode up the gangplank. Richard was still aboard.

'You'll stay to dinner?' he offered as he passed the boy.

288

'Yes, sir. Thank you.'

With a wave, the captain headed for the cabin to prepare. There was plenty to do.

★

The Calcotts were good company and the carriage ride passed swiftly. Coming back to London was like visiting an old friend, and in the pleasant weather Maria kept the window down and watched one house after another slide by. As they pulled up outside Thomas's sister's residence in Piccadilly, Maria saw Georgiana skulking in the long upstairs window. She waved, but the girl's face disappeared as she dodged out of sight. It was poor manners to gawp at a carriage.

Augustus handed her down. This felt, Maria realised, like being ten again and arriving with nothing in the big city, climbing down from a strange carriage unsure what to expect. Lady Dundas's home was only two streets away.

'Shall I?' Augustus gestured towards the door.

'Thank you.'

It was strange, Maria thought. She'd rather face the earthquake in Chile again than this. And yet there would be a scandal if this wasn't the first place she came to. If she didn't lodge here while she was in town. Her bereavement tied her to Thomas's family.

The door opened and Georgiana's butler, Billingham, peered into the street.

'Mrs Graham,' he said. 'Miss Graham will be delighted. Please come in.'

Maria waved at Miss Calcott, still ensconced in the carriage. The girl smiled and nodded.

'I have seen you safely delivered.' Augustus bowed. 'You must call on us at your convenience.'

'I will, Mr Calcott.'

Everything must seem formal where it might be overheard.

Clutching her manuscripts, Maria stepped into the hallway. The air felt cool. Billingham closed the front door and dodged ahead, leading the way upstairs past familiar furniture and family portraits. Georgiana was in the drawing room, bent over a small tapestry, apparently engaged in working it. She was dressed in a mourning gown.

'Maria.' She rose as if she was surprised. 'You have come home.' Her eyes took in her sister-in-law's travelling dress and her lips tightened. 'You look well.'

Maria smiled. If the house had not changed, Georgiana certainly had. She was thinner and older than when the Grahams had quit London a little over three years before. Her eyes were steely and small lines had appeared at their fringes. Georgiana was a good five years younger than Maria, but a stranger would have guessed she was the widow.

'Now you are here, you must see the plaque I raised to dear Thomas.' The girl took a little gulp of air as if she might burst into tears.

'He would be so glad,' Maria said.

It was a lie. Probably not the last she'd have to voice. Georgiana patted the chair next to her and a puff of violet scent rose from her sleeve. Thomas had joined the service when he was ten. He had been home scarcely more than two months at a time since.

'You must tell me everything,' she said. 'How he died.'

'It was as I wrote to you,' Maria parried, sitting a little further away than Georgiana might have liked.

Tears welled in the girl's eyes. Maria looked down. The tapestry Georgiana was working was a representation of the *Doris*, Thomas's ship. *Dear heaven, she has thought of nothing else,* she realised.

'We must be brave,' Maria managed to get out. 'It is what Thomas would have wanted.'

'I'm so very glad you're back.' Georgiana gave a half-smile. 'It is so much more fitting, Maria. London is where you belong. And who would want to marry me with a sister-in-law who is gallivanting halfway round the world, expressing her opinions in print?'

Maria ignored the implication. A man would have to be half mad or desperate to marry Georgiana – she had not had an offer since she was seventeen. That was a good fifteen years ago and had been scotched, from memory, at Lady Dundas's insistence. No man, it seemed, would ever be good enough for Georgiana Graham or, at least, none yet had proved himself so.

Georgiana clasped her hands. 'We should have a memorial service now you're here. Another one.'

Maria sighed. Downstairs, she heard the door and movement in the hallway. Billingham appeared. 'Lady Dundas,' he announced.

News travelled at speed in Piccadilly. Georgiana had probably sent a message the moment she spotted the carriage.

If Georgiana looked older than when Maria last left London then the reverse was true of Maria's aunt. In her mid-fifties, Catherine Dundas could pass for ten years younger. She spent, Maria knew, a good deal of time and effort effecting this illusion. Her speedy arrival belied her immaculate dress. In a swathe of carefully worked silk, she swept into the room.

'Maria,' she said. 'You may kiss me.'

Maria did so obediently. Lady Dundas sank onto the sofa. 'Tea, Georgiana,' she said. 'Would you, Billingham?' Her eyes fell to the pile of papers that Maria had deposited on the side table. 'Oh really,' she said with distaste. 'Another of your books. At least you have come home. Now we must make plans.'

'Plans?'

'Yes. For your future.'

Maria sat back. 'There really is no need. I shall leave for Brazil, Aunt Catherine, in three weeks. I have found a position.'

'You have no need of a position,' Lady Dundas spat. 'The Dundas trust will provide for you and, as Thomas's wife, the navy will furnish you a pension. Really, Maria.'

'The position I have secured is at the royal court,' Maria continued smoothly. 'I shouldn't like to defy Her Royal Highness the Empress of Brazil.'

It was a trump card. Lady Dundas raised an eyebrow. This was a tricky decision. Naturally, Her Ladyship was staunchly in favour of the monarchy – indeed, she stood in awe of all royal institutions – but the lady to whom her niece had just referred was undeniably foreign.

'I am to be the governess to Princess Maria da Gloria, you see. I shall live in the palace in Rio de Janeiro.'

Georgiana looked even closer to bursting into tears.

'We shall see about that.' Lady Dundas turned her attention to the tray that Billingham was delivering to the low table at one side. She poured a cup of China tea for each of them, adding both milk and sugar.

'Who was the gentleman who delivered you?' Georgiana asked as she took a sip.

Lady Dundas sat straighter, were it possible. 'A gentleman?'

'Augustus Calcott. I am a friend of his sister.' Maria smiled. 'There was some difficulty with the stage from Bristol. Mr Calcott kindly came to our aid.'

'Oh really,' Lady Dundas sneered. 'At least I know the Calcotts. One never has any idea what you will come up with next, Maria.' She downed the cup of tea and, looking around, rose to her feet. 'Well, I imagine you want to unpack and settle in. I wanted to lay eyes on you, that is all. I shall send a carriage tomorrow. You must come for luncheon.'

'I shall have to deliver my manuscripts to Mr Murray, but I can call on him very early. And also, Aunt Catherine, I need to replace my luggage. There was a dreadful misadventure and the sum of my possessions is as you see – on my person. I have lost everything. Perhaps you might help me to pick out some items? Her Imperial Highness has opened a line of credit for me at her London bank.'

'My dear.' This raised a smile on the old lady's thin lips. Her whole life she had relished the occasion of shopping. Still, she couldn't quite bring herself to endow approval on her wayward niece. 'You see what trouble you get into with all this nonsense of yours. Nonetheless, if you wish, you shall come at eleven o'clock. We shall go to Covent Garden.'

The clock struck two as Lady Dundas swept out of the room. Maria could not tell if the old lady was happy – perhaps placated was the most she could hope for.

Georgiana laid down her cup and saucer. 'I wish I had been there. On board. When Thomas passed,' she said sadly.

'Shall I tell you how it happened?' Maria offered.

This was going to be trying, but it seemed it must be borne. These women, after all, were her family.

293

'Oh yes.' Georgiana sounded rapturous. 'Please. Tell me everything. I miss him so dreadfully, you see.'

*

There was no Old Street Bridge or, at least, none that spanned the Thames marked on the map at the captain's disposal, which was only a tattered affair showing St Paul's and the surrounding area. It was also a good forty years out of date, for it had belonged to his father. With a sigh, Henderson stowed it beside the ship's log. He was trying to bring a deal to the table, but he had no idea of the table's location. There was nothing for it but to ask directions, and the captain preferred to do that in advance. Knowing what he was heading into would be an advantage.

The captain stepped smartly off the *Bittersweet* and flagged down a skiff touting for business along the bank. The boatman brought his craft close to the water's edge and held up a hand to help the captain on board. 'Where are you headed, sir?'

Henderson held his ground. 'I want to go to Old Street Bridge. Do you know where that is?'

'Old Street Bridge.' The boatman pulled his hand over a grizzled chin. 'Yes, sir,' the man lied. When the gentleman did not step aboard, he gave directions to Old Street to encourage him. 'It's on the other bank. I'd let you off at St Magnus, guvnor, St Magnus the Martyr.'

'And from St Magnus?' Henderson asked.

'You need to walk past Eastcheap and across the Cornhill. Old Street's a mile north off the quay. No further. It won't take more'n half an hour – with luck, twenty minutes. The fare's a shilling. The tide is with us this time of day. That's a blessing.'

Henderson declined.

'All right.' The boatman bargained. 'I'll do it for less'n a shilling. How about ten pennies?'

'Do you know what's on the bridge? What's it like over there?'

The pilot paused and spat a gob of tobacco that landed on the green water like a parcel of pus. He didn't want to dally longer without assuring his fare.

'You want to go over or not?' the fellow asked, his voice cheery but his eyes dead. Ten pennies was his best offer – he wouldn't make the journey for less.

'Not till later,' Henderson admitted.

'Well, you'll see what it's like then, won't you?' The man moved to punt away.

Henderson caught the side of the little boat and held it to the shore.

'Woah,' the boatman shrieked.

'I said, what's it like over there?' Henderson repeated calmly. 'It's a civil question.'

'I wouldn't say a gentleman such as yourself might like it. But there's those as would reckon they was after the adventure. Gaming. Women. Men too,' the man spat viciously. 'Whatever your vice, they got it over on Old Street if you got the money.'

'Is the bridge famous for anything?'

'Nah,' the man said. 'There ain't no bridge. It's just Old Street, you stupid cuss. And all it's famous for is docks and scum, like most places east of London. Now let go my boat.' He raised his oar to demonstrate he'd strike. At the dock, a rope punctuated by tiny birds jumped to life and a little flock took off.

Henderson turned back towards the *Bittersweet*. Strange – Will had been adamant about the bridge. Wherever it was, surely it must be on or near Old Street, and by the boatman's description, there was no question of the area being home to a respectable business at night. He decided that taking the goods with him was out of the question unless he brought a posse of men to act as guards. Even then, the skeleton crew left on board were not the ones he'd pick for such an outing. He'd deal with the investors alone and arrange to pay the money separately.

Will had made the Old Street Bridge sound cosy – the inn was the Rose and the ale was excellent. The investors were benevolent. But then, the boy had been at home among all manner of roughness, Henderson now realised. In fact, Simmons liked it rough – after all, he'd bought a girl on the sand dunes, not that he could be blamed for that or, indeed, what happened next. Still, look at how handy he'd been with a blade. Simmons fell into place now the captain had seen England, or at least parts of it – the layer of the city that was tucked like a filthy sheet below the clean stucco frontages of Covent Garden and Piccadilly. Will had been savvy and now Henderson must be savvy too. He'd expected that dealing with smugglers would be the easy thing, but it appeared not. It crossed the captain's mind that perhaps it was best that he hadn't shaved this morning before he left White Waltham – it would give him a rougher appearance – and he'd need to change out of his smart clothes too. By the sounds of it, a man would fare better along Old Street if he was ready for anything. He'd count the gemstones, weigh the gold and calculate his margins on the cacao beans. He required the figures at his disposal so he could make a quick decision. No doubt the merchants at the Old Street Bridge would drive a hard bargain.

★

As the captain emerged on deck later that evening, the light was fading and the men had lamps already hoisted. Intending to cross the river that night after dark, he had changed. The crew fell to their evening occupations to the strain of a melancholy squeezebox playing a Welsh shanty below decks. Beer had been brought aboard and the deck was humming with contentment as the crew filled their tankards and pursued idle chatter, board games and the following of a tune. Two were whittling blocks of cherrywood, slumped against the mizzen, alternating their attention between knives and tankards to a steady rhythm. It was easy to blend into the background. Henderson had searched out a grubby suit of clothes that ensured an overall impression of disarray. He had the air of a down-at-heel ruffian who was not to be tangled with.

Beyond him, Richard stared down the wharf, taking the evening air and watching, curious about the hostelries that spilled noisily onto the beaten earth. People were eating dinner outside rather than in their miserable hovels, and fast-looking gentlemen – perhaps naval officers – were slumming it, on the lookout for women. The boy appeared able to ignore the whores, which, in a young man of his age, was impressive. The doxies promenaded along the quay, which meant business tonight on the high street must be quiet. They called up, making eyes over their pale shoulders. Richard passively regarded the trade. Strangely, Henderson noted, the lad looked like he belonged on the deck of the *Bittersweet*.

Tripping up the gangplank, the cabin boy arrived laden with the evening's provisions. In one hand he carried a bag of bread and pears, bought from the jumble of stalls on the high street. In his other hand he grasped a pewter dish, fetched from the inn. The boy made for the galley, from where, despite the absence of Big Al Thatcher, all meals were served.

'That's your dinner, gentlemen,' the mate announced. 'I ordered pottage. With the cook away . . .'

Fry followed Henderson to the cabin, ready to eat at the long polished table. The captain's dowdy shirt and jacket made him look out of place as the cabin boy, far cleaner and tidier, poured the wine. The boy commented on the captain's scruffy appearance. 'Some get-up.'

'I need to blend in tonight.' Henderson shrugged off the observation. 'I've a deal to make.'

'It's lamb, I reckon,' the cabin boy announced, placing the tureen on the table with a long serving spoon.

Henderson lifted the lid. There were carrots and potatoes in a dull-looking sauce. He stirred. There was some kind of homecoming about food here. Some kind of extraordinary comfort. 'Can't see much lamb,' he said. 'Though it smells good.'

Fry poured some Rhenish from the decanter. Henderson spooned them a portion each and then paused. He wanted to voice his curiosity. It was the boy's first time in the big city. There was a bond forming, the terms of it as yet unclear. 'You're still aboard, Richard,' he announced. 'And you're drinking wine.'

Fry's eyes flashed. 'I hoped you wouldn't mind,' he said. 'I know you have business in London, sir. I hoped you might let me help you with it.'

'Still trying out another life, then?'

'Aren't you?'

The captain looked down at his costume. 'Look, son, this venture may be dangerous.' He shook his head. 'I'll have enough to do looking after myself. Hitting a target is different from the real thing.'

Fry pulled back his shoulders. The captain had heard of his prowess. 'You might need someone to cover your back.' The boy took the knife from his pocket. He fiddled with the blade, folding and unfolding it with one hand and then perusing the edge. The food lay cooling. 'It's late for you to be making deals is it not? After business hours?'

Henderson shrugged. 'Your father . . .' he started. 'I can't imagine he'd be glad of you—'

'He wouldn't approve,' Fry agreed. 'Not of the Rhenish either. Did your father approve of your wildness when you were my age?'

Henderson sighed. 'Yes. He encouraged me.'

'Well, that's commendable,' the boy managed to get out. 'A fellow ought to be given a chance to try new things. You can't spend your whole life green.' He raised his cup. 'I promise that I'll be useful, Captain Henderson, if you can find a use for me. All I'm asking is a chance to discover things for myself.'

Henderson shook his head. 'You'll stick out a mile on the other side of the river.'

Fry considered this. Then his face lit up. 'No. Wait.' He sprang to his feet, dashing out of the door.

He returned with a bundle of clothes that emanated a musty odour. As he unrolled them, the captain coughed.

'My brother disguises himself to find out what other

chocolate makers are up to,' he said. 'And I use these. To go places I wouldn't otherwise be welcome.'

As understanding dawned, Henderson whooped. He was glad, in a way, to see gentlemen were not of a muchness and the rules governing them were bent with more regularity than might be the expected. Maria believed the world so black and white, or at least that's how it seemed. Perhaps he might yet find his way. Fry's complexities were interesting.

'Well, one of you is sharp enough – at least your brother stands to make some money.'

'I win at cards. And dice.'

'Put it on.' The captain sat back in his chair. 'Show me.'

Fry scrambled into the clothes. 'I tousle my hair and spread it with goose fat. I don't want to appear too clean. Look, I want to stay awhile, Captain,' the boy pleaded. 'I want to learn. We Frys work hard, sir, and here is something intriguing here. Let me come with you. Please.'

'You'd be a liability, son.' Henderson's voice was flat. 'The trade takes a while to pick up and, believe me, the learning isn't pleasant – not for a gentleman. The *Bittersweet*'s got no business here, besides. Clarkson will refit and resupply. He's probably seen to most of it by now. There's nothing much to learn on board.'

'But you'll reload, surely?' Fry asked. 'You'll take on cargo to ferry back to Brazil. Fine silk from India perhaps? Tea from China? Or British goods – engines, pottery, bales of wool?'

Henderson paused. He might reload. He had not thought of it. 'There are some people in London with whom I'm looking to make a deal,' he admitted. 'Investors.'

'Well, perhaps I could help you there.'

300

The captain considered. Will had said something about meeting the investors at night, because it was then that the gentlemen tended their business. That hadn't seemed strange at the time, though now, having seen London, no respectable business operated after dark. The city at night was a pleasure ground of carriages, dinner, dancing and music for anyone from the upper echelons. The dark sky shrouded London's guilty delights – illicit women, certainly – and the shops closed early; the bonds were all done and only the hostelries and their ilk had an open door come nightfall. The truth was that the investors were clearly smugglers, though both Sam and Will had called them gentlemen. Henderson already felt the sting of superiority – he wasn't a smuggler any more. He took a deep breath and decided to confide in the lad.

'I want to make a deal with the investors who paid for the beans I sold your father. I know nothing about them except that the area where they reside is of the lowest and they undertake most of their trade at night. They are smugglers.'

Fry's eyes shone. 'Smugglers?' he breathed.

'I had a partner in the cargo I sold to your father. He died in Brazil, and tonight we must return his effects and come to an agreement with the fellows who backed him. They are my investors only by inheritance.'

'Who are they?'

'I understand them to be gentlemen, but we have never met and the more I hear about the Old Street Bridge, from where they do business, the less I like it. I do not mind whether they are gentlemen or not. I am accustomed to dealing with difficult characters. But, generally, I restrict myself to the reasonable.'

Richard stood straight. 'It'll be dangerous,' he said.

'I shouldn't take you, by rights, but if you're really set on doing something, Richard, perhaps you might be able to help me find them? Or, like you said, you could watch my back, and for that, you're right, this get-up of yours might be handy.'

Fry's eyes shone. 'I tell you what. I'll cut a deal with you, Captain Henderson. Let me come now, where it interests me, and I'll help you in the real bear pit. I know why you're really in London – it's Mrs Graham, isn't it?

Henderson felt himself blush. He cursed silently. Maria had said he had been too obvious about his feelings. That Fry knew at all was evidence of that.

The boy continued. 'I can help. I know how to woo a lady. I have been tutored in etiquette, deportment and elocution. My education has been finished and finished and finished. Show me the ins and outs of your world and I'll show you mine. I want to see what it's like – a deal that doesn't take place in the offices of my family's manufactory.'

The captain considered. He could understand Fry's curiosity – admire it, even. Maybe the boy could offer some assistance in the matter of developing a modicum of respectability. 'I am considering penning a treatise,' he admitted.

'On what subject?'

'Cacao.'

Fry nodded. 'It must, of course, be illustrated.'

Henderson had not considered this, but now he'd said it, he realised the boy was right, and this presented a challenge. 'Yes.' He leaned back. 'I had not thought.'

'Perhaps Mrs Graham might know someone who could help,' Richard suggested. 'Illustration is often a matter accomplished with the help of ladies. Or do you think she might wish to illustrate the work herself?'

Henderson could not bring himself to explain that Mrs

302

Graham would be deeply offended by the notion. She was, after all, an accomplished author, far more competent than he was ever likely to be. Quite apart from the fact that he was, at present, hardly her favourite. 'I had hoped that John Murray might publish me,' he continued. 'I called on him yesterday evening, but we did not discuss it. There were other matters to attend.'

Richard smiled. The captain's exploits continued steeped in intrigue. 'Matters such as the matters tonight?'

Henderson did not reply immediately.

'Mrs Graham was offended,' he said after a pause. 'I used her name to gain admittance. I had hoped to find her at Murray's address.'

Richard looked quizzically at the captain. 'Might I enquire, sir, are you and Mrs Graham betrothed?'

Henderson shook his head. 'I have been refused,' he admitted. 'She is now, of course, very angry.'

For the first time on board the *Bittersweet*, Richard Fry looked shocked. The men might target practise their deadly skills, the captain might treat with smugglers, but this was beyond the pale.

'You hoped to find her at the residence of a male acquaintance and yet you are not . . .' he stuttered.

'I know. I know.' Henderson brushed away the words. 'In Brazil it is different. In fact, I expect, nowhere else in the world must a fellow behave in such a circumspect manner, but here, I understand, such niceties are important. I never finished my education and I am ignorant of the way it works. I am mired in guilt, Richard. I realise that my behaviour has been . . .'

'Mrs Graham must be . . .' The boy's voice trailed.

'I understand,' the captain repeated, this time with finality.

'I see it now – women so afraid of meeting a man's eye that they walk instead with their eyes on heaven. I mistook what was possible. She's absolutely right. I should not have presumed.'

There was no question he could do with Richard's help in the drawing rooms to come, if not on the streets this evening.

'You are sure you can endure the East End, whatever its horrors? We don't know what we're going to.'

'I'd like to.' Fry's eyes were bright.

Henderson considered. It might do the boy good. 'All right,' the captain said. 'I'll take your deal.'

Fry grinned. He held out his hand and Henderson shook it.

The pottage proved an elegant dish, smooth, silky and rich. The captain murmured as he dipped a piece of bread into the gravy. Fry scooped a spoonful of carrot and beans. The atmosphere felt relaxed – almost confessional.

'And after, will you run more cacao?' the boy asked.

The way Richard discussed business had an air of the Fry factory, where all men were decent and most likely knew each other socially. Henderson considered momentarily.

'To sell to your father?'

The boy nodded.

'I don't know. I've decided to stay in London for at least some of my time. I like it here.'

'Father would definitely buy more,' Richard observed. 'Especially the wild beans. He was exceptionally excited by them. You should consider it.'

Henderson had thought of it already and had decided that the quality was the thing. He might, he reasoned, come to some arrangement with Thys. If he ran two shipments a year from the Bagdorf estates, he would have a reasonable income as prices stood now in England – certainly enough for a house in Soho and the maintenance of a wife. Having seen John Murray's residence, however, he wondered if he should perhaps be more ambitious. Ideas were stirring that might result in crystal chandeliers of greater proportion, libraries of leather-bound volumes, and exotic handwoven carpets in extraordinary Oriental hues. Why not?

'It is a great shame the journey is so long,' he commented.

Fry smiled. 'The beans wouldn't be worth as much if we could farm them in Sussex.'

Henderson shrugged. 'The Atlantic crossing must be reckoned a matter of six weeks at a minimum. I have an excellent source in Trinidad, but I should much prefer to run something closer if I can.'

'Spices from Maroc, perhaps? Ivory from Africa?'

'My expertise is with cacao.'

The men finished their meal.

'What time do we venture out?' Fry wiped his mouth.

The captain stood up. Outside, the sun had sunk and the water was a glossy stream of jet, far more attractive than the murky daytime river.

'It is time,' he said.

The sailor at the gangplank gave a salute that looked odd from the shore, as the two shabby fellows (surely more accustomed to a life of receiving orders rather than giving them) left the vessel. Clarkson smiled from the shadows in a pall of tobacco smoke. 'Blow me,' he whispered. 'The lad got what he wanted.'

Within three hundred yards of the *Bittersweet*, the sound of church bells punctuated the night air. Ten bells. The moon sidled up an alleyway, but Henderson and Fry kept to the shadows. A woman stepped between them. She smelled of sweat and syrup. 'Time for a bit of fun, lads? I'll do both of you together. Come on.'

The men strode faster.

'You'll get a rowing boat further up,' Henderson said. 'Take it to St Magnus the Martyr. On a quiet night like tonight, and in your get-up, you'll be able to haggle a good price. Here are two sixpences, but you'll only need one. Engage the sorriest-looking boatman and say you're on an errand. I'll follow.'

Fry's eyes gleamed. 'Yes, captain.' He grinned. This sort of thing was exactly what he hoped for. 'I won't let you down.'

24

Piccadilly

Maria sat on Murray's canary-yellow sofa and took in the drawing room. Dinner had been magnificent, but she could scarcely recall the exact menu, for the fare that most delighted her was the company. There were ten at the table, most of them men and Murray authors. The conversation sparkled. History. Literature. Science. Art. Having been sequestered from society for almost three years, Maria had catching up to do.

'Only in London. Only in Piccadilly. Only in Albemarle Street. At number 50,' she teased Murray. 'Only here.' This last most contentedly.

Murray motioned the footman to serve Mrs Graham another liqueur as she moved a flat ochre pillow so it settled in the small of her back. 'You must not become too comfortable, my dear,' he said. 'We rely on your travels for news of the world. Your manuscripts inform us.'

Maria looked suddenly serious. She had sent the manuscripts to Murray that afternoon. 'Have you read them already?'

'I have read Chile.' Murray's blue eyes focussed. 'In one sitting and at speed. I sent it to press. The Brazilian journal will follow tomorrow. They shan't be on the shelves before you depart, Maria, but I shall send your notices.'

When Murray's invitation to dinner had arrived, Georgiana had declined it.

'I shall attend,' Maria had said stolidly.

Georgiana scowled. 'Well,' she said, 'at least this afternoon you will visit the monument I raised to Thomas's memory.'

Maria acquiesced.

The tree was in the grounds of the local church, only a few streets away. The minister of the parish had greeted the ladies enthusiastically. The Grahams and the Dundases were his most generous parishioners.

'And what ghastly stories can we expect?' Miss Graham had enquired on the carriage ride home. 'What revelations of a woman travelling alone? What was in those horrid papers you sent round to Albemarle Street?'

When Maria told her, Georgiana looked pained.

'Oh really,' she sighed. 'You tar us all with this brush of yours. I do wish I had been clever enough to snag an admiral or a duke. I don't suppose now there will be any hope.'

'Will neither a captain nor an earl suffice?' Maria posited, and then cursed herself for being so uncharitable. She reminded herself she ought to pity her sister-in-law. 'Why don't you join me and dine at Murray's tonight?' she offered. 'You can change your mind.'

'Don't be silly.' Georgiana snapped shut her fan. 'Why on earth would I want to dine there?'

Still, the conversation had left Maria nervous about what she might have produced. No one had read the manuscripts. She craved Murray's opinion. If the books garnered poor notices, they would cement her family's low opinion of her.

That said, Lord Dundas, her late uncle, had insisted the notices of her previous publications, both good and bad, were removed from his morning paper before the footman brought it, to save him the distress of having to read them.

'And the manuscripts are not too personal? I worried that I had put in too much of myself,' she enquired nervously, shifting on the publisher's sofa, eager for his reply.

Murray's eyes sparkled. 'Not at all. They will stand with the work of gentlemen, my dear, if that is what concerns you. In many regards, my view is that the touch of a personal detail engages any intelligent reader. Tell me, how long will you be in London?'

A vision of the grand but cold hallway of Georgiana's mansion entered Maria's mind's eye. 'Not much longer,' she admitted.

'I shall endeavour to have proofs produced as soon as I can. Perhaps we shall manage that at least before you go,' Murray said kindly. 'Not bound, I'm afraid, but I will send them on. And your charge in Brazil?'

'The Princess Royal,' she confirmed. 'She is only three – though she will be four, I expect, by the time I return. I shall be taken up by my teaching duties, which will not be onerous for the time being. I hope I might pen you something while I am in Rio – a memoir of court life. Its practices and customs.'

Murray's lips curled upwards. Such an enterprise would surely please the ladies as well as the gentlemen. So many books appealed to only one gender, but this was of more general interest and books with a wider audience sold more copies. 'What a good idea,' he said. 'You must see how you get along.'

Maria sighed contentedly and sipped a tiny glass of liqueur.

The cut crystal caught the candlelight and magnified it. Already there was part of her that knew she would miss this side of London. After a difficult afternoon, this felt like home again.

'Who was that fellow?' Murray enquired, cutting into her thoughts.

'Which fellow?' Maria put down the thin-stemmed crystal, with a cold shadow stealing over her.

'The fellow who dropped you at Georgiana Graham's? I was not snooping, but my dear, I was so glad to have news of your arrival. My man said he was a tall chap with a pale-green cravat.'

Mrs Graham breathed more easily. In London people noticed everything, but, that being the case, she was glad Murray hadn't brought up Henderson's unseemly intrusion the other day. She was not entirely sure she would be able to remain bluff about her feelings.

'Augustus Calcott?' She smiled. 'He is a painter – rather a good painter, I think. I have seen some of his work in oils. His sister and I are acquainted.'

'We must encourage him to have you sit.' Murray smiled. 'A portrait would be a good idea.'

Maria's eyes danced. 'I've asked him about the matter of a miniature. I should like to have one of my father, though the likeness will be difficult to capture. I have described Papa from memory and Augustus has kindly said he will make it a priority in his studio, so I can take it with me when I return to South America.'

'A miniature?' Murray had never known Maria to care for such fripperies. 'I understood you did not like much in the way of paraphernalia.'

Maria's colour heightened. In the past she had, indeed,

disdained these items – comforts of home. She had always thought them vanity. And yet, it would seem it was time to own a portrait – only a small one. Maria had not forgotten her lonely walk in Bristol and the feeling of being groundless. Augustus had arranged a visit to his sister's dressmaker, where a feast of satins was promised, including evening gloves and pumps and maybe even a headdress.

'A bronze and gold extravaganza,' Calcott had mused, as they rode towards London. 'You will suit regal tones,' he smiled. 'A bright ostrich feather in your hair, most certainly. And dark-brown velvet for the gown. The colour of chocolate, perhaps.'

Maria had blushed. Calcott could not have known that, to her, chocolate meant Henderson.

In any case, that afternoon, while listening endlessly to Georgiana eulogise her brother, Mrs Graham had resolved if not to change her ways, then to slightly alter them. She was to be based in Rio at court, so it was entirely fitting that she should enhance her wardrobe and carry mementos. She was considering an entire box of books, only for herself, and perhaps two evening outfits – the brown that Calcott suggested and another in blue to replace the dress that had been stolen.

'Oh yes. Blue,' Augustus had pronounced. 'It is a tremendous colour.'

'You seem . . .' Murray hesitated, searching for the right way to express the changes in Maria Graham that had occurred, as far as he was aware, in the hot-blooded Latin American provinces. Seldom did words elude him. They wouldn't dare. But tonight he could not quite put his finger on it. 'Well, well, in any case, I'm glad that you're happy.' London's most prominent publisher finished his drink.

311

Maria smiled and demonstrated a previously undiscovered touch of the Mona Lisa. She missed Thomas, of course, but she had discovered that life and London went on.

The publisher motioned for his glass to be topped up. Murray wondered if this Augustus Calcott fellow was of more than merely artistic interest. Now, that would be something. Imagine if Maria Graham were to fall in love again. How affirming. He must speak to his wife on the matter and look into Mr Calcott's portfolio.

'Once I'm settled,' Maria said, 'I must go to the Royal Society. I have some samples and sketches to give them.'

'I shall see to it that the first copies of your editions are sent to Sir Humphry,' Murray promised. 'Might you not consider talking at a meeting? I could look into it. Such an undertaking would fire interest in your new publications. If you have time.'

Maria, however, appeared distracted. She was gazing into the grate. 'Do you think that I suit chocolate?' she said quietly.

At once, her attention was miles away. Thousands of miles. Aboard a ship. Love was a long river, and difficult to outrun. The last nights, lodged at the inn, she had dreamed of James Henderson, but in her gruesome imaginings he was dead, like Thomas and her father. She had raised a brass plaque to Henderson's memory in the church on the main square in Natal. It was too strange. The dreams hovered on the fringes of her mind. They pulled her in between bursts of real life. They seeped between the cracks in her anger.

'Chocolate? Whatever do you mean?' Murray laughed.

'Oh. Nothing.' Maria's attention dropped back into his lap like a ball. 'Now,' she said, 'we were going to further discuss these experiments Basil Hall has been undertaking, were we not? Where is that astronomy fellow, Mr Pond?' Maria looked around. 'Mr Pond.' She accosted a small but well-dressed man with a receding hairline. 'You must come and assist us in our scientific endeavours. Have you read about these experiments of Mr Hall's? Please, do join us.'

Pond peered.

'Mrs Graham,' he said, 'I have heard that in Chile you measured an earthquake. That is of far more interest than Basil's calculations. Pray, tell me how you did so.'

Murray cut in. 'Mrs Graham shall be presenting that at the Society, I'm sure, sir.'

Maria glowed. She widened her shoulders. 'Now, now,' she said, 'we can surely trust Mr Pond. His expertise in difficult calculations will be invaluable. And, I admit, it was tricky.'

Murray gave way. Pond sat by the fire, his cuffs wilting in the heat as a lavender haze rose from his linen. Maria leaned in conspiratorially. She must put James Henderson out of her mind. 'I'll tell you, Mr Pond, on condition that you will help me confirm the calculation.'

Pond nodded and Maria waited only an instant, just until the men were not quite sure that she was going to speak. Murray looked as if he might tip out of his seat.

'Well, here is how I did it . . .' she said.

★

Richard Fry's first thought when he pitched up at St Magnus the Martyr was that he ought to procure a lamp for the captain. Between the darkness and the thin fog curling off the water, he could scarcely make out the church's facade, which was a grubby shade of white punctuated by round windows. The black rounds looked like empty sockets from which unnatural eyes had been prised. Was it fashioned to look like a ship, he wondered. Perhaps.

Fry's instinct was to investigate the lie of the land, but he had been instructed to wait for Henderson, so instead he hovered, observing that the area was more down at heel than he had expected. The smell took him by surprise. The river wound round the dock like putrid entrails spilling from a corpse. The rank air was riddled with damp, the low, mildewed buildings rotting and all of them, save the church, as good as invisible against the dingy backdrop of the East End. The slim byways, however, were busy. Black shadows flitted from one alleyway to another, creeping like silent, jagged ghouls.

The place felt indescribably heavy, like a huge black manacle locked onto the side of the river. It came to him that poverty in Bristol was lighter. There might be no easy way out of the slums, but back home at least a fellow had some kind of chance. Here, the residents did not appear to live in these black houses as much as infest them. It certainly did not feel like the location of a business run by gentlemen. Richard shuddered. Henderson would not be far behind, the boy assured himself as he squatted against the wall.

In five minutes, three gentlemen came off a skiff with a lamp strung high. They disembarked with a sense of extraordinary purpose and strode into the darkness, two of them holding fierce-looking cudgels. Thin shadows lying in wait moved in a wave towards such a promising shore. Fry noticed four boys, feral and stalking like predatory birds, ready at any moment to pounce. As the gentlemen rounded a corner, the flock followed. Fry was glad of his disguise, and that he did not have a light after all.

When Henderson finally arrived, there were no ripples in

the night. The captain disembarked so quickly, the boat hardly stopped. Henderson's rough edges played to his advantage here. With his two-day beard he cut the air of a fellow who, though not from this place, could fight his way through it. As the captain slipped towards St Magnus the Martyr, the skiff's lantern receded along the river. Henderson touched Fry's arm but made no other sign that he recognised him. The boy fell into step, a few paces behind.

Straight up towards Eastgate, hostelries poured their customers onto the highway on a tide of purl and gin. Here was the raucous laughter of women interspersed with the cries of youngsters left to fend for themselves. The men slowed their pace. Two girls begged a ha'penny from the captain, who waved them off with an appropriate hint of leering cruelty. An eager-eyed child fell in beside Fry.

'Wotcha following him for?' he hissed. 'He got somefink?'

'Get off or I'll bash ya,' Fry promised, in his best low-life drawl.

'I was only askin',' the boy exclaimed.

A flash of Fry's eyes worked as well as drawing a blade, and the boy backed away.

Unlike Regent Street and Oxford Street, there were no names carved into the walls by which to navigate – it was unlikely that many of the locals could read. Still, it put a stranger at a grave disadvantage. As the men crept away from the river, the air felt cleaner – or, Fry pondered, perhaps he was getting used to the stench. At least his stomach was no longer turning.

At Old Street, the captain stopped. The road was wide, with buildings on both sides, most of them shrouded in darkness as the rash of public houses dissipated, the night's ominous smooth blackness reinstated. The low moon made it feel like a mythical highway. There wasn't anyone around and it was easy to imagine that Old Street might go for miles, leading out of the city, an endless road to God knows where. Henderson squinted as a solitary figure approached from the opposite direction.

'Is this Old Street, friend?' the captain asked.

'Aye. Who're you looking for?'

The captain pulled his pipe from his pocket, establishing himself as a fellow who was ready for a civil chat. He needed information, and the best way to get it was to dally. The man was dirty in appearance but not the poorest wretch they'd encountered, nor the drunkest. He probably worked on the docks.

'I don't know who I'm after,' Henderson admitted. 'Is Mallow Street close by?'

The fellow laughed, and the sound scooped into the thick night air, removing something. 'Up there, stranger.' He pointed to the left, openly staring at the captain like a hungry dog. 'Keep going.'

'You heard of the Rose?'

'Yeah.' The man's voice was deceptively bluff. 'It's the ticket.'

'I was told to have a drink there by a friend.'

'You do everything your friends say, you'll land yourself in trouble.'

Fry crept against the wall, out of the moonlight's reach. Henderson's manner was relaxed as he stood smoking. By the light of the moon, the captain's skin looked almost translucent. He might, Fry supposed, be taken for a ghost. The fellow in the street had no such concerns. His interest was in this world, not the next, and he had clearly surmised that Henderson might be of value. 'Who did you say you're looking for?' he asked again.

316

'I don't know. Friend of a friend. An importer. I don't have a name.'

'Round here? That sort got offices at the dockside, mate. Your luck's out, I reckon.'

Henderson laid the silence on the ground between them, like a tomcat offering a mouse.

'If you're looking to import something, perhaps I can help you,' the man tried.

'How might that be?'

'I know some people. Who's this friend of yours, if you don't mind me asking?'

'Will Simmons.'

'Never heard of him.'

If the man didn't recognise Will's name, there was probably no more information to be had. The captain turned, but the fellow wasn't done. He caught the sleeve of Henderson's coat, determined not to let an opportunity turn into Mallow Street and be lost for ever. 'And what is it you're after?'

Fry reached for his knife.

'A word with a friend of a friend is all.' The statement had finality. Henderson jolted back his arm and continued to walk away.

The man had scented money, though, and if he couldn't have it by guile, he'd have it by force. As he got ready to punch, the captain spotted the movement out of the corner of his eye. He dodged the first blow and managed to lay his hand on his knife, but the stranger was fast. The fellow moved in with a sharp kick to the shins.

'Give me your cash. You got money, ain't you?' The man's voice was aggressive, but there was an undertone of anguish. 'You gotta have a wad if you're looking for an importer. At night as well.'

317

'I've got nothing but a blade for you, friend, and I'll slip it in your skin if you don't stand off.' The captain's voice was flat as a stone and just as hard.

The stranger didn't move until suddenly he seemed to make a decision, his desperation outweighing his good sense as he lunged.

Without hesitation, the captain struck out like a piston, stabbing the stranger in the shoulder with such force that his blade stuck and he ended up simply abandoning it in the other man's flesh. Like an enraged bull, the man bellowed, fired up by the injury.

'Fuck you,' he spat and, ignoring the wound, he started beating Henderson with his uninjured fist.

Henderson dodged, punching twice and catching the fellow on the nose so that blood spurted down his shirt, but the man didn't give up. He landed two solid punches to Henderson's chest, which winded him.

'Shit,' Fry breathed from the shadows, thinking this had gone far enough as he fumbled in his pocket and withdrew the flick knife. This was just what he'd been practicing on deck. He opened the blade and ran forward, a shadow scuttling out of the blackness.

Henderson tried to wave him off, but Fry launched the knife just as he had been shown on the *Bittersweet*. It hit its true mark on the man's torso. The fellow stopped in his tracks. Grasping his chest, he fell to his knees, blood seeping between his fingers.

'There.' Fry grinned, taking the opportunity to stroll into the scene of the affray and retrieve his blade, as if this was only target practice. But the injured man was not done. As the boy turned to form a nonchalant comment, the stranger

318

lashed out a final time. He had a weapon concealed – a razor. In pain, he drew it from his boot. The captain grabbed Fry and pulled him out of the way. If the man had hit true, the deadly edge would have caught the boy in the base of his spine.

'I'll not lose another one,' Henderson said under his breath. 'You stay out of the way unless I call on you, do you hear? You're on captain's orders.'

Fry nodded. His fingers were quivering, but he managed to snatch the razor from the fellow's hand and stow it in his pocket. The man fell back, an untidy pool of blood blackening the dirt. The stranger's eyes were no longer hard, or even anguished. He simply stared between long, slow blinks, waiting to see if they would finish him.

'Mallow Street,' Henderson directed, peering off to the left.

Fry kept his eyes on the wounded man. 'Is it kinder . . .?' He was shaken now.

Henderson shook his head. 'It's murder, is what it is. At least this way he stands a chance.' He pulled the boy further up the street towards the turn-off, leaving the man to his fate.

Mallow Street was not so wide as the highway. While Old Street was bathed in cold white moonlight, the Rose cast a glow over the bottom of the road. The indistinguishable babble of voices that emanated from the inn was comforting. Fry glanced over his shoulder, but the dying dock worker was out of sight. His stomach fluttered. He had been in fights before, but he'd never killed anyone. Men were hanged for murder. He felt sick. Henderson stared at the boy, checking his fitness for duty. Putting one hand solidly on Fry's shoulder, he motioned him towards a shuttered window.

'Wait here,' the captain said.

'I won't let you down.' Richard's voice was a dim echo of when he'd sworn on the *Bittersweet* – a blustering youth in search of adventure.

'I'll sort you out when I get back.' Henderson opened the door.

This wasn't working out quite the way either of them had expected.

★

Inside, the Rose was well kept. In addition to purl and porter, there were casks of brandy stacked alongside the inevitable bottles of cheap gin, which was the drink of choice in this locality. Henderson was glad his entrance did not cause much notice. Later, if the stranger died in the street, there would be questions. Only one or two of the men had turned, and more of the women. One girl, he noticed, was sewing her tattered hem by the fire. In the candlelight he checked his coat for the spatter of blood, but he appeared to have got away without marking himself with evidence of the affray. With luck, he'd be able to do his business quickly and get Fry back to the ship. Henderson turned his attention to the matter in hand. A handy-looking fellow, no more than forty, and wearing a bright-yellow waistcoat, was filling jugs of purl behind the bar as he smoked a cheroot.

He nodded. 'Stranger, what can I get you?'

Henderson indicated that a tankard of purl would be welcome. He handed over a coin and took a deep draught. 'I'm looking for a friend of Will Simmons,' he enquired.

The man removed the cheroot from his lips and contemplated this statement. 'Will Simmons? Nah. Not 'eard of 'im,' he pronounced. 'Does he live round here?'

Henderson shook his head. 'He had business here, though.'

From further behind the bar, a middle-aged woman emerged. She was sporting a flash of grainy rouge that gave the appearance of a rash across her cheeks and she wore a grubby peach ribbon in her hair. Both the hair and the ribbon looked as if they belonged to someone younger. 'What's he after, Titus?' she asked.

'Fellow called Simmons.'

The woman looked Henderson up and down. 'Mr Simmons,' she greeted him.

The captain smiled. 'No. I'm a friend of Will Simmons. He had business hereabouts and I was hoping to get in touch with his associates. There are some gentlemen, I believe.'

Titus stood a little straighter – only a fraction, so that from a distance no one might notice, but Henderson saw it. Meanwhile, the grubby woman stared with a look of such intensity that she took on the bearing of a waxwork.

'If you were aware of such gentlemen, I'm sure they'd be delighted to hear the news I bring.' The captain popped his empty tankard onto the bar. 'A fine pint.'

'Betty and I keep a cellar beyond the means of the immediate area.' Titus nodded. 'Another?'

Henderson shook his head. 'I've got to find Simmons's friends. If you can't help, then I'd best be on my way. Simmons recommended your beer. He was right.'

The woman unfroze suddenly. She motioned the captain to approach, her nose wrinkling and twitching like a rabbit's. There appeared to have been a lot of news arriving for the gentlemen of late and she itched to find out at least some of it. 'I might know who you're looking for. To what does your news pertain, sir?'

Henderson betrayed not a flicker. 'If you know where they are, then you had best tell me.' His voice was flat.

Titus looked as if he might lay down his cheroot and take action, for even a hint of a threat was a hint too much, but Mrs Wylie touched his arm lightly. She was, after all, intruding on the gentlemen's privacy, or at least trying to. Someone would tell her what was going on – sometime soon. In the meantime, the appearance of the stranger was interesting. He did not look like a fellow for the cards and in no way fine enough to sit at table with Hayward, Fisher and Grant, who were dapper to a man and well above her sort. She leaned in further.

'You'll find 'em directly across,' she whispered. 'It's the black door – the shuttered house. On the first floor. Right over the road.'

25

Old Street

The Bridge Club had summoned Sam Pearson that evening. They were insistent that, having had a full day to consider the matter of their stolen cargo, they would be ready to issue instructions. Sam had arrived early or, rather, he thought with a smile, right on time. When he spotted the captain and the boy on Old Street, he fell in behind. This encounter was an unexpected bonus. From the shelter of a broken-down doorway, he calmly watched the men disarm the fellow who tried to rob them and slash his sides. Once they had moved on, Sam followed, still limping from his encounter with Mrs Wylie the day before. He passed the injured man without stopping as the poor creature tried to haul himself towards Shoreditch, where, no doubt, if he could make it, help would be at hand. He was, Sam noticed, making decent headway, and by the time Pearson slipped silently into Mallow Street, he'd moved a block, which was a promising sign for his prospects.

Pearson's attention, however, was directed to more important and pressing business. He cut as close as he could into the shadows as he rounded the corner and was just in time to witness the figure of Fry crouching in the indent of the

323

window and the captain disappearing into the Rose. The very sight of Henderson made Pearson's blood boil. He had a hot temper at the best of times, but he had been humiliated on the *Bittersweet* so the fires burnt with a particular ferocity. He couldn't go into the Bridge Club without the captain's lookout seeing him, so by default the boy became his target. By Sam's reckoning, the lad was carrying two weapons and, of course, there were his fists, but then not only was he shorter than Pearson, being just at the age before the final filling out of manhood added girth to height, but also Sam had the advantage of surprise. The boy's gaze was fixed upon the Rose. Sam smiled. Silently, he cut back the way he'd come, sneaking around the alleyway to the rear and creeping behind Fry, not so much a shadow as a levitating spirit, hovering over the manure-strewn side street. In one stealthy swoop, he kicked the boy over with his good leg and, not without skill, held him down by the throat. In this position, he frisked Fry efficiently, removing both the flick knife and the stolen razor from his keeping. Fry squirmed but could not call out, for Pearson had him pinned by his windpipe so that the street's stinking sewer oozed against his ear. Richard's eyes flashed. It was only natural for him to assume that this attack was related to the skirmish on Old Street only minutes before, but then in the East End, it was becoming apparent that you could be mugged twice in five minutes, easy.

Pearson leaned down. 'Stay quiet and I won't kill you.'

With this ominous warning, Pearson hauled the boy to his feet. He pinned Fry's arms behind his back with a vice-like efficiency that could only come from experience. Next, he guided the fellow in the direction of his choice. It was an effective technique and in less than a minute Pearson had bundled Fry across the road, through the door of the Bridge Club and up the wooden stairs.

In the club room, the gentlemen were still and silent. The only movement came from the trickle of smoke that trailed upwards from Hayward's and Grant's cigars.

'What have we here?' Hayward enquired.

'He's here,' Sam said. 'The captain of the *Bittersweet*, the blaggard. He's over the road in the Rose.'

'And this scrap?' Grant enquired.

'Was covering his back.' Pearson couldn't help grinning. 'I thought it best to bring him up.'

Fry squirmed unconvincingly and a glob of mud fell from his face onto the bare floorboards. It was difficult to say what this place was, but at least these were gentlemen. In Richard's experience, the presence of gentlemen meant he was safe. He considered telling them that Henderson had come about their investment, at which point, forgetting his appearance, he anticipated the offer of a drink.

The boy was on the point of speaking when instead he became intrigued as the men in the room shifted, wordlessly. Grant laid his hand on his ebony cane and moved his palm backwards and forwards over its fox-shaped head. Fisher rose slowly and adjusted his cravat, while Hayward stayed absolutely still. Mesmerising, the men's movements had the air of a tableau being set. It flashed through Richard's mind that this wasn't how the Frys did business. These gentlemen were unlike any others he'd encountered. It was as if they were playing out some kind of deadly ballet. Then, in a flash, the scene switched from something half-familiar to a nightmare. In a swift, unanticipated motion, Grant brought down his cane across the boy's legs.

The sound that came from his mouth was not one Richard Fry recognised. For a second, it seemed the whole world disappeared and only a strangled, desperate yell hung in the air. When his eyes were able to focus once more, the boy struggled for breath. He thought he might vomit. His legs felt as if they had been shattered, and his brain raced with fear and confusion. In Bristol, when he'd fought, it was with boys his own size in the main and no one had weapons to speak of. Fisher stepped forward, taking charge of the interrogation that was to follow the assault.

'What's your name?' he asked calmly.

'Richard,' Fry managed to get out, the word so guttural it clanked against his teeth.

Fisher took his time. He appeared to be enjoying himself immensely. 'Well then, Dick, enlighten us. What is it you're doing here?'

'The captain's come to arrange payment. You're Will Simmons's investors? He's come to return Simmons's effects and pay your share.' This time, the words came in a loose babble, difficult to discern, like filthy water flowing too fast. He ended with a sigh, the last of the air leaving his lungs. His legs stung like fury. There was no reason for this, he thought, only badness.

The men stayed stock-still. Grant's eyes were like embers. He raised the cane once more with such ferocity that a loose lock of his greying hair swung sharply like a horse's tail at a gallop as he brought down the ebony. This time he cut Fry's leg higher and Richard didn't make a sound. After a tiny pause that he would later put down to shock, the tender skin on his thighs burst into tiny flowers of pain. The boy could feel the bruises forming – dark weals blooming in a line the colour of

326

blackcurrant jelly. His legs quivered. *If I can feel them shake, can they truly be smashed?* he thought. It was clearly some kind of misunderstanding. He tried to speak, but he was winded and only let out a sigh like a candle guttering.

'Good of your captain to pitch up,' Fisher commented viciously. 'But it's not up to him to make a deal. Not now.'

'He paid the excise,' Grant hissed under his breath. 'He hijacked our goods, damn him, and paid the bloody excise.'

Fry was scrambling and out of his depth. It was difficult to think. Henderson had said the men were smugglers, but that made no sense. Who the hell tried to avoid excise? Surely not gentlemen such as these? What was it these men actually wanted? And was there any way he could warn Henderson what was waiting for him? There was something grotesque about the room. Something awful.

Fry had come up with no answers as a heavy knock sounded on the door to the street. The men shifted, refocussing. It occurred to him that they were acting together like a pack of wolves – no, not that, for wolves would surely not be so malicious. These fellows were enjoying their cruelty.

The knock was repeated more urgently a second time and this was somehow gratifying to them. Fisher, Hayward and Grant shifted. Sam Pearson let go of Richard's arms and Fry slumped, his injuries causing his legs to give way beneath him. His thighs ached, but his fear of what might happen next dampened the pain. At Grant's nod, Pearson answered the door as Richard's eyes darted between the three gentlemen, desperate to foresee what would transpire. He'd given his word to watch the captain's back.

'It's not often we have a visitor who knocks,' Fisher drawled.

When the gentlemen laughed, it was a murmur. Fry's eyes

bounced from one to another. Should he attempt to disarm Grant, who, as far as he could make out, was the most violent and certainly most heavily armed? He made a move, trying to grab the man's stick before Henderson could enter. It was a brave attempt, but Grant, who had appeared not to be looking, was too quick. With a vicious thrashing motion, the ebony came down on Fry's shoulder, and this time the blow came from the end with the silver ornament. It knocked the boy over and his ribs cracked sharply on the floor. The pain seared through the thin material of his jacket and Grant loomed above him, ready to continue the beating if he moved.

'Well, he's spirited, I suppose,' Fisher commented as Fry let out a sob and the hammering of feet on the staircase introduced the captain.

Henderson entered ahead of Pearson and, noting Richard's prone body, nodded brusquely. If he realised Richard was hurt, he showed no sign of it.

'Ah, there you are,' he said, seemingly relaxed. 'Gentlemen.' He lowered his body into a half bow. 'I'm glad to have tracked you down.'

Grant moved back towards the group, but Hayward was the one who spoke.

'Captain,' he said. 'If you had not come to find us, we surely would have visited you. Where in damnation are our goods, sir?'

Grant was leaning heavily on his stick and Fisher appeared to be toying with some kind of cord – not a rope, but a red-silk affair. Henderson noticed it and wondered if it was a rosary. In the low light, it was difficult to tell.

'Disposed of at profit, gentlemen,' he said smoothly.

'All of our cargo?'

Henderson smirked. 'Well, the beans, which are, if I'm not mistaken, not quite everything. Do you wish to discuss this matter in company?' He nodded towards Pearson and the boy.

Hayward stepped up. 'You are correct. Mr Pearson was not aware of the other matter. He is loyal, however, if not fully informed. And the boy is your concern. Damn you, sir. First, you abscond with our cargo and then—'

Henderson cut in. 'Not at all. I delivered your cargo, or, rather, Will Simmons's cargo, for I had no real detail of your involvement until I arrived. From Cornwall on, I had your representative aboard in the person of Mr Pearson. He chose to leave the ship, thus depriving me of any natural means to find you. Luckily Will had mentioned Mallow Street and enquiries have proved . . . well . . . fruitful. Here I am and not too shabby. I've been in London two days. I think I have found you promptly.'

Pearson started to object to this version of events, but Grant moved his stick to forbid it and motioned the captain to continue.

'I cannot see, gentlemen, what else you might have expected me to do. In fact, I think you owe me thanks. Not every captain, upon the death of the man who had filled his hold, might go to the lengths I am going to now to make good on a deal he made thousands of miles away with the representative of people he had never met. Oh, and here are Will Simmons's effects.' He drew a packet out of his pocket. 'I'll not rob a dead man.'

The Bridge Club ignored this gesture.

'You paid the duty,' Grant said baldly. 'The boy cannot have left you that much in the dark.'

The others agreed, but Henderson remained bluff. 'I did,

sir. I paid it. As captain, that was my decision. And I am here to arrange repayment of your investment as a result.'

'And then there's the other matter,' Hayward pointed out.

'The gemstones and the gold. Yes, there's that too.'

Fisher poured himself a drink. 'We are expecting a good return,' he said.

Henderson smiled. He motioned for permission to sit. He kept one hand in his pocket, on the handle of his knife.

'To business, then? Well, I expect a commission for brokering the deal Will made when he bought the beans. He and I agreed that, and I have already taken it. And then there is the matter of transporting and disposing of your goods at profit, for which there will be a fee. I also expect to be paid for my honesty, gentlemen. And I expect to be paid well, because I have done a good job.'

'But the duty,' Grant repeated.

Henderson did not deny what Grant said, but he did ignore it. 'In the matter of your rather singular block of chocolate, I have removed the gemstones and gold and I expect a fee in respect of delivery. A generous fee, in fact. Most men would have gone off with that kind of prize.'

Hayward sat down. Henderson's tone was impressive and his argument was not without merit. He may have been misguided in paying excise, but he seemed a decent enough rogue. He was here, after all. 'Captain, why did you pay the excise?' he enquired. 'Did Will not explain the nature of our operation?'

Sam cut in. 'I explained. I told him.'

Grant silenced the boy with a look that cut through the low light like a flaming arrow.

Henderson shrugged. 'It's a captain's job to make decisions.

To tell the truth, I didn't deem it worth the risk. As it turns out, I made a profit the other way. I can't tell, of course, if I might have made more by smuggling the beans, but I expect the quality of the goods helped to sell them. It was not, by my thinking, an unreasonable act to keep the law.'

Hayward considered this. 'Well, well. We were looking for a reliable captain, were we not?' he murmured.

'We need a fellow who can do things our way,' Grant said.

'He could do it our way,' Hayward concluded. 'Couldn't you, Captain? I'd say you've run goods in your time. Look – he's calm as a tame ferret. Seems reliable enough. You'd run for us, wouldn't you? It's our intention to regularise this route.'

Pearson looked furious. He shuffled his feet.

'I'm here to conclude this deal, gentlemen.' Henderson smiled. 'That is all.'

'We pay very well, Captain,' Fisher said.

'We insist.' Hayward leaned across the table. 'You'll see.'

'No,' Henderson said. 'It's a kind offer. Thank you. But I have plans.'

'The Old Street Bridge Club does not brook disagreement on such matters,' Grant replied flatly. 'In the matter of this first shipment, we may have been mistaken, Captain.' Here he paused to stare at Pearson. 'We may not have realised that under the right orders you could be a considerable asset. In the past we have had problems with unreliable fellows. Captains in particular.'

'Indeed,' Hayward concurred. 'We may require your services. With your help we can bring in goods regularly from the Brazils. We'll put you on a generous percentage. It will be worth your while.'

Fisher hovered at Henderson's back. He was fondling the red-silk cord.

'Gentlemen.' Henderson smiled. 'I'm here to conclude the arrangement I made with Will, and after that I have my own plans. I'm sorry.'

He had not quite finished speaking when Fisher made his move, slipping the garrotte around the captain's throat and pulling it tightly enough to bring Henderson to his feet, struggling against the cord. His eyes bright with panic, Henderson desperately tried to paw away the rope. 'Do it, Fisher,' Hayward encouraged.

Fry moved to help, but Sam held him down. He kicked Sam's injured leg and Pearson retaliated by punching hard, landing a stinging blow on Fry's bruised shoulder. As the boys scrapped, the Old Street Bridge Club remained focussed on Henderson, Fisher still tightening the red cord around the captain's neck. The captain's face was flushed, his eyes hard as he tried to figure out how to get out of the deadly lock. Hayward appeared mildly troubled, while Grant peered with an eager expression, his blue eyes bright. They did not anticipate what happened next. Struggling for breath, the captain moved unexpectedly. Instead of jerking against the cord, he jerked his whole lower body with it. In doing so, the captain kicked the chair from beneath him, catching Fisher an agonising blow to the groin and toppling him. The red cord fell. Grant moved in with his cane raised, but the captain was too quick. Instantly, he landed a knockout blow on the bridge of the Scotsman's nose. Grant went over on top of Fisher. By the time Hayward presented himself, Henderson was armed with Grant's cane, a potentially lethal weapon, and swung the silver head hard. The gentlemen became subdued.

'Stop,' Henderson shouted to the boys over his shoulder. 'Are you all right, son?'

Fry extracted himself from Pearson's grip and shakily hauled himself to safety. 'Aye, sir,' he said.

'Look.' Fisher rose to his feet, objecting, as if trying to make a point in court. He had, earlier in his career, trained at the bar.

Henderson wasn't listening. He fetched a full swipe, landing Fisher in the stomach and knocking him over. 'Jesus. I came here to make a deal. I hesitate to call you gentlemen. You are lucky I don't smash your skull, sir, and finish you. I'm not sure who you are used to dealing with, but, whoever they are, I pity them.'

Grant's eyes opened as he came into consciousness. There was a dark bruise purpling his face and his expression was hard. He looked an entirely different man, no trace of the Charming Charlie he generally presented to the world. He stared at Hayward as if accusing him of not controlling the situation adequately.

'There are three of us,' he said bluntly.

Pearson stepped forward, as if to announce himself a fourth, and Henderson raised the cane a little higher. He had the measure of them now. They were used to dealing with men who were not able to defend themselves against the will of their betters. They were bullies who used their station to get whatever they wanted. Henderson, however, had spotted a crack. Between this world and the West End, there was a weak spot.

'Here are the terms I will offer, gentlemen. I have returned Will Simmons's effects and I will double his stake money. In addition, I will keep half the jewels. You can take my offer or leave it. I might have come to more accommodating terms, but you just tried to bloody throttle me, so damn you.'

'We triple our money,' Grant growled. 'That was the deal with Simmons and it's the deal with you.'

'Not when you try to murder the bearer of the goods. You're lucky I'm offering you anything.' Henderson turned to the only member of the Old Street Bridge Club he could name. 'Mr Fisher?'

Fisher nodded cursorily, casting a sideways glance at Hayward, who had named him.

'I shall conclude this deal with you then, sir, at your residence. Where shall I call?'

Fisher objected vigorously. 'We conduct our business here.' His voice was raised.

Henderson smirked. His instinct was good. This East End hideaway was a secret. 'If you think I shall come here again then you take me for a bigger fool than I have ever been in my life.'

'You cannot dictate—' Hayward started.

'I can, sir, and I do. Should you object to these terms and seek me out, you will forfeit your share and get nothing. If you pursue me after I have made payment, I shall look in more detail into why you conduct your business here and where in polite society each of you resides. And then I shall see to it that polite society hears of your place of business on Mallow Street. That's the three of you, do you hear? I'll track you down and name you, I swear it.'

'Blackmail,' Hayward blustered. 'Damn blackmail.'

Henderson delivered a devastating grin. 'Just be glad I don't throttle you with that cord, sir. I am sorely tempted. Better blackmail, I'll warrant, than that. I don't know who you are accustomed to dealing with, but, frankly, you take an unfair advantage and I shall have some of it back. Have you a wife, sir? And will she relish hearing about this little exchange? Well, behave honourably and it will never come out. You will still make a profit, gentlemen. Those are my terms.'

Grant made to rise in furious objection, but he got no further than his knees before Henderson fetched him a blow to the side of the head that sent him reeling.

'I mean it,' the captain said firmly. 'I'll dishonour you so soundly no house in London will receive you or your families.'

Fisher and Hayward stayed stock-still and in shock. No one had ever threatened the Old Street Bridge Club.

'Can you walk?' the captain asked Fry.

The boy nodded. His shoulder was in agony and he'd be limping, but he could move to get away.

'Go down,' Henderson instructed him. 'Wait by the door.'

As they listened to Richard's unsteady footsteps descending, Henderson leaned in. 'If you follow us, I'll hound you. Do you hear me? It's a good deal less trouble just to let go of the likes of me. And if you attack either Richard or me tonight, you'll never get your money. As it is, you'll have your share and the jewels inside a couple of days, Mr Fisher. Think on that and be done with us.'

He could not tell as he backed out of the door if the gentlemen concurred. Respectability was an excellent weapon, he thought. In a way, Maria had taught him that – she was a skilled practitioner at using etiquette to her advantage. As the captain swung out of the front door, he barrelled Richard down the nearest alleyway, away from any vestige of light. The route back to the water was a decent walk and the boy was badly injured. Back on the highway, they'd be vulnerable.

335

At the other end of what was effectively a dark tunnel, there was a carriage on the main road running east to west, with two coachmen bundled in dark greatcoats. Henderson peered around the corner. One of the footmen was holding a whip and the other a cosh. The carriage was of good quality, but old. A lamp hung on a long hook and a family crest adorned the door – white and red plumage around a helmet. It had to belong to the gentlemen, he realised, or at least one of them. Henderson squinted to read the name in the low light. Hayward. Fisher and Hayward. Now he had two of them. One of the footmen stamped his feet. It was getting cold. Henderson sneaked back up the alley just as it began to drizzle. Fry was leaning against the wall.

'Here.' He put out his arm so that Richard could lean on it. In the darkness, the boy's heart was hammering – he could feel it. Tiny drops of cold rain sat on Richard's hair like a dusting of icing sugar. 'Are you all right?'

Fry nodded.

'Well.' The captain motioned. 'We can't go past the coach, and the highway feels too obvious, for I would hate to meet our friends again – either the gentlemen or the chap you knifed earlier. So we need to go this way.' He jerked his head into the darkness beyond the inn. 'It's a case of cutting down the backstreets. For a while at least.'

Walking the whole way was out of the question. Between the dangerous pockets lay long, empty roads. The river was safer, but as late as this and as far out it might be difficult to find a boatman. Still, they had to try.

From above, in the direction of the Bridge Club, a muffled cry rang out – a desperate yelp of pain. Without saying a word, they both knew it was Sam Pearson.

'At least he'll keep them busy,' the captain murmured as he led the boy down Mallow Street.

Across the road, a lonely voice singing an army song emanated from the Rose. Richard thought of his family home, the house silent on a night such as this, everyone safe in bed, their sheets starched, a glass of milk on the night stand.

'We'll get to the river and pick up a skiff.' Henderson took the boy's arm, setting the pace. As the two of them rounded the corner, a church to the east sounded its bell. Henderson's face was shrouded in darkness, but Fry caught his expression as they passed through a slice of moonlight. He was focussed, absolutely intent on escape.

26

Covent Garden

Maria settled into a leather chair in the bookshop. She felt almost disloyal, but it was interesting to peruse the titles of, well, other publishers. Murray's list, while undoubtedly the most impressive, was not comprehensive. Blackwood's, for example, brought out some wonderful books. She told herself that Murray wouldn't mind – and, to calm herself, she breathed in deeply. The smell of an English bookshop was a comfort – dense paper, the occasional waft of vellum and the thick scent of leather bindings, the gold tooling glowing from the shelves like a magical totem. There was no library in Georgiana's mansion. Maria had discovered a few old books laid about the drawing room, nothing more. As yet, she had not had an opportunity to peruse them, for Georgiana talked endlessly about her brother, enquiring about the details of his death again and again. Maria was finding it troublesome to explain Thomas's short illness over and over. It was distressing and, when it came to it, there was a limited amount she could say. His temperature had soared. She had nursed him, but he had died.

In addition, Georgiana had not housed Maria in the room to

338

which she and Thomas had been accustomed, with a married bed, nor indeed in either of the other two vacant guest rooms with an aspect. Instead, she billeted her widowed sister-in-law in dreary smaller accommodation to the rear of the house with a slim single bedstead and a thin fireplace. Maria had no real objection, except to wonder quite what Georgiana meant by it. Such a placement could not possibly be good for the spirits. In the event, she was glad to have business to see to and, hence, reason to go out. When Maria announced she must write some notes and make some appointments, Georgiana treated it as if each letter on the page were the harbinger of a suspicious assignation. When Maria lingered on the sofa after breakfast, she suggested an outing to church.

'How very French,' she said when Maria proposed a trip to the Dulwich Gallery instead. In her grief, the girl had come to despise not only pleasure, but anything normal. 'Don't you cry for him, Maria? I haven't seen you weep,' she said.

Maria thought of those days in Chile, breathless and panting when, finally alone she not only cried, but howled. She had been unable to stand, instead sinking to the floor. It had felt animal. Visceral.

Georgiana dabbed her eyes with a handkerchief. 'I cry every day, you see,' she sniffed. 'In his memory.'

Maria had almost been relieved when the time had come to join Lady Dundas and set out for Covent Garden to replace her baggage.

Now, her aunt having refused to join her in a trip to a bookshop, Maria lingered in the calm of Mr Thin's excellent establishment off Regent Street. There, she relished the quiet and the calm. Quite apart from a decent pile of books, she also set aside a stack of the *Edinburgh Review* to save for the outward voyage. Her sojourn at her sister-in-law's house at least made her appreciate the places that she was welcome.

'Always a pleasure, Mrs Graham.' Mr Thin encouraged his illustrious customer. 'But I need not attempt to sell you anything. You know your mind. Catching up, eh?'

Mr Thin stocked back copies of all the reviews for just this purpose. Anyone who'd been abroad might easily miss a year or two of scientific debate and politics. Thin's was stocked to have a fellow up to speed in no time, or a lady, for that matter.

'Such interesting articles,' he promised, leaving her to leaf through some diverting scientific journals that she had already agreed to purchase.

Maria reached down with her gloved hand and pulled a copy from the bottom of the satisfyingly large pile. There must be a dozen quite besides the political news-sheets. After she had read and reread them, the magazines would be set upon by the English community in Rio when she landed. News of home always came at a premium. Beside her, a skeleton clock on the mantel whirred and a gentleman checking his pocket watch glanced at the books she had set aside, reading the titles. His eyes lingered on the unusual lady who had requested such august tomes.

'Can I help you, sir?' Mr Thin enquired, emerging from the storeroom.

'I'm only checking the time, Mr Thin,' the gentleman admitted, doffing his hat with one hand as he clicked closed the watch's face. 'It's a wonderful timepiece.'

This was exactly why Mr Thin had invested in the clock. The hypnotic movement of the spokes and spirals drew customers. Gentlemen arrived to set their pocket watches by

Thin's timepiece every week, and each week some of them were tempted by the latest releases or volumes of seasonal interest, which the wily old bookseller placed within perusing distance, as if at random.

Mrs Graham looked up from the *Edinburgh Review*.

'I'll take all of these as well.' She patted a pile to her right. 'A Latin primer and also a Greek, please. In addition, I'm looking for material relating to botanical gardens – tropical ones. Her Imperial Highness is establishing such a concern in Rio de Janeiro and requires detailed information. Succulents are of special interest. And orchids.'

Mr Thin's mind whirred, as if powered by a mechanism not dissimilar to the one on his mantelpiece. The old bookseller was a living compendium of every book that had ever passed through his highly experienced hands. This was one of the reasons Maria loved to visit his tightly packed emporium. She adored Mr Thin fetching her things. Occasionally she had found a gem of a book as a result of the old man's encyclo-paedic knowledge.

'Ah yes,' he said. 'I have something. It may, however, be somewhat out of date. I'll bring it up and you can decide if it's suitable. There is a directory of orchids with some wonderful illustrations too. I'll search that out as well, shall I?'

He turned to go down to the cellar. The gentleman, having set his watch, and finding this state of affairs beyond him, nodded politely and left. Maria flexed her ankles and flicked through the *Review*. In moments of quiet reflection such as these, James Henderson came to mind. She remained furious with him, and cross at herself that she continued to consider him. But there it was. Any small matter might provoke it – an article about plantation ownership or a costermonger offering

341

leg of lamb as she passed by with her aunt. She had not expected it.

Dragging her attention back to the present, she watched the women striding past Mr Thin's carefully stacked windows and, far more diverting than dusty books, finding themselves attracted like magnets towards the milliner's next door.

When Thin comes up, I'll ask him for another two, she decided. *A history of Spain and something on the subject of zoology.* With the Empress's letter to the bank, there was no need to stint – new books were a necessity to do the job well, rather than a luxury, and the princess may still be young, but whatever Maria purchased would be useful in time. Mrs Graham settled into her seat and opened the *Review* again, endeavouring to find something that had no connection whatever with Captain James Henderson.

She was deeply engrossed in an article on Mr Plunket's speech about Ireland when the shop door opened and a girl swept in. She was wearing a dress the colour of bluebells. Maria caught a flash of it out of the corner of her eye. The colour was lovely – hadn't Augustus said something complimentary about blue? This induced her to glance further, upwards, in the direction of the girl's face. Then that face smiled, the girl touched Maria's glove and Mrs Graham jumped to her feet. It was unjust, but she could not help cursing Captain Henderson. Here he was, called to mind again.

'Why, Miss Bagdorf,' she exclaimed.

There was no forgetting Miss Bagdorf's elegant features, which were framed in such an expression of delight that it was clear that, for her, the memory of dinner at the plantation in Trinidad was unencumbered by dubiety. She was clearly delighted to see Maria.

'Mrs Graham.' Ramona clasped Maria's hand firmly, the clean scent of blackberries swirling around her. 'How nice to run into you.'

In London, Ramona's Danish accent seemed more pronounced than it had been in the tropics, but she was just as beautiful. Perhaps more so, Maria mused. The girl had retained something of the vivid equatorial air. Against the backdrop of shelf upon shelf of leather covers, she stood like a vision, her blonde curls cascading beneath the brim of her hat like a golden exotic plant.

'I had no idea you would be in Europe so soon, my dear,' Maria said.

'Neither did I.' Ramona grinned. 'But the letter Thys and I were waiting for when you came to visit arrived only two days after you departed. I made my journey on the *Jury* shortly after you left. I was sorry that it didn't fit together more seamlessly. It would have been preferable to travel with you aboard the *Bittersweet*, of course.'

Maria blushed. Ramona's presence would have changed matters. The inappropriate intimacy of dinner on deck, for a start. 'So you packed quickly in the end.' She remembered the girl's nonchalance at Henderson' suggestion for her speedy departure.

Ramona shrugged. 'I had help, of course, but packing is so tiresome, don't you agree? I occasionally wonder how many dresses one can actually wear,' she whispered, as if the matter were a scandal. 'All the fuss. Dressing and dressing and dressing endlessly. As my aunt is an invalid, however, I am spared the greater part of such troubles. We do not eat a formal dinner and I expect I shall venture out rarely.'

The door opened once more and a footman entered,

343

carrying two boxes parcelled with brown paper and string.

'Dawson is looking after me,' Ramona smiled brightly. 'Aunt Birgette insisted that I should not go shopping by myself. So English.'

Dawson bowed and Maria noticed the stern expression on the man's face. The girl's life here must be quite different after riding across the tropical hills discovering native customs, being the mistress of her own home, and given her head by a tolerant brother. She felt a flood of sympathy for Ramona's confinement.

'Are you enjoying yourself?' she enquired.

'Oh, London is one of my favourite cities,' Ramona declared, quite unperturbed. 'If I end up living in Europe, I hope I live here.'

'Do you still ride in the park, Miss Bagdorf? I recall you said you'd learned while you were here as a child.'

Ramona shook her head. 'No. Not this trip. Not yet.'

'And how is your aunt's health?' Maria enquired.

'She isn't at all well,' the girl admitted. 'That is why I have come today. I hoped to find something to read to her. She can sit up in bed but would find it difficult to manage a book on her own. It will take her some time to recover, I expect. It's always nice to listen to a story while you're convalescing, don't you think? Like being a child again.'

Mr Thin emerged from the cellar, a pile of books in his arms. He balanced them on the side table beside Mrs Graham's chair.

Ramona addressed him. 'Sir, I'm looking for a novel. Something diverting for an elderly relative. Mrs Graham, can you think of something for us?'

'Scott,' Maria suggested. 'Does Sir Walter have something new?'

'*Kenilworth*.' Mr Thin perused a shelf and slid out a volume. 'It's an historical romance of the Tudors.'

Maria said nothing and was careful not to show her distaste. She'd have chosen poetry.

'*Kenilworth* will be perfect,' Ramona enthused, quite oblivious. 'We shall both love it. History is so diverting and a romance will restore my aunt's spirits. I hope it ends happily.'

'Or *Maid Marian* by Mr Thomas Love Peacock, perhaps.' Mr Thin produced another book as if from nowhere, like a magician. 'It has proved very popular with many of the ladies and if you like a history . . .'

'I shall take them both.' Ramona smiled gratefully. 'We shall have plenty of time for reading and I expect a story that my aunt hasn't heard will be most beneficial. How helpful. Thank you.'

The footman moved forward to pick up the books, which Mr Thin was already parcelling.

'What are you buying, Mrs Graham?' Ramona enquired.

'Books for my charge, mostly. I shall be a governess when I return to the Brazilian court. We require a library of educational publications for the Princess Royal.'

Ramona smiled warmly. She picked up the Latin primer and turned it over in her palm. 'How lovely to be around children.' She paused momentarily. 'And how is Captain Henderson?'

The words escaped as if casually. Maria found herself perturbed by the question – not so much the enquiry itself as the stab of jealousy that accompanied it. Why must every mention of Henderson provoke a physical response? No good could come of it.

'I have scarcely seen the captain,' she said. 'We docked at

Bristol and since then I have only bumped into him once. We do not move in the same circles.' After this last, she found she was biting her lip. She did not want to sound uppity.

'But he is in London?'

'As far as I am aware.'

'I hoped I might see him again.' Ramona shrugged. 'What a shame. I'm glad I ran into you. I'm staying on Fitzhardinge Street. Number 12,' she volunteered. 'It's close to Manchester Square. Please call if you're in the neighbourhood. I can't offer fried chicken and chilli, but the cook is from Scotland and makes excellent scones.'

Maria nodded. She was transfixed by Ramona's eyes – the girl had extraordinarily long lashes. 'I will,' she said. 'How kind. I hope your aunt is feeling better soon.'

Later, with a large box of books set to be packed for travel and dispatched to her lodgings at Georgiana's townhouse, and a conversation during which Mr Thin said he would be delighted to stock Maria's new editions and would stack copies in pride of place, close to the clock, Maria emerged onto the sunny street. At the corner, she engaged a cab to the village of Kensington Gravel Pits, and her next appointment. Taking her seat, she snatched a glance at a man in a dark frock coat and, for a ridiculous moment, her heart skipped a beat. The spectre of Henderson was everywhere. She must get on.

The cab was dusty and worn. Dirt ingrained the threadbare seats, but Georgiana hadn't offered the use of a carriage and Maria had not liked to ask. Mrs Graham had not anticipated that London would be so trying. Still, as long as it was road-worthy, the state of the cab hardly mattered. The journey west was pleasant. The light on the road became dappled with shadow as the busy London streets shifted to a more suburban state lined with trees. Maria opened the grimy window and considered the frontages on some of the newer crescents. She tried to focus on the horticulture instead of thinking of him, but it was impossible. Miss Bagdorf, she realised, would make the captain an excellent match, and he, she. And there it was again, that tearing feeling, uneasy, in her belly. Maria cursed quietly. Amid the buying of the books and the interest in her work, it was difficult to accept that she was stuck or that things were difficult. *I can't have my cake and eat it,* she told herself. In short order she'd be leaving for Rio, and yet, there was no denying it, if she couldn't have Captain Henderson, she preferred that no one else would.

Maria had never been illogical in her life. She prided herself on her ability to think things through and abide by what she knew to be right. But now it seemed she was cursed by an inability to play by the rules. At the gates of Hyde Park, she suddenly realised she was set to arrive at Miss Calcott's empty-handed. She tapped the roof of the cab to stop the driver and descended into the sunshine to buy a posy of lavender and rosebuds. Beyond the railings, children played with their nannies on the grass. Prams were wheeled in the open air. A little boy was being taught to ride a pony by his family's groom. She felt at a great remove from such comfortable domesticity – miles away from Murray's townhouse and all its cultured conversation. Beyond, Miss Bagdorf's lodgings were not far, on the other side of the grass, in Marylebone. Maria stole aboard once more and set off into the countryside.

The village wasn't far. The first sign of it was a line of carts hauling stones from the pits and transporting them to town. They pulled to the side to let the carriage pass until Maria's cab drew up on the pebbles that lead to the double-fronted brick house where the Calcotts resided. She climbed down and, after paying the driver, took a moment to collect herself, taking in the clematis that rambled up the facade. The flowers were in bloom, cascading on a wave of summer sun. Before she could even knock, a maid opened the door and, bobbing a curtsey, led her through a wide, pleasant hallway and upstairs. The house smelled of beeswax and peaches and the light streamed through the well-appointed windows. As Maria entered the bright drawing room, she noticed a vase of garden roses placed on the piano, blousy petals spilling across its surface. On the table there was a white dish of red apples with their leaves attached. All so English. The Calcotts did not favour the fashion for exotic or Oriental furniture and the room was set with comfortable chairs, oak cupboards and tables of English design. Though close to town, Kensington Gravel Pits felt like the country.

Miss Calcott jumped to her feet as Maria entered, laying a ring of embroidery onto her pink velvet chair. 'My dear Mrs Graham, I have missed your company,' she declared, and rang the bell for tea, which arrived so quickly it must have already been on its way up.

A plate of sandwiches was laid on the table next to a silver teapot and delicate porcelain cups. Maria set the flowers beside her friend's chair and tried to relax. It was a good day, or at least it should have been. Arriving at the Gravel Pits was diverting. Here, somehow, life seemed less complicated. Perhaps because it was a home rather than a residence, or maybe because Miss Calcott was truly glad to see her. Two painted landscapes had pride of place over the simply carved mantel, but they could not divert her from what was truly on her mind. Maria's stomach turned. It was shaming and unfair of her to keep hold of Captain Henderson. She must let go.

'I'm so glad you have come. The dressmaker will be along in a little while. In the meantime, Augustus left you this.' Miss Calcott passed across a blue box, tied with an ivory ribbon. 'He had to see to a portrait commission. He's frightfully dedicated, you see. He said to send you his regards and to invite you to accompany us to see Mr Bourgeois's portrait collection at Dulwich on Friday. Might you come, Maria? I'm sure you will like it.'

Maria smiled. Augustus Calcott was everything you might hope of a gentleman. She'd wanted to visit Dulwich. 'Yes. Friday,' she said as she sat down on the long sofa, then eased the thin ribbon to one side and slid the top of the box open. Inside, staring up at her, lying on a bed of straw, there was a likeness of her father in miniature. Calcott had dressed him in naval uniform with the horizon in the background, sea, sky and, in the distance, a ship – it looked like the frigate *Juno*, which had been his favourite command. Mostly blue, the miniature was set in a carved oval ebony frame that set off Captain Dundas's dark hair. Startled, Maria let the box fall into her lap. She gasped. For a man who had never met her father, the likeness the painter had captured was astonishing. Augustus had even caught the little mole that she'd described, by the cleft of her father's chin.

'Oh.' She let out every pocket of breath in her body. 'Oh.' Tears flooded and she scrambled for her linen handkerchief.

Miss Calcott leaned over and touched her arm. 'Augustus was sure it would please you, my dear. Don't fret, I beg of you. If it is wrong, we shall have him paint it again.'

349

Maria put out her hand. 'No. It's absolutely perfect.' She picked up the tiny picture. It fitted exactly in the palm of her hand. 'This is the first painting I have ever owned.' She smiled. 'I shall take it with me everywhere.'

As Maria clutched the miniature, she comforted herself that she was doing the right thing. London was paramount. Her father's likeness showed that as surely as if he'd laid a comforting hand on her shoulder and whispered into her ear from beyond the grave. She should be proud of herself – she was a royal tutor and an accomplished writer. A respectable widow. Georgiana was only in mourning, that was all. Lady Dundas would, if not come round, at least come to accept her decision. Ramona, poor girl, was perhaps a little lonely. Soon, she'd be gone on a royal commission. Maria ran a finger over the portrait's frame like an old woman stroking a cat. She sniffed. Coming home had made her terribly overwrought.

'I honestly think it is the best gift anyone ever gave me.'

Miss Calcott poured the tea. 'Oh good,' she said. 'I thought something was wrong.'

'I'm sorry. I didn't mean to make a fuss.' Maria sat back on the pale-green pillows. She stared into her father's eyes. 'I'm very glad to be here.' She picked up a sandwich. 'Ham is quite my favourite.'

'Well,' said Miss Calcott, 'the dressmaker will be along directly. And Augustus says I must order myself a new day dress as well as your evening gown. He has arranged the colours. We need only agree them and submit to measurements. Won't that be nice?'

Maria smiled. How thoughtful. Soon she would be travelling again.

'Yes,' she said. 'What a perfect afternoon.'

★

The Old Street Bridge Club was not in the habit of meeting anywhere other than Mallow Street, but in the present circumstances the gentlemen made an exception and congregated at Fisher's residence near Leicester Fields. Grant lit a cigar and eyed the crystal decanter on the sideboard. He ignored Fisher's dogs – two terriers, which were crowding at his feet in hope of attention. Fisher poured three glasses.

'Down,' he ordered the animals, to no avail.

Normally he'd ring and have the dogs taken away, but with Hayward and Grant here, he did not want staff in the library. The men were careful not to be seen in public together and certainly not as more than passing acquaintances. He casually put out his foot and kicked one of the dogs away. The animal whimpered.

'They belong to my wife,' he explained, his brown eyes phlegmatic as he passed the brandy.

None of the men had yet slept. The business of the evening before was most disconcerting, and all had cried off social engagements in order to come to an understanding.

Hayward downed his brandy in one. 'That's better,' he said.

'Well, whatever are we going to do?' Fisher asked. 'The captain said he was coming here.'

Hayward remained steely-eyed. For almost two hours after Henderson and Fry had left the club the night before, the men had interrogated Sam Pearson. It had started as a bloodletting, but it quickly became clear that there was real mileage in it. The boy had spent time aboard the captain's ship and, although he had been restrained below decks, he had seen and heard plenty. Hayward's jaw flexed. He was the one who had realised, of course – Fisher was little more than an idiot when it came to

351

it, and Grant, while having an excellent brain for logistical matters, had no understanding of people, least of all himself.

'We have to kill Henderson, whether he pays the money or not.' Grant couldn't restrain himself. 'He has threatened us.'

'Yes. We can't have that,' Hayward agreed.

'Not at all.' Fisher shook his head. 'But if we can secure the money as well as the fellow's death, it would be preferable. I like to balance the books.'

'Quite.' Grant nodded. 'And he says he's coming here to pay. So it seems that is entirely possible.'

Fisher looked around his grand library. He was accustomed to behaving quite differently in these surroundings from his persona at the Bridge Club. While the thought of the captain's presence in his home made him uncomfortable, he still felt a frisson at the idea of killing someone here.

Hayward stood up and served himself from the decanter without offering either of the others. 'Gentlemen, I see another possibility,' he said. 'Why kill the fellow when we can still have him? He's the most useful captain I've seen in years. Not only can he throw an effective punch, but he's clever too. This Brazilian run has been troublesome. I think he may still be the answer to our problems. The chap is a natural smuggler. We must only tame him.'

Grant and Fisher looked nonplussed.

'What do you mean, Henry?' Grant enquired gently, as if Hayward might have gone mad. 'He is coming here to pay us, but we cannot suffer the fellow to live. He knows who we are.'

Hayward smiled. 'Yes,' he said. 'But I think we may have something to parry with. What Pearson said last night. You know. The woman.'

Grant's eyes narrowed. He couldn't grasp what Hayward was talking about. 'What woman?'

'The woman aboard his ship. Pearson said she was a lady. Weren't you listening?'

Fisher lit a cigar. 'Yes. The captain's mistress,' he said glibly. 'The men said there had been an affair.'

'Not only an affair. Didn't you hear how they had put it? The captain was doe-eyed, and the lady a widow recently returned from South America,' Hayward said slowly. 'A lady who has been travelling in Brazil? Don't you fellows follow the news? It is Mrs Graham, I'll warrant. The writer. She is the toast of Piccadilly. Do you not see?'

Fisher had clearly never heard of the woman, but something stirred behind Grant's eyes. He recognised the name and, therefore, the glimmer of possibility.

'If our captain has feelings for this lady then we may counter his threat with one of our own,' Hayward announced with a flourish. 'He will not want to see her fall – why, he is probably relying on her position in society to advance his own plans. And, in that case, we have him quite as much as he has us. In fact, we have him more so, don't you see?'

Grant nodded slowly. 'Yes,' he said. 'We could expose her. That's brilliant, Hayward. Quite brilliant. We could kidnap her. We could do anything.'

Fisher squirmed. 'Ruin a lady? I say, that's a bit much. And who's to say the captain would spring to her defence? He's a grubby chap. No, I don't believe it. A lady with . . . that man. I say we take the money when he delivers it and then we kill him.'

Both Grant and Hayward ignored Fisher's objection. The men were a tight threesome, but the two of them were at its core. They did what they wanted when it came down to it. Fisher was like putty – easily moulded. He was there by inheritance alone, although admittedly he was useful for some of the Old Street Bridge Club's more hands-on jobs. It was Fisher who had been charged with dumping Sam Pearson's body into the Thames only two hours before. The boy was a hopeless case – not nearly perceptive enough to bring off the job.

'If Henderson loves the woman, he could not risk her disgrace. We'd have him as our captain as long as we wanted.' A grin slit Grant's face as the idea settled. 'We can keep the money. We can have whatever we want.'

'No, no.' Hayward raised a finger. 'We mustn't be greedy, for there is something more valuable here. We shall insist upon three times the stake, as usual, but the captain must run for us. He will be our man. We will make a fortune or,' he added smugly, 'another one.'

'Who is this woman?' Fisher tried to keep up. 'It seems rather a lot to go through on her account.'

Hayward regarded his friend. They had known each other all their lives. 'You do not understand love,' he said simply. 'Mrs Graham shall be our insurance policy. You will see.'

Fisher slumped into a leather chair. 'I think I shall organise my own little insurance policy,' he insisted. 'In case the captain does not fancy your deal. That's if he turns up at all. He may run, of course.'

'I account him a man of some honour. I think he meant what he said,' Hayward pronounced.

'Let's give him a day.' Grant looked at his nails. 'No more than one. It would be good to secure the money, whichever way it turns.'

Fisher extended his leg to once more remove one of the terriers from his notice. 'All right,' he said. 'I will stay at home today. And if the captain arrives, I'll try your ruse with the lady. Mrs Graham, is it? What kind of a woman writes?' His voice dripped with distaste. 'Really, I can't see that this plan of yours will work at all.'

St James's Street

In the normally restrained atmosphere of Boodle's gentlemen's club, John Murray's colour was rising. Firstly, he had been summoned like an errant schoolboy, and now he was being given a dressing-down.

'We simply can't have it,' Sir Horace Strange, notable member and Tory peer, tutted, spit flecking his collar. He was furious. 'A woman. What are you thinking, sir?'

Murray stood up for himself. 'I am thinking that Mrs Graham has one of the most interesting minds of our age and, furthermore, that excluding her from speaking at the Royal Society on account of her sex is ridiculous, given the woman's talents. Her writing is marvellous and her scientific observations I'm sure will prove valuable. She is an adept geographer. Her books are widely regarded.'

Strange glared. The club was undergoing a long process of refurbishment and several workmen were engaged in the hallway, renovating the plasterwork to a design by the celebrated architect Mr Papworth. Strange had met Papworth on several occasions. He appeared to be solidly English, but the chap's predilection for ornamentation of a most continental nature was causing Sir

Horace some difficulty. Classical design was to be commended, but the proposed statues of nymphs were beyond the pale. Today, under pressure from all sides, the gentle tapping of the workmen's tools and the smell of fresh plaster that emanated from the hallway were particularly infuriating.

'A woman at the Royal Society? I won't allow it, sir. I have spoken to Sir Humphry, among others,' Strange insisted.

'I was not aware you were in charge of the Society,' Murray said smoothly.

'There is much, Mr Murray, of which you are unaware,' the infuriated peer spat. 'The prattling of ladies, even of ladies who travel, is not of interest to the Society's members. We are serious fellows. Ladies, sir, lower the tone.'

'You cannot have met Mrs Graham.' Murray kept his voice low through sheer force of will. 'I, however, have known her for some years. She has never, in my experience, prattled. She has instead written several books, which I am proud to publish. She is a keen observer of life abroad and her work sells in numbers. I will happily send copies so you can evaluate them for yourself.'

Strange made a sound that was more reminiscent of a furious animal than of a member of the English aristocracy. 'A woman's place is not at the lectern, and while you are entitled to your opinion, I have heard that Mrs Graham's writing is weak and self-serving. A lady's thoughts are simply not designed for the rigours of intellectual discourse. It's not their fault. Nature has made them that way, and Mrs Graham would do better to turn her hand to fiction, perhaps, or to poetry, if she must. She has a second-class mind and we will not lower ourselves by listening to her arguments.'

Murray took a deep breath. 'And who, might I enquire, is "we"?'

Strange stopped. This publishing fellow was quite unreasonable, but the Scots were invariably difficult. Murray had been born in London, but his father was Scottish. Such fellows had their uses, but they were not known for their understanding of social matters. That was the main thing.

'Mrs Graham is quite unprotected, sir. Her husband and her father are dead. You will not be allowed to make a fool of her,' Strange insisted.

'Whereas you are happy to discard her knowledge and try to make a fool of her that way. The idea, sir, that members of the fairer sex have little understanding is beyond me. What of Mrs Wollstonecraft, Sir Horace? What of Miss Herschel? Mrs Somerville?'

'Pah.' Sir Horace dismissed these examples of female intellect. 'Why, the Wollstonecraft woman tried to kill herself more than once, and Miss Herschel assisted her brother with his calculations – ably, I'll grant you, but nothing more. Miss Somerville is interesting, but the idea that a lady might originate a theory is outrageous. They are not built for it.'

'Mrs Graham has certainly originated more than one idea. I stand by her observations of life in South America, and she has, through hard work and scientific endeavour, come up with a notion of measuring earthquakes. It is an astonishing achievement.'

'Well, the Royal Society – the Royal Society,' Strange repeated, 'does not exist for such female folderol. And that's the size of it, Murray. Neither Mrs Graham nor her ideas will be appearing. A woman. Really.'

The fact that Sir Horace had been designated as the person

to make this point, rather than Sir Humphry, as president of the Society, was telling. Murray backed down. 'I see,' he said. 'That's most disappointing.'

Strange took Murray's retreat as some kind of threat. From the hallway, there was the sound of something breaking – a muffled crash. A shout went up from the workmen.

'What now?' He lost his temper.

'Diana, I imagine. Shattering,' Murray said drily.

'I look forward to reading the reviews of Mrs Graham's latest work.' Strange couldn't help continuing his attack. 'Should there be any notices, of course.'

Murray got up. If Strange organised some kind of campaign against Maria's books it would be most unjust, and rather more energetically pursued than Sir Horace's usual hobby horses. But if Murray stayed and provoked him, perhaps the vindictive old sot might find the time.

'I bid you good day, sir.' He bowed. 'I will apprise Mrs Graham of your views. She will be leaving shortly, to take a position with the Brazilian royal family.'

'What position?'

'The governess of the young Princess Royal.' Murray made for the door.

'Now that is most suitable for a widow.' Strange raised his hand in farewell. 'The Royal Society, sir, does not, and never will, admit women.'

Murray restrained himself from saying anything further. Instead, he collected his outerwear from the servant on duty at the club's entrance. Maria would be disappointed, but he would have to be honest with her. Perhaps the next time she returned he would see if they might take another tack. A member of the Society could present Mrs Graham's theory on her behalf, perhaps. The battle was lost for now.

As he headed up St James's Street towards Piccadilly, Murray cursed himself for not being more effective. He could have cited women who had attended the Royal Society in the past. He seemed to recall there had been one in Pepys's day – a titled lady. He had not arrived at Boodle's prepared to tackle Sir Horace's fallacious argument, for no one had informed him what Strange wanted. It was infuriating. Maria was so seemly – who could possibly be offended by her? It was true that occasionally scientific ladies were harridans and that some women (and men as well) had submitted scientific papers that upon examination had proved unoriginal, or inaccurate. But Maria? Intelligent, educated and now, of course, widowed, there was simply nothing to which a reasonable man might object. Murray puffed. There, he thought, might lie the problem. What London needed was a club for reasonable fellows. He must make a note of it. Such an institution would be graced with a dignified name – not called after a head waiter, like Boodle's, but named after something worthwhile. An institution of erudition and learning.

'The Athenaeum,' he smiled.

Should such an enlightened edifice ever open its doors, Murray decided, it would not admit the likes of Sir Horace Strange.

*

London might have been large, but finding a gentleman was surely not too difficult a business, nor a lady for that matter. Captain Henderson restrained himself, however, from seeking out Maria. For one thing, he had realised his erstwhile behaviour was quite unacceptable. The more time he spent in the city the more he realised that Maria was right. In the circumstances, she had been both patient and generous with him, and he did not know how to proceed. For another, the business of dealing with the Old Street Bridge Club was consuming and Maria was best kept out of it. Still, he could not help but notice the next morning, with a twinge of pride, that Mrs Graham's journals would be on sale shortly, as advertised in the London *Times*. *Journal of a Residence in Chile* and *A Journey of a Voyage to Brazil*. Hot off the press at twelve shillings a volume and available to order in advance from booksellers nationwide.

'So we are going west to conclude this business?' Fry asked when he rose on the *Bittersweet* to find the captain reading a newspaper he had sent Clarkson to procure and sipping a coffee of inordinate fortitude at the long cabin table.

Henderson looked up. 'You don't have to come, Richard. You've done quite enough.'

Fry shook his head. The smell of lavender salve, smeared onto his injuries the night before, was pervasive. 'No,' he said. 'I promised. This is my part of the deal. The wooing of the ladies and the dealing with the gentlemen. You took me to Old Street; let me take you to Piccadilly.'

Given what had transpired, it did not feel a fair exchange. 'How are your bruises?' Henderson enquired.

Fry sat down with only the tiniest cringe. 'They're better than last night, though I expect I'll avoid ball games for a while,' he said, employing the gentleman's art of understatement.

When they had finally returned the night before, the city had felt dark and dangerous – an inescapable metropolis only remitted by the memory of his brothers and, once Clarkson had administered some morphia, a fantasy of chocolate.

Henderson's extraordinary idea for a chocolate bar was still with Fry. If he could find a way to set the stuff, Richard realised, he could cast shapes like edible sculptures. That aside, if he could sweeten the chocolate and cast it into little blocks, how many men might carry one with them at all times? Past two bells in Henderson's cabin, exhausted and sated upon cheese, bread and scalded brandy with opium, Fry had clung to dreams of commercial success as he descended into a sleep that blacked out the world.

Now the sun was long up. Outside the cabin window, the dock at Greenwich was alive and the Thames was bustling. It felt odd to be back to a regime of such normality. To wake to baskets of pears on the dockside, children running along the quay and the summer sun glistening off the white buildings further along the water was like wakening into a different world – one that had been swapped in the night and bore no relation to the pain-ridden, stinking hours he'd spent near Old Street. Outside, it was light and everything was possible.

At the turning to the high street, there was a girl selling flowers. She was blonde and plump, in a worn dress the colour of sapphires. She looked like the factory girls at Fry's, except more ragged. She made Richard think of home. From this great distance, it seemed unthinkable that the Fry manufactory was still churning out its produce and that sweet Mary was preparing a tray for his father mid-morning at his desk. Fry looked down at his grimy hands. 'I shall need to scrub myself rather cleaner,' he said.

'We can see to that.' The captain was good-natured.

Fry sniffed. The coffee smelled enticing, though he was used to chocolate of a morning. And toast. Slowly, testing himself, he tried one leg after the other. His limbs were stiff, and the thought of touching the bruises made his stomach turn. His shoulder ached.

'We can fetch a doctor if you need one,' Henderson offered.

'No. There's no stabbing pain.' The boy bore up. 'No broken bones. It'll take a while to heal, that's all. I can take laudanum.'

Henderson nodded. The boy was certainly plucky.

'Perhaps I'll try a cup.' Fry motioned towards the coffee pot.

'At breakfast, the custom in Brazil is to drink it with milk,' Henderson said, 'though I prefer it as black as they can make it. The natives favour cakes or doughnuts, but we only have the bread left from last night. I hope Thatcher comes back soon. He's a good cook and will improve matters.'

'Captain?'

'I think, after last night, you ought to call me James, don't you?'

Fry moved painfully. 'Last night, you saved my life, sir. I'm indebted to you.'

'I put your life in danger, so it was only fair to get you out.'

'Do you think they'll come after us?'

'I don't know. I have to find Fisher. That's the first thing. And track down the other – Hayward – as an insurance policy. I'd like to find the name of the third, were that possible. One thing's for sure – they'll come if I don't keep the bargain I made. And fair enough. But if they come anyway, I want to be prepared. At least they won't find you, Richard. They have no idea who you are.'

'Do you always do business like this?'

Henderson shook his head. A strand of dark hair slipped across his face and he pushed it back. 'Nothing like it. I admit

I have smuggled goods into America. But I've never come across the like.' He smiled. 'And I prefer the Fry way.'

'Me too.' Richard would never have thought it.

There was a knock on the door and the cabin boy entered, carrying a jug of hot water.

The captain rose from the table. 'We'll need more than that, I'll wager. See if someone can get a proper pot boiling and bring soap, a scrubbing cloth and a large basin for Mr Fry.' Henderson passed his hand over his face. 'Time for a clean shave, I expect.'

'To be a gentleman again,' Fry mused. It flashed across his mind that he might ditch his pauper's clothes. Maybe he'd burn them. 'Right,' he said, taking a sip of coffee and shuddering as it went down. 'Best get started.'

★

By late morning, Henderson and Fry, arrayed like gentlemen, skirted Pall Mall. The streets were busy in the morning sun. Gentlemen of the court were about their business, scurrying to and from St James's with a tremendous air of purpose. Several well-dressed ladies dotted between establishments, shopping and dodging carriages. They looked as if they were fashionable engravings come to life. The rain the night before had perked up the city. On a corner, flower sellers offered their wares.

'Ha'penny a button'ole and a posy of lavender.'

A gentleman stopped and bought a fragrant bunch of rosebuds before turning off for the Strand.

'Normally you'd find a chap at his club, of course,' Fry said wistfully as he guided the captain across the road. 'Either that or you'd know the coffee shops he frequented.'

Neither he nor Henderson belonged to a London club, unless, in Fry's case, you counted a meeting of Friends, which he did not. And as for coffee shops, London was knee-deep in such establishments. You could scarcely round a corner without coming across one. The air was scented by roasting beans, not sweet like chocolate but still musky and fragrant.

'Fisher is a common name,' Fry mused, touching his hat, which felt curiously out of place after the shenanigans of the night before. None of his clothes felt like his own. 'Hayward might be a better bet.'

'And the last one – the third,' the captain added. 'Don't forget him.'

'Do you think any of them might be a member of the Royal Society?' Fry tried.

It was difficult to imagine. The prevailing memory of Fisher was of the man wild-eyed and throttling Henderson, the others intent that he did the job thoroughly. Surely members of the Royal Society didn't carry red-silk garrottes and assault helpless urchins with their walking sticks.

'The Society? I'd like to see it,' Henderson admitted.

The men crossed the road and cut down towards the river and eastwards to the grand edifice of Somerset House. Outside the Society rooms, a bill was posted announcing forthcoming lectures on the subjects of 'Bitumen in Stones' and 'Fluid Chlorine'.

'Some Friday night. Can't they find someone to talk about something interesting?' Fry commented with a smile as a footman admitted them to the hallway.

From a back room, a man emerged, pulling on a dark frock coat.

Henderson accosted him. 'Excuse me, I'm looking for two

gentlemen. Fisher and Hayward. Might they be members?'

The man squinted, as if considering this matter seriously. 'My dear fellow,' he said, his wide vowel sounds betraying his Scottish origins, 'I can't be expected to know everyone.'

He made for the door, but Fry fell into step. 'Fisher and Hayward have a friend we're keen to get in touch with. He's a Scot, like you.'

The man turned. 'And, pray, why are you so anxious to find these gentlemen?'

'We were playing cards, sir,' Henderson said. 'There was drink taken. And reparations must be made, I fear.'

'I see.' The fellow nodded. The footman opened the door. 'This last man? The Scot. What is his name?'

'That's the trouble. He's of medium height with red hair going grey. But his name eludes me. He was carrying a black cane with a silver fox-head.'

The man's face split into a grin. 'Why, Charlie Grant. The devil. He never plays cards, surely? Calvinist to the core, I always believed. Gentlemen, you have made my day.' The fellow bowed cheerily.

'Grant,' Henderson said, catching the man's arm. 'Yes. Thank you. Do you know where we might find him? And do you think he might be with the other two – Fisher and Hayward?'

'No.' The fellow shook his head. 'Those names don't ring a bell. I don't know a Fisher or a Hayward. But you'll find Charlie all right. He's a regular at Rules – they've generally got Galloway beef, on the bone, and sometimes partridge. Charlie lives on his own, poor fellow, on Tavistock Street. He prefers to dine out. I don't expect it's worth keeping a cook.'

'Thank you.'

The man headed into the sunshine with a grunt.

'Fisher, Hayward and Grant.' Fry smiled in the doorway.

'It's a start,' Henderson said. 'Now we must find them.'

'Well,' Fry ventured, the stale bread and milky coffee having worn off, 'I suggest we start with lunch.'

Outside, they cut towards Covent Garden. More ladies out shopping passed with parasols held aloft – there seemed an interminable supply of smart women, all ribbons, sashes and bows. Outside one establishment, a footman bundled parcels into a carriage, dropping one onto the dusty paving stones and brushing it clean.

Service for luncheon was just starting and Rules restaurant as yet was quiet. In a corner, a gentleman was pouring a glass of port for a woman who could not, in all honesty, be called a lady. The sound of her laughter gurgled between the empty tables. The air smelled of fine cigars and roasting meat ingrained over the ages.

'Do they have partridge in Brazil, Captain?' Fry enquired.

'No. Perhaps that's what we should order.'

The waiter pointed the gentlemen to a table in the furthest corner from the courting couple.

'Claret,' Fry said. 'And do you have game bird and potatoes?'

The waiter nodded. 'And some cheese?' he suggested hopefully.

Henderson shook his head. 'No – just game and potatoes will be fine. And a pudding to follow. Something English.'

The waiter looked startled at the suggestion that Rules was an establishment that might indulge in the service of foreign food. 'Yes, sir,' he mumbled, and headed for the kitchens.

'So.' Fry leaned over the table. 'We have at least one of our gentlemen smugglers in our sights and we'll find the others. Worst ways, we can employ the means my brother would – servants talk endlessly about their masters and their masters' friends. The serving classes know far more about our lives than we know about theirs. You wouldn't believe how much we've picked up – recipes, techniques – all by chatting to a housemaid. But, Captain, that's only a portion of what I promised. There is, in addition, the matter of Mr Murray and the lady. You were hoping to raise the value of your stock with Mrs Graham, were you not?'

Henderson nodded silently. He had behaved unforgivably. The glimpses he had seen of polite London confirmed the gravity of his actions.

Fry continued. 'So, in that case, you must first call on Mr Murray. In your own right. You want to write your treatise, don't you? We must see to that and make no mention of Mrs Graham. Not a word. If Murray commissions your idea that itself will raise your stock. And after that, we'll address ourselves to your suit.'

Henderson was suddenly unsure what his suit might be. Maria seemed beyond him now. Seeing her name printed in *The Times*, he had realised how great were her achievements. He had offered a mere promise to replace something concrete and most certainly worthwhile. He had been selfish, childish even. Still, as Fry said, there were other matters in hand before that need be considered.

'We've got to get on with finding these fellows.' The captain caught sight of a waiter approaching the table with a promising salver of meat and potatoes. Behind him, another man bore a bottle of claret.

Fry's eyes gleamed as the food and drink was laid down. He accosted the waiter. 'I'm looking for an old friend. A Scotsman named Grant. He eats here often, I believe. Lives on Tavistock Street. You wouldn't know the number of his residence?'

The waiter shook his head. 'Mr Grant. No, sir. But Tavistock Street is only round the corner beyond Covent Garden. I'd try there. His neighbours will know of him.'

Fry stuck his fork into a crisp potato. 'I suppose they will,' he mused. 'Very good, we'll give that a try.'

*

Fortified by claret and an excellent meal that culminated in a sticky, raisin-studded pudding the like of which was only available in England, Fry and Henderson burst onto London's streets. English vittles were most satisfying. The captain resolved he must see that Big Al Thatcher was supplied to produce such delights.

It was early in the afternoon and Mr Grant had not chosen to dine at Rules. Watched eagerly by flocks of small boys loitering on the pavement, drays pulled by enormous carthorses delivered barrels of beer to public houses on the fringes of Soho.

'Tavistock Street,' Fry directed, and they turned towards Aldwych.

Henderson was happy to let the young gentleman have his head. Fry seemed capable of negotiating this side of London with ease – Maria's world was like a spider's web. The captain's sense was that if you really knew your way in Piccadilly and Covent Garden, you could fashion the world to your specifications. In London, anything was possible.

In a haze of red wine, it was easy to block out the filthy streets that lay behind the veneer and to ignore the pickpockets and ne'er-do-wells hovering on the fringes, peering from behind Covent Garden's colonnades as the men cut towards Grant's residence. Tavistock Street was highly respectable and far grander than the back street where Henderson had been brought up. Here the buildings were wide and ran to four storeys, occupied by fashionable families of all stripes. At this time of the day, society was making its calls in many of the fashionable first-floor drawing rooms. So many carriages waited outside the more popular residences that the footmen jostled to smoke in peace as they attended the pleasure of their masters and mistresses. The horses kicked the cobbles, forming a veritable herd that left the road only open to one-way traffic.

'Do you know, by any chance, which of these houses is occupied by Mr Grant?' Fry enquired of a man who was brushing a horse's mane.

The footman declared himself ignorant. 'Never heard of him. Here, Rodney,' he shouted along the row. 'You 'eard of a Mr Grant?'

'Scotch fellow,' Fry added, helpfully.

Rodney peered from inside the next carriage. 'No,' he said, mystified. 'Sorry.'

Further enquiries proved no more fruitful. Fry was pragmatic. 'What we need is a house where no one is at home.' He crossed the street to view the line of first floors. 'That one.' He pointed at number 34.

The windows were dark and, on the first floor, the drawing room was apparently unoccupied. A rap on the brass knocker was answered by a jolly-looking maid with an air of competence. The girl's frame filled the open space so that neither

Fry nor Henderson could see into the hallway behind. She bobbed a solid curtsey, emanating a scent of polishing wax and potato peelings.

'I need some help.' Fry's smile was charming. 'I'm looking for Charlie Grant. He lives along here. Man on his own. Scotch. Might you be able to help?'

The maid's smile spread like soft butter and she glowed at the prospect of being of assistance. 'Yes, sir. Mr Grant is at number 18. But he'll be out, I expect. Perhaps with Mrs Hamilton at 25.'

Henderson laughed as the door closed and the men turned back onto the street. Society had a tiny orbit – inexplicable from the outside but, for those in the know, a very comfortable club. He wondered about the nature of Grant's relationship with Mrs Hamilton. Fry strutted towards number 18.

'Francis always says servants are the key. He befriended Menier's bootboy. It proved the key to uncovering the French process.'

'The bootboy knew his master's chocolate recipe?'

'No. But the bootboy knew two of the girls who worked in the manufactory. Servants see everything. All the comings and goings. All the secrets and the lies.'

At number 18 it seemed no one might answer, until a thin butler appeared in the doorway.

'Is Mr Grant at home?' Henderson asked, trying out this bluff world of gentlemen.

The butler paused. 'No, sir. Shall I say who called?'

'Thing is,' Fry said, 'it's not Mr Grant we're after, but his friend, Mr Fisher. Might you be able to direct us to Mr Fisher's residence? We are hopelessly lost, old man.'

The butler's lips pursed as if this was a great inconvenience.

Gentlemen were expected to know the whereabouts of other gentlemen. That was the nature of the club. 'I'm sorry, sir. I am unacquainted with Mr Fisher.' The man barely opened his lips.

'Or Mr Hayward. Hayward would do,' Fry said. 'But we simply must track down one of them. It's a matter of an important investment.'

The butler weighed this up. Mr Grant seldom received callers – as an unmarried gentleman, he was invariably the one to call on others. The man's eyes flicked towards Mrs Hamilton's house, where he knew his master to be engaged in the matter of society. 'Investment? I see.'

'Well, if you know where Mr Grant is, we can call on him directly, but it's Hayward or Fisher we need to speak to.' Fry appeared nonchalant. 'When will he be back? We heard he was with Mrs Hamilton. I suppose we could call on him there.'

The butler paused before deciding that Mr Grant would not wish to be troubled by a financial matter. Giving the details for one of the master's acquaintances to two gentlemen callers of good standing was one thing, but allowing him to be disturbed while he was out was quite another. 'The Hayward family, I believe, resides nearby,' the man drawled. 'The house is on Exeter Street.' The butler pointed along the pavement. 'Go to the end and turn right. It's about halfway along.'

Fry doffed his hat. Given two choices, a good servant would almost always decide not to trouble his employer. 'Most obliged.' Fry smiled. 'Thank you.'

Exeter Street was smaller and quieter than Tavistock Street. Both sides of the pavement were in shade, so that the street felt like a tunnel. The Hayward residence stood out without having to make any enquiries – halfway along there was a lamp adorned with the same coat of arms that had been displayed on the side of Hayward's carriage the night before. It was painted so thickly that the feathers were a nondescript crust and the visor of the helmet would be impossible for a knight to see through. Still, it was there.

'Do you expect they're in?' Henderson craned to see if there was any movement in the upstairs windows.

Fry shrugged and approached the knocker. This time, the door was answered immediately by another butler, almost a carbon copy of the man in charge of Grant's household. Henderson wondered momentarily if the men were brothers. The hallway revealed behind him was exquisitely ornate. It framed the tiny man as if he were a painting – something modern.

'Sir.' The butler peered along the street, as if he had been expecting someone else. 'I'm afraid there is nobody at home.'

'I wonder if you can help me. I called on Mr Hayward only because I'm looking for his friend, Mr Fisher. Could you direct me to Mr Fisher's residence, please?'

'Lord Hayward.' The butler could not help but correct this mistake.

'Yes. Yes. Met the fellows over cards, you see.' Fry brushed off the correction casually. 'Do you happen to know His Lordship's friend Fisher?'

The butler shook his head. 'No, sir. I am not acquainted with that gentleman.'

'There's a Mrs Fisher,' a female voice said from inside the house. The butler turned and a lady's maid appeared from a side room. 'Mrs Fisher calls on Her Ladyship from time to time. She lives in Garrick Street. Towards Leicester Fields.'

The butler cut her off. 'Thank you, Brownleigh.' Fry got

the impression she was going to say more but, as far as the butler was concerned, that was quite enough.

'Ah, Garrick Street, of course. Yes.' Fry sounded bluff. 'Thank you, miss.' He peered around the butler's legs. The maid was pretty. 'How helpful.'

The butler closed the door and the men set off.

'Mr Grant, Mr Fisher and Lord Hayward,' Fry smirked as if ticking the names off a list. 'We have found them out.'

As they walked back towards the main road, Henderson pondered that this round of social calls to a series of opulent houses located on London's nicer streets and run by efficient staff was like being given a tour of the life to which he might aspire. This was a place where everyone knew everyone else, or at least knew of them. Still, it occurred to him, not one of the grand residences had felt like a home – each had the atmosphere of a lodging. Perhaps it was only people who could bestow the title of home upon a residence. Perhaps, it occurred to him, it was love.

*

On Garrick Street, there were several gaps in the line of houses and construction was underway. The area was mixed, in part on the rise but lapsing in places into what could only be described as slums. Some of these more tumbledown buildings seemed to be in the process of demolition, while others, rickety and half-timbered, were alive with activity. Boys flitted to and fro with messages and women gazed laconically out of the grubby windows, hoping for trade of one kind of another. Many of the street's front doors lay open and led onto what looked like public houses. Up side streets, signs jutted overhead – B. Bowman Wigmaker and Oliver Bradstock Purveyor of Fine Haberdashery. The newly built stone residences on the main street were more formal. Fry enquired of a maid, about her business with a basket on her arm, where Mr Fisher resided and was pointed to a grand edifice of Portland stone on the corner of Rose Street. It was far larger than the homes of Hayward or Grant. Fisher had clearly decided to risk a more mixed area, further from town, in order to secure all but palatial accommodation. They had picked just the right fellow to threaten with disgrace. He clearly cared about how things appeared.

'Do you think he will be in?' Fry asked.

'I hope so.'

The windows were dark but that was not conclusive.

'If someone was set to call on me with a large sum of money and a wrap of gemstones, I might tarry,' the captain said.

'Come on then.'

Henderson laid a hand on Fry's chest to stop the boy advancing any further. 'You're not coming in, Richard. Wait for me over there.' The captain nodded at an overflowing public house across the road.

'But—' the boy objected.

Henderson stopped him with a raised hand, as if he was training a dog. 'No,' he said firmly. 'You've helped enough. The connection to your family is too vulnerable and they think you are a pauper. If they hear you are a Fry, it will only arm them. This is my business. Go. Play dice. These are dangerous men. If I'm not out directly, then come looking.'

Fry nodded curtly 'All right,' he said unwillingly. 'I'll be your lookout.' He turned to cross the road.

Henderson took the steps and, checking the boy was out of sight, knocked on the wide front door. It creaked as it opened, revealing a lavishly attired footman. The man had wide shoulders. He looked like a chap who could hold his own in a fight, though his ornate costume belied it.

'Is Mr Fisher at home?' Henderson asked.

'Who shall I say is calling?'

'An old friend from Brazil.'

The man hesitated before disappearing inside. Henderson took a deep breath. He must get this right. Almost immediately, the fellow returned to usher the captain across the impressive hallway, tiled in black and white. Inside, if anything, the house was grander than its exterior. The captain's footsteps echoed around the high ceiling. Ornamentation dripped from the balustrades. The sconces were sculpted in crystal and the plasterwork was gilded. It was like visiting a palace or a cathedral. The street was sunny, but inside the temperature dropped. Henderson shivered as if someone had walked on his grave. The footman guided the captain into an empty library, which was lined on all sides with tall bookshelves. Henderson perused the titles and took in the leather chairs placed at intervals and the mahogany desk tidily stacked with papers. Behind it was a wooden upright chest sporting several brass locks.

'The lair of a gentleman,' he muttered.

The air was so heavy with the smell of musty paper and leather that it was difficult to breath. His heart speeded up. He peered out of a mullioned window onto a small garden at the rear. A maid was hanging laundered sheets on a line strung between two trees. Everything here murmured tradition. The captain was disturbed by a cough, which came from behind.

Fisher stood four-square in the doorway. He was wearing a burgundy frock coat with brass buttons and the rest of his outfit was buff. As Henderson took in the man's appearance, he noted that Fisher was pretending not to be nervous. He felt exactly the same, though he hoped he was more effective at hiding his feelings. His skills at poker would stand him in good stead. At Fisher's heels, two fat terriers waddled in and curled up by the fireplace.

'My wife is out for the afternoon.' Fisher closed the door. 'The dogs belong to her.'

Henderson nodded. This was not a social call. There was no need to waste time. He reached inside his coat and withdrew three large pouches. Fisher crossed to the desk. 'It's all there,' Henderson said. 'Half of everything.'

'We are due two-thirds.'

The captain remained silent. The men stared at each other. Then Fisher opened the pouches and poured the contents onto the desktop. The money was satisfying, but it was the rush of gemstones and small gold bars that held the attention.

'I have a buyer.'

'That concludes our business then,' Henderson said.

Fisher looked up. 'Not quite, Captain. The thing is, you have threatened our reputations. We do not take that lightly.'

'I shall do so no longer, sir.' Henderson smiled. 'And I should point out that you tried to kill me. I hope our paths do not cross again.' He turned towards the door.

'Ha!' The noise came out of Fisher's mouth like a short, sharp blast on a foghorn. 'No, you do not understand. You owe us another portion and we will have you run for us on the same terms. We have not changed our minds. The club is quite decided.'

'I will not be pressed,' Henderson replied, his eyes hard.

'And I'm surprised that I need to remind you that you should not press me, given what I could reveal.'

'And what might we reveal of you, sir?'

'I have fought you off once,' the captain started. 'Do you really want to . . ?'

Fisher pulled out a copy of *The Times* from the drawer of his desk. 'Mrs Graham,' he said, his brown eyes searching for a reaction. 'What might she make of this?'

Henderson's blood ran cold, but he held his poker face. 'What do you mean?'

'Man, your own crew belie any denial. They talk of scarcely anything else but this tawdry affair of yours. The lady shall be quite done for if it comes out. Why, if you care for her at all, you shall deliver our two-thirds and do as we ask. It's not so bad, is it? The Brazilian run has proved profitable for you already. Did you really think we would not find something to hold over you when you nestled our reputations in your grubby hand? You look like a gentleman today. Myself, I'd choose a different waistcoat. But you aren't a gentleman, are you? And, when it comes to it, Mrs Graham is no lady. Do you want the world to know?'

The captain's mind raced. In such a situation, he knew that if he showed his hand Maria would lose everything. By having her at their mercy, they had him as well. And these men were pitiless. The only way out, he realised, was to make Fisher believe that he did not care. He raised a smile.

'You are at least half correct in your assumptions. Mrs Graham is not a lady, sir,' he said, the words turning in his gullet. 'And if you thought to hold me by threatening her, then you are sadly mistaken. Such women are ten a penny. Bitches, all.'

'You deny the affair?'

'No, sir,' he said strongly. There was no point. Who knew what they'd heard from the crew. 'Nor do I deny it is over. If you wish to tar Mrs Graham with your brush, then go ahead. I shall, of course retaliate with what I know. The secret society enjoyed by yourself and your fellows will capture the imagination of the scandal sheets far more than a fallen woman – a bluestocking, at that. People will wonder what you get up to in Mallow Street. They will wonder if what I say about you is true even if you never set foot in the place again. My guess is you couldn't afford that, could you? Not with such a fine mansion to keep up. A place like this. You must keep the shipments arriving.'

Fisher puffed. A small vein in his temple throbbed – a tell. He had not expected Hayward's ruse to work. Now he set it aside and decided he could not let the captain leave. He'd wanted to kill him all along. Laconically, he turned and opened a hidden door concealed in the spines of a set of books. Inside was a drinks cabinet. He poured a glass of brandy from a crystal flagon and gulped it down. 'Would you like one?'

Henderson shook his head.

'It's a good year, from the cellar of a friend.' Fisher ignored the captain's refusal. He refilled two glasses and handed one over. 'It's bad luck to drink alone. You are off the hook, sir. And you cannot blame a fellow for trying.'

'I can and I do,' Henderson objected. 'I have never known the like and I've been running goods for more than a dozen years into America.'

'Ah, Americans,' Fisher declared with distaste. 'Why, they do not even choose a king when they have the chance. Please. No hard feelings.'

Henderson picked up the glass. The liquor was the colour of toffee and it smelled of burnt sugar. He sipped. Fisher was right. It tasted good.

'A fellow has to try,' the older man continued. 'My wife, you see, can be demanding. It takes two-thirds to keep her happy. I hoped I might reason with you.'

'You can't try to murder a fellow and expect to negotiate what you want. I came to your offices in good faith and I have delivered in good faith too. But I'll not haggle or be subjected to this kind of blackmail – and on the good name of a lady! I have no care for Mrs Graham, but, still, it is both low and unnecessary.'

Fisher changed tack. 'How is the boy? Dick, isn't it?'

'He'll recover.'

Henderson downed the drink and laid his empty glass on the desk. Fisher looked pained; his shoulders dropped.

The captain continued. 'Now, to be clear, I spent the day visiting the houses of Mr Grant and Mr Hayward. Or Lord Hayward, isn't it? So, Mr Fisher, I recall to you the terms of the deal that you are accepting, by dint of the payment I just made. This matter is concluded, sir. And should you choose to pursue it, there will be revelations and damn Mrs Graham in the crossfire. My intention – my hope, rather – is that I might simply disappear from your notice. I'm certain you must have more important business.'

Henderson's thumbnail was cutting into the cushion of his hand so sharply he feared he might draw blood. He examined Fisher for any sign that he had not played his part. He hoped he had saved her. There was still time to backtrack if he had to. He held Maria's face in his mind's eye.

'Very well,' Fisher snapped.

Henderson smiled. 'I hope Mrs Fisher will be happy.' He turned. 'And with that, I bid you good day.'

Fisher emerged from behind the desk as if to walk the captain out. 'I built the place to my own design,' he said. 'I like an old-fashioned library. You'd wager it had been here a hundred years, wouldn't you?'

Henderson laid his fingers on the handle of the door. His palm was clammy, he noticed, but then he had had a shock. Fisher closed his left hand over the top of the knob. The captain squirmed. He pulled back, but he wasn't quick enough, and at close quarters Fisher's right fist hit him square in the face, slamming the back of his head hard against the wood. He felt woozy, but he lashed out, knocking Fisher onto the patterned carpet. The dogs barked but didn't move from the fire. Fisher laughed, heaving the sound from deep inside his chest. He pulled himself up as the captain staggered to his feet. Henderson thought he might vomit. A bitter taste was building. It seemed to come from his chest.

'You won't last more than another minute,' Fisher said. 'It's the oldest trick in the book. Powders in the glass.'

Suddenly, behind Fisher's head, the window appeared to sparkle as if the garden was beset by fairies. Henderson blinked, his eyelids heavy. How could he have been so naive?

'You won't get what you want if you kill me,' he blurted. 'There's no more money that way.'

'We won't be unmanned. We can't have you threatening us.' Fisher smiled, pressing a button so that a door clicked open in the wall of books. 'My design,' he continued smoothly. 'Ten feet by ten feet, and no one knows it's there.'

He returned to put an arm around Henderson's shoulders and, with his elbow jabbed painfully into the captain's ribs, he guided him towards the hidden room. The captain had lost the capacity for speech. His mind was crowding. He couldn't remember exactly what he was doing here. In the windowless gloom, Henderson made out a stack of paintings of naked women – why were none of them Maria? His eyes dimmed. Fisher's voice was an echo.

'My wife wouldn't like my little collection,' he admitted, pushing the captain into a corner.

He fetched a length of rope and tied Henderson's arms. The terriers were still yapping, though it sounded as they were further away, in the street perhaps. Henderson tried to lift his head, but it was too heavy. The room heaved. Were they on a ship? Were they at sea? What had he done to her?

'Jewellery,' Fisher said contentedly as he tied the knot. 'That's what I always say. Copious jewellery and your attention over breakfast. Keeps any woman happy and you can do whatever you like.'

Piccadilly

Maria arrived a little early for Murray's salon, at the publisher's own request. She took the news of Sir Horace's refusal of her talk, and the resultant unlikelihood of her being accepted at the Royal Society, rather better than Murray expected.

'My goodness.' She smiled, her eyes bright and with a look that Murray could only describe as mischievous. 'You've caused a stir, John. Perhaps we must simply come to terms with the fact that certain of our friends will never accept the notion of a lady with a mind of her own.'

Nervous of Maria's reaction, Murray had downed half a bottle of port before she arrived and now it was spreading a pleasant tide of warmth through his body. His eyes were round as soft-boiled eggs, halved and ready to be consumed. He had thought Maria would be distraught. That she would blame him. Now, he smiled.

'The truth is that a lady must do what she can,' Maria continued smoothly, 'and in this situation, we can only hope the books will be well received by those broad-minded enough to read them without judgement. As you know, that does not include members of my own family, who disregard the good notices of society because I am a woman. As for the glory of the Royal Society, well, it was a lot to hope for and I am not entirely convinced it would be a pleasant excursion. They gave Margaret Cavendish a dreadful time.'

'That was over a hundred years ago,' Murray said. They had called her Mad Madge. 'Some lady must be first,' he commented.

Maria got up. She walked to the window. The muffled sound of hooves on beaten earth reached her as the carriages creaked by. Albemarle Street was bathed in summer sunlight. It hadn't rained for two or three days.

'Well, it's hardly a battle worth engaging in. I shan't be in London much longer.'

'If you were a gentleman, you would not take this sleight so well,' Murray pointed out.

A ghost of a smirk played across Maria's face. 'If I were a gentleman, I would call Sir Horace out, I expect. And as I cannot, you are angry on my behalf?'

Murray nodded.

'You men – always after blood. If Sir Horace is mistaken, I'm sure it will not be the first time or the last. And in this matter, I believe he is mistaken,' she said coolly. 'That is enough, don't you think?'

A laugh escaped Murray's lips.

'We cannot,' she continued smoothly, 'exact our revenge on such people. Why, we would find ourselves at war with half the world.' Maria sat tidily on the yellow sofa with her ankles crossed and her hands in her lap. Her mind flitted to Georgiana and, for that matter, her aunt. It was the same over and over. One could not be held up by it. 'It seems to me, Mr

Murray, you don't comprehend what it is to be a lady and a writer. That is the matter.'

Murray laughed. 'Pray, tell me. How is it?' The publisher leaned forward.

'Sir, I'm a widow. I shall never have children. But I can leave my writings and I can teach the Princess Maria da Gloria. One day she may rule millions of people and perhaps some of my teachings will help her to make sound decisions. It sounds grand, I know. But how many childless women can leave such a legacy – not money or mere gossip or a flight of poetry, but something that might have a bearing on the world? Her Majesty wishes me to teach the princess not only sketching or deportment, but geography, history, mathematics, languages. A proper education. Can you imagine? We women are bred to fall in love, to put on charm alongside our other vestments – one as important as the other. This is a chance to educate a young woman who might someday be an Elizabeth! Sir Horace be damned. That and being able to write my journals gives me a voice – one that you amplify by publishing my words. Men such as Sir Horace may not listen, but that does not downplay the fact that I have said what I wish. I have seen the world. These are my concerns. And while there are things I must give up for that – the good services of my family, perhaps – it seems to me that for a lady lucky enough to have such opportunities, the Royal Society and Sir Horace Strange are by the by. I shall see the world and I shall understand as much of it as I can.'

And there it was. Murray sat back. She was simply the most admirable woman. Upon occasion, there was something historical about her. He published everyone, but some of his authors were simply made for posterity.

'Have you everything you need, Maria? You know that if there is anything . . .'

Maria turned. There were two dresses still to arrive from the Calcotts' seamstress, but they were on their way and Murray would not wish to be troubled by trifles. In addition, her finances looked remarkably healthy. Murray had put a most generous price on her books. Maria had visited a few private galleries and strolled round the new public gallery at Dulwich with the Calcotts. She had amassed a small library to take back to Rio and had called on almost all her old acquaintances. She had also bought a leather pouch to house Calcott's miniature of her father, which she had taken to carrying with her at all times. It was nestled now in the drawstring bag she had laid on Murray's side table. Lady Dundas was surly but as close to placated as might be hoped. Georgiana was beyond help. All in all, Maria was set. There was no place for Henderson in her future. There could not be. This fact still stung her, but no progress could be made without some losses. She bore up.

'I have your friendship, sir and your role as a staunch supporter besides. What more might I require?'

The question hung.

The butler came into the room. 'Mr Smyth is here, and Mr Gulliver,' he announced.

'Afternoon tea?' Murray offered. In Maria's flight of passion, he had forgotten there were other guests. 'Oh. Yes. Bring them up.' He waved off the butler.

'My dear.' He leaned in confidentially, knowing only a few seconds remained before they would be in company. 'You will promise me, though, should you have another chance for marital contentment . . . You are still young enough . . . and what is a life without love? You would not give up that, I hope.'

Maria's hand lighted on the drawstring bag. Her stomach jumped. He didn't know. He couldn't. Had she given herself away? She searched Murray's face and realised that the enquiry was general. She put his mind at rest. 'Another fellow like Thomas, you mean? I can't imagine I should ever be so fortunate,' she said. 'I am content, John. Really I am. I have made my choices and they are good ones.'

Murray wavered. It was on the tip of his tongue to enquire as to Maria's happiness. Goodness was important, but, still, it was happiness that made a life. Then the door opened and Mr Smyth entered with his hand held out and John Murray abandoned the idea. It had, after all, probably been foolish.

*

In Garrick Street, Fry had decided to wait half an hour before he took any action. He bought a tankard of small beer at the bar and eyed a game of crown and anchor that was under way in the corner of the room between keeping a check on Fisher's front door. It was, he was positive, no more than twenty minutes after Henderson had disappeared inside when the door opened and Fisher emerged and slipped into the back of a carriage that pulled round. Fry considered. Fisher had left the house alone, which meant the captain must still be inside, and that, most assuredly, was not right.

He laid his tankard on a table. There was no evidence of any wrongdoing visible through the house's black windows, but Fry was curious. Leaving a coin for the serving girl, he crossed the road, dodging the stinking manure that had built up in the absence of a sweeper. Garrick Street was too mixed to merit the prompt attention on offer for gentlemen traversing the roads around Piccadilly. Fry turned the corner. On Rose Street, Fisher's house had a side gate, but it was locked. He peered over the top. The back garden was laid to grass and he could see no movement in the windows beyond it.

Returning to the street, Fry knocked on the front door and awaited the sturdy footman. 'My friend, Captain Henderson called here earlier,' he said when the door opened. 'I'm looking for him.'

'The gentleman from Brazil?'

'Yes.'

'He left, sir. With Mr Fisher.'

Fry studied the man's face, which was entirely impassive. There was something of the bulldog about him. Fry knew better than to argue with an English footman, valet or butler in the matter of who was or wasn't home. There was no bringing them round. 'I see. Thank you,' he said. 'I'll look for my friend elsewhere.'

The footman closed the door. Fry tarried on the step, considering his course of action. There seemed nothing for it but to get inside the house. Henderson was definitely still inside. He turned smartly towards the side gate, where he paused to check that he had aroused no notice. Then, with some effort, he pulled himself over the top. Without hesitation, he dodged between the lines of drying washing and sneaked towards the rear. From the basement, a wispy cloud of steam rose from a vent in the kitchen window and inside there was a flurry of activity as a maid and a cook fussed over the long table.

Fry looked up. Ahead of him, on the ground floor, there were three rooms to the rear, one of them a library. With

Fisher out, there would be no resident of the house in there. The library was the domain of the master. This made it the perfect point of entry. Looking round, he fetched an empty barrel that lay to one side of an outhouse and levered himself onto the windowsill. Then he painfully smashed his elbow through one of the small mullioned panes and reached gingerly through the ragged glass to open the window and step inside.

Mrs Fisher's dogs were stationed by the fireplace. As Fry's feet landed on the carpet, they sniffed the air. One of them let out a solitary bark as if in greeting and then the terriers waddled over, tails wagging. Richard dropped to his haunches and petted them.

'There, there,' he said, comforting himself as much as the animals, his stomach was turning over. If he was caught here, God knows what they might do to him. 'Now,' he said to the dogs, 'where's the captain?'

By logic, Henderson must be restrained. In a house such as this, there might be any number of storerooms and cupboards, the most secure of which was usually near the kitchen and housed the silver. It would be tricky to get into. Richard crossed the room and the dogs trotted at his side. When he reached the door, he listened and put his eye to the keyhole. The dogs barked. 'Shush,' he said.

The hall appeared deserted. Richard listened. If they had taken the captain, he would fight and there might be some kind of noise. On the other side of the hallway, a grandfather clock ticked loudly. Apart from that, the silence was absolute. Richard steeled himself and was about to hazard crossing the hallway to investigate when, behind him, the dogs barked again and one of them made a whining sound. He turned to reprimand the animal. It might be a large house, but a barking dog might draw attention. Both terriers were on the other side of the room, one of them bouncing up and down against a bookshelf. Fry laughed. The little animals were eccentric – quite loveable really. Still, he must get on – Henderson needed him. He decided to search methodically – the top of the house (where there should be fewer people and, therefore, where he should be safer) to the bottom.

Fry turned the doorknob and was about to slip into the hallway and make for the stairs when he heard a maid approaching. His heart pounding, he curled back into the room and squatted, watching the girl through the keyhole as she crossed the black-and-white tiles with a bucket of coal in her hand. The dogs had stopped barking now, but one of them was still knocking himself silly off the row of books.

'What on earth are you up to?' Richard hissed as he crept across to investigate.

The terriers appeared to be interested in the writing of Plato. Fry touched the book. The dog barked again and its fellow appeared by its side as Richard grabbed its snout. 'Shhh,' he whispered.

One terrier wagged his tail as the other continued to butt himself against the classics. With half an eye on the door, Fry removed a book. 'Plato?' he asked.

This was foolish. Then he noticed the rim of the bookcase. It was flush, but the edges were split. You had to be close to notice it, but there was a thin outline the size of a door embedded in the frame. Fry grinned. He stroked the dog. 'I don't suppose you feel like telling me how to open it?' He looked around.

But before he could go any further, he heard footsteps

approaching the door. Quickly, he dived under the desk. One of the terriers followed him, but Fry kicked him off firmly and the dog trotted behind the maid as she entered the room and filled the coal scuttle. Fry kept the girl's feet in his sightline as she bent to replenish supplies.

'Brent will come for you. He'll let you out later,' she scolded the little animal as she lifted her bucket and left the room.

So, there wasn't long. The dog returned to Fry's heel, wagging its tail enthusiastically, as he scrambled back to the bookcase. Richard tried to pull the door open, heaving from under one of the shelves. When that didn't work, he removed more books at random, but none of them seemed connected to a latch. His mind raced as he considered the dilemma. Where might a fellow want the opening mechanism? Smiling, his eyes lit back on the desk. He picked up the inkwell and blotting paper, running his fingers around the edges of the drawers. Then he dropped to his knees and examined the underside, where he'd just been hiding. There was an ormolu knob at the top of one of the legs that he had missed in his haste. He pushed it. The door popped open, hitting a terrier broadside. Fry's fingertips tingled. He didn't know how long he had and his heart was beating like a pump. This was exciting.

Peering inside Fisher's secret room, the boy found what he was looking for. There was Henderson out cold, tied up on the floor with the dogs sniffing around him, licking his face. Fry checked the captain was breathing. Then he loosened the knots and slapped the man around his face. 'Come on,' he urged.

Henderson didn't stir. Fry considered a moment. The captain was always so strong and competent. To see him like this was disconcerting. The boy's mind raced. He had to get Henderson out of here, whatever it took.

'Blazes,' he murmured, taking a deep breath, as with difficulty he hoisted the captain onto his shoulder and half carried, half dragged him into the library. Appraising the situation, Fry realised that, having knocked out the captain, Fisher would be coming back, most likely with the other members of the Old Street Bridge Club. His first priority must be to get Henderson out of the house and back to the *Bittersweet*, but he also needed to send a message to the gentlemen, who were no doubt on their way. He had to make a statement.

He looked around. On the carpet were the volumes of Plato he had removed. Fry scooped them up and dumped them in the wide baronial fireplace, then he returned to the secret room and removed several of the smaller paintings. Behind one there was an indent, a mere ledge, and on it a leather-bound notebook. On impulse, he grabbed it and stuck it in his pocket. At the fireplace, the boy stacked the small paintings in a well-constructed pyramid so that the flames would catch and then he reached for the tinderbox on the mantel. It took a minute to spark a flame and then, breathing in, he let it fall onto the books, kindling the bonfire from the bottom. Old Mr Fry would be horrified. This was some kind of ultimate evil. Books were sacrosanct. Fry felt his pulse racing even faster as the paper crinkled. He fetched more volumes and wedged them in, making sure the fire spread to the paintings above. He eyed the naked nymphs as they bubbled and cracked. The dogs settled contentedly in the warmth.

On the desk, he picked out a piece of paper. *If you come looking,* he wrote, *next will be Mallow Street, then Grant's residence and Hayward's. Fire spreads.* Fry blotted his words. He reached inside his pocket and took out the notebook, ready to throw it on the flames, but the grate was jammed. 'It won't burn if air doesn't circulate,' he chided himself. A schoolboy error.

He stuck the notebook back in his pocket and hoisted Henderson onto his shoulder. Ignoring his aching bruises, he hauled the captain across the room and silently opened the door. The hallway was deserted. Fry kept his eye on the rear, where the servants' stairs emerged into the main house. In a feat of precarious balance, he hauled Henderson's body to the front door, thrust it open and continued outside into the sun. On Garrick Street, there were so many drunken gentlemen that the captain's condition was unremarkable. As Fry manoeuvred down the steps, three men were singing outside one of the taverns. They pointed and waved. 'Got your dad there?' one of them shouted. The others laughed.

Fry searched for a sign of movement from the house or any whisper of Fisher's return to the street. The showy carriage in which he'd left was nowhere to be seen and the boy kept moving. Half a block down, he hailed a cab. 'Take me to the river,' he instructed. 'I need a skiff to Greenwich.'

The driver alighted to help bundle Henderson inside. 'He's had a skinful,' the man said. 'What's he celebrating?'

Fry shrugged. It seemed best to make light of it. He hoped the captain would wake soon. 'He likes a drink is all.'

The boy looked back at Fisher's. There was still no sign of the club's return and the boy worried that the blaze might spread. He had left the dogs in the library. As he looked down, he realised his hands were shaking. He leaned against the frame of the carriage. He had wanted to send a warning – he was right to do so. Besides, it was too late to go back now. He suddenly felt a shaft of ice run down his arms. His fingers were freezing. Would the gentlemen come looking? He tried to dismiss the thought, but he knew this was an escalation.

The captain showed no sign of stirring. Joseph Fry's words rang in the boy's ears – *A Fry always thinks things through.* Well, he'd saved Henderson's life. That much at least was good news. With one final look at the Fisher residence, Richard mounted the grubby interior of the cab and set off for the *Bittersweet*.

29

On board the Bittersweet

Henderson was plagued with strange dreams. When he woke, he was in his cabin, it was dark and he had a ferocious thirst. He blundered out of bed, not sure what was real and what imaginary. By the light of the moon, which cast a cold stripe across the boards, he poured a drink from the decanter on the table. Immediately he had emptied the glass, he realised he had not been able to taste a drop. Then he fell to his knees and vomited into the chamber pot. When he found he could scramble to his feet again, he felt driven to check the stones and the gold he had secreted under the cabin floorboards alongside the main portion of his money. He prised his way into this hiding place and delved inside. Everything was where he'd left it. Hurriedly, he secreted his prizes again and, trying to stay calm, laid a hand on his stomach. At last, resting against the wooden wall, he took a moment to think. He had eaten with Richard and they had visited several houses in town and, it came to him suddenly, there had been a small dog. Yes, it was Fisher's dog. No, Fisher's wife's dog. He had delivered the goods and then . . . Suddenly the captain remembered exactly what had happened.

In a panic, he burst out of the cabin and onto the deck. Two sailors on watch sprang to their feet, their faces pale and startled in the light of the thin moon. Over the side, Greenwich was calm and all but silent, and the frantic captain appeared out of place. A seagull called a way off.

'Sir.'

'How did I get here?'

'Sir?'

'Who brought me back to the ship?'

'Mr Fry, sir.'

'Where is he?'

'Abed.'

'And were we followed?'

'No, sir.'

'Is there any news of Mrs Graham?'

The seamen looked at him blankly.

On the high street, the church bells struck five of the clock. Henderson's mind was a rush. The dock was deserted. The gangplank was up. Everything seemed normal and yet he was engulfed by dread. He had ruined the best of women. The beasts would do anything they could. She had been right all along and now there was no way back.

The morning air was fresh and soon the sun would rise. He could hear the wash of the water against the side of the ship, a lazy slap against the boards. Towards town, further up the river, there were the first peeps of life in the city – a lamp on a skiff or a passing carriage going home very late, a flame in the window of the bakery. Mostly, London was sleeping. But somewhere over there, be it in the East End or the West, the Old Street Bridge Club was no doubt discussing his disappearance.

'Have I slept round the clock?' Henderson asked.

'You came back in the afternoon, sir.'

'Keep a close eye. There may be men,' the captain ordered, waving them off. 'We may have to fight.'

Henderson left the deck. Without knocking, he burst into Richard's cabin. Fry sat up sleepily, his hair tousled.

'Captain,' he cried. 'You're well.'

Henderson grabbed the boy by the sleeve of his nightgown. 'They know about Mrs Graham,' he said desperately. 'They know . . .' His voice broke. 'And they will expose her. I must send payment immediately. I must run goods on their behalf. I must placate them.'

Fry let this sink in.

'They had talked somehow to the men.' Henderson's tone was desperate.

'It's rumour, then. Backstairs gossip. Nothing more.'

The captain shook the boy by the shoulders. 'Her book is to be published, Richard. Her book about Brazil. And they will name her for a harlot – a fallen woman. What matter the proof of it? Her friends may not believe it, but the rest of London . . . a rumour is enough.'

Fry nodded, understanding settling. 'Oh God,' he said. 'James, I set a fire of the fellow's books and some of his paintings. When I took you, I thought to leave a message, and to underline it I set a blaze in the grate. I threatened them.'

Henderson's temper flared. He pushed Fry back on his bunk. 'You fool!' he spat.

'I saved your life,' Fry shot back. 'I didn't know they'd uncovered your affair.'

A stream of rising sunlight seeped round the edges of the shuttered porthole as the day dawned.

Fry looked sheepish. 'I'm sorry,' he said.

Henderson was about to lash out, but a muffled knock sounded on the door. It was one of the men from the deck. He was holding a sheet of folded folio. 'It arrived at first light, sir, only a second ago. A message boy,' he said, his eyes avoiding both men as he handed over the missive.

Henderson opened the seal. The writing was clear. The message clearer.

Men in wooden ships should not start fires.

'Those bastards will kill every man on board,' Fry said.

Henderson sank onto the edge of the bunk. He turned over the paper and considered as it dawned on him there was something there – a hint upon which he might hang a negotiation.

'These men are bullies and they will strike one way or another.' He spoke slowly as he reasoned it out. 'But still, if I read it right, this is not a statement – it is an invitation. If they wanted to set fire to the *Bittersweet* then they would have done so. No – they are hoping for a response. What you have done is up the stakes, Richard. I don't expect I can simply pay them off any more but still . . .'

Henderson opened the shuttered porthole and peered out to see if the delivery boy had loitered. The quay was deserted apart from a cat curled up asleep on a low wall. There was movement on one or two of the ships at anchor as the sailors stirred, used to getting up with the sun.

'The only way to save her is to kill them.' Fry squared up to the problem.

Henderson turned his gaze back into the cabin and stared at the boy. 'No. That kind of vendetta would be insanity. In that case it will become only a matter of how many people end up dead. You. Me. Clarkson. The fifteen men aboard. Fisher. Grant. Hayward. The staff in each of their houses. Perhaps even Maria. God knows. That way leads to the gallows and it is impossible to call who might win such an engagement. We don't know their resources and, in any such activity, luck plays its part. It is too dangerous and uncontrolled. No. I will tackle it another way. I must face my responsibility.'

Fry got out of bed, ready for action. The captain held up his hand.

'Not you, Richard. It's time for you to go back to Bristol. I'm not prepared to put you in harm's way any longer. You can't help with this, boy. Not now. You've done enough.'

Fry looked appalled. 'I'm not a coward,' he insisted.

'I'm not telling you to run away. You're being ordered out of the line of fire. Like a soldier. You've done an admirable job. You saved my life, whatever might transpire.'

Richard's eyes were surly. He had thought fondly of his home in the last few days. It surprised him how often he'd wanted to share his ideas with his brothers or listen, at least for a little while, to his mother's impassioned tittle-tattle chock-full of unreasonable opinion. Still, he didn't want to be made to go back. 'I'm not a child.'

'Not any more.' Henderson smiled. 'You will return to the safety of your family and stand taller amongst your brothers, I expect. But you will go. I am captain of this ship and I am issuing a command.'

Richard bit his lip. 'But the men are in danger, sir. I must stay to help.'

Henderson shook his head. 'Enough. And no more petty actions, Richard. Setting a fire in the fellow's study. What good is such revenge? We must keep our eyes to the main matter. You are a man now.'

'If I go home, I won't be a man. You think I am a fop.'

'I know most certainly you are not. I have seen you near kill a man. But if I am going to play this game and win it, then I need to play it alone.' The captain stood up. 'Come on. You'd best get your things. Go and say goodbye to Clarkson. I dare say he'll miss you.'

Richard's eyes narrowed. He jumped out of his bunk. 'I'll find Clarkson then,' he said.

As the door closed, Henderson felt his heart sink. The least he could do, he told himself, was save the boy. He sat on the edge of the bunk, facing what lay ahead. He had men and he had weapons. That at least was a start. He'd never backed down from a fight in his life. From his pocket he pulled out the flick knife he'd carried with him – his London blade. He opened and closed it.

Then his eye fell to the desk that jutted out from one side. On it, there was a small leather notebook. He'd never seen Fry with that before, he thought as he picked it up and opened the first page. Inside, columns of figures trailed a ragged line – calculations divided by three and marked by place names. Calais, Natal, Bombay, Canton, Constantinople. Henderson flicked through the pages. Venice, Copenhagen, St Petersburg, Murmansk. Every one a trading port. His fingers tingled. There was only one place Fry could have got this. Henderson started to laugh.

'That boy is a plague of God. I swear.'

He held the note that had arrived in one hand and weighed it against his discovery.

'This is an invitation,' he said. 'And this is what will save Maria Graham's reputation and my life.'

His sense of hope reinstated, Henderson sprang to his feet. He burst into the corridor. Fry was returning to the cabin with a canvas sailor's bag with which Clarkson had evidently provided him.

'You've supplied me ammunition, boy.' The captain grinned. He flung his arm around Fry's shoulder and hugged him. Then he crossed the corridor, closing his door and locking it without waiting for a reply.

'What? What do you mean?' Fry's tone betrayed his bemusement.

Even later, when the boy had dressed and packed and loitered on deck as he completed his target practice one last time, the captain didn't stir. Leaning to listen at his cabin door, all Fry could hear was the scratching of a quill and, intermittently, the captain striding up and down, muttering. Then, at two of the afternoon, Henderson left the *Bittersweet*. He had the air of a man for whom there would be no turning back.

'I have business to see to in town,' he said. 'When I get back, son, no offence, I don't want to see you here.'

★

With the library unusable due to the lingering odour of burning oil paint and leather, the gentlemen congregated in the day room. Fisher was in such a filthy mood that it wasn't surprising his wife had vacated the house to visit her sister in Oxford, taking her damn dogs with her. The staff had seen to her packing while Fisher had sent a note to the artists' agent Mr Notman, whose discretion in the matter of a gentleman's particular collection was always assured.

'It took me years to find just the sort of thing I like,' he complained. 'And the books were worth a fortune. I shall replace them, of course, but the expense.'

'It's not as if you read,' Grant pointed out.

'I might want to,' Fisher snarled.

He hoped that the leather notebook that was missing lay burned amongst the ashes. The fire had been so damnably effective that he could not tell which books had been consigned to the flames, nor could he admit his concerns to Grant and Hayward. Their agreement was that there should be no records. Fisher tried not to think on it and instead focussed on his losses. 'We could have forfeited our lives in this business,' he exploded. 'Lighting flammable material in an unattended room is madness. The carpet is entirely singed,' he said petulantly.

'We shall have him now. Never fear,' Grant soothed. 'We shall hire men.'

Hayward, however, did not want to rush. Fisher was hopeless at most matters – everything except strangling an unsuspecting victim, he thought as he silently reviewed the state of affairs on Garrick Street through the long windows. He should never have left the matter of Henderson in Fisher's lily-fingered grasp. The situation clearly required subtlety. On the street, the new buildings reminded him of a monochrome engraving, one of Robert Wilkinson's finest – a picture of a new London. The sun was at its height and today His Lordship felt that he might manage to consume luncheon. He wondered if Fisher's staff would serve them. The fire had thrown the household into disarray. The butler had not even taken his hat when he arrived, and when Hayward had put it into the man's hands, he had not immediately understood what was required. Mind you, Hayward had never visited the

402

Fisher residence before yesterday and he had not encountered the butler at all on that occasion. It may be that the man was simply poorly trained. The house was grand, but it lacked something. He could not quite put his finger upon it. Hayward strained to see as a message boy approached the door and his missive was taken in.

'Ah,' he said, 'we have a reply.'

The men formed a group around the fireplace. When the footman brought the note, Fisher held it up. It was sealed with green wax and written in a good hand. Fisher turned it over and shooed the man away. As the door closed, he cracked the seal.

'Well?' Grant strained.

Fisher read quickly and handed over the paper. 'Bastard,' he said.

Gentlemen, I firstly want to assure you that the fire of yesterday was not set by me. When my fellows rescued me, they were understandably vexed on my behalf. I only heard of their actions upon rising after a long sleep induced by your brandy. I wish to apologise heartily for what they did, but if you will persist in trying to kill me, I expect such matters will continue. I also wish to issue an invitation to Lord Hayward – a peer of the realm and a fellow I hope I can trust. Sir, if you would like to finish this matter to the satisfaction of us all, I suggest we meet tomorrow morning at 11 at the offices of my acquaintance, Mr John Murray, at 50 Albemarle Street, Piccadilly. I have chosen this address because if you were to attempt to kill me there, you would certainly be charged, and if I were to harm you, the same would apply. It is a gentleman's address and I hope we will all behave as gentlemen while we are there. Mr Murray is unaware of our situation, but he is an accommodating fellow. Will you risk it? I admit you have a great deal held over me, but you will find I am not unarmed. If you carry out your threat against my ship, I promise you a bloody breakfast, and if you carry through your threat against the lady's reputation then I will do worse. It would be better to parlay. I hope I can bring us to agreement and will spend today endeavouring to arrange the means to do so.

Grant let the letter drop from his fingers into the fire and watched it curl in the iron basket. His eyes were alight. 'How interesting. Do you think he might give us more money? *The means to do so.* Is that what he's referring to? If so, we should get our hands on that before we do anything else – the third share that was owing.'

'To hell with that. If we go tonight, we can burn him alive in his ship,' Fisher spat.

Hayward sat on a richly upholstered chair. He sighed. His eyes fell to a chessboard, which was in play on the other side of the room. Even from here he could make out the best move. Fisher must play with his wife – only a woman could possibly mount such a vulnerable defence. He could mate in two moves in two different ways. The peer got up and played black. It was disappointing that both his business partners so lacked vision.

'He's intriguing, isn't he? Well, Fisher, I think for once you are right. Let's see what the fellow has to say for himself. We can disgrace the woman afterwards if we want to. I think I shall meet him before deciding what's best. I'll go to Murray's tomorrow, and if we still want to kill the man afterwards, what's to stop us?'

'You mean at Murray's?' Fisher sounded shocked.

'Certainly not. But we can pull him into a carriage if we choose and take him to Mallow Street. He thinks an address in Piccadilly will save him? The impudence of it! Still, I'd like to hear what he has to say.'

'I shall come with you,' Grant swore.

Hayward nodded. 'If you wish. You can wait in the carriage. But I say let's play his game for now. I, for one, am intrigued.'

Fisher licked his lips greedily. 'And if there is more money—' he started.

Hayward cut in. 'If there is money to be had, then we shall have it, dear fellow.'

Fisher wandered over and stood on the other side of the chessboard. He played a white bishop to the front lines. 'All right,' he said, resigned 'Should I come too?'

'You have enough to do here, I imagine, old man. Leave this to Grant and I. We shall send news as soon as we have it.'

The truth was, Lord Hayward wanted to keep Fisher out of the way. This had to be dealt with competently and, though deadly in the confines of the Old Street Bridge Club, Fisher didn't have what it took to kidnap a man in the street or, indeed, blackmail a fellow effectively enough to assure the best outcome. Henderson had escaped from his house after he had administered poison. What kind of fool could still lose from a position of such advantage?

'And if you take him to Mallow Street?' Fisher enquired.

'We will wait for you. Of course,' Hayward promised as he brought up his queen. 'Checkmate,' he announced.

Grant laughed. It was a cruel sound, and Fisher fumbled with his cravat. 'Very well, very well,' he said, saved from his humiliation by the butler announcing Mr Notman, who provided an immediate excuse to motion his friends to the door. 'Yes, I have quite enough to see to,' he said airily. 'There's a great deal to do. But we will kill him, Hayward, will we not?'

Hayward knocked over the white king.

'Oh yes,' he said. 'I'm only curious, is all. And this way is neater. I'd hate to miss our mark and tomorrow, at least, we know where he is going to be.'

30

St James's

John Murray rode out in the morning. He enjoyed a canter in the park. It put his mind in the right frame for a few hours' work until it was time for his salon. On Rotten Row, he greeted fellow riders as he passed, for Hyde Park was a hub of sociable encounters. The light was exceptionally pleasant today. There really was nothing quite like an English summer. The trees cast long and complicated shadows, and the sky was a pleasing shade of blue. The smell of grass, which a small army of gardeners were presently scything, rolled in waves towards his nostrils, and the sound of horse brasses, hammering hooves and voices raised in discourse floated back and forth. Much of London society was arrayed in smart riding gear or seated elegantly in glossy leather-upholstered buggies, open to the air. The Sidmouth sisters raced their mounts, and gentlemen passing time with their mistresses slowed the pace so they could talk. Some ladies preferred to walk, their parasols aloft, but most of the excitement was around the track as people made the best of their last week or two in town. Soon London would all but empty as society took off for the countryside in the wake of the good weather. The Thames had already started its summer stink and in London a fellow was never far from the river. It was not only unpleasant to stay but also dangerous. Murray was set to visit relations in Scotland for a month. Mrs Murray had been looking forward to it.

When he had had taken the air, London's foremost publisher trotted back to Albemarle Street. The costermongers were out in full force and several of the kitchen maids had been sent up to street level to avail the household of the best of the fruit from London's market gardens, coming into season. Murray hoped his cook had thought to buy peaches and perhaps some raspberries, of which he was particularly fond – spots of bright blood in the sea of cream on his plate. As the publisher handed over his mount and strode into his shady hallway, the butler approached.

'Captain Henderson is waiting in the drawing room,' he said.

Murray searched to recollect the name. Ah yes, the fellow who had called for Maria. An early visitor. Whatever might he want? Murray handed over his hat and gloves and took the stairs at a stride. The ride had been most invigorating.

Henderson was stationed by the long windows, one eye on the street. As Murray entered, he held out his hand.

'Might I interest you in some refreshment, Captain?' Murray enquired.

Henderson professed himself perfectly satisfied. 'I come with a project in mind, sir. I wondered if I might discuss it?' he said, his tone serious and yet convivial, just as he'd practised with Fry.

It had all been leading to this morning. If he put a foot wrong, he might be dead by lunchtime, and Maria ruined too. He hoped that Murray would never know the half of it. But this was the only respectable place in London he had a reason to call.

The publisher's blue eyes sparkled. He never tired of new proposals. It was part of his success that even when for weeks on end not a single idea was of interest, he still gave consideration to whatever came his way. Many of Murray's most popular publications were the result of a chance meeting or an unsolicited manuscript. Miss Austen, whose books had received limited critical acclaim but sold by the gross, and, for that matter, many of the scientific publications that he had produced, which provoked debate worldwide, had their genesis in moments of chance, just like this one.

'Certainly.' Murray smiled. 'What had you in mind?'

'I have been based in Brazil, as you know, and what I have in mind is cacao. It's a fascinating plant and a delicate one, difficult to farm – an exotic crop that has been a luxury here for hundreds of years. I was brought up in part on a plantation and chocolate has been my cargo for the last fifteen years. I should like to write about it. I will have to search out someone to illustrate this venture – the seedpods are quite beautiful and lend the plantations a particular wildness. There are native recipes that employ chilli or nutmeg, which they use for ritual purposes – meditation, and medication too. The drink has a reputation in Europe for lavishness and allure. From the seed to the cup, I thought. Do you think such an endeavour might be of interest?'

Murray took a seat by the fireplace and considered Henderson's appearance. The fellow was well dressed, and the rough edge he had, the sea captain in him, suited him well. At least this time he hadn't mentioned Maria. Murray thought of the books already available on this subject. Sloane had written a great deal about cacao, but that was almost a century before. There was nothing of popular interest that he could think of.

409

'I should need to see how you write, Captain, before I can commit myself, but yes, readers often enjoy discourse of a botanical nature and there are many chocolate devotees. Mrs Murray, herself, is one. Such a book could do well. How might you approach it?'

'The different varieties of cacao produce different flavours. There is criollo from Brazil and elsewhere in South America. Trinidad has its own varieties – all different to cultivate. I'd like to write about that. The farms, the methods and the processing of the beans, as well as their uses in the kitchen and out of it.'

Murray nodded. The more he thought of it, the more he liked the idea. In addition to the botanical element, London loved to read about foreign climes. Good travel books sold in numbers and everyone was interested in the medicinal qualities of food.

'If you could compose it as a personal journey, visiting plantations and describing what you find – the people who work there, the customs and superstitions as well as the botanical issues and recipes – then, yes, if you would do me the honour, I should very much like to read what you produce with a view to publication.'

A grin split the captain's face and quite suddenly he had the air of a boy who had scored a point at a ball game. Smiling, he continued to hover at the window. 'Thank you,' he said. 'I was hoping that my friend Mr Fry of Bristol might write an introduction.'

Murray had heard of the Frys, but a botanist would be better than someone in trade – the author of the foreword should be eminent. Such a decision might make or break a book. There was no point in tackling that issue now, however.

Instead, the publisher brushed it off. 'We shall see. I may find a fellow to pen something for you.' He crossed the room to lay a hand on the globe by his desk, where he peered at South America. Henderson joined him and helpfully pointed out Brazil and Trinidad.

'Cacao only grows in tropical conditions,' he said. 'The latitudes form exact boundaries – there is no chocolate above or below them. The terrain must be perfect or the entire enterprise fails.'

Murray considered the area in question. 'And longitude?' he enquired.

'Well, it stops at the sea.'

Henderson moved the globe. The latitudes he had pointed out ran across the Atlantic and his finger lighted upon the west coast of Africa. Something stirred. It occurred to him suddenly – might cacao be able to grow there, in another place along the correct latitude, but on the other side of the ocean? Henderson twitched as a candle lit in his mind. It was providence, surely. Almost as if the regions were somehow related – distant cousins torn apart. It might be possible. Imagine if it were.

Murray, oblivious, retreated to his seat, and Henderson tore his attention away from the Ivory Coast and recalled himself to the matters in hand. Out of the corner of his eye, he could see movement at Murray's front door distorted through the uneven glass. The second and more dangerous part of his plan was coming into play. The church bells struck eleven of the clock, the hazy chimes from nearby Warwick Street sliding over the slates.

'You have had a pleasant morning, then?' He made idle conversation.

411

'Riding,' Murray admitted, still pink-cheeked.

Henderson waited. The clock on the mantle ticked. He felt his heart pumping as the butler entered the room.

'Sir,' he announced. 'Lord Hayward is here.'

Murray stood up. 'Hayward . . . Hayward . . .' He was trying to recall the name.

'That's for me,' Henderson said. 'I sent a note to His Lordship. I wanted to introduce him, Mr Murray.'

Murray nodded, as acquiescent as expected. 'Send him up, then,' he said. 'Any friend of yours is most welcome, Captain.'

This was how Henderson had seen it playing out. He steeled himself.

When Hayward entered the room, he was not in a friendly frame of mind. His eyes impassive, he made a slight bow in Murray's direction and then blurted, 'Well, sir. I am here, damn you.'

Henderson laughed, as if Hayward was a naughty child or simply in his cups. 'I summoned you, Lord Hayward. I apologise for that.'

Hayward glared. He had come as bidden, but he would not put on a show for Murray. In fact, he looked as if he might strangle the captain with his bare hands. Henderson, however, remained calm, convivial even.

'When I last met Mr Murray, I lacked manners,' he admitted. 'I hoped my acquaintance with a peer of the realm might reassure him. I wanted to introduce you.'

Murray put up his hand to allay any such assumption. 'In this residence,' he said, 'ideas are of paramount importance. I like the idea of your book, Captain. It is always a pleasure to meet new friends, however. Lord Hayward might I offer you—'

'Brandy,' Hayward said, his eyes still on the captain.

Murray looked around. The decanters were not out – it was early. He rang for service and, frustrated, went to the door. 'I shall have them fetch some,' he said as he disappeared.

Hayward's eyes lit up. 'Your guard dog has gone.' He smiled ominously. 'And if you think you are protected here or anywhere else, you are greatly mistaken, Captain. We shall have you.'

Henderson knew he only had a moment. 'I am trying to come to an accommodation where every one of us does not end up bloody, beaten or burnt, Lord Hayward. If you have me, I shall have you back, and how many of us will end up in an early grave? You strike me as the most intelligent of the gentlemen at Mallow Street, so let me put something to you. A proposition. Murray is not my only guard dog, sir. I have left letters in the event anything should happen to me or to the *Bittersweet* or, indeed, to Mrs Graham. They will be dispatched if you cause harm. And, sir, I have a record of your dealings. This is no longer a mere matter of reputation. It is a matter of the law. And what I have will see you swing.'

Hayward drew a slim cigar from his inside pocket. 'Letters? Pah,' he said as he lit up. 'There are no records of our dealings, sir.'

Henderson shook his head. 'I beg to differ. I found exactly that at Mr Fisher's residence. Did you not know of it? It goes back years. A gross of silken cloth from Murmansk and a shipment of green tea from Canton in the last few weeks alone. A notebook.'

Hayward was a chess player, not a fellow for the cards. He betrayed his shock. These were indeed the last two shipments that had passed through the Bridge Club's hands. *Damn Fisher,* he thought as his heart plummeted. The fool had been keeping accounts. He was obsessed with money – of course he had.

Henderson ignored Hayward's distress and continued smoothly. 'Until now I have been merely a captain in your eyes – a drudge – but Murray is commissioning me to write for him. I am to be established in London. So I am a gentleman, sir, like you. As such, we must come to terms.'

Hayward looked as if he might not take the trouble to remove the captain from his shoe, had he stepped on him. He grabbed Henderson by the lapels. 'Gentleman,' he spat. 'I'll kill you, and I'll kill bloody Fisher too.'

'What you do to Fisher is your business. But if you make me fight, I'll unmask you,' the captain growled, his face against the peer's. 'If anything happens to me or to Mrs Graham, the details will be released and you, sir, and your fellows will swing. The letters I have written are detailed. I have had them notarised. They are addressed to the chairman of every club in London and to the editor of every paper. To the magistrates and to the Bishop. To the coffee houses. Oh, and to your wife and to Fisher's. Your secret is a scandal, and there will be no escaping it if you have me. I promise. We'll be like two men with loaded pistols pointed at each other's temples. It's the safest way, if you have the nerve for it. Which, from what I know of you, I'm sure you do.'

Just at the moment Hayward understood the captain's proposal, the door opened and Murray returned, the butler in tow. Hayward stepped back, his eyes flitting. The captain had considerably upped his game.

'Brandy, was it?' Murray smiled as he poured the pale

liquid into the crystal balloons. The carved facets amplified the light into sharp pinpricks, like tiny suns.

'I was just saying,' Henderson said smoothly, 'should you publish my discourse, Lord Hayward knows more of me than most. He could make or break my reputation.'

Murray handed Hayward a glass and he held the brandy to the window to examine its colour before sipping. He appeared to be thinking. Having perused the liquid in his glass, he now turned his attention to Henderson, or, more accurately, his attire, which he checked up and down coldly. Then he leaned confidentially towards Murray. 'The captain can be fiery, you know.'

The publisher beamed. 'Yes. I noticed his passion when he was discussing cacao. Well, that may be all to the good for the manuscript.'

Hayward finished his glass.

'Might I accompany you down?' Henderson enquired.

Murray rose, still without an inkling that anything untoward had taken place. 'It is a pleasure doing business with you, gentlemen.' He nodded happily. 'I shall look forward to reading your book, Captain,' he called, already making for his desk. 'Please call again.'

At the bottom of the stairs, Hayward and Henderson collected their hats and gloves.

'I should still kill you,' Hayward growled. 'I'm tempted to chop you up, bit by bit. A finger first, then a nose, and the devil take us all.'

'That's why I arranged to meet you here.' The captain had no illusions. 'I expect you'll calm down in time.' He spoke with the lightness of a fellow who was not at all disturbed by gruesome threats. Likewise, the butler's face betrayed not a whisper of concern as he assisted the gentlemen with their attire. It was as if he hadn't heard them. Where did Murray get such exemplary staff? Hayward wondered.

'You have written the letters and lodged them?' he asked.

'With a reliable and well-paid solicitor. Should anything untoward happen to me, or to the *Bittersweet*, there will be revelations, and the force of the law will hear of your operations. Men swing for smuggling, sir, as you know. And should you escape the penalty of the law, you'll be done for in society. Still, I have no interest in pursuing you and your friends. As far as I am concerned, the deal is done – you have been paid. I should like to be left alone. And though Mrs Graham is nothing to me, it is only fair you should leave her alone too. That was a low blow, sir. She is a lady.'

The butler opened the door and the gentlemen turned down Albemarle Street towards Charing Cross. Hayward took a minute to break the silence, but when he did so, he had come to a conclusion. 'You have a deal,' he said with a curt nod.

The fellow had presented a clever solution. The Old Street Bridge Club had never done business with one of their own. Not in all the years. Perhaps this was why. Hayward wondered if Henderson might best him at chess.

'We wanted you to work for us,' Hayward said, as if he was excusing his actions. 'We might have made a very great deal of money.'

Henderson shrugged. 'And I respectfully decline. No measure of harm in it. I am simply not available.'

'I shall follow your lead, sir. I shall address letters to Murray and to the Lord Advocate, outlining what we know of you. Your shadier dealings. Smuggling and even piracy, from what

I understand. I shall unmask Mrs Graham's moral failings. I shall lodge letters safely and see her ruined and you hanged if you do not keep your word. How about that?'

'I suggest you do,' Henderson insisted. 'That's the spirit. Fire ahead. I prefer the chances of two fellows equally armed, don't you? I knew you'd get the hang of it.'

Hayward's eyes narrowed, but he kept his head.

At the street corner the carriage with his coat of arms was waiting. Inside, Charming Charlie Grant sat, both hands on his stick, a man in the shadows. His eyes lit on the captain and he leaned forward greedily, ready to help Hayward force him inside. He had a knife drawn and, furious as he lunged, he plunged it into Henderson's forearm. The razor-sharp blade cut through the fabric of the captain's jacket and a stream of blood shot up from the gash. Henderson called out, more in fright than in agony. His heart was pounding. Hayward lifted his hand and roughly pushed Grant away.

'No,' he said.

Grant spluttered.

'I shall tell you on the way,' His Lordship drawled. Fisher would feel the sting, he swore silently. The fool had compromised them all. Hayward hated to trust anyone.

Henderson pulled back. He drew a handkerchief from his pocket to bind the wound. Later Big Al Thatcher could stitch it and the pain would settle.

'Apologies,' Hayward said, though he clearly didn't mean it.

The captain held out his good hand, but His Lordship declined to shake it. The captain pressed him. 'I insist. It will hurt me more than you, I'll warrant.'

Slowly, Hayward grasped Henderson's fingers.

'What became of Sam Pearson?' the captain enquired.

'He'll recover,' Hayward lied.

'He's loyal, you know.'

'I hope, Captain, we do not meet again.' His Lordship shrugged as he mounted. 'I hope that wound is infected and you die of it.'

Henderson stood on the pavement as the door slammed and the coach drew away.

As he walked down Charing Cross Road, Henderson could not help but feel that Hayward was still there, on his shoulder. He realised it was a sensation that might take a while to shift. The Old Street Bridge Club was nothing if not memorable, but, he thought, smiling, he had brought them to terms. He had done it.

It was a short stroll to Mr Thin's bookshop, but the captain felt like the walk. He was a free man. He wondered if the old bookseller might have an atlas – specifically, now he thought on it, maps of west Africa. The idea that had lit beside Murray's globe was growing. Fluid, it trickled around his mind. However a gentleman made his money, surely the most important thing was to be able to pay your bills. London welcomed new ideas, Maria had said. Henderson wondered how well London welcomed new money. He checked his pocket watch and wondered if Maria had received the parcel he had sent her. He had wanted her to have the present, no matter how his meeting with Hayward transpired. He shrugged. Later, he'd return to the *Bittersweet*. He hoped she had sent a note.

The sun was at its height. A ghost shivered by, a shadow of his mother creeping along the shady side of the street. Henderson smiled. There was a long way to go, but at least he had started. He must lay his plans now and investigate the profits available under a hot African sun – closer to London and nowhere near as developed as Brazil. His new life was starting. He had discovered a new land here – a place of possibilities. England. As he passed a newsstand, he picked up a copy of *The Times*. The headline was of Admiral Cochrane's victories on behalf of Brazil. The war, it would seem, was over, and the Emperor's throne secure. *I might never see it,* the captain pondered silently. *I might never return to South America again.*

31

Mayfair

In the window seat at Georgiana's mansion, Maria pored over the newspaper reports of the South American war for almost an hour. However, there was nowhere near enough detail. Nothing was mentioned about Rio, or at least only in passing. It appeared Cochrane had not yet returned to the capital, which meant, she expected, that he had set off on some other mission. It was most frustrating not to know. Her things were almost packed and in two days she intended to leave for Portsmouth, where she would take a berth across the Atlantic. She considered writing to the editor and asking if she could read the original report upon which the article had been based. She might well have done so had there not been a delivery.

The package arrived in a small pine packing-box that she opened by means of Georgiana's letter knife, retrieved from the desk. Inside, packed in straw, was a bar of chocolate and a note. *The Spanish way,* it said. She smiled. Then she fetched a little sharp from her vanity case and drilled into the bar, immediately hitting something solid. She looked over her shoulder and then began to mine it. Maria peered, wide-eyed, realising there was gold inside, just as the note had promised. And there was only one person who might have sent it. Grinning now, she worked quickly, scraping off the chocolate in long curls to reveal a substantial necklet of almondine garnets that twinkled darkly in the room's low light. The stones were the colour of claret, but there was an appropriate hue to them – a shadow the colour of chocolate. The necklet was set in thin gold cups with links between them. Maria detached the bottom garnet and turned it around, realising it might be used as a brooch to sit on the lapel or in a hairpiece. She sank back on her haunches and sighed. It was beautiful – with more substance than any opal. It was as if he knew. Her face was flecked with chocolate scraps and her hands were brown as she scrambled through the box, spreading straw and chocolate shavings over Georgiana's Chinese carpet. At the bottom, she found Henderson's note.

This gift is for you, Maria. I do not expect us to meet again and I want you to have something to remember me by. I apologise for my imposition and thank you for inspiring me to improve. Anything I may achieve would be impossible had you not shown me the way. 'Don't you want something better?' you asked me once. Now I have seen what that means and the answer is that I do. It is thanks to you that I have discovered my path. Given my behaviour, most ladies would have shunned me from the moment we met. Your generosity and patience are not disregarded. Both have changed me, and I shall ever be your friend, should you need one. More than that – your protector, I hope. Thank you.

Your friend, a gentleman, James Henderson.

She sank onto a side chair and read the note twice, slipping the paper quickly into her pocket as Georgiana bustled into the room.

'Ah, Maria, dear,' she said. 'Whatever is that? My, what a state.'

'A gift.'

'From Augustus Calcott?' Georgiana almost spat Calcott's name. She was clearly of the view that, with Thomas dead, it would be preferable for Maria to never speak to a man again. 'How very French,' she sneered, predictably.

Maria felt her hackles rise. 'Actually, it isn't from Augustus. It came from the captain who brought me from Brazil.'

Georgiana's eyebrows arched and her gaze fell to the drawing room floor. 'Well, it looks like a dog's dinner or worse, and so do you. We should visit Thomas's memorial again before you go,' she said. 'I shall have one of the maids pick rosemary and forget-me-nots from the garden. We can do it before you have to go to Mr Murray's. You intend to attend his salon this afternoon, do you not?'

Maria hesitated only a second. Georgiana had insisted they visit the tree she'd had planted in memorial for her brother several times now. Church services and memorials were not Mrs Graham's way, and she'd seen the damn thing four times, and on each occasion had been held in conversation by Reverend Green – a further punishment, were one required. Georgiana's constant haranguing was too much. She had lost a brother, it was true, but Maria had lost a husband. When Maria next visited London, she would stay elsewhere.

'Perhaps tomorrow,' Maria replied smoothly, clasping the necklet round her throat. It fitted exactly. 'Today, I have a meeting to attend. Cook can use the chocolate. I believe it is of very good quality.' And with that, she swooped out of the room to fetch her hat and gloves.

Outside, as if bewitched, Maria picked up a cab to the Thames, where the stench after several days of sunshine was almost overwhelming. She put her handkerchief to her nose as she picked across the moorings, the seaweed floating like arms outstretched, beckoning her to cross the river. It was a simple matter to hire a boatman for Greenwich. The journey would take twenty minutes, and she settled in the bow in a state of mild agitation, curling and uncurling her fingers and flexing her wrists. Her heart was pounding. He didn't expect to see her again. What might it be like when he did? Succumbing, she thought of the cabin, of stretching like a long cat in the sunshine, of the warm blue skies of their voyage and the clear starlit nights of being herself. It was as if London had evaporated. She must see him once more. Only once.

At Greenwich dock, she disembarked. The *Bittersweet*'s distinctive outline took only a short time to find among the hotchpotch fleet at anchor. She was not sure that she would go aboard. Perhaps, she thought, it was best to watch from a distance. In the event, however, she had no choice. Clarkson spotted her amongst the hurly-burly of the dock. She wondered momentarily if she ought to have brought the captain a gift, but it was too late now. Her heart was hammering as the mate waved and came down to escort her

'Mrs Graham.' He bowed. 'Might I see you aboard?'

'Is the captain here?' She had not anticipated this. Not fully. 'Yes ma'am.'

'I'm not sure . . .' Her voice trailed. The chance was a sweet windfall apple, if only she would allow herself to taste it.

Clarkson was insistent. 'We can't have you in Greenwich and not see you aboard, ma'am.'

It was what she had come for, after all. She steeled herself. Clarkson offered his arm and Maria allowed him to escort her up the gangplank. Several of the sailors saluted.

'My,' she said. 'You've polished her up, Mr Clarkson.'

'We've been at dock a good week and more,' the mate explained, handing Mrs Graham towards the cabin and rapping on the door.

Inside, Henderson was at the table. Books and charts were laid around him. A mere glance confirmed that he was different. Something had changed. Maria couldn't put her finger on it. Certainly, today, just from this glimpse, he might be a naval officer after all. Her skin began to tingle. *I must stop,* she thought. *It's as if I am a schoolgirl.*

'Maria.' Henderson sprang to his feet. 'Please. Come in.'

She took a deep breath. The cabin smelled familiar – a musky mixture of shaving soap and boot polish, wood and coffee. She moved forwards. 'I'm not sure . . . that is to say . . . I don't know why I came, except to thank you for the gift.' She had not intended this. Not really.

'Do you like it?'

Her cheeks coloured. 'Yes. It is very generous, especially given how we last parted.'

Henderson's shoulders squared. 'You were quite right on that occasion. I have learned my lesson. I hope you will forgive me. I shall never intrude again.'

He pulled out a chair and motioned for her to sit down. She would never know how close she had come to disgrace, he thought with the merest blush. He'd saved her that, at least.

Maria noted his effects had been put away. The cabin

seemed darker than when she'd stayed here and she felt suddenly smaller. No longer the great Maria Graham, a figure in London society, but simply herself.

'What are you reading?' she asked as she sat peering over the table with its array of scattered papers.

'About Africa. The strangest thing. I am wondering, well, several things. Topaz is mined in the west and diamonds in the south – as in South America. I wondered if I might be able to procure gemstones there. The voyage is shorter than across the Atlantic and it will be quicker. But now I'm considering something quite different, though I fear it may be foolish.'

Maria shrugged off her jacket and gestured to him to continue.

Henderson faltered. 'It is nothing,' he said. 'It doesn't matter.'

She stared. It felt good to be back. 'Go on,' she insisted. 'Tell me.'

Henderson let out a sigh. 'It's only that if cacao is grown between distinct latitudes in certain conditions in tropical countries in South America, might it be possible to cultivate the beans in African countries between the same latitudes? Where the same conditions prevail?'

He pushed over a map and indicated the areas to which he referred, rolling the names around his tongue with relish. There was an attraction in the Dark Continent – a place of possibility, however dangerous. It was somewhere new. Maria's face lit up. 'Ah, I see what you mean. But in Africa, surely, whatever might be botanically possible would be subject to other difficulties.'

'Such as?'

'We are at war there.' Maria indicated the location on the

map. 'With the Ashanti tribes. And some of these other territories are Dutch, Danish and French.'

'They would not welcome English investment?'

'It's hard to say.'

'But they might welcome Dutch or Danish money?'

'They might.'

Henderson looked up. 'I'm so sorry,' he said, 'I have forgotten my manners. Might I offer you some refreshment?'

Maria flushed. The captain was quite changed, it seemed. He appeared more distant, though his manners had improved. His arm was bandaged near the wrist, as if he'd cut himself.

'It's nothing,' he insisted, following the line of her eyes.

She wanted to touch it. Instead she drew her attention to the point. 'Is there chocolate?' she asked.

'I'll see.'

He disappeared, and Maria pulled the map closer. She glanced furtively around the cabin, her eyes lighting on the bed, which was unmade. Every part of this wooden room reminded her of the long, hot nights and the breezy afternoons – a time when she had almost melted. When Henderson returned, she was so deep in thought that she was startled.

'Is your book out soon?' the captain enquired, sitting back at the table. 'I hoped to take a copy with me.'

'It will be published in the next few weeks.' She waved off her success and changed the subject. Henderson's interest in Africa intrigued her. 'I notice there are regions in the African interior that are unmapped,' she said. 'You might like to speak to the Royal Horticultural Association about your theory. They may know someone who has spent time there and has an idea of conditions.'

'Thank you.'

'It seems to me that the most promising area will be around the Gulf of Guinea. The Ivory Coast, which is French, and the territories next to it – Danish, I think. Further inland, it gets drier, if I'm right, which I think is no good for cacao?'

Henderson nodded. 'I will need partners. I wondered if Thys might be interested. I shall write to him. He has the requisite nationality, and I trust him.'

Maria smiled. Henderson was impressive. He had transformed. She admired that, but it held a tinge of sadness. He would never approach her again. He had attained his place, or at least an idea of how to find it. But then she had changed too. She had her portrait. Maria paused before she made the decision. She must be generous. She flexed her fingers, as if she was letting something go, and then nonchalantly she said, 'I bumped into Thys's sister. She is staying with her aunt in Marylebone. Off Manchester Square. The aunt is unwell and Ramona is nursing her. She is collecting English recipes as if they are a curiosity.'

'I shall call,' Henderson said lightly.

Maria felt her stomach turn. 'Indeed,' she replied. 'I am sure she would welcome that.'

The cabin boy entered with a pot of chocolate. 'Are you back, ma'am?'

'Only to visit.' Maria raised a smile.

The boy popped the pot on the table and Henderson poured two draughts. The dark scent of hot milk, cacao and a sprinkle of cinnamon pervaded the cabin.

'Are we at peace then?' Henderson asked.

'I do not recall ever being at war, sir,' Maria replied.

'Do you not?'

She sipped. The rich liquid slipped down her throat, and

for just a moment it was like being on a star-strewn deck, in the middle of the ocean. Then, as she opened her eyes on the English afternoon, Henderson smiled.

'I hope you make your mark, Captain Henderson,' she said. 'I only came to say thank you.'

She got up and offered him her hand. For an instant, it seemed he might bow and kiss it, but he simply took her palm in his and shook instead. Maria's disappointment sent a tiny ache through her ribcage. This afternoon, that emotion wasn't even tinged with relief. Once, when she was a very young child, her father had left for sea in winter – was it the first time? The rooks that weighed down the bare branches took flight suddenly as his carriage drew away. She watched him leave the sullen February driveway, past the naked trees. The birds were ominous black smudges in the sky ahead. She had been bereft. All that day and all the next, she had thought, *He will come back. If I wait he will be around the next corner, teasing me.* But Captain Dundas had come home more than a year later. She had waited for him every day. Now, the memory came to fetch her. She left Henderson a moment of clear space, a brief few seconds that offered him one final gap in which to strike like lightning.

The captain bowed. Maria waited. He moved to hold the door.

'You are a gentleman, sir,' she said.

'I have certainly found something new here, Mrs Graham.'

She waited again. An instant only. Under her skirts, her knees clicked as she stood on tiptoes.

'Well,' Maria Graham said, wondering how she might bear it. 'I must be getting on.'

32

Further along the river

Richard Fry did not adopt a pauper's guise, but he certainly made himself as inconspicuous as he could. He had sworn that before he left London he'd eat jellied eels and that he'd visit Mallow Street again. He did not want to feel he'd run away. As he came into the East End, the place was frantic with workmen. The sound of the dockyards echoed through the streets, and he could hear the unloading of the ships and the shouts of the stevedores. The highway that had been deserted late at night was now busy with carts and drays, transporting goods further along the shore and into the city. It hardly felt like the same brooding, deadly part of town where he'd half killed a man and almost lost his life.

Richard cut down Mallow Street at a nip and stood outside the door of the Old Street Bridge Club. In the sunshine, it did not seem half so sinister. He worried that they had got away too lightly. Richard wanted a solution that bled, not one that lacked teeth.

On a whim, he decided to pop into the Rose and avail himself of some luncheon. Inside, behind the bar, Mrs Wylie was cleaning the gantry, her hair a rat's nest of ribbons. A few quiet tables of daytime drinkers keeping out of the sunshine gave a background hum to the bar.

'Good day, sir,' she called out cheerily.

Fry ordered a pint of porter and enquired after the menu.

'I got pie and cheese, sir,' Mrs Wylie offered.

Richard nodded peremptorily. He wondered if any of his blood was still out there on the cobbles.

Mrs Wylie served the pint and then disappeared into the rear to fetch a plate. Fry contemplated his surroundings. The Rose was clean and well kept. Today it was pleasantly cool inside, if a little dark. From the back, three doxies watched him, but Fry was never tempted by women. Today he even ignored the game of dice that was under way by the door. Settling to drain his tankard, however, he felt a twitch, as if a tiny mouse had climbed his britches. He swung round and caught a barefoot boy, the child's skinny fingers deep in Fry's coat pocket.

'Most people wouldn't feel it.' Fry grasped the youngster's wrist firmly. 'But you picked the wrong gentleman.'

The boy squirmed, trying to get away.

'Sit down,' Fry growled.

The boy stopped moving. One of the slatterns in the shade shouted, 'Pick on someone your own size.'

Fry ignored her.

'I didn't take nothing,' the boy spat.

'You want me to fetch someone?' a man on another table offered, coming over to clip the boy about the ear.

'And let them imprison him for not picking my pocket? You, boy, be more careful who you try to rob.'

He waved the boy off and the child disappeared like quick-silver across a mirror, into the street. The most valuable thing

430

leaving London in his possession, Fry pondered, was the idea of a chocolate bar that could be eaten without having to cook it. It would keep the third floor of the factory busy for months, if not years, to come. Richard had a sudden pang – he wanted discuss the idea with Francis. He considered how much he might reveal about his London adventures. Would his brother realise how much he'd changed? He had a sudden vision of being at home sitting in an armchair, reading.

Mrs Wylie returned with the food. She had the manner of a retired slattern. Someone on the lifelong make. 'Is that all right, sir?' she enquired, nodding at the barrels dotted around the room.

'Fine,' Richard said.

This was his final calling place. But still there was an echo, a whisper of unfinished business – the glimmer of a small revenge. Henderson wouldn't want him to stir up trouble – to land the gentlemen in something – but, given the opportunity, it was difficult to resist.

'I heard of your establishment from my uncle,' he confided, leisurely cutting into the pie.

'Oh yes?' Mrs Wylie, ever eager, leaned forward.

Yes, she's perfect, he thought. 'He is a member over the road at the club, you know. Lord Hayward?'

Mrs Wylie's eyes widened. 'His Lordship,' she breathed. 'Hayward. Here.'

'Not that you must ever tell him. Heavens, my aunt would quite expire if she knew that a gentleman of his standing . . . Well, you understand. It is only that he is so fond of his friends. The other members. Mr Fisher and Mr Grant.'

Mrs Wylie's countenance took on a beatific glow. She had found them out, at last. 'Oh, of course, sir. Their secret's safe with me.' She smiled. 'They're good customers, the gentlemen.'

Fisher. Hayward. Grant.

Fry downed the last of his porter. He felt suddenly, entirely satisfied. Whatever he had come to London to find, he had got it. Sated, he pushed the last of the pie to the edge of the plate.

'Good day, madam.' He left a shilling and headed onto the sunny East End highway, where he turned at last in the direction of home.

EPILOGUE

Maria stood on the deck of the *Valiant*. The quay at Portsmouth was alive with activity, none of it on her account. Both Georgiana and Lady Dundas had refused to see her off. 'Really,' Lady Dundas had said, 'I worry for your reason, my dear, but we cannot gainsay Her Imperial Majesty, can we?'

Maria was glad of their absence at least. She directed herself to the open water, her stomach curling in excitement. She put a hand to her cheek, just thinking of it, and passed her fingers through the dark fringe she had cut into her hair. She would be in Rio inside eight weeks. She knew she had made the right decision. This was what she had lived for, and Henderson. . . Well, he had passed.

Aboard the *Valiant*, the captain had not given up his cabin, and Maria glanced along the deck, where she was billeted in tiny quarters on the starboard side, her room crowded already with books and copies of the *Illustrated London News*. Earlier that morning, she had discovered that, with care, she could stretch on the bed, the tiny window casting the last squares of English sunshine onto her legs.

Behind her, on the dock, the other passengers mounted the gangplank. First, a thin gentleman with a moustache, determined, no doubt, to make his fortune in Brazil. After him, there was a glassy-eyed priest and two children in his charge, being sent to an aunt in Recife. The little boy, dressed in brown velvet, kept peering over his shoulder, his last glances of home, as if he hoped someone might fetch him. The little girl's lip wobbled, her eyes following the line of the long boards.

Maria stepped forward to introduce herself. The gentleman with the moustache bowed elaborately and swirled his hat as he tipped it. He was an engineer, he said, investing in the country's mines. 'And anywhere else I might see an opportunity, madam.' He smiled.

His conversation was like a *pas de deux*, heavily choreographed. Maria doubted he might ever surprise her. She knew the Brazil he hoped for – rich provincial towns where gold and diamonds were ripped from the red earth. He would live in an ornate stucco house, find himself a beautiful Brazilian wife and contribute to the building of a rococo church on the town's square. Many such gentlemen arrived and most of them prospered. There would be more now that Brazil was independent and greater openings were available for English investment.

Captain Birse swept forward and welcomed the passengers to the ship, directing them to their cabins. He all but ignored the children. Maria caught the little boy's eye and smiled. He could be not much more than seven, and his sister no more than a year older. She crouched down and addressed both youngsters. 'Perhaps you might like to learn a little of the language of the place where you're going. I could tell you stories.'

The girl lifted her gaze from the deck's pristine planks and nodded slowly, her lips a sombre straight line. 'I shall enjoy that.'

Maria nodded.

'Mrs Graham,' the priest assured her, 'there really is no need.'

'I insist.' She smiled. 'I must practise. In almost three weeks in London, I have hardly spoken a word of anything but English.'

The priest looked perturbed at the very idea and swept his charges towards their cabin, the little boy distracted by the wide-winged wheeling of the gulls high above.

The last of the supplies were loaded. They were not promising, Maria noted, consisting mostly of smoked, dried meat, hard tack and sacks of potatoes. This captain was not a connoisseur. On the dock, a woman was selling the first of the English strawberries. The bright fruit was packed in wooden punnets and glistened on the straw like luscious rubies. Maria gave a ragged cabin boy sixpence and sent him to fetch a punnet. 'Make sure they smell ripe,' she said.

Dallying near the gangplank, she watched him handing over the coin. Behind her, the captain directed the crew. The tide was ready. As the boy came aboard and handed over the fruit, the gangplank was raised behind him, and Maria turned, suddenly unwilling to watch England shrink and everything become smaller.

'Thank you,' she said.

She'd give some to the children, she decided. The wide blue sky was beautiful out to sea. That was what she must think on. She banished the encroaching picture of Henderson, the way his hair flopped over his face when he was concentrating. The *Valiant* was another ship entirely and she had chosen to make her journey upon it.

'Goodbye,' she murmured under her breath, and then, managing a smile, she remembered she had a brand-new journal to start, its leather bindings fresh and its blank pages full of promise. A new story. One she would share with the world in due course.

'I shall be in my cabin,' she told the captain as Maria Graham, governess to Princess Maria da Gloria, and one of John Murray's most celebrated authors, took the world in her stride as she swept away.

WRITER'S NOTE

I don't have a single view on what is acceptable when using historical fact in a fictional story. My ideas vary over different novels and sometimes I surprise myself. However, I always find archive material and written history both inspiring and fascinating, and I love finding an echo of someone from two or three hundred years ago – a letter or a diary that is so fresh and well written, it brings the writer once more to life, as if they're standing next to me.

Maria Graham is one such figure. I am struck absolutely in admiration for her achievements. To continue her (real) story from where it leaves off here (in fiction): she did not last long as the tutor to Princess Maria da Gloria. The English fell out of favour at the Brazilian court and she left Rio just over a year after she arrived. Returning to London, she rented a house at Kensington Gravel Pits and shortly after married Augustus Calcott (soon to be Sir Augustus Calcott), with whom she travelled across Europe. Maria continued to write books for John Murray and died childless aged fifty-seven. She is still remembered today, though, like many extraordinary people (and particularly extraordinary women), her story is not widely known. Her letters show her tremendous good humour and also her seriousness in the matter of defending her reputation. She was an admirable and extremely brave worldwide traveller at a time when few women journeyed more than a few miles. After she arrived back in London, her ideas were presented at the Royal Society and caused a furore, but she stood up for herself and, in addition, was backed by Charles Darwin, among other gentlemen.

Of the other real-life characters that appear, John Murray, Augustus Calcott, Admiral Cochrane and Richard Fry are heavily fictionalised. However, the details about Dutch presses and the intrigue and espionage in the chocolate industry are not. The advances Henderson dreams up all come to pass – Danish investors farming cacao in Africa, a new process that produces eating chocolate and, of course, the Fairtrade movement.

Cochrane is a national hero in both Chile and Brazil today, where they honour his memory far more than in the UK. He is said to be the character upon which Captain Jack Aubrey, of Patrick O'Brian's *Master and Commander* series, is based.

Although it was initially Maria's story that interested me, I became drawn to the core of this novel – Henderson finding his identity not only as a man, but as a gentleman too. It has ended up being his story in many ways, as much, if not more than hers. James Henderson is entirely fictional, but the social difficulties he encounters are not, and unlike many who fell through the cracks in Georgian society, I'm delighted that he hauls himself back aboard. One of my favourite eras is 1820–1845. It gurgles with life and is full of have-a-go heroes (my favourite kind).

Lastly, I want to thank all those who helped. My agent, Jenny Brown. Lisa Highton, who gave me sterling editorial advice. The kind readers who suggested improvements along the way. Members of staff at the John Murray Archive at the National Library of Scotland (who I hope are not too horrified by my fictionalisation of their wonderful facts) and also Creative Scotland, which, as an organisation, has solidly supported my work for many years and did so in particular with this project by funding research and development work. Research tips, support and cups of tea provided by Joe Goodwin were also gratefully received. And lastly, to the wonderful team at Black & White Publishing, who have brought the book to print, I say thank you very much.